WHAT COULD POSSIBLY GO WRONG

THE CHRONICLES OF ST MARY'S BOOK SIX

JODI TAYLOR

Published by Accent Press Ltd 2015

ISBN 9781910939468

Copyright © **Jodi Taylor** 2015

First edition published 2013

Thanks and Acknowledgements.

I would like to thank the following people for their help and encouragement with this story.

Thanks to Professor Tom Coulthard and Stephen W. Cross whose theories inspired the Valley of the Kings story.

Staff at Leicester City Council's Information Office who pointed me in the right direction over my queries with the car park.

Emma Lay, Marketing and Events Manager and Rachel Ayrton, Learning and Interpretation Manager, both from the King Richard III Visitor Centre, for their patience with my queries about car parks and tarmac.

The *Leicester Mercury* for their article about the painted letter 'R' in the council car park and the subsequent discovery of Richard's body.

Phillip Dawson for his helpful advice on the range of handguns and the correct procedures to be followed when encountering late-night policemen in Leicester car parks.

Cat Camacho, my editor, who is never anything other than patient and helpful and is very sound on chocolate and its role in the creative process.

Accent Press – of course.

Jan and Mike for their hospitality.

List of Characters

Dr Edward Bairstow

Director of St Mary's Institute of Historical Research.

Mrs Partridge

Kleio, daughter of Zeus, Muse of History. PA to Dr Bairstow.

History Department

Dr Tim Peterson

Chief Operations Officer.

Mr Clerk

Historian.

Miss Paula Prentiss

Historian.

Mr Tom Bashford

Recently rescued historian.

Miss Elspeth Grey

Ditto but strangely reluctant to resume her duties.

Mr Gareth Roberts

Historian.

Mr David Sands

Historian and possessor of the world's worst collection of knock-knock jokes.

Miss Rosie Lee

PA to Chief Operations Officer.

Trainees

Dr Maxwell	Chief Training Officer. Also Mrs Leon Farrell.
Mr Phil Atherton	The quiet one.
Mr Laurence Hoyle	The mysterious one.
Miss Constance Lingoss	The misfit.
Miss Celia North	The perfect one.
Miss Elizabeth Sykes	The psycho.
Mrs Shaw	PA to Chief Training Officer.

Technical Section

Chief Leon Farrell	Chief Technical Officer.
Mr Dieter	The other Chief Technical Officer.

Security Section

Major Ian Guthrie	Head of Security Section.
Mr Markham	Security guard and winner of the one-handed bra-unfastening competition.
Mr William Randall	Security guard.
Mr Evans	Security guard.

Mr Gallaccio	Security guard.
Mr Cox	Security guard.
Mr Keller	Security guard

Medical Section

Dr Helen Foster	Suffering nicotine deprivation and possibly even more unstable than normal.
Nurse Diane Hunter	Recipient of Mr Markham's affections
Nurse Fortunata	Junior nurse.
Professor Andrew Rapson	Head of Research and Development.
Dr Octavius Dowson	Librarian and Archivist.
Miss Polly Perkins	Head of IT.
Mrs Theresa Mack	Kitchen Supremo.
Mrs Mavis Enderby	Head of Wardrobe.

The Time Police

Captain Matthew Ellis	Looking for trouble and choosing not to find it.
Dr Kalinda Black	Liaison officer to Thirsk University.

Vortigern	Agoraphobic kitchen cat reluctantly participating in vital historic research.

Key Historical characters

Herodotus	Father of History, Father of Lies, and a complete bastard.
Joan of Arc	Not having a good day.
Richard Plantagenet	Dick the Turd.
Henry Tudor	A man who would drink his own bathwater.

Sundry Egyptian tomb-builders, Neanderthals, Homo sapiens, mammoths, citizens of Rouen, the entire city of Bristol celebrating in the streets, various medieval armies, and a couple of passing policemen.

Prologue

I think I'm one of the most privileged people on this planet.

To do what I do – go where I go – see what I see – it's a wonderful, unique, never-to-be-taken-for-granted privilege.

However with great privilege comes great responsibility. There's nothing in our contracts about this, but it's clearly understood nevertheless. Should anything go wrong, the responsibility for putting it right rests with us. Solely with us. We know this. We know it's the only reason History allows us to do what we do.

And if we don't step up – if we don't put right the things we've caused to go wrong – then it will be done for us. And possibly to us.

So when you're pursuing a fanatic with a gun, hell-bent on changing the course of History, it doesn't matter if putting it right *might* cost us our lives, failure to put it right *will* cost us our lives.

One

I stared at Dr Bairstow.

'I'm sorry, sir. Could you say that again?'

A bit of a mistake there. He doesn't like to repeat himself. We're supposed to pick things up the first time around.

'Which particular part was unclear, Dr Maxwell?'

I took a deep breath.

'The bit about the American, sir.'

'Really? I thought I expressed myself perfectly clearly.'

'You did, sir. It's the concept rather than the words that I'm not quite clear on.'

'I have five trainees for you, Dr Maxwell. As Chief Training Officer, I had expected more enthusiasm. Not to mention gratitude.'

'As you must know sir, enthusiasm and gratitude are my default state. It's surprise that I'm wrestling with.'

'And I have no doubt you will gain the upper hand any moment now.'

I sighed. 'Upper hand gained, sir.'

'There will be five of them – two men and three women.'

3

'Excellent, sir.'

'And one of them is from America.'

'So – an American, sir?'

'Normally, the answer would be yes. As you so rightly point out, a person from America is usually an American. But in this case – no.'

'So – not an American then, sir?'

He smiled. I suspected he was winding me up and while I believe that senior managers should be given every opportunity to display their frivolous side, it should not happen at the expense of their newly appointed Chief Training Officer.

'Perhaps,' I said cunningly, 'as someone new to this country, it would be helpful if she could spend a period of time at Thirsk University, acclimatising herself, so to speak.'

As if St Mary's was perched atop the Andes.

'Actually, Dr Maxwell, she is a he.'

'Well, that's no good to us, sir. We need more women. The History Department is unbalanced enough as it is.'

'At last, we are in agreement over something. As you know, I always maintain that if two parties discuss their difficulties in a rational and sensible manner, common ground always emerges.'

This breath-taking hypocrisy from someone whose style of management had passed autocratic years ago and was entering the foothills of dictatorship left me temporarily speechless and while I was attempting to regroup he stooped to conquer.

'I am at a loss to understand your consternation, Dr Maxwell.'

'Well, the borders have been closed for some time now. How did he get out?'

'Through the Canadian Corridor, I believe.'

That shut me up for a bit. The Canadian Corridor is not a stroll in the park.

I tried again.

'Will he be able to understand us, sir? It's a foreign language over there. I've heard they spell plough with a "w"?'

'I share your horror,' he said, 'but since I have the strongest doubts that anyone in the History Department can spell the word plough in any language, I do not feel this is an insurmountable barrier to admission at St Mary's.'

'And he's probably called Otis P. Hackensacker III. Or Spiced Tea Bag. Or something like that.'

He pretended to consult his notes. 'No, he gives his name as Laurence Hoyle.'

'What sort of name is that for an American?'

'I believe we have covered this already, Dr Maxwell. He is not an American.'

'You said …'

'I said nothing of the kind. He is British and found himself caught there when the borders closed. He has, apparently, devoted the last two years of his life to returning to this country.'

I said sceptically, 'What was he doing there in the first place? Is he a spy? Why would he want to come here to St Mary's? Really, sir, it's all very suspicious. And annoying.'

'Strange though it may seem to you, Dr Maxwell, I do not believe Mr Hoyle smuggled himself out of

America, crawled along the Canadian Corridor, transported himself across the Atlantic, and hitch-hiked his way across this country for the sole purpose of annoying you.'

'So who has he come to annoy?'

There was a bit of a silence.

'In an organisation that already contains you, Dr Maxwell, the acquisition of any further irritants would be superfluous.'

He was effortlessly hacking the ground from beneath my feet. I made a last valiant effort.

'Do we know why he was in America in the first place, sir?'

'It's no secret. He was undertaking some research and was overtaken by events when the borders closed. Which makes him half way to being a member of the History Department already, I think you'll agree.'

I nodded, gloomily. He had me there.

'Five trainees for you, Dr Maxwell, arriving in ten days' time. Will you be ready for them?'

I brought up the data stack.

'The training schedule is complete, sir.'

'Talk me through it, if you would be so good.'

'As you can see, sir, the focus is on getting our trainees out there as soon as possible.'

'Not too soon, I hope.'

'No indeed, sir. They will undergo the basic training, of course. Theory and practice, getting themselves fit, self-defence, first aid, outdoor survival, all the usual stuff. However, instead of waiting until after they've worked their way through the theory and practice-of-pods module and the endless simulations, I propose to introduce a number of small jumps quite early on in the process. These jumps will be purpose-oriented. For instance, the first jump, the one to the Valley of the Kings, will incorporate mapping and surveying skills. The third, to Thurii, will cover interacting with contemporaries, and so on. Obviously, I'll need to liaise with Dr Peterson, because this will all be subject to pod availability, and the needs of the History Department will take priority, but these new procedures mean we could knock months and months off the training period.'

He frowned. 'These jumps, especially the early ones, will, of course, be heavily supervised?'

'Oh yes, sir. Either by historians, the Security Section, or a combination of the two, and I or a member of the History Department will personally be present at each jump.'

'There is a certain amount of risk involved in sending inexperienced and only half-trained people on real-life assignments.'

'Agreed, sir, but it works both ways. If there's a problem with any of our trainees, surely it's better to discover this fairly early on in the programme, rather than after we've spent a fortune on getting them trained up. Or worse, suppose they go to pieces halfway through their first assignment when others may be depending on them.'

He stared at the stack for a while. 'Very well, Dr Maxwell, the schedule is approved. Work it up into a full training programme. Involve Dr Peterson, of course. As Chief Operations Officer, he will be providing the backup. Mr Markham will provide the security.'

I flattened the data stack and looked up.

'What about Major Guthrie, sir?'

'He may not be available for a short period. He has requested permission to spend some time at Thirsk.'

Elspeth Grey was at Thirsk. It struck me suddenly that she had been there for a long time, now. She and her partner, Tom Bashford, had recently been rescued after being missing for ten years, and had gone off to Thirsk for a few months to get themselves reoriented. Bashford had returned and was noisily among us. Seemingly, he had acclimatised himself to his new world with no problems at all. Not so Elspeth Grey, apparently. I couldn't find it in my heart to criticise. Bashford had been semi-conscious throughout their ordeal. Most of it had gone way over his battered head. She had been the one who battled to keep them both alive.

I kept my face as non-committal as I could. 'Well, the Major never takes any leave so perhaps it will do him good.'

'Perhaps,' he said levelly.

'Sir, may I make a suggestion?'

'Of course.'

'You asked me to select someone to represent us on the Belverde Caves expedition.'

He looked up. 'The Botticelli paintings?'

I crossed my fingers for luck. 'If they're still there, of course.'

He smiled. 'I think the world would know if they had already been discovered, Dr Maxwell.'

'True. Anyway, sir, may I suggest Miss Grey? It could be a stepping-stone for her before returning to full duties here. Perhaps it would give her a chance to regain her confidence.'

He seemed to consider the suggestion. 'I believe you were to nominate Mr Sands?'

How does he know these things? Yes, I had been considering David Sands but I didn't remember mentioning it to anyone.

He smiled faintly. 'Miss Prentiss and Mr Bashford are scheduled for 11th-century Coventry. Mr Clerk and Mr Roberts are putting together the Riveaux assignment and as the only historian not currently assigned, that really only leaves Mr Sands. I am not, actually, omnipotent, Dr Maxwell.'

'Alas, sir. Another illusion shattered.'

'As is, I believe, the large window in R&D. May I expect a report on the History Department's latest catastrophe in the very near future?'

I replied with all the confidence of one no longer in charge of an erring History Department. 'A trifling episode, sir. The result of a – vigorous – discussion between Dr Dowson and Professor Rapson on the long-standing question of torque versus tension.'

'And was any decision reached?'

'Still undetermined, sir. It was direction control that got away from them this time. Literally, you could say. However, on Dr Peterson's instructions, any further experiments are to be conducted outside.'

'Very wise. And how are you settling into your new position, Dr Maxwell?'

'Absolutely fine, thank you, sir. Dr Peterson and I

always work well together.'

'That wasn't quite what I meant. I was enquiring into your new status.'

I blinked. 'Sorry?'

'Chief Farrell?'

'Oh.'

Oh. Yes. Leon Farrell. Chief Technical Officer. My ... husband.

Yes. My husband. I was married. To Leon, I mean. I still had difficulty with that. Not being married, I mean. No, that wasn't what I meant. I mean ... oh, I don't know. Start again, Maxwell.

Leon and I were married. Something neither of us ever thought would happen, and I'm damned sure no one else thought it would happen either and then, suddenly, right out of the blue, it did. On a wonderful starlit evening, surrounded by friends, we'd been married. We'd slipped away when no one was looking, driven off into the magical night, and ten minutes later we'd been assisting the police with their enquiries. A tree had been involved. Leon and I had history with trees. Apparently, the whole thing had passed into St Mary's legend, and unkind people were still making jokes at our expense.

'Everything is fine, thank you, sir.'

And it was. Mostly. There were the usual – discussions – that would always arise when two people, very accustomed to solitary lives, were suddenly living together, but this was easily overcome. In my new position, I wouldn't see as much of him as I had when I'd been Chief Ops Officer. I was almost nine to five these days. He left me a cup of tea in the mornings when he departed and I often wouldn't see him again until the evening meal. And Dr Bairstow had requested that, as far as possible, we didn't both go on the same assignments, which made sense, so we were gently working things out as we went along and so far, marriage wasn't anything like as bad as I thought it would be. Still, give it time.

I picked up the personnel files from Dr Bairstow's PA, Mrs Partridge, took everything away, and went through it all very carefully. There were the usual discrepancies between the information provided by the trainees themselves and that uncovered by Major Guthrie's detailed background checks. The things people don't mention are always more interesting than the things they do. Still, on paper at least, they all looked relatively normal. Even the non-American.

There were five of them. Alphabetically, we had Mr Atherton, Mr Hoyle, Miss Lingoss, Miss North, and Miss Sykes. All were single – in fact, come to think of it, I was the only married person I knew. And Leon, of course. Atherton, the oldest, had been briefly married. Very briefly. She'd left him and he'd kicked his banking job into touch and returned to his first love, History. He'd come to us via Thirsk.

The non-American, Laurence Hoyle, was only in his mid-twenties, but looked older. Every time I looked at his photo, he reminded me of someone and I just couldn't think whom. He was thin-faced with a long nose, a wide mouth, and deep, dark eyes that gave nothing away. I searched his features for any signs of humour and found none. If asked to guess his profession, I would have said monk. Or fanatic. He had a fragile look about him. I suspected possible childhood illness. He was another one who'd come to us from Thirsk. In fact, he'd been specially recommended by our liaison officer, Kalinda Black. Despite that, he looked harmless enough.

Not so Miss Lingoss.

'Wow!' said Peterson, appearing alongside and staring at the photograph on the inside of the front cover. 'She's eye-catching.'

I nodded gloomily. He was right. Historians, like librarians, sometimes labour under an unfortunate image. Quiet, mousy, hairy skirts, thick stockings, glasses on a chain round their necks – and that's just the blokes.

Miss Lingoss wore her thick black hair in a Mohican that added a good six inches to her height. She wore a short, tight leather top and an even shorter and tighter leather skirt. Her stockings were ripped; her heavy boots unlaced. Although, yes, maybe she was historian material after all because she certainly was wearing a heavy-duty chain around her neck. For what purpose I could only guess. Don't ask me what she looked like. There probably was a face under all that make-up. She stood in her photo, hands on hips, challenging …

'Does she have a first name?' asked Peterson, peering over my shoulder.

'Um …' I flicked the file.

'Doesn't matter,' he said, grinning. 'They're going to call her Connie,' and disappeared, laughing his head off.

And if Miss Lingoss looked like trouble, next up was Miss North. Celia North came from a good family background, had had the best education money could buy, and contrary to the usual spoilt-brat behaviour, had more than exceeded everyone's expectations. Perfect, was the word that described everything about her. Perfect grades, perfect appearance, perfect life. It would appear that Miss North had only to set her sights on something for it to fall into her lap. This would be interesting.

And finally came the one I suspected would be the biggest troublemaker of all. Elizabeth Sykes was the baby of the group. Short and dark, the face in her photo smiled up at me angelically. I knew that look. I should do. I held the patent.

I sighed. What had seemed a perfectly straightforward exercise on paper suddenly seemed a great deal more complicated now that I actually had trainees.

On the positive side, as usual, none of them had children or close family ties. I was particularly pleased about this because if my plan to get them out there as quickly as possible came crashing to the ground – and it well might – we could tie a brick around their necks, throw them into the lake, and move on to the next batch as quickly and quietly as possible. This was bound to appeal to Dr Bairstow – quick, efficient, and with minimum expenditure and fuss.

I estimated training time at around six months. Give or take a few weeks for the odd wound to heal.

Just six short months. Get them trained up, hand the training section back to Peterson, and return to what I still thought of as my real job as head of the History Department.

I thought it would be safe. Dull, even. The perfect way to spend my period of medically imposed light duties. I would engage our trainees with a little gentle lecturing in the morning, and then they would go off and spend the rest of the day either with Leon, learning about pods; or with Markham, learning self-defence; or in the Library, studying something or other. I had a lot to learn about teaching, because the reality wasn't like that at all.

There's a surprise.

Two

The big day dawned. I stood in the window, watching as they trickled up the drive, and were security wanded and signed in by Mr Strong, our caretaker. I sent them to be kitted out in the trainee-grey jump suits, ushered them to Sick Bay where they were medically probed, handed their blood-donating schedule, and vaccinated against everything in the world because Dr Foster likes to get all the bad stuff over in one go.

I'd sent them for lunch, after which they'd endured the terrors of Dr Bairstow's allegedly welcoming monologue, and now they stood in the Great Hall, bemused, expectant, and lightly traumatised. And waiting for me.

My plan was to give them a moment to absorb the ambience, and then usher them into the training room for my own carefully thought out 'Welcome to St Mary's' speech. However, from that moment in the Great Hall to the day the survivors graduated, it would be fair to say that very little went according to plan.

We're St Mary's. We don't scream. Although we do tend to be a cause of screaming in others. So when a yelping Bashford raced past, followed by a stampede of St Mary's staff, all of them shrieking contradictory instructions, you could say my attention was caught.

'My feet are melting! My feet are melting!'

I gestured to my trainees to remain where they were. The sooner they got used to this, the better. I had no clue what was going on. Given those involved, it could be anything from a reconstruction of some medieval torture device to a re-enactment of the famous scene from *The Wizard of Oz*.

As I said, we're St Mary's. To give us our full title, we're the Institute of Historical Research based at St Mary's Priory, just outside of Rushford. We're part of the University of Thirsk. We research major historical events in contemporary time. Yes, time travel. As would soon be experienced by the innocents in my charge.

I cleared my throat to regain their attention.

A waste of time. Before I could continue, Dr Dowson erupted from the Library, trailing his own staff, all of them eager to become involved, and considerably adding to the confusion.

He planted himself firmly in front of a hopping Bashford, demanding, 'What's going on here? What's the old fool up to now?'

He meant Professor Rapson. The Professor and Dr Dowson are old adversaries. Or old friends. Whichever it is, they delight in winding each other up.

'My feet are on fire! Aaaagghh!' yelled Mr Bashford, possibly feeling that not enough attention was being paid to his pain.

In one smoothly synchronised movement, Mr Clerk tackled him to the ground and Prentiss rolled him over and sat on his chest. I felt a glow of pride. It's not often we historians manage to achieve that level of coordination. Roberts and Sands wrestled off his boots. Mrs Mack and her team emerged from the kitchen with ice packs.

Professor Rapson found his spectacles, took up the boots, and examined them closely, apparently quite oblivious to the curses of Bashford, now encased in ice to his knees and probably in imminent danger of frostbite.

Dr Dowson was, as he frequently is, beside himself. 'What on earth is going on? May I remind you – again – Andrew, that this is an educational establishment and as such ...'

He got no further. Bashford, feet encased in ice, interrupted him. 'It might have been my own fault, sir. I think I may have overheated them.'

Professor Rapson frowned. 'I told you, my boy, ten seconds for every stone of body weight.'

'Stone? You said pound!'

'Did I?' he said vaguely, already drifting off back to Planet Rapson. 'Dear me. What was I thinking?'

'Well, they work, sir.'

'What works?' demanded Peterson, pushing his way through the by now quite large crowd, because St Mary's will stop working at the drop of a hat.

'For the expedition to the prehistoric age,' said Miss Prentiss, comfortably ensconced on Bashford's chest and obviously in no hurry to move. 'Heated boots.'

'Oh. Cool.'

The professor sighed. 'Well, no actually, and that's what appears to have been the problem. Sadly, it looks as if I shall have to go back to the drawing board and I have to say I was rather proud of these. Heat exchangers, you know.'

Peterson took a boot from him and subjected it to close scrutiny. 'Like the human nose, Professor?'

'Something similar, yes, although I based this design on the human testes. I'm sure you're all familiar with the pampiniform plexus which cools and reheats the blood to ensure optimum delivery of seminal ... well, never mind that now.'

Miss Prentiss got up in a hurry. 'I'm not wearing anything whose design is based on Bashford's testicles.'

'You could do worse,' said Bashford indignantly, from ground level.

'Not according to what's written in the ladies' loo on the third floor. And there's a diagram on the wall, as well.'

'Really?' said Bashford smugly. 'The entire wall?'

'Most of it seemed to be contained in an area approximately equivalent to that of a postage stamp.'

'What?' He struggled indignantly to his ice-wrapped feet.

Once, I would have had to deal with this. Now, however, as Chief Training Officer, I could sit back and let others take the strain.

My trainees stood nearby, mouths slightly agape. It was interesting to study their reactions. Hoyle, North, and Atherton looked slightly taken aback. Hoyle particularly so. If he had been expecting hallowed halls of learning, he was in for a bit of a shock. Lingoss had acquired a boot and was peering closely at the sole. Sykes was a picture of bright-eyed mischief. I made a mental note to keep an eye on her.

Detaching them from the inevitably vigorous discussion that was building nicely, I led them into the training room.

They say it takes a teacher a whole term to sum up her class. They also say it takes her class a whole minute to sum up their teacher. I wondered what they saw when they looked at me. A short, ginger historian in a blue jump suit, still leaning on a walking stick (Not so much because I needed it, but because I thought it gave me gravitas. And it was something to wield should my teaching skills prove unequal to the task in hand.) My name is Maxwell. I was Chief Ops Officer and then I had to have a partly new knee. I mean a partial knee replacement – so I'm on light duties for a while. Tim Peterson had the History Department now. Good luck to him.

Anyway, I ushered them into the training room and stood looking down at them. I remembered Dr Bairstow's trick of standing silently for a while. They looked at me. I looked at them. There were a lot more of them than there was of me.

I let the silence gather.

'Welcome to St Mary's. My name is Maxwell. I am your primary trainer.'

I paused to let that blow sink in.

'As you will remember from your interview with

Dr Bairstow, we investigate major historical events in contemporary time. Don't call it time travel. If Dr Bairstow overhears you referring to it as time travel, then I'm afraid I won't be able to save you.

'If you would consult your organisational charts, please, you will find a list of the different departments and their functions. St Mary's is a large establishment, but most people are easily identifiable. As you can see, trainees wear grey. Historians wear blue. The Technical Section wears orange. Security wears green. IT wears black. The Admin department wears whatever it likes – and members of R&D wear protective clothing, wound dressings, and a dazed expression.

'Moving on to your timetables now … you will see that your schedule is divided into three areas. The first part of your training should take around four to six weeks and will consist of self-defence, first aid, and outdoor survival, all supervised by the Security Section. Then you will have pod familiarisation with Chief Farrell, followed by a number of practice assignments with me. The third part of your training, consisting mainly of the calculation of spatial and temporal coordinates, will be with Chief Farrell again and Professor Rapson – yes, you met him just now. The one with the hair.

'There are weekly examinations every Friday afternoon which will cover everything learned that week. The pass mark of eighty per cent is rigorously applied. There are no resits. One fail and you're out.'

They nodded. No one spoke and I worried I'd frightened the living daylights out of them before we'd started. To reassure them and give them something pretty to look at, I brought up the Time Map.

The Time Map is a thing of beauty – not just for what it represents, but also for what it is. Two twisting turning double cones of light and swirling colour. I could look at it for hours.

'Ladies and gentlemen, this is our Time Map. Please come closer and have a look.'

I stepped back to give them a moment.

'Those of you who successfully complete their training will be designated Pathfinders. Maintaining this Time Map will be part of your responsibilities.'

They were staring up at it, mesmerised.

'What does it all mean?' said Lingoss. Her voice was blunt Yorkshire.

'Well. The vertical axis is the Timeline. The horizontal axis represents Space. The point where they intersect is Here and Now. Ground Zero, if you like. Everything above Now is the future, and below Now is the past. The lines radiating outwards from Now delineate the boundaries of the cones inside which we must work. We use the Time Map to plot historical events and their coordinates. Having done that, we can then chart the relationship between them. Here, for instance, if you look at the year 535AD – The Year of No Sunshine – you can see that event is linked to massive upheavals around the world – climate change, crop failure, drought, floods, the Pope died – not sure of what, but it didn't help – plague swept around the world, empires fell, and new religions rose from the ashes.'

I pointed to the silver filigree of lights connecting larger, different-coloured areas, tracing the lines from one event to another.

'What are the tiny blue dots?' asked Lingoss, peering closely.

'Those are Pathfinder jumps. For instance,' I brought another area into focus, 'the date of the fall of Troy was not precisely known. The Pathfinders jumped about until they were able to pinpoint the exact location and date. Armed with that information, we launched two major expeditions. One to survey the city before the arrival of the Greeks and one to observe the closing stages of the war. Those are the two bigger red spots here and here. If you expand them,' I did so, 'you can bring up the coordinates and assignment numbers. From there you can access details of the mission. You can also see silver lines radiating outwards – these represent events leading up to and those occurring after the fall of Troy, because, of course, nothing happens in isolation.'

'It's very bottom-loaded,' said Atherton, pointing. The Map shimmered as he touched it. 'The top cone is virtually empty.'

'There has been one jump into the future but the coordinates have been withheld.'

'Why?'

'We're historians,' I said. 'Most of us are not interested in the here and now, let alone the future. Besides, jumping back into the past, while possessing its own hazards, is considerably less dangerous than the future. For a start, how do you know there is one? Let us say you decide to investigate London one

22

hundred years from now. Suppose, however, in fifty years' time, London is destroyed in a nuclear blast. Or the entire planet is destroyed by an asteroid. Where will you land? Empty space? A meteor field? A radiation field so severe you can't safely return to St Mary's for fear of contamination?

'Or, if this is easier, think of the future as a glittering vortex of infinite possibilities, all bunching up to pass through the chicane of Now and become reality. Obviously, most of these possibilities never come to pass. They just quietly fade away into non-existence, which is only a problem if you happen to be an historian visiting that particular possibility. In other words, nothing is real until it actually happens. Personally, I prefer the certainty of Hastings in 1066 where all you have to do is remember not to look up.'

They thought about this.

'And on a practical note,' I continued, 'who here knows for how long they will live? Suppose you jumped into the future and you were still alive? The consequences would be catastrophic. For that same reason, we don't usually jump less than one hundred years into the past. The official reason is that that way your younger selves, parents, and grandparents are all safely avoided. As I say, that's the official line. The unofficial reason is that Dr Bairstow won't let us go back to tease Stephen Hawking.'

I paused. I might as well get it over with now.

'While on the subject, you should know that there are areas to which we cannot jump. Temporal hot-spots if you like. Sites of Special Significance.'

'What?' said Hoyle, sharply. 'I mean – which

areas?'

'Anything to do with religion, mostly. We can only visit Jerusalem at certain times. Or Mecca. Or Bethlehem. Or Medina. Or Benares. Or Bodh Gaya. That's what those all those three red triple S's are.'

I pointed to various spots on the Map.

'Why not?'

'We're not in the business of propping up ancient belief systems.'

'But,' said Sykes, 'you could prove once and for all ...' She stopped.

'Yes?' I said. 'Go on.'

'Well, if you could prove that the crucifixion actually did take place ...' she trailed away. 'Oh. Yes. I see.'

'I'm glad you've grasped the point so quickly. Imagine the worldwide consequences of confirming the crucifixion did take place. Would they be more or less catastrophic than if we could prove it didn't?'

The room sat silently as they worked out the implications.

'For that reason, there are certain areas to which a pod will not – cannot – go. It's built into the programming.'

'What would happen if you tried?'

'The pod would warn you – just once – and then after a short period, if you did not extricate yourselves, the pod would automatically instigate emergency evacuation. Whether you were inside or not.'

'So we would be ...?'

'Stranded forever with no means of getting home,'

I said, deliberately brutal, because some rules are unbreakable.

'So how does the Time Map work?' persisted Lingoss, still fascinated. She was tracing a tiny silver arc with her finger.

'No idea,' I said cheerfully. 'Historians and Pathfinders upload the info to Professor Rapson and he and Dr Dowson incorporate the findings into the Map.'

I wasn't sure they were taking it in. Hoyle appeared to be in a world of his own and Lingoss was making love to the Time Map.

'There are patterns,' she said, dreamily.

'That's part of what we do,' I said. 'We look at History as a whole and try to establish patterns or recurring themes. After all, they do say that History repeats itself.'

I could see the wonder in her eyes.

'So we don't actually get to build it?' She sounded disappointed.

'Well, no. The practical stuff is usually done by R&D, Dr Dowson, and the IT team,' I said, pleased to have this opportunity to showcase inter-departmental cooperation and, wisely I think, skipping over the disagreements, the shouting, and the sometimes quite major academic tantrums.

I shut down the map and they resumed their seats.

'You will be obliged to nominate a specialist subject. I believe you have already discussed this with Dr Bairstow. Mr Atherton – the Age of Enlightenment?'

He nodded.

'Mr Hoyle – The Late Middle Ages with especial reference to the Wars of the Roses and the Tudor succession?'

He nodded. I held his gaze for a little while. Who did he remind me of?

'Miss Lingoss – The Machine Age?'

She nodded.

I couldn't help myself. 'Why?'

She grinned. Her big black Mohican was tipped with blue today, to match the History Department's jumpsuits.

'It's fascinating. All that giant machinery. The noise. The smell. Wondering whether the equipment will be a success or blow up taking half the factory with it. I built myself a steam pump in college.'

I remembered she had been born in Halifax, centre of the cotton and wool industries with their giant machines and steam-powered mills.

'Miss North – The Renaissance?'

'That is correct.'

Hers were the cut-glass tones I had been hearing around the building all morning. I wondered how long before they started to grate on people's nerves and then kicked myself. As a trainer, I shouldn't allow myself to be irritated just by her voice. I was sure there were plenty of other things about her that would irritate me as well.

And Miss Sykes. She grinned at me amiably.

'The Dark Ages?'

She nodded.

'Dr Dowson, whom you also just met, is in charge of our Library and Archive and will order you anything you require to keep abreast of your specialised areas. Are there any questions so far?'

Miss North's hand was first up. Of course it would be.

'How long before we actually …?' She hesitated.

'Jump?' I said.

'Yes. Jump.'

'That depends entirely on the progress you make. If you don't make any then you won't jump at all.'

I could see her deciding she would be the first to jump. I could also see Lingoss watching her from the corner of her eye and grinning.

Hoyle put up his hand. 'About the … coordinates?'

'Yes.'

'Do we work them out?'

'Usually they're provided by IT and laid in by the Technical Section, although obviously, it makes good sense for you to be able to calculate your own. Learning to do that is part of your training.'

'Do we … jump … alone?'

'No. We very, very rarely initiate solo jumps,' and remembered not to say that that was usually because we needed someone to bring the body home. Too early in the schedule for historian humour.

I paused but there were no more questions.

'A special note for the ladies. You will be required to learn to ride sidesaddle. See Mr Strong for a schedule.'

I paused, struggled, and then completely failed to resist temptation. You can only channel a certain amount of goodness in one day.

'I recommend old Turk as your horse. I did my

own training on him and he knows his business.'
Which was perfectly true. It's just that his business
was dumping any rider into the nearest bramble bush
and then pushing off, leaving them to do the walk of
shame back to St Mary's. He was lean, mean, and
carnivorous. An unfortunate encounter with Mr
Markham some years ago had soured his already evil
disposition even further. Markham, on fire at the time
and understandably having other things on his mind,
had run full tilt into Turk's bottom, and knocked
himself unconscious. It would be interesting to see
how they handled him. Turk, I mean. Markham was
generally reckoned to be unhandleable, and as
Peterson always said, 'Who would want to anyway?'

'You will all be required to grow your hair. Ladies,
as long as possible. Gentlemen, around chin length.'

Atherton raised his hand. 'No short hair at all?' He
had the same accent as Kalinda. Broad Manchester.

'Not unless you contract lice or mange. Then, I'm
afraid it all has to come off.' I paused significantly.
'All of it.'

Lingoss grinned at him. 'What a great title for a
book –*St Mary's and the Inadvertent Brazilian.*'

He looked horrified, although whether at the awful
joke or the actual thought of follicle trauma was
difficult to say. Speaking of which …

'With regret, Miss Lingoss, the Mohican must go.'

She nodded, presumably unperturbed. 'Can I get it
out on high days and holidays?'

Sykes snorted and attempted to turn it into an
unconvincing cough.

'Of course. Any time there's an X in the month.'

My com unit bleeped.

'Right, everyone, you can leave your stuff here. We're going to Hawking Hangar. Members of the History Department are about to set out on their next assignment. I thought you might like to see the reason we're all here.'

I led them down to Hawking and installed them out of harm's way up on the gantry. They fell silent, looking down on the scene below.

We have eight regular pods, numbered – amazingly – one to eight, and a big transport pod – TB2. Pods are our centre of operations. From the outside, they look like small, unobtrusive stone shacks. Inside, there's the console with two seats whose design has apparently been stolen from some medieval torture chamber. Above the console is the screen so we can see what's going on outside. Lockers contain the equipment needed for whichever assignment we're on. The first-aid kit is huge and situated next to the kettle so we have all of life's necessities together in one place. Thick bundles of wiring and cables are bunched around the walls. Think shabby hi-tech. They can sleep two or three people in moderate comfort, or four to five in extreme discomfort. We live and work in them during whichever time period we've been assigned. They're slightly claustrophobic, the toilet never works properly, and they smell of cabbage. They're frequently eye-wateringly squalid. I once went to the Cretaceous for three months and when I got back, the Technical Section swore blind the smell was making the paint on the walls bubble.

Orange-clad techies were running around, lugging umbilicals out of the way, and carrying out last-minute checks. I saw Dieter checking things off on his clipboard and talking to someone inside Number Three.

I nudged Atherton and gestured to the historians approaching from the other end of the hangar. Prentiss and Bashford, now apparently fully recovered from boot trauma, were off to 11th-century Coventry to look for evidence of the Godiva legend.

Personally, I thought this was just asking for trouble – a view shared by Peterson who had warned Prentiss for God's sake to keep an eye on Bashford, saying that he would hold her personally responsible for any trouble that might arise during this assignment. A warning to which the two of them had responded with looks of almost supernatural innocence.

'You do know that's where the legend of Peeping Tom originated, don't you?' I'd said to Peterson afterwards. 'And he went blind.'

'If Bashford comes back even mildly short-sighted, there will be trouble,' he muttered. 'Seriously, Max, I'd forgotten what a pain in the arse your people are. Can I have my old job back?'

'No. Close the door behind you.'

Anyway, Prentiss wore the usual nondescript woollen dress in muddy brown. Forget television and sweeping around in beautiful flowing gowns. Ours were always ankle length. If you had ever seen a medieval street then yours would be ankle-length too. Or possibly, you'd wear a hazmat suit. Piss, entrails, rotting vegetables, wet straw, dead dogs – yes, you'd definitely want your hem sweeping through that little lot, soaking up the good stuff and then wrapping itself around your legs for the rest of the day.

Prentiss's head was covered in a grey hood that extended down over her shoulders. No hair was showing. She carried a wicker basket.

Bashford wore matching mud tones, boots, and carried a staff.

I turned to my trainees. Time to start earning my meagre pay.

'Miss Prentiss and Mr Bashford. Off to 11th-century Coventry. What we call a basic bread-and-butter jump. Someone at Thirsk will want some information, so off we go. You will notice the unobtrusive dress. We never stand out. Our behaviour is always discreet and unremarkable.'

I paused for a moment in case I was struck dead on the spot but no, as usual, the god of historians wasn't paying attention.

'Concealed about their persons will be – for defensive purposes only – a stun gun and pepper spray, together with water-purification tablets, a compass, and anything else they feel appropriate. This is a two-day assignment. They're due back tomorrow, around three.'

It was Atherton who asked the question. 'What if they don't come back?'

I turned to face them because this was important.

'Then we go and get them. We take everyone who can be spared, and we go after them and we bring them back, because we're St Mary's and we never,

ever, leave our people behind.'

Sykes said in her deceptively soft Scottish accent, 'I heard a couple of people were lost for ten years.'

Bugger! I had forgotten that at St Mary's, rumour defies the laws of physics and travels considerably faster than the speed of light.

'Yes, that's true. But it was ten years for us. Not for them. According to Grey and Bashford, they were only missing for a few hours. And we found them in the end. We always do.'

Yes, we always did. Even when it was four hundred years too late and we were staring at a broken body folded into a box and left for us to find centuries later. Schiller was buried properly now, in our little churchyard. A peaceful sunny spot, marked with her name.

I stood with my trainees and we watched Bashford and Prentiss walk down the hangar. There was the familiar banter and the dreadful jokes. They entered Number Three. Dieter, the other Chief Technical Officer, followed them in. I couldn't see Leon anywhere.

Five minutes later, Dieter exited the pod and waved his team back behind the safety line.

I stepped to one side to watch my trainees, because I wanted to see their faces.

The pod blinked out of existence in its usual unexciting manner and people filed past me until the gantry was empty except for us. Slowly, Hawking returned to normal. Orange techies shouted to each other and began to heave the umbilicals back into place. Somewhere, a metal tool tinkled on the concrete floor and someone cursed.

They still stood, all five of them, staring at the spot where Number Three had been. North drew a long breath and turned to look at me. Naturally, she was far too cool to show any unseemly excitement. Not so Sykes, who had a huge grin from ear to ear and said, 'Wow!'

Atherton nodded. Hoyle's face showed no emotion, but I noticed his white knuckles as he gripped the handrail. Apart from his questions to me, he'd barely spoken, just standing quietly and watching everything around him. He spoke now. 'How long? How long before that's us?'

'That,' I said, 'is up to you. Not this afternoon anyway, so you may as well all go and get something to eat. We're finished for today. Please be in Training Room 2 at 09.30 tomorrow for your first session. Dismissed.'

They disappeared.

Down below, the radio started up again and somewhere, I could hear Polly Perkins, head of IT, calling out figures to someone unseen. Just another day.

I turned to go and found Leon standing directly behind me. For how long had he been there?

He drew me away from the railing. 'What's the matter?'

'Nothing. Nothing at all.'

He didn't speak.

'Well, maybe just a faint stab of nostalgia. I might call in and see Dr Foster and see if she'll put me back on the active list ahead of schedule.'

He didn't move.

'Something wrong?'

He sighed and looked around, but we were quite alone.

'Leon, what's wrong?'

He took my hand. 'You know I would do anything you ask?'

I nodded. This sounded serious. 'Yes, I do know that.' I tried to lighten his mood. 'That's why I never ask you for anything. Too easy!'

He tightened his grip. 'So you know why I never ask *you* for anything, either?'

'Yes.'

'Well, I'm asking now. I'm going to ask you for something.'

'All right. Ask away.'

'Are you sure?'

'Yes.'

'I know you're desperate to get back to your old job. I don't hold it against you and when the time comes, I'll encourage you to get back on the horse – or into the pod – but you have six months off. Take it. I love knowing you're here. I love leaving in the morning knowing you'll still be here when I come back. We have six months and I really, really want us to have this time together. I'll happily let you go when the time comes, but please, Max, just give me these six months.'

I swallowed, then nodded. 'All right, I will.' I grinned at him. 'What will you do when you discover that after only six weeks you can't stand the sight of me?'

'Six weeks? That long?'

'Techies have a short attention span. I was giving you the benefit of the doubt.'

Three

Their first assignment.

I'd compressed months of training into just a fraction over seven weeks. A little longer than I'd anticipated, but we'd had two sprained ankles and a dislocated shoulder to contend with. Leon had whirled them through the first part of the pod familiarisation course. The Security Section had beaten the basics of self-defence and first aid into them, and under the erratic but usually benign supervision of Professor Rapson, they had immersed themselves in the theory and practice of nearly everything. In my day, we'd been obliged to have secondary areas of expertise as well as our primary subject but I'd kicked all that into touch. They'd nominated their primary specialities and that would do for the time being. It would mean a lot of intensive research for individual assignments, but we'd address that later.

Today, they were about to start work on their first assignment. This was when we would begin evaluating the success of the new training programme. *My* new training programme.

I stood in front of them in one of the small rooms off the Hall. The sun streamed in through the windows, highlighting the dancing dust. Outside, late winter was thinking about giving way to early spring. I could hear the comforting roar of the History Department at work on the other side of the wall. There were worse places to be on a Wednesday morning.

'Good morning, ladies and gentlemen. If you open the folders in front of you, you will find details of your first assignment.'

I could almost feel their little shiver of anticipation. They opened their folders. Inside was a single piece of paper, which read:

Assignment: SM/TC46/VOK
Objective(s):

- ➢ To survey and map the Valley of the Kings.
- ➢ To identify any previously undiscovered burial sites.
- ➢ To record their location.
- ➢ To pass details to the University of Thirsk for future exploration.

They looked up at me.

'There are many pharaohs whose tombs have yet to be discovered. It may be that some of them lie in the Valley of the Kings. Or not. That is for you to ascertain. You will survey the Valley, note the position of anything previously unknown, and pass details to Thirsk for them to check out at a later date.

'I've deliberately not given you any other instructions because you will have complete responsibility for planning this assignment and I want to see how you set about it. You will decide the date to which you will jump. And the location. Yours will be the selection of personnel and equipment. On your successful return, you will work up your findings and present them to Dr Peterson for onward transmission to Thirsk.

'Today's session brings together everything you have learned over the last month. You may work alone or as a team. At the end of the day, we will look at what you've produced. This is your first assignment, people. Let's see what sort of a job you make of it.'

They were already reaching for their scratchpads.

'Right, the time is 09.45. At 15.00, you will present your findings to me, answer my questions, and muster all your powers of persuasion. Please bear in mind that your work today will be subject to intense scrutiny by me as your primary trainer, Dr Peterson as Chief Operations Officer, the rest of the History Department, and the Security Section. To say nothing of Dr Bairstow. So no pressure. Good luck.'

It was interesting to watch them. They were terribly polite to each other to begin with, which was disconcerting, but that wore off quite quickly and relations soon deteriorated to normal as they scornfully rejected each other's proposals in favour of their own plans.

In my mind, I had already decided that North and Lingoss would probably work alone. North wouldn't want to share credit and Lingoss was naturally independent. Atherton and Sykes might work together. Hoyle, even after seven weeks, was still unknown territory.

I stayed with them for about half an hour, just in case anyone had any questions or there was a fistfight – they didn't and there wasn't – and as they began to build their data stacks, I left them to it. There was the faint possibility there would be a bloodbath as soon as my back was turned, but they had to learn to work with each other sometime.

I was in my office, formulating the questions for Friday's examination, when Markham wandered in.

'Can I have a word, Max?'

'Sure. What's the problem?'

He wandered around the office, reading old notices on my board and fiddling with my calendar before coming to a halt in front of my desk.

'Do you remember – last year – our little unpleasantness at Old St Pauls?'

'I do, yes.'

No need to say any more. None of us would ever forget our little unpleasantness at Old St Paul's during the Great Fire of London. The entire History Department had been ambushed by Clive Ronan and Isabella Barclay and trapped in the burning cathedral. Sands had been left unconscious. Schiller murdered. And that wasn't the end of it. Events had rumbled on, culminating in my being shot at our Open Day.

He said nothing. More was obviously required from me.

'Yes, I do remember it, but we've had the Security Section on every salvage operation since then and there haven't been any further problems. Have there?'

'No, but that isn't what I was talking about. We've missed something. We've been so busy ensuring something like that could never happen again that we haven't given any thought to how it managed to occur in the first place.'

'Sorry, I'm not with you.'

He turned from the window.

'How did they know we'd be at St Paul's? On that date. In that place. How did they know?'

'Well, I …' I stopped. It hit me like a blow. How *had* Barclay and Ronan known where and when we'd be? With all of History out there – how had they known? How could they have known?

'I – I don't know.'

But I did know. I just didn't want to say it. To think it, even.

'Yes, you do.'

'Are you saying …?'

'Yes, I am. There's no other explanation. Someone tipped Ronan off.'

'Someone here. From St Mary's?'

'Yes.'

'But how?'

'Easy enough. Ronan hooked up with Barclay. Why not someone here as well?'

It came out as a whisper. I almost couldn't bear to put the thought into words. 'Who? Who could it possibly be?'

'No idea. Virtually everyone was involved in the Old St Paul's assignment and certainly everyone in the unit knew about it. It could be anyone.'

I clutched at a straw. 'Thirsk knew. It could have been someone from Thirsk.'

'They didn't know the coordinates. Only someone

here could have accessed those and passed them on.'

I stared at him. 'Do you know what this means?'

'I do, yes. It means we have a traitor here.'

I did what I always do in a crisis. I went to see Peterson who took one look at me and asked his current assistant, Miss Lee, to make the tea. She immediately disappeared out of the door on some unknown errand somewhere.

'I don't think you're doing it right,' I said, smugly. 'My Mrs Shaw brings me chocolate biscuits as well.'

'I blame her previous owner,' he said, putting the kettle on. 'Why are you here? Have all your trainees run away? I have to say, I was hoping they'd last a little longer than this. My bet was eight weeks.'

I dropped into the visitor's chair and baldly recounted my conversation with Markham.

He handed me a mug and said thoughtfully, 'Well I wondered …'

'You never said anything.'

'What could I say? No one else said anything. Dr Bairstow, especially, never said anything. I concluded I was an idiot and forgot about it.'

'Well, you got one thing right.' He threw a paperclip at me. 'If there was anything to it then surely the Boss would have said something.'

'Not necessarily. Last year was all about putting St Mary's back together again. The last thing he would want would be rumours that someone in this unit was tipping off Clive Ronan. Can you imagine the way people would look at each other?'

I sipped my tea. 'Should we say something to him,

perhaps?'

'I don't think so. If there's any possibility of it being true then he'll already be all over it like a tramp on a kipper. He won't want us getting underfoot. If he wants any input then he'll ask for it. But we could keep our eyes open.'

'For what? I asked, bitterly. 'It's more than six months ago now. If there ever was any evidence, it's long since been disposed of.'

'Maybe we could look at motive. Why someone would do such a thing.'

'Revenge. Jealousy.' I stopped suddenly.

He finished it for me. 'Money.'

My first impulse was to deny it. My second was that he might be right. We're not well paid. In Markham's case, what with all the Deductions from Wages for Damages Incurred forms he's signed over the years, he's barely paid at all. And money is a powerful motive.

'No, surely the first thing the Boss would have done is to check everyone's bank accounts.'

He sighed patiently. 'Max, there are many ways of concealing a large amount of money other than shoving it in a bank account.'

'I bow to your superior knowledge.'

I was joking, but the implications were frightening me.

He finished his tea. 'What have you done with them?'

'Who?'

He grinned at me and signalled downstairs with his eyes.

'Shit!' I leaped from my chair. I had forgotten all about my trainees.

'Please promise me you and Leon will never have kids. There won't be a shop in Rushford that hasn't got a tiny Maxwell outside, crying in the cold, forgotten and abandoned in her pram.'

'Very funny. Can I have my old job back?'

'No. Close the door behind you.'

I raced back, half convinced there would be blood up the walls by now, but when I peered in through what dear old Mr Strong always referred to as a viewing aperture, they were all still working, heads bent over their data stacks.

I went for some lunch.

I spent the afternoon compiling the Friday afternoon examination questions. We'd all been through this. Now, however, I was the one setting the questions. Trying to find the balance between testing their knowledge without being too harsh. It's a fine line. If they can't handle the workload then now is the time to find out, but if I were too harsh, then in forty-eight hours I'd have no trainees left at all.

At 14.30, my assistant, the lovely Mrs Shaw, brought me a mug of tea and a ton of paperwork. I signed and sipped.

At 15.00 on the dot, I was walking through the classroom door. Whether they had finished or not, it was presentation time.

I had been right. North had worked alone. Sykes and Atherton had worked together and surprisingly, after a while, it seemed the conventional Mr Hoyle and the unconventional Miss Lingoss had combined their efforts as well.

I made myself comfortable and we began.

Not surprisingly, they'd all opted for a period of around the end of the 18th dynasty, one of the most famous and powerful dynasties in all of Egypt's long history. Famous Pharaohs included Hatshepsut, the female pharaoh, Akhenaton, the heretic pharaoh, and of course, Tutankhamun. Egypt was at the very height of its power and influence. By the end of the 20th dynasty, around one hundred years later, the ancient civilisation of Egypt had begun its long decline and the Valley of the Kings was slowly abandoned, the tombs desecrated, destroyed, or forgotten.

All of them had selected sites looking down into the Valley. North, Sykes, and Atherton had selected the south-eastern slopes and Hoyle and Lingoss had gone for the hillside to the south-west, arguing that this would give them a better chance of identifying the owners of the large number of anonymous tombs in that area. Both sides defended their position vigorously and we all enjoyed twenty-five minutes of spirited academic debate and abuse.

Other than that, the two scenarios were reasonably similar – as they should be – with only minor differences in equipment and allocation of personnel. Naturally, everyone had placed themself in charge. I could have appointed any of them as mission controller, but out of curiosity, I nominated Lingoss. I wanted to see what she could do. She'd get some grief from North who seemed quite shocked that she hadn't been chosen and it would be interesting to see how that manifested itself and how Lingoss would deal with it.

I passed the details over to Peterson who said, 'Rather you than me,' but allocated me Roberts and Sands to help spread the supervisory load. From there I wandered down to Markham who was drooping with boredom behind a paper-laden desk and welcomed me with enthusiasm.

Since we would be well away from the areas patrolled by the Medjay - the official Egyptian police, who patrolled the Necropolis and the Valley itself, he agreed we didn't need the full might and majesty of the entire Security Section and we settled for Markham himself, Randall, and Evans.

That made a total of eleven people, plus all the equipment, scanners, laser measuring devices, recorders, whatever. That meant at least three pods, probably four, which was just asking for trouble half way up a mountain, so we settled for our big transport pod, TB2.

I've already said that pods are our centre of operations. We live and work in them. I usually go on to say how small and squalid they are, but that's not true in the case of TB2, which is *big* and squalid and, despite being of fairly recent construction, and to my certain knowledge never hosted any sort of cabbage derivative in its entire life, still manages to smell of boiled brassica. It does, however, have the benefit of a large working area, should we be overtaken by sunstroke, dust storms, plagues of locusts, rains of frogs, or whatever the ancient kingdom of Egypt felt like throwing at us. Actually, I've been to Egypt before, and it's quite pleasant. So long as you stay away from the Nile crocodiles, of course, and what were the odds of finding one of those half way up a mountain?

We spent two days being instructed in the use of geological mapping and surveying equipment by the Technical Section. And how to repair it. It would seem they had very little confidence in our ability not to break anything.

We assembled outside TB2 and I surveyed the troops. We were all dressed in desert camouflage. In contrast to our well-worn gear, the trainees' fatigues looked stiff and uncomfortable, although they'd had the sense to break their boots in. I remembered Markham telling me that when he'd first started here, they'd used the old-style boots, and the only way you could soften them up enough to get them to bend was to reverse a lorry over them. Which, he had gone on to inform me, had led to the unpleasantness with the former wall outside Hawking and an irate Major Guthrie.

'Really?' I said. 'So there's no truth in the claim that Randall told North the best way to soften them up is to pee on them.'

Randall, standing nearby, grinned. 'I made the offer,' he said. 'She turned me down, can you believe, and I even told her she didn't have to take them off if she didn't want to.'

I tried to imagine North standing quietly by while Randall peed on her boots, failed, and ushered them into the pod.

'All laid in,' said Dieter, running an eye over the console. 'Who's driving?'

'Me,' said Sands, stowing his bag in a locker. Dieter had the grace not to look too relieved, but we all knew it was far too early in their training to let the trainees drive.

I stood against the lockers, out of the way, and watched them get on with it. Roberts did the head-count and Sands began to flick switches. Dieter wished us luck and left.

'Everyone set?' said Sands.

I heard the sound of five collective breaths being drawn. Here we go. If anyone was going to panic …

'Computer, initiate jump.'

And the world went white.

We landed with only a very gentle bump, but almost immediately, we tilted. Someone gasped but before we all descended into full-blown panic or slid down the mountain, or both, one of the hydraulic legs automatically extended, and we were level again.

Sands busied himself shutting things down.

'Right,' I said. 'Who can tell me what just happened?'

As usual, North was ready to speak, but was pipped at the post by Lingoss.

'We landed successfully,' she said, 'but the terrain wasn't level and one of the legs extended to keep us stable.'

'Correct. Can anyone tell me what happens next?'

Again, North drew breath, but Sykes got in before her.

'We should carry out safety checks.'

'In the form of?'

North was speaking even before I'd finished.

'We should check the readings and use the computer to confirm we are where and when we should be. We should angle all the cameras to check for any possible hazards outside the pod. We should check the proximity alerts. We should each inspect our equipment and carry out a com check. On permission from Mr Sands, we exit the pod.'

'Anything else?'

She shook her head. They all looked at each other, mystified.

I sighed. 'Welcome to the glamorous world of the historian, people. Yes, everything Miss North has said is correct, however …'

I paused. They still looked mystified.

'So you've all been to the loo, have you? Checked you have enough water? Applied your sun cream? You have, presumably, noticed the outside temperature?'

Sheepishly, they shuffled off. You have to drill these things into people. They must be made aware it's the little things that could get them killed. An unfortunately timed comfort break at Thermopylae had once nearly changed the course of History.

Finally, they were ready.

'In your own time, Mr Sands.'

The ramp came down and they got their first glimpse of a whole new world.

I gave them a moment to get their heads around it. Everyone's first jump is a special occasion. There is nothing in the world to compare with the moment you exit the pod and take your first look around at a new time and a new place, and realise that this is what all that training has been about. The first jump used to be a solo affair with a few hair-raising scenarios thrown in, just to sort the historians from the boys, but that was something else I'd discontinued. In terms of time and cost, we simply couldn't afford to get that far in the training schedule only to have someone bottle out right on the verge of qualification.

Those of us who'd done this before all grinned at each other, stood back, and watched their faces. Just for once, they were simultaneously struck dumb. They stared about them, blinking in the hot, hard sunshine. We were three and a half thousand years ago and sometimes, you need a moment to process that fact.

The red rocks around us were silhouetted darkly against a gloriously blue sky. Above our heads, an eagle screamed faintly as it was mobbed by other birds and climbed higher to escape them.

I looked around us. Our site was perfect. From our vantage point, we could look directly down into the Valley of the Kings – or, to give it its correct name, the Great and Majestic Necropolis of the Millions of Years of the Pharaoh, Life, Strength, Health, in the West of Thebes. That's the Egyptians for you. Brilliant builders – crap at naming things. I think we'll stick with Valley of the Kings.

We had arrived – we hoped – at the end of the 18th Dynasty, at the height of tomb building. Looking down, the area teemed with people, all of them beavering away in the hot sunshine. Some wore loincloths, others wore short tunics. Most had covered their heads, either against the sun or to mop up the sweat.

In the distance, the Nile glittered in the late-autumn sunlight, cutting a broad swathe through the desert. A hundred little boats – feluccas – plied their trade. Those travelling south to north were using the flow of the Nile; those travelling in the opposite direction had raised their triangular sails.

A wide band of cultivated land ran along each riverbank, gloriously green against the desert red. The dividing line between the two was quite abrupt. It was perfectly possible to stand with one leg in the Black Land (the fertile river plain) and the other in the Red Land (the desert). The flood season – inundation – was ending. Patches of standing water reflected the sky. Sowing would soon begin.

The air was crystal clear up here and I could make out individual areas of cultivation, groves of palm trees, irrigation channels, irrigation devices – or shadufs, small buildings, even a line of camels being taken down to drink. A flight of large, white birds flew gracefully over the Nile and alighted on a sandbank.

In contrast, the Valley itself was thick with dust, kicked up by the feet of beasts and men. Work was progressing simultaneously in several areas and even at this distance, I could hear the ringing tap-tap-tap of chisel on rock and hear the occasional shout or a donkey braying a protest. Piles of stone blocks stood around at regular intervals, waiting to be dressed or incorporated into current building schemes.

The ever-present dust, however, could not conceal what looked like scores and scores of tomb entrances. Best of all, in the centre of the Valley, at its lowest point, exactly where it should be, a fresh scar indicated the entrance to the tomb of Tutankhamun. We had jumped to exactly the right time. The Valley was still occupied – extensive tomb robbing had not yet led to the tomb entrances being concealed either deliberately, or by Nature herself. The presence of the feared Medjay was sufficient deterrent against thieves, but that worked both ways. There would be patrols everywhere. We would have to be careful.

Markham drew me aside. 'Who's in charge, here?'

'Me.' I said, 'But for the purposes of this exercise, Miss Lingoss. Please tell your people that unless she wants them to do something really stupid, they are to take their instructions from her.'

The warning wasn't necessary. Miss Lingoss already had everyone lined up outside TB2 and was requesting the Security Team carry out a reconnaissance. While they were doing that, she herded everyone else into their teams, reminded them of their duties and responsibilities, made them carry out their com tests again, checked they had sufficient water with them, and despatched them to their allocated positions.

I liked her. Despite what I suspected was an inclination to solitude and independence, she showed all the signs of a natural leader. I had high hopes of her, despite her unconventional appearance. The Mohican was covered by a camouflage hat with an assortment of pens and pencils rammed into the band. Without make-up, her face was pale, angular, and determined.

'Not bad,' said Markham, joining me on the ramp in the shade. 'What's the matter with the tall one?'

'You mean Miss North?'

He nodded.

'She thinks command should be hers. She's now trying to work out whether doing as she's told and displaying team qualities will stand her in better or worse stead than displaying initiative by challenging her temporary boss.'

He grinned. 'She does know there's no correct answer to that one, doesn't she?'

'Hopefully, by the time she's worked it out, she'll have realised she doesn't need to work it out. Shall we go and see what's happening?'

We stepped out into the bright sunshine. Autumn in Egypt is actually quite pleasant, especially up here with the cooling breezes.

We set off.

I've visited the Valley of the Kings as a tourist several times, and the difference between then and now, as always, takes some getting used to. For example, in this time, the floor of the Valley was rough – not the artificially smooth surfaces constructed for tourists – but piled up with naturally occurring rocks and spoil from the tombs. The floor itself was much lower than in modern times, as well. Innumerable flash floods would wash silt and debris down into the Valley, building up the bottom and burying the tomb of Tutankhamun, thus keeping it nearly intact for that all-important future discovery in the early 20th century.

I gave myself five minutes to enjoy the panorama below me and then, with some regret, resumed my Training Officer role and concentrated on my charges.

I spent an hour or so with each team. Atherton, Hoyle, and Roberts were detailed to cover the south-east corner. There were any number of anonymous tombs in that area that we hoped to be able to identify. I could see Hoyle twisting his viewfinder, trying to home in on a line of carving over a lintel.

Lingoss, North, Sykes, and Sands were covering the western side of the valley where there was another cluster of unidentified tombs to survey.

They'd all found themselves shelter and shade and assembled their kit. They were working quietly together, dictating, recording, and surveying. Except, of course, for North who was trying to do everything herself. Sands, as per instructions, was letting her do things her way. He grinned at me as I passed.

Markham and I spent the afternoon toiling between the two teams and then, as the shadows lengthened, I instructed Lingoss to pull them back to TB2, because this was only half of the job. Now they needed to assimilate their findings, update their records, liaise with the each other, and decide on their next day's order of work. You can only plan so far ahead and some decisions must be made on site.

Back in the pod, they ditched their packs with sighs of relief, had a good drink, and made themselves comfortable. I watched Atherton and

Sykes working quietly together. After a moment, they were joined by Hoyle and Lingoss, comparing their findings. The four of them had their heads together and then one called a question to Sands, who responded and passed over a data cube.

Only North seemed to keep herself apart. I sighed. She wasn't going to last long at this rate. I know from personal experience – it's just too much work for one person alone. You have to have a partner. I wondered how long it would take her to realise this, or even, gloomily, whether she would realise it at all. Should I say something to her, or leave her to work it out for herself? There was no doubt she grated on my nerves. How happy would I be to see her fail? I hesitated and then the decision was taken out of my hands by Atherton, who called her over to confirm something on his scratchpad. Once there, it was only natural for her to sit down and start collaborating with the others. I mentally awarded a couple of extra points to Atherton the Peacemaker.

We got our heads down early that night and awoke ready for the new day.

Four

There was the usual healthy bickering over who was responsible for making the tea.

'Actually,' said Hoyle, 'can I have coffee? I don't like tea.'

The world stopped spinning on its axis. Ten people eyed him with expressions ranging from condemnation to compassion via outright bewilderment.

'Was it when you were in America?' asked Roberts, sympathetically. 'Did they make you drink coffee there?'

'No, I didn't like tea before I went to America. Never have.'

'So, you don't drink tea at all?' persisted Roberts, adrift in the unknown.

'No.'

'Why not?'

'Well, it tastes awful.'

Ten people recoiled at this heresy. Sands tightened his grip on his mug as if fearing it would be torn from him and coffee would suddenly become compulsory.

Hoyle seemed unaware of the consternation around him, calmly spooning coffee into a mug and topping it up with boiling water. I watched him as he sat quietly, sipping his devil's brew and, as usual, taking very little part in the conversation around him. Even after all this time, he was the trainee about whom I knew the least. He was quiet, polite, and hard working, he caused no trouble at all, and yet every time I looked at him, I felt a stir of unease. Who did he remind me of?

The Security team did another quick recce as they loaded up their equipment. Apart from reminding them to make sure they had enough tapes and water, I hardly had to do a thing. I could get used to this training lark.

To make sure we were all on the same page, I asked Miss Lingoss to lay out the day's schedule.

'We think we may have identified an opening on the south-eastern side of the valley. There's a cluster of three tombs together – KV60, KV20, and off to one side, KV43. However, at a fork in the path, close to KV60,' she stabbed at the map, 'we've identified a stone formation that looks suspiciously regular. We've consulted modern maps and there's nothing shown. We think there's a possibility that over the centuries, whatever is there will be concealed by the spoil from KV19, which, of course, hasn't been built yet.'

'Satisfactory work,' I said. 'Who identified the site?'

Without hesitation, she nodded across the pod and I was pleased to see she had no difficulty bestowing credit where it was due. 'Atherton.'

'Well done, Mr Atherton. I shall look forward to viewing your findings this evening.'

They loaded themselves up with equipment again and we stepped outside into the early-morning sunshine. The air seemed close and still. I wiped sweat from my forehead. It was hotter than yesterday. Much hotter.

Markham and Randall reported the area clear. Lingoss directed them to their original sites and they dispersed.

I gave them half an hour, then picked up a water flask, and settled my hat firmly on my head. I was just exiting the pod when I met Markham coming towards me from further up the trail.

'We may have a problem.' He gestured.

He was right. We did have a problem.

Over to the northeast, clouds were building on the horizon. Big, ominous bubbling clouds of purple and dirty grey. I remembered this area was prone to heavy winter rainfall.

'I think we should get them all back,' he said. 'We'll wait things out inside the pod. I know it looks a long way off, but the autumn storms in this area can be ferocious.'

I nodded. These were trainees. We weren't taking any chances. 'I'll recall them now. How secure is the pod?'

'It's big and solid and waterproof. I'll get the lightning rod up. We may have to power down for a while, but we'll be perfectly safe.'

I stepped aside and activated my com. 'This is Maxwell. We have a heavy weather warning. Pack up your gear and return to the pod. Immediate action. Maxwell out.'

Markham had crawled forwards to look down into the valley. 'Max. Come and look.'

Any doubts I might have had about whether I was being over-cautious were dispelled when I saw what was going on below. Controlled panic. Workers were scurrying around, shouting orders and instructions. Tools and valuable items were being loaded onto protesting camels and donkeys. This was not people battening down for a storm. This was an evacuation. They were leaving as quickly as they could. Canvases were hurriedly thrown over valuable but immovable items, their flapping corners secured. Everyone seemed in a big hurry to leave.

Even as we watched, the wind got up, blowing stinging dust and sand into our eyes. I reached for my sunglasses and Markham pulled his scarf around his neck. In the sky, clouds boiled angrily, enveloping the sun, leaving only a frilly golden glow around the edges. A big weather front was coming through. I clambered to the top of a nearby rock and looked anxiously for my people.

Atherton and Hoyle were first back, escorted by Roberts and Evans. All of them were staggering slightly under the weight of all their gear and Atherton, a true historian in the making, was complaining bitterly at having to break off his work for something as trivial as life-threatening weather.

I could see no sign of any of the others. They should have been right behind them. Even as I opened my com, North spoke in my ear. 'Dr Maxwell, we have a problem.'

If I had a hundred pounds for every time I'd heard that …

'Report.'

'Mr Sands has fallen. He's not badly hurt, but his ankle is twisted.'

Markham rolled his eyes. 'Who's with him?'

'Me, Lingoss, North, and Mr Randall.'

Markham nodded. 'On my way. The rest of you, continue back to TB2.'

'But, sir …'

'An order, Miss North. Immediate action.'

He closed his com. 'Looks like it's you and me again, Max.'

Of course it was.

He turned back to the other team and raised his voice over the wind. 'All of you stay here with the pod. No one leaves. I don't want us heroically rescuing Sands, to get back and find you lot have wandered off and fallen down a ravine. Mr Roberts has command. Come on, Max.'

They would, of course, have to be the team that was furthest away. I pulled my scarf around my face and we set off, clambering over rocks and scrambling along goat paths. Neither of us bothered about whether we could be seen from the valley. Down there, they had more important things to worry about than us.

We met North and Sands making their way towards us. The others, burdened by all the equipment, would be making slower progress. She had his arm around her shoulders and was supporting him as best she could. It had to be North. Sykes was too short and Randall knew better than to leave two trainees unescorted.

I raised my voice above the wind. 'What happened?'

'He slipped on a rock and hurt his leg.'

Sands was red with effort and mortification. 'Sorry, Max.'

He'd lost his left foot at the Battle of St Mary's. He had his bionic foot now and he always swore it would never be a hindrance but today it was, because he'd twisted his good ankle.

'Not your fault. Get back and help them to secure the pod. Where are the others?'

'Not far. Back up that trail. Struggling a bit with all the equipment.'

'Go. We'll give them a hand and be right behind you.'

They disappeared back to the pod and we found the others about a hundred yards further back, carrying tripods, mapping equipment, and recording devices. Markham took a heavy case from Lingoss and I grabbed a tripod and slung a recorder around my neck.

Around us, the wind had picked up again. The frilly border around the clouds had disappeared. The furthest hills had vanished in the murk. It was noticeably colder.

Markham led the way and Randall brought up the rear.

It wasn't easy, making our way along the path with all our kit. The wind blew stinging dust everywhere, but we weren't doing too badly and we certainly weren't in any immediate danger, which made a nice change, and then it all went wrong.

Just one – then another – then another – huge raindrops began to splatter to the ground, raising little craters in the dust. Some hit the ground so hard they bounced straight back up again. One or two fell on me and then, with no other preliminaries, the storm was upon us.

It wasn't rain. It was a solid torrent of water. I was drenched in seconds. We all were. The noise was overwhelming. Rain hammered into the ground and bounced off the rocks around us. And it was cold. The temperature had plummeted.

We put our heads down and did the best we could and we weren't doing too badly despite our burdens and the reduced visibility and then Randall, dependable, reliable Randall, bringing up the rear, slipped on a wet rock and went down with a terrible crash that was audible even above the noise the vertical water was making.

I turned. He lay, sprawled awkwardly and cursing fit to burst.

Markham ran back. 'You two,' he gestured to Sykes and Lingoss, 'pick this lot up and get it back to the pod. We'll follow on behind.'

Lingoss opened her mouth. 'But what about …?'

'Do it now, Miss Lingoss.'

They gathered up all the gear and staggered off into the rain.

He was right. It was vital they got all the equipment back safely. This was one of the most heavily excavated areas on the planet. We couldn't possibly leave behind a theodolite or a recorder to be discovered by archaeologists in the future. Quite apart from the archaeological furore it would raise, Dr Bairstow would quite simply kill us. And then deduct the cost of the equipment from our wages. We had brought metal detectors with us to ensure that our final foreign object search would be rigorous. This was the FOD plod (Foreign Object Damage), when we meticulously went over and over the ground to ensure we were clear, because leaving anything behind was a hanging offence.

I felt quite confident letting Sykes and Lingoss go on ahead. They didn't have far to go. The pod was only just around the corner. They couldn't come to any harm. Despite the rain pounding down on our heads and the rising wind, I still didn't feel worried.

Markham was examining Randall, shouting above the noise of the storm. 'How the hell did you manage this, you plonker?'

Peering through the rain, I could see he hadn't just tripped. He'd put his foot down some sort of hole, all the way up to his knee. He was half-kneeling, half-sitting, and still cursing.

'Does it hurt? Is anything broken?'

'No. Not much. But I can't get it out.'

No, he couldn't. He'd fallen with the whole weight of his body, which had rammed his foot into this tiny space, and he was wedged.

'We need a crowbar,' said Markham, and opened his com. 'The rock is quite soft. It's not a problem. We'll jimmy you out.' He turned away, talking into his com.

I stood up and walked a few paces up the path, meaning only to see how much distance remained between us and the pod. I still couldn't hear anything over the pounding rain, but something made me look down. An inch of running water covered the path. It doesn't sound much, but an inch of fast-flowing water is a lot. It only takes two feet of water to wash away a car. Don't ask me how I know that when I still can't tell you who the current prime minister is. Not that that really matters. The bit about the prime minister, I mean. Knowing how much water will wash you away to your death is always useful. Whereas knowing the name of the prime minister rarely is.

I looked around at the surrounding rocks as if seeing them for the first time. Saw the deep channels carved by fast-flowing water. Remembered that this area was notorious for its flash floods. This country might only receive one inch of rainfall a year but it looked to me as if they got it all in one go. I looked around at the Theban Hills, all magnificently designed to channel vast quantities of water into the valley below. And we were standing in a very deep but above all very narrow gulley. And while I'd been working all that out, the water around my ankles was running faster and deeper. We were quite low down. In the foothills. Up there, hidden in the curtains of rain sweeping down from the skies, were the high hills, from which, any minute now, thousands of gallons of water would be pouring. And a substantial amount would find its way into this gulley.

I turned back to Markham and said urgently,

shouting above the noise of the rain, 'We need to get him out. We're going to be in trouble any minute now. Flash flood. And we're right in its path.'

He pushed his wet hair back and looked around at our surroundings.

'There should be more water, surely. There have been huge amounts of water through here once upon a time. Where is it all?'

I shrugged and wiped my wet face.

'Dunno. Maybe there's been a landslide further up and something is blocking the flow. Whatever it is, we should be grateful. But we still need to get him out as quickly as possible.'

We both looked at Randall, still trapped, but the water flowing past him was still well below his waist. We had time to get him out.

Sykes and Lingoss reappeared out of the curtain of water. Sykes was clutching a crowbar.

My first impulse was to enquire sarcastically why it took two of them to carry one crowbar, but I had second thoughts. Get Randall out first. Yell at them later.

Randall's position was awkward. He couldn't sit, he couldn't stand, and the water streaming past him was knocking him off balance. Lingoss and Sykes kept him upright as best they could while Markham hacked away at the rock, which was, as he had said, quite soft. It wouldn't be long now. We would get him out.

I put my hand on Randall's shoulder. 'We'll get you out.'

He nodded, wiping his face on his sleeve.

And then, of course, just when you think things can't get any worse, they do.

Another voice in my ear. Sands, this time.

'Max?' He sounded worried.

'Busy here. What's happening?'

'Max, I'm sorry. We're going to have to go.'

My heart thumped painfully in my chest. If it's one thing every historian fears, it's being left behind. That your pod, for some reason, goes off without you. You're stranded and if it doesn't come back, you're stranded forever. We tell ourselves we're St Mary's and we never leave our people behind, but always, deep down, there's that fear ... This situation was deteriorating with every passing moment.

I kept my voice calm. 'Why? Is someone else hurt?'

'Worse.'

He paused.

'What, for God's sake?'

'It's TB2. We're blocking the flow of water down your wadi.'

'And don't think we're not grateful.'

'No – it's worse than you think. The pod is so big that we're actually diverting a bloody great riverful of water and it's flowing down the wrong side of the mountain.'

'And that is bad because ...'

'We're diverting a substantial amount of water away from the Valley of the Kings and all the debris and silt and gubbins that goes with it will be deposited somewhere else. I don't know where, but it won't be the lowest point of the valley. What I'm saying,' he said, making things crystal-clear for his idiot boss, 'is that it won't cover Tutankhamun's tomb.'

I heard Dr Bairstow's voice from long ago. 'The act of observing changes that which is being observed.'

In other words, by being here, at this time, we were blocking the passage of water. Without this flash flood, all the debris and loose rock would not crash down into the Valley of the Kings to cover Tutankhamun's tomb and keep it safe down the centuries, ready for Carter and Caernarvon to discover millennia later. The tomb would be exposed all throughout the winter. Visible to anyone who cared to stroll past with a view to a little light tomb robbing that night. We knew it should be covered over during this autumn, the one following Tutankhamun's spring burial, because the remains of seasonal flowers had been discovered amongst the spoil during the excavation. This was almost certainly the storm that led to that serendipitous burial, but we and our giant pod were in the wrong place at the wrong time and had screwed everything. The diverted water would carve fresh channels in the hillside. Future floods would also flow down the wrong side of the mountain. The tomb might never be covered over at all. We were about to have a major impact on History. If we prevented this tomb from being safely buried – if this, the most important tomb ever discovered – was left exposed to the same fate as every other tomb in this valley, then we would be changing History and History won't let that happen.

Ever.

If TB2 stayed put, then it and all of us, including Randall, would be at risk from History.

If TB2 jumped, the original flow would be restored and Tutankhamun's tomb should be safe. And Randall would drown. A great torrent of water would come racing down this wadi. Randall would drown but the tomb would be safe.

I had a decision to make.

I looked down at Markham who had paused from his efforts to free Randall to look up at me. The implication was clear. The decision was mine and whatever decision I made, he would support me without hesitation. Therefore, I'd better get it right.

I sighed. There were no procedural issues here. This was a moral dilemma. My duty was clear. My conscience would not be.

If possible, the rain came down even harder. I was blind with the force of it and shivering with the cold. Even without the unwitting protection of TB2, the level was nearly up to Randall's waist. Lingoss and Sykes were struggling to keep him kneeling upright as cold, dirty water surged past us.

'Max?' It was Sands, back in TB2, awaiting instructions.

I caught Markham's eye. He nodded briefly and then redoubled his efforts.

I took a deep breath and gave the order.

'Initiate the jump.'

There was a pause. I knew what he was thinking.

'Say again, Max.'

'Initiate the jump. Return to St Mary's. My

authority.'

'Copy that,' he said, with no expression in his voice at all, and closed the link.

Randall had closed his eyes.

He knew what this decision meant. We all knew what this decision meant. Not only were they going off and leaving us, but as soon as the pod jumped away, an enormous torrent of water would be unleashed, and a vast wall of water would race down this narrow gully, bringing down everything in its path. If Markham, Sykes, Lingoss, and I managed to keep our feet, it would be a miracle. The only one who wouldn't be swept away was Randall, still with his leg firmly trapped. Since at that point, the water would probably be a good two feet over his head, this would be small comfort, but I had no choice. We were badly parked. We were diverting floodwaters away from their natural course, which was down into the Valley of the Kings. And if I didn't correct the situation, History would correct it for me.

I leaned down so he could hear me. 'We won't leave you. We're St Mary's and we never leave our people behind.'

He was white and shaking. I didn't blame him. He couldn't see any way out of this and neither could I, because there wasn't any way out of this.

Markham squatted in front of him. 'Not going to let you die, mate.'

He gave a weak smile and nodded.

Raising my voice over the downpour, I shouted, 'Sykes, Lingoss, get yourselves to higher ground. Now. That's an order.'

Sykes was staring at me.

'But …'

Well, looking on the bright side, the original purpose of this assignment had been to foster team-building and planning skills. Now, I was presenting them with an excellent opportunity to see what happens when everything goes tits up, and however unpleasant remedial action might be, when History is involved, there's never any choice. It was a lesson that had to be learned and today was as good a day as any.

Neither trainee moved.

I shouted, partly over the rain, partly over the noise of Markham still hacking away at the rock and, judging by his occasional shout of pain, Randall himself. 'Did you not hear me? Higher ground. Go. Now.'

If TB2 had already gone – and if they hadn't then they'd be answering to me later – then any minute now a great tsunami of water was going to race down this wadi, bringing God knows what with it. If they didn't get out of here, it was very possible that it was their remains that Howard Carter would be digging up in 1922. And on a more personal note, I was bloody sure I wasn't going down in St Mary's history as the person who lost two fifths of her trainees on their very first assignment. I'd never hear the last of it, Dr Bairstow would be unhappy, and worst of all, there would be Paperwork.

'No,' said Lingoss in a tone of voice that was not defiant or disobedient but definite. She wasn't going to budge and there was nothing I could do about it. I looked at Sykes.

'Nor me,' she said. 'Team spirit, remember.'

There was no time to argue. The flood was upon us. Even over the downpour, I could hear approaching thunder. We had only seconds left. It was too late to get them out.

I shouted, 'Brace yourselves.'

And suddenly, here it was.

I stood behind Randall so any pressure of water would force him back against me and keep him upright. In an effort to shield him from the worst of it, Sykes stood as I did, but in front of him. Lingoss braced herself against the rock face with one hand and seized Sykes's belt with the other. We all clung on to each other, apart from Markham who continued to batter at the rock with frenzied blows and truly awful language.

I was enveloped in a sudden deluge of icy, foul-smelling water. If I hadn't been hanging on to Randall then I'd have been swept away in the initial impact. The shock of it made me gasp. I felt loose grit and stones shift beneath my feet and for a moment I thought I would be washed away.

People who've never been caught in a flood think it's just water. Cold and unpleasant, but just water. But it isn't. A flood of this magnitude picks up everything in its path and brings it all down with it. Dead branches – no idea where they came from half way up a mountain – swirled past me in the muddy torrent, scratching at my face and threatening to poke my eyes out. I could feel rocks banging away against my legs. Even with Randall protecting me to some extent, it still hurt.

We all hung on to each other, trying to fend off the worst of it and protect ourselves, but even so, we nearly lost our footing in that first relentless surge of water.

Within moments, Randall's straining head had disappeared below the surface. I heard Sykes shout something. She appeared to take a deep breath and then she too disappeared beneath the swirling torrent. I thought she'd been swept away, but I couldn't free a hand for her. I could feel her moving beneath the surface. Ten seconds later, she reappeared, sucked in another massive breath, and then disappeared again. I saw Lingoss tighten her grip on the rock and her face creased with the strain of holding on. I realised what the pair of them were doing. In a desperate effort to keep him alive, Sykes was giving Randall underwater mouth to mouth, and Lingoss was hanging onto her for dear life.

While all this was going on, Markham had never let up in his efforts to prise Randall's leg free, but something must have hit him below the waterline. I heard his cry as he lost his grip on his crowbar, which whirled past me and was lost before I could grab at it. I could only hope it was well and truly buried and rusted away before anyone had the chance to find it.

Markham himself tumbled past me. Without thinking, I reached out an arm and grabbed him by the scruff of his jacket. So to recap, Lingoss had hold of the rock and Sykes. Sykes was hanging on to Randall. I was hanging on to Randall and Markham and Markham was flattened against the rock face, which at least took some of the strain off my shoulders.

While all this was going on, Sykes was surfacing, sucking in air, and submerging again. Keeping up a rhythm. Her hair was plastered to her head and her eyes were two dark holes in her white face. Lingoss was gritting her teeth and just hanging on. I could see her arms quivering with the strain. The noise was tremendous. I had no idea how long we could keep this up. And what of Randall himself, still submerged underwater? I could feel no movement from him. Impossible to believe he was calmly kneeling there with the water twelve inches over his head while someone else did his breathing for him. I couldn't have done it. Was he even alive? Were we all risking our lives for a dead man? I pushed that thought away. With luck, he was unconscious, which would make everyone's job easier.

Red water poured past us even more furiously. The stink was amazing. We were buffeted on every side. I could see Lingoss bracing herself hard. Her knuckles were white with strain and her eyes squeezed tight shut. Sykes kept up the rhythm. Head above water. Suck in oxygen. Disappear. Reappear. Gasp for breath. Do it again. The force of the water was pushing them all against me and it was only a matter of time before I lost my footing. I couldn't hear myself think over the noise of the rushing water. Something hard hit me on the arm and I nearly lost Markham. He shouted something. He and I were fending off the floating rubbish as best we could but the flow was unending. There was no escape from it.

We were all hanging on for dear life. I could only hope that when the initial surge had passed then Randall's head would be above water again. Whether he would be alive or not remained to be seen.

And still the rain poured down on us. Surely a storm of this ferocity must wear itself out soon. That's the thing with flash floods. Soon started – soon over. I couldn't help remembering last year during the Great Fire of London, when we were all slowly cooking to death and I'd wished for an assignment that involved plenty of cool, clear water. They say you should be careful what you wish for. I decided to shut up in future. If I had one.

Sykes was still carrying out her mouth to mouth. I've done it myself. I know how exhausting it can be. She couldn't keep it up much longer. I began to formulate plans to change places with her without us losing our grip and being swept away. At the moment, however, there was nothing we could do but grit our teeth and endure.

Markham shouted again. He was trying to tell me something. I looked around. I looked down. Surely – yes – the water level was lower. Much lower. The initial surge, the one released by TB2's departure, was subsiding as quickly as it had come. Even the rain was letting up.

Randall's head appeared. His face was very white. Dark bruises showed clearly on his cheekbones. A deep gash ran across his forehead and up into his hairline. His eyes were closed. His hair and ears were filled with mud. Sykes fell sideways into the water, exhausted. I braced Randall's head and Markham scrabbled to clear his airways. We were all cold, but Randall's skin felt icy. I assumed he was breathing on his own. Either that or he was dead.

Markham had lost his crowbar and the crack was filled with silt and stones. There was no way we could get him out ourselves. We could only wait for rescue. For TB2 to come back.

All around us, I could hear the sounds of splashing water. There were small, recently formed waterfalls everywhere. A chill wind still blew.

Through chattering teeth, I said to Markham, 'Is he alive?'

'As far as I can see, yes. But my hands are so cold it's hard to tell.' He turned to Sykes, who was showcasing this year's drowned rat look. 'Well done.'

I nodded. 'Yes, excellent work the pair of you,' and considered what to do next.

Sykes had collapsed against the rock face. I was still taking Randall's weight and dared not move. I knew Markham wouldn't leave us so that just left Lingoss.

'Miss Lingoss, are you able to get further up the wadi and meet the rescue party?'

She hesitated, looking from me to Markham to Randall. I understood. 'They will come, Miss Lingoss. I need you to advise them to bring rescue equipment and guide them here. Quick as you can.'

The wadi still ran with water, and the going was rough, but she splashed her way up the path and out of sight.

I turned my attention to Sykes. 'Are you hurt?'

She opened her eyes and grimaced. 'Something hit

my shoulder. It hurts a little.'

'We'll get you checked out as soon as we get back.'

She nodded. 'Is he alive?'

I could hear the note of anxiety in her voice and liked her all the better for it. And I liked that she hadn't given up. She had no idea whether Randall was alive or dead, but she hadn't given up.

Markham nodded. 'He's unconscious – whether because he was walloped by something hefty or lack of oxygen or both, I've no idea. But he's bleeding so he's still alive.'

She closed her eyes again and sagged against a rock.

Time passed.

My earpiece crackled.

'Dr Maxwell?'

It was Lingoss.

'They're here, ma'am. TB2 is back. They've come back.'

'Told you,' I said. 'Bring them down here – quick as you can.'

Barely minutes later, they tramped around the corner. Peterson and Clerk in the lead and half the Security Section behind them, flourishing crowbars, hammers, and various implements. Behind them trudged Helen and Hunter, slipping and cursing as they came.

They clamped an oxygen mask to Randall's face and turned their attention to his leg. With four or five of them at it, Randall was soon free. It wasn't a painless process so it was just as well he was unconscious. They heaved him out and carted him up the path.

Hunter checked over Lingoss and Sykes. Markham and I seemed comparatively unscathed and there's a phrase I never thought I'd ever get to use. We followed along behind.

'So,' said Helen, staring at the twenty pounds of Egyptian mud adhering to her boots as we squelched our way through the still-ankle-deep water. 'Just to be clear. You nearly drowned half way up a mountain in a country that has one inch of rainfall a year.'

I considered this. Yes, a perfectly accurate statement.

'So what's next? A trip to the Namib Desert so you can contract hypothermia?'

Markham shivered. 'Don't give her ideas.'

Back in Sick Bay, they whisked Randall away, Sands had his foot bandaged, and we had our numerous bumps and bruises treated.

Someone put a mug of tea in front of me and I sat down for a moment to get my breath back.

'You OK?' said Markham, sitting himself down beside me.

'Fine. How's Randall?'

'About as well as can be expected for a bloke who's just had half a mountain wash over him. Concussed. Sprained ankle. There's also crowbar-related trauma – I missed a couple of times and hit him instead.'

'He'll never let you hear the last of that.'

'I hope not.'

He shifted in his seat and we fell silent, because for a moment up there, it had looked as if Randall might never get to complain about anything again.

'Anyway,' said Markham, 'I'd say those two have the makings of true historians. Disobeying instructions and doing the right thing. North doesn't look very happy.'

No, she didn't. There had been Drama and she hadn't been involved.

Helen wasn't happy either. I could hear her snapping and snarling at everything within reach, including the furniture. I assumed that was because Randall was still only semi-conscious and couldn't hear her, so she was taking things out on everyone else, but even so …

'What is the matter with her?'

He looked furtively over his shoulder even though she couldn't possibly hear us. 'Well …'

I inched closer. 'What? Tell me?'

'Hunter says she's given up smoking. Started yesterday.'

'No!'

'Yes.'

'Oh my God. We're dead. I'm dead. You're dead. We're all dead. We might just as well stop breathing now. The only one likely to survive is Randall and that's only because there's some sort of medical code that says you're not supposed to attack patients in your care, even if you are in the throes of nicotine deprivation.'

'That reminds me, he's asked to speak to you.'

'Who?'

'Randall.'

'It's really not necessary. And anyway, if he wants to speak to anyone, it should be those two.' I jerked my head at the two miscreants over in the corner, drinking their tea and trying to look as if they weren't there. 'Which reminds me ...' I got to my feet.

'Be gentle with them,' grinned Markham. 'It's not as if you yourself don't have form.'

'Not the point,' I said.

I ushered them into the women's ward where we were to spend the night under observation. We sat down because my bruised legs hurt.

'Well?'

They played dumb. 'Well what?'

'What was that all about?'

'You would have left them?' said Lingoss. Straight into attack mode. That's my girl.

'No, I wouldn't. I ordered you to.'

'I couldn't go. I was mission controller.'

'*I* was mission controller,' I said, tightly. '*You* are a trainee. Trainees follow orders. I ordered you to go.'

'If we'd gone then Randall would have died. And maybe you and Markham as well. You ordered me to go and it was the wrong decision.'

'No, it was the right decision. We were lucky. The priority was keeping you alive. Randall understood that. And you endangered Sykes as well.'

'I can endanger myself,' said Sykes, indignantly.

I ignored her. 'Both of you could have been swept away at any moment. And don't give me any garbage about calculating the odds and deciding the four of us could keep Randall alive when two of us couldn't.

80

You were lucky.'

'Yes, I was. We all were. What is the problem with that?'

'The problem is that I can't rely on you. Either of you. How can I give an instruction and not be able to rely on you to carry it out?' I took a deep breath. 'Have you not been here long enough to realise that trust underpins everything we do here? We all trust each other to perform our function.'

'I do know that, but you always say, "We're St Mary's and we don't leave our people behind." So I didn't.'

I was left without anything to say.

She mistook my silence. 'Look, I'm sorry. Yes, I disobeyed your instructions. I admit it and I am sorry. I apologise. I don't know what the punishment is, but I'll accept it. But please, don't punish Sykes who only followed my lead.'

Sykes opened her mouth to protest vigorously and by the sudden spasm of pain on her face, I guessed she had just been kicked under the table. They glared at each other.

Silence.

'You just redeemed yourself,' I said quietly, and got up to go.

Outside I could hear Helen giving some poor sod absolute hell.

'That's it?' said Lingoss. 'I thought there would be some sort of punishment.'

Helen's voice was drilling through the wall and getting closer every second.

'There is,' I said. 'Dr Foster has, apparently, given

up smoking. Today is her second day in. Enjoy.'

And abandoned them to their fate.

Five

I should have been tidying up the Valley of the Kings assignment. I'd passed the relevant details to Thirsk but now, instead of looking over their reports, I was doodling on an old piece of paper and staring aimlessly out of the window. The historian at work.

I hadn't really given Markham's theory about a traitor a great deal of thought – not because I didn't believe him, but because I just didn't *want* to believe him. I didn't want to believe that anyone here at St Mary's could be involved in the murder of one of their own colleagues. That was bad enough, but to stuff the body in a lead-lined chest and bury it for us to discover four hundred years later was something I couldn't to get my head around. Every time I tried to think about it – to try and get inside the mind of someone who would betray St Mary's for money – my thoughts refused to focus and just slid away.

I sighed, brought up Sykes's Valley of the Kings report, and started on the first page. Two paragraphs later and I hadn't taken anything in. This was ridiculous. I looked down at my doodles. I had drawn a giant pound sterling sign and embellished it with tiny curlicues. Very pretty but not very helpful.

I took a fresh sheet of paper and drew a square, carefully coloured it in, and began to scribble names. I started with the Housekeeping people and deleted them almost immediately. There was no way they could have accessed the coordinates and if any of them had approached Polly Perkins for them, I had yet to hear of it. I deleted Housekeeping. Ditto the caretaking team for the same reasons.

What about Admin? They'd been involved with Dr Dowson's research into the project, but again, approaching IT and asking about coordinates would have been such an unusual thing for any of them to do that someone would have remembered.

Well, this was progress. One third of the unit eliminated already.

I crossed out the kitchen staff. And Wardrobe too, which left Security, the Technical Section, R&D, the Library staff, and the History Department.

I stared at the list, and after a while, circled R&D and the Library staff and placed question marks alongside. Possible but unlikely.

The Technical Section included IT, so anyone there could have accessed the coordinates without rousing any suspicions at all. I sighed, imagining Leon's reaction if I went to him with this. Most of his people had been with him for some time and they were as tight as the History Department.

The same could be said for the Security Section. Major Guthrie ran a tight ship. Background checks were more than rigorous. I looked at the list of security guards. Guthrie had saved my bacon at Troy. I'd yanked him and Markham out of the Cretaceous

Period. Randall and Evans had been with me when we sorted out Mary Stuart. The whole team had saved Peterson and me when we were having our throats cut in Nineveh. It was impossible to believe any of them would betray St Mary's to Clive Ronan.

Which brought me, inevitably, to the History Department. If I couldn't believe the traitor was a techie or a security guard, then how much more difficult was it to believe a member of my own team was responsible? That someone had set in motion a series of events that had culminated in the murder of an historian?

No. This was woolly thinking. If it was anyone, it was someone from those three departments. It had to be. Pull yourself together, Maxwell, and concentrate.

I listed the members of the History Department and stared at them.

Peterson – no. That was the end of it. It wasn't Peterson. It just wasn't.

Nor Bashford. He hadn't even been with us then. I crossed him out too.

Nor Grey, for the same reason. Delete Grey.

Clerk? In my mind, I saw his open, freckled face. Surely, he wouldn't ...

Or Sands? Possession of the world's largest supply of unfunny knock-knock jokes admittedly made him someone to be shunned socially, but didn't necessarily make him a traitor.

And then there was Roberts, still skinny and squeaky and still, despite his best efforts, looking about twelve years old.

And Paula Prentiss, with her huge grin – the one

like a slice of melon. Calm and capable. How could it be her?

It wasn't as if any of them hadn't shown their loyalty to St Mary's hundreds of times over. I remembered them at the Battle of St Mary's, injured, bloody, and defeated. They'd given their all that day. They'd fought. We'd all fought. Everyone had lined up to defend the unit. Even the civilian staff.

Wait a minute. No. No, they hadn't. One person hadn't fought. True, there was no compulsion. Dr Bairstow had stated very clearly that it was volunteers only. Everyone had volunteered except for three people. Old Mr Swanson from R&D who could barely see properly and was, believe it or not, in charge of the poisons cupboard. Mrs what-was-her-name Midgeley, from Housekeeping, recovering from having her appendix removed.

And Miss Lee. Rosie Lee hadn't fought. I remembered Mrs Shaw telling me. Rosie Lee hadn't fought at the battle of St Mary's. She was young, she was fit, she could see. I didn't know if she had an appendix or not, but she hadn't fought. And she wasn't any kind of conscientious objector, either. Rosie Lee was one of the most aggressive and unlikeable people I knew.

I saw her now, her dark wavy hair, her hostile stare, heard her grating voice, but mostly I remembered her shabby appearance. She wasn't untidy or scruffy. Markham was scruffy. Bashford was untidy. Rosie Lee wasn't. She was ... I struggled to put my mind picture into words. There was never enough money. Her clothes were clean and neat but never new. Her shoes were shined but much repaired. The coat hanging behind the door was practical but not pretty. Her hair hadn't been styled for ... ever. She wasn't desperately poor, but she had the appearance of one for whom the cost of everything was of the first importance. That day-to-day, never-ending struggle to keep her head above the financial waters. The constant robbing of Peter to pay Paul and hoping that somehow, Peter could be repaid when the time came. That desperate, soul-sapping, endless struggle to make ends meet. No small treats. No little guilty pleasure to reward herself with at the end of a long, hard day. No pleasures at all. Every penny ruthlessly accounted for and spent. Go to work. Draw your money. Pay as many bills as you can. Don't give way to despair. Do it all again next month. And the next. Until you give in. Or die. Or, of course, until someone steps in to help, with the promise of a sum of money that will change your life forever and all you need do to have your problems solved at a stroke is just this very, very tiny thing, Miss Lee, and no one will ever know ...

I stared at her name on my sheet of paper. Of all the people at St Mary's, she was the one I could believe capable of this crime. People didn't like her. No one liked her. She was very unlikeable. Prickly, defensive, rude, hostile ... and she'd been my assistant. How easy for her to access the coordinates from my own files. A quick telephone call to an anonymous number and job done, thank you very much, Miss Lee, payment as agreed.

And she'd had the sense not to appear with a new

hairstyle and smart new clothes. She hadn't suddenly given in her notice nor done anything to arouse suspicion. She'd quietly taken the money and continued as normal and then sometime in the next eighteen months or so, when Schiller's death and her own leaving were too far apart to be connected, she would quietly hand in her notice. No one would stop her. In fact, the huge sigh of relief would probably blow her over. Then she would pack her bags and walk down the drive to a new life abroad. She would get away with it.

No. Not now she wouldn't. I saw Schiller's body, brutally crammed into that lead chest, heard the gasp of shock as she was discovered. No, she wouldn't get away with it. I didn't know what to do, but I'd think of something, In the meantime, I too would do nothing out of the ordinary. I'd carry on as usual. Two could play at that game. I could wait. Wait and see.

With both historians and trainees busy with Leon one morning, I wandered down to Peterson's office for a mug of tea. We both put our feet up and were competing in the traditional St Mary's 'Who's got the worst job?' competition when Leon almost erupted through the door, slamming it behind him. Both of us stopped in mid-argument because this wasn't something you saw very often.

It was clear that Leon ... my ... husband (note to self: work on this phrase) really wasn't very happy about something or other and I was at a bit of a loss because the traditional irritants – me and Peterson –

had been in here all morning, well out of the way.

He stood, hands on hips, glaring at the pair of us.

'Bad morning?' I enquired, displaying the perceptive insight for which I was famed.

Peterson, always the more conciliatory of the two of us, crossed to his illegal chiller and pulled out a soothing can of beer.

Averting his eyes from the big red **ELECTRICAL APPLIANCE TEST FAILURE** sticker plastered across the door, Leon sank into the nearest chair and drank deeply. It didn't seem to do him a lot of good.

'What's up?' I said.

He breathed heavily. 'You! And you!'

Peterson blinked. 'Max I can understand, but what have I done?'

'Never mind him,' I said. 'What have *I* done?'

'You – the pair of you – you're both in charge of that bunch of … of …' He paused. As many do when beginning a scathing indictment of the History Department without the aid of a thesaurus.

'What have *they* done?' As far as I knew, they'd been down in Hawking for a pod familiarisation session this morning. What could possibly have gone wrong?

'We thought …' said Leon, in a voice heavy with restraint. 'We thought that since one or two upgrades have tested successfully, that this would be a good opportunity to introduce both historians,' he nodded at Peterson, 'and hopefully future historians,' he nodded at me, 'to the heroic efforts made by my section to make their lives easier.' He paused. 'I don't know what I was thinking.'

Neither did we, but it hardly seemed the moment to say so.

'We herded them into Number Five because we could just about fit them all in. To make things easy for them to comprehend, I was doing the talking and Dieter was doing the demonstrating.'

Peterson unwisely intervened. 'You mean like cabin crew doing the safety demo.' He waved his arms in the theoretical direction of the theoretical emergency exits.

Leon eyed him coldly. 'No.'

Peterson subsided.

'We'd planned it all quite carefully. Bearing in mind the limited intellectual capacity of the History Department, we thought we'd start with the decontamination strip and work up.'

I nodded. Decontamination was vitally important. On both outward and return jumps. We had a nasty blue lamp to neutralise any germs we might be carrying, the pod walls were painted with that special anti-bacterial paint – and there was a strip of it just inside the door that sterilised our footwear, too.

'Well, with historians' giant feet stamping on the strips day in and day out, we've discovered they need daily top-ups. A dozen or so spray canisters are to be stored in the lockers for this very purpose. As we never got to inform them.'

Peterson and I made conciliatory noises. A waste of time.

'From there, we intended to demonstrate the new computer upgrades. More capacity means functions that are more intuitive. Enhanced memory means historians can spend less time wandering around wearing headsets and walking into walls. And the newly installed uplink means you can contact the computer directly and it will download any info required straight to your earpieces.'

'Neat,' said Peterson.

'Furthermore,' he said, getting into his stride, 'you can record an image, send it back to the pod, and the computer will identify it for you.'

'Even more neat,' I said. 'What did they say to that?'

Now he stared coldly at me.

'We'll never know.'

Oh ... dear.

'And then, we were to demonstrate the Sonic Scream, a modified version of which is now fitted to all our pods.'

The Sonic Scream is brilliant. It's a soundless way of dispersing unwanted crowds, ravening beasts, teenagers, politicians, and any other of the unpleasant but frequently encountered nuisances of life.

'After the unpleasantness in Hawking when you nearly destroyed the place, it's been modified so that now it doesn't actually shatter every piece of glass within a hundred yards, cause ears to bleed, or stampede livestock.'

'So quite dull, actually.'

I was ignored.

'So,' said Peterson, unwisely. 'If all of that is what didn't happen – what actually did happen?'

Leon crushed the can in his fist.

I moved around to join Peterson behind the safety of his desk.

'We ushered them inside. They're all lined up – breathless with anticipation, I'd like to think – and Roberts, whom I've always considered to be one of the more harmless idiots in your department, suddenly squeaks, 'Oh! Wow! Cupholders!' and the whole bunch of them surge forwards, exclaiming in wonder, and pulling them in and out until, of course, they break one, and when they try to fix it without us seeing, they manage to break the other one as well. They mill around the pod, mewing in confusion, and Dieter and I have to drive them out and shut the door on them before they break anything else. Or each other. God knows where they are now, and I don't really care.'

He got to his feet. 'And get rid of that chiller before it electrocutes the pair of you and I get the blame.' He stopped. 'Is anyone even listening to me?'

Peterson and I were staring at each other in excitement. 'Oh! Wow!' said Peterson, a huge grin on his face.

'I know,' I said. 'Cupholders!'

And so on to assignment number two, the purpose of which was for them to undertake research, learn to give briefings and present their findings.

I passed details of the assignment around, enjoying the looks on their faces, and allocated responsibilities.

'Mr Atherton. You will undertake the initial research and be responsible for briefing your colleagues. Mr Hoyle will assist you.

'Mr Hoyle, in addition to assisting Mr Atherton, you will be responsible for making the final presentation of your team's findings. Be aware your audience will comprise your fellow trainees, members of the History Department, and anyone else from St Mary's who cares to turn up.'

He nodded. No visible reaction.

'Miss North, you and Miss Lingoss will observe and document the flora and fauna of the period.'

I had been expecting at least a murmur of complaint from North, in case she considered herself overlooked again, but she was running her eyes down the briefing note. Given some of the fauna she would be observing, there really was very little to complain about. Lingoss was already grinning in anticipation. I looked forward to seeing how the two of them would work together.

'Miss Sykes.' She looked up. This mission was really all about her. Lingoss had proved herself, now it was Sykes's turn. I wanted to see how she would set about this. 'You will be mission controller. Put together your teams as you think fit.'

I could almost feel her excitement from here.

'Are there any questions?'

They shook their heads. Sykes was already bashing away at her scratchpad.

'Very well. Report back here in forty-eight hours. Professor Rapson, Dr Dowson, Dr Peterson, Major Guthrie, and I are already on high alert so don't be afraid to consult as widely as you like.'

'Consulting' is such a useful word. Now they could legitimately ask as many questions as they wanted. In fact, they would gain points for doing so.

They scattered to their various tasks and I made my way back to my office and the endless avalanche of paperwork that trainees generate. Sadly, and I never thought I'd use that word in conjunction with doing paperwork, I never got around to it that morning, because when I got there, I had a visitor waiting for me.

Elspeth Grey. Back from Thirsk.

Technically, she wasn't now one of mine – she belonged to Peterson, who was derelicting his duty again by jumping back to suss out the political background to the War of Jenkins' Ear. Typical.

'Hello, Elspeth,' I said, closing the door behind me. 'When did you get back?'

Unasked, Mrs Shaw put up the red light outside, signifying I wasn't to be disturbed, and made herself scarce. No help there, then.

Elspeth sat quietly, her light hair picking up colour from the sun. Despite her lengthy visit to Thirsk, she looked pale and heavy-eyed.

'Yesterday.'

I was surprised and to cover it, I made a business of sitting at my desk and shunting some files out of the way. She'd been back for nearly twenty-four hours and I hadn't seen her in Hawking in any of that time. In fact, I hadn't seen her at all.

I decided to plunge straight in. 'Have you been down to Hawking to say hello? Or to Security?'

'No.' She shook her head. 'That's what I wanted to talk to you about.'

I sat still and said nothing.

I could guess what the problem was. It had never happened to me, but it did happen and I suspected it had happened to Grey. Normally, you can't keep historians out of a pod. Any pod. They jostle each other in the doorway. They bicker over who sits in the favoured left-hand seat, but if Grey had been anywhere near a pod since her return from Roman Colchester then I had yet to hear of it.

To say she'd lost her bottle would be unfair and unkind. She and Bashford had been snatched by Clive Ronan and dumped, unprepped, almost right under the bloodstained hooves of Boudicca's approaching army, which was enough to cause anyone temporarily to mislay their bottle. True, Bashford appeared unaffected by the experience, plunging happily back into the noisy maelstrom of the History Department at work, but he'd had a bad blow to the head and for most of the time, he'd been cheerfully oblivious to what was going on around him.

Elspeth Grey had not had that luxury. As many people often do, she'd risen to the occasion and then, afterwards, as the implications began to sink in … I could imagine her lying in bed at night, torturing herself by imagining what would have happened if we hadn't turned up and saved them. That happy feeling of invulnerability that every historian carries with them … that *nothing can ever happen to me* feeling had been well and truly shattered …

And then, they'd returned, to find that ten years had passed and things had moved on …

'Elspeth, talk to me.'

She said nothing.

'Would you prefer to speak to Peterson?'

She shook her head. 'I don't want to speak to anyone.'

'But you must. If only so we can help.'

She remained silent.

'All right then, *I'll* talk.' Never a problem for me. 'You're afraid to go on assignment in case the same thing happens again. Like any historian, you're not afraid of death or injury, but you've discovered there are worse things than that. You were thrust into a situation of extreme peril. Even if you'd survived the bloodbath that was Colchester, you faced a future where you had no hope of rescue. No one knew where or when you were. You would have been condemned to a short and very brutal life out of your own time. At that moment, you were too busy saving yourself and Bashford to give it any thought, but now you've had time to work through the implications and you've decided, not unreasonably, that you never ever want to set foot in a pod again. Am I right?'

There was a horribly long pause and then, reluctantly, she nodded.

'Elspeth, it's not a problem. If you feel you want more time, I'd be happy to speak to the Boss for you. You and I both know he's not unreasonable. I'm sure he'd be happy to give you the time you need.'

'It's not that, Max. I don't … I don't want …'

Silence.

Shit.

I said quietly, 'You don't want to do this any longer, do you?' and I think it's to my credit that my first thought was not, 'Bloody hell, there goes fifty per cent of our female historians.'

'Well,' I said, 'it's not a problem because I've had a brilliant idea.'

She blinked.

'Yes, I know,' I said. 'Sometimes I amaze even me. I was going to mention this to you anyway. It's the Belverde Caves expedition next month. They invited us to send a representative. Would you like to go? You'll be gone about two months, possibly longer. Perhaps, when you return you'll be able to see your way more clearly. Even if you don't, at least you'll have a few months' thinking time.'

She nodded, still not looking at me. 'Thank you. Yes.'

'All right. I'll speak to Peterson and Dr Bairstow. You'll have to speak to Major Guthrie. Just promise me one thing, Elspeth.'

'What's that?'

'That you will come back. Even if you're leaving St Mary's for good, come back and tell Ian to his face. Don't leave him again.'

Tears began to slide down her face. I suspected we had arrived at the real problem.

'He's not the person I left behind.'

I said, gently, 'No, he wouldn't be, Elspeth. You were gone for ten years. People can change a lot in that time.'

She began to cry. I reached for one of the many boxes of tissues Peterson had warned me that training officers needed.

She continued. 'But for me it was only a few hours and I came back and he's different. Everything's different. It's no one's fault, Max.' She gulped. 'I just don't know where I fit in any longer. And now he'll hate me.'

'No he won't. There are many solutions to this prob– situation. Go to Italy. Participate in the greatest archaeological find of the decade. Clear your mind. Make a decision. Come back here and tell us what it is.'

'I will.' She stood up suddenly, 'Thank you, Max. I feel ... much better.'

'Glad to hear it.'

Bloody hell, I'm good.

On his return from the intricacies of Jenkins' Ear, I invited Peterson for a drink. A statement that completely fails to convey the speed and enthusiasm with which he whirled us both into the bar and got the drinks in. I sipped my Margarita and brought him up to speed on Grey. That done, we fell back on having a good moan about our staffing issues. Being early evening there weren't many people around and I had a good thirty minutes before meeting Leon for something to eat. Peterson was avoiding Helen whose nicotine deprivation was laying waste to everything around her, so it was a rare moment of peace for both of us. We both sighed, sat back, put our feet up on the battered coffee table, and relaxed.

The explosion blew in the windows at the far end of the room. The curtains billowed inwards. Tables were overturned. Glass lay everywhere in glittering fragments.

Peterson and I, neither of whom had relinquished

the grip on our drinks even for a second, were quite surprised by this. As was everyone else in the room. The only sound was the final tinkle of falling glass.

And then the fire alarms went off.

Major Guthrie raced through the bar, shouting, 'Stay here, everyone,' kicked his way through the shattered French windows, and disappeared.

Peterson drained his drink. 'Come on,' he said, and we followed Guthrie outside.

My first thought was that the Time Police were back for some reason. I always associate them with explosions. I'm told they have a similar opinion of us. My second thought was that Professor Rapson had really excelled himself this time. But no, this particular Big Bang had come from outside St Mary's.

A big, black mushroom cloud of smoke hung over the grounds. There was a terrible smell. A truly terrible, terrible smell.

The traditional smoking crater occupied the space where much of the South Lawn had once been.

Unidentifiable lumps of concrete lay everywhere. Some had come down with considerable force and gouged great lumps out of the tiny part of lawn that was still hanging in there. Burning branches and leaves were dotted around all over the place. People were stamping on the smouldering grass, trying to put out the fires and still, there was that terrible smell. Well, at least no one seemed to be hurt.

Wrong.

I caught Peterson's arm. I could see three figures on the ground, horribly still. One was clad in the smoking remains of a green jumpsuit and the other two in blue.

'Shit,' said Peterson, under his breath and we ran to investigate.

Markham, Bashford, and Roberts were lying spread-eagled on their backs. Their faces black, their eyebrows gone, their clothing smouldering. My finely honed historian senses told me that they and this unexplained explosion were somehow linked.

Peterson was bending over them. They were alive, but only temporarily. Any minute now, the less-than-stable Dr Foster would be among us, closely followed by Dr Bairstow, unreasonably demanding explanations. I would have advised them not to start watching any long-running TV series, but they wouldn't have heard a word I said. Guthrie was there as well, alternately yelling at them and checking them for fractures and the like. They smiled hazily at him. Evans was patting out their smouldering clothing.

Given the damage around them, they seemed miraculously unscathed. Markham must have extended the umbrella of his invulnerability over them.

Faintly in the distance, I could hear sirens. The emergency services were on their way. The Chief Constable would be on the phone. None of this was good.

'Oh God,' said Peterson. 'Not again.'

I said, 'You go. Head them off if you can. I'll see to this.'

I could see Helen and her medical team jogging across the former lawn. She was probably so weighed down with nicotine patches that she couldn't run any faster. At that moment, I wouldn't have been Markham or Bashford or Roberts for any money.

Out of corner of my eye, I could see two grubby, grey figures, Lingoss and Sykes, endeavouring to fade into the background. Of course I could. Just as I was congratulating myself that for once, none of my people could possibly be involved.

'You two – front and centre. What happened here? And more importantly, what is the extent of your involvement?'

Lingoss shuffled her feet. 'There was a rat and it might have been my idea.'

I set my teeth. 'Go on.'

'We saw a rat.'

'Who are "we"?'

'Mr Markham, Mr Bashford, Mr Roberts, and us. It ran into the shrubbery over there. We had to do something. They're vermin, you know,' she added in an explanatory tone.

'I'm a training officer. I'm familiar with vermin.'

She pointed to the ex-shrubbery at the top of the drive, now just a series of sad stumps. 'It ran into those bushes there. Those bushes that used to be there. We thought we'd flush it out – and any others, of course.'

Enlightenment landed as heavily as the lumps of concrete must have done. I mustered all the restraint I could find.

'It's the old septic tank. No one wanted the bother of digging it out so they planted the shrubbery to conceal it. You blew up the septic tank.'

'We didn't know that,' said Lingoss. 'None of us knew. Anyway, aren't we on the mains?'

I loomed. Quite a feat when you're as short as I am, but I was in a looming mood. 'We are now. We weren't then. Continue with this sorry tale.'

'Ah. Well. If we'd known that then our actions might have been a little different. It's not our fault we didn't know.'

'Can we get back to the rat?'

'Yes. Sorry. Well, it ran into the shrubbery which we now know concealed the septic tank.'

'Yes, we've covered that. Move on.'

'Actually, we were going to shoot it but Mr Markham said that might be quite dangerous and I had a brilliant idea. We got some bottles, filled them with just the very tiniest drop of paraffin, and plugged them with an old rag.'

I groped for words. And that doesn't happen often. 'You *what*? Have you never heard of methane?' I demanded, with all the confident knowledge of one who has experienced an exploding manure heap at first hand.

'Well, yes, obviously, but we didn't know there was methane because no one told us about the septic tank. Really, it's not our fault.'

I could feel the beginnings of a headache coming on.

'We'll have signs made,' I said nastily. 'Go on.'

'We made up a few more bottles ...'

'Molotov cocktails ...'

'If you like, yes.'

'How many?'

'Only a few.'

'How many?'

'Hardly any.'

'HOW MANY?'

They stepped back. 'Six.'

I breathed heavily.

'We could see this bit of broken concrete over what looked like a hole in the ground and we reckoned the rat had gone down there. Mr Bashford prised it up and we tossed in the five bottles. Then we lit the sixth and tossed that in as well.'

She stopped. A born storyteller.

'And?'

'Nothing. Nothing happened. So Sykes and I started to leave because we've got exams tomorrow and we had to revise,' she said virtuously. 'Anyway we'd only gone about ten paces when there was this God-almighty bang and we were flying through the air. I curled into a ball because I could hear things hitting the ground around me.'

'What things?'

'Bloody great lumps of what we now know to have been septic tank, mostly,' said Sykes, helpfully, 'but some other stuff as well.'

'What other stuff?'

'Probably the contents of the now-known septic tank. Great flaming lumps of congealed … organic matter. Bits of burning bush. Fortunately, we were pretty well out of range. Not so the others of course.'

Helen and her team had the Three Stooges on their feet. Bashford was wandering in a small circle humming gently to himself. Peering blearily at the world in a semi-conscious daze appeared to be his default state.

I wandered over.

'Hey, Helen. How's it going?'

I had meant – how's it going in relation to our three casualties, but she obviously had the tunnel vision common to all those weaning themselves off cigarettes.

'Did you know,' she demanded, apparently abandoning her medical responsibilities, 'that when Raleigh returned from his travels with potatoes and tobacco it was potatoes that were deemed to be hazardous to people's health?'

I did, actually, but now hardly seemed the moment to engage her in a discussion concerning the risks of starch versus nicotine.

'No,' I said. 'Really? How interesting.'

'Apparently, the potato was responsible for, among other things, scrofula, excessive farting, and general overindulgence in matters carnal.'

'Well, that accounts for the Security Section's love of chips.'

She sighed.

'So, other than that, how is it going?'

'Oh, fine. Not too bad at all. Fortunately, I don't seem to be falling prey to the sudden and irrational bouts of head-bursting rage that inflict lesser mortals giving up cigarettes. Bashford, I swear if you don't stop doing that this minute, I'm going to tear off your head, reach down your neck, and rip out your testicles from the inside.'

It's all very well saying smoking can damage your

health but giving it up damages everyone else's.

We watched as she shepherded them back into the building where they would be nursed back to health ready for almost-certain execution by Dr Bairstow.

I was struck by a sudden thought and turned back to the perpetrators.

'And what of the rat?'

'Actually, we think the rat might have got away.'

I looked around.

In the distance, I could see Peterson arguing with a group of firemen. A big, red, shiny vehicle with a ladder panted at the gates. For some reason, they all wanted to come in.

Mr Strong, on his knees at the edge of the pretty impressive crater, was keening over the remains of his South Lawn.

In their panic, the horses had knocked down a section of fencing and bolted. God knew where they were.

The swans appeared to have taken refuge in a nearby tree. I don't know if other people's swans can do this but I swear ours can go up a forty-foot beech tree faster than a banker can collect his annual bonus.

People were standing around, grinning. Except for Hoyle who had on his Queen Victoria face. He was definitely not amused. Perhaps this was the final straw and he would leave. I had the grace to feel a little ashamed at the thought. But only a very little.

Before I could make my escape, Mrs Partridge appeared at my elbow and contemplated the scene before her.

She said nothing in a manner that conveyed

volumes.

I said nothing in a manner that I hoped conveyed my complete innocence.

She said nothing in a manner that conveyed her disbelief in my complete innocence.

I said nothing in a manner that conveyed my hurt at this lack of trust in me.

She said nothing in a manner that effortlessly conveyed the message that Dr Bairstow wished to see me at his earliest convenience and to collect Dr Peterson while I was at it.

I said nothing in a manner that conveyed there was actually a very reasonable explanation for all this and she'd laugh when she heard it.

She just said nothing.

Six

The next day, we were assembled in the larger training room. With Messrs Markham, Bashford, and Roberts still off the active list – to say nothing of the still recovering Randall and Sands – a certain amount of people jiggling had been going on, but we'd assembled a crew in the end. I sat at the back where I could keep an eye on all of them.

Major Guthrie dropped into the seat alongside and grinned evilly. 'Markham's not fit for purpose, so you've got me.'

'A dream come true,' I said, just to annoy him, and indicated that they should begin.

Atherton opened the batting. He fumbled with his papers, dropping some to the floor. North tutted, but no one would catch her eye. Everyone sat quietly and waited patiently for him to sort himself out.

He began a little nervously and, as with everyone not accustomed to public speaking, had an air of astonishment at the sound of his own voice.

'Good morning, everyone. As we are all aware, our next assignment is to the Pleistocene Period, some fifty thousand years ago. The Pleistocene is an age of severe climactic change. Ice advances down from the poles not once, but many times. There are many extinctions during this period, but we hope to catch a glimpse of sabre-tooth cats, woolly bears, woolly rhinos, and, of course, mammoths.'

He paused, took a deep, calming breath, and continued, still in an artificially high voice. 'Also around at this time are, we very much hope, our cousins, the Neanderthals, whose fate has always been a bit of a mystery. There's a great deal of controversy over whether they just dwindled away; whether they died out because they were unable to cope with the rapid changes in climate and living conditions; or whether our ancestors – Homo sapiens – hunted them to extinction. Nobody knows so let's see what we can find out.'

He breathed again. 'We've chosen this location because it's a known site. The bones and hand tools found here have been dated to this time, so we know it was inhabited. Whether it's been inhabited continually or only for seasonal hunting is something we hope to ascertain. And, of course, by whom it is inhabited.'

He was speaking more naturally now and without his notes. 'At this time, summers are short, so the chances are that we'll find ourselves in a winter tundra environment and will dress accordingly. Please report to Wardrobe to get yourselves kitted out.'

He paused and grinned, confident enough now for a small joke. 'Normal footwear will be worn.'

There were faint cries of disappointment. I, however, was grateful that my boots would be based on the conventional design and not related, in even the smallest way, to anyone's testicles. And there aren't many jobs where you can make that statement.

He began to distribute files. 'Here's the brief, people. Professor Rapson has put together detailed information so make sure you read it. Miss Sykes is in charge of the assignment and she will now provide details of personal responsibilities.'

With relief, he sat down. He hadn't enjoyed his presentation, but he hadn't made a bad job of it. Best of all, he'd kept it short.

Sykes had no confidence problems at all. No nerves. No notes. And she kept her briefing even shorter than Atherton's.

'Right, everyone. Teams are as follows: Team One – Maxwell, Guthrie, and Atherton. Team Two – Hoyle, North, and Gallaccio, and Cox. Team Three – Sykes, Lingoss, Evans, and Keller.'

It was North who said, rather nastily, 'No historians?' knowing full well that Prentiss and Clerk were elsewhere, Sands was still limping, and that Bashford and Roberts were still on their backs in Sick Bay awaiting the return of their equilibrium. Personally, if I'd been their equilibrium I wouldn't have bothered. It was only a matter of time before it was blown somewhere else. Probably even before it had had time to unpack and do its dirty washing.

It would take more than North, however, to throw Sykes off her stride.

'We don't need them.' she said calmly. 'The assignment is to record and document only. Positively no interaction. Didn't you understand the brief? I can prepare you a simpler version if it's easier for you.'

North opened her mouth but she swept on. 'We're taking TB2. As Atherton has said, Arctic gear will be worn. Here is a list of equipment to take. Please ensure it's all fully functional before we jump. Any questions? Right – assemble in Hawking at 11.00 tomorrow morning. Thank you, everyone.'

My personal opinion was that with trainee historians, mammoths, cave bears, woolly rhinos, and sabre-toothed cats all gathered together in a small space, there weren't enough security people in the whole world to cope with that little lot, but what did I know?

The next day I stood quietly in Hawking and watched them organise themselves. Sykes seemed to be making a reasonable job of things and even North was beginning to think twice about tangling with the tiny terror.

Dieter wandered past, wearing a tool belt and carrying the inevitable clipboard.

'Now then, Max.' He nodded towards my noisy charges. 'Are they getting the hang of things?'

'Of course not,' I said, adopting the traditional trainer's optimism. 'We're all going to be dead ten minutes into this assignment.'

He looked me up and down. 'What the hell are you wearing?'

I looked down at my natty cold-weather gear, all in the colours of dirty snow. 'Fifty shades of grey.'

'What?'

'Never mind.'

'Bearing in mind your last little expedition, should I be issuing lifejackets as well?'

'Look, I get enough grief from Leon. I don't have to put up with it from you too, Mr Dieter. Shouldn't you and your fellow techies be making sure the clockwork motor is fully wound-up, rather than insulting hard-working historians?

He grinned down at me. 'Given your track record, I'm just saying.'

Dieter is the biggest man at St Mary's. Possibly, even, the entire country. He blocks the light wherever he goes. Sometimes it's like having a portable solar eclipse around the place. He fell heavily for Kalinda Black about twenty seconds after laying eyes on her. Typically, they've defied all the rules that say long-distance relationships don't work. She's at Thirsk – he's at St Mary's – and they meet regularly for weekends together, from which they both emerge dishevelled and grinning their heads off. Apparently, their stated ambition is to have head-banging sex in every room in every hotel, motel, and B&B in every county between there and here. According to Kal, if neither of them actually manages to kill the other, they're well on target. Despite his enormous stature, his good nature was legendary, so I took full advantage, demanding to know why I was taking fashion tips from a man swathed in orange and accessorised with a Phillips screwdriver and a roll of gaffer tape.

'Better than looking like a pile of perambulating slush. What happened to the infamous heated boots?'

'We're not sure. Left overnight, they were discovered the next morning, half-melted, in a corner of R&D. Rumour has it that Dr Dowson knows more than he's letting on. However it happened, Dr Bairstow put his foot down – no pun intended – so thankfully, today we're all in bog-standard footwear.'

He grinned suddenly. 'Not Dr Dowson, no.'

I stared suspiciously. He was a techie, after all and I wouldn't put anything past that lot. Before I could say anything, however, he nudged me towards TB2. 'Are you going to gossip all morning or would you like to get yourself and your bunch of shambling misfits into TB2?'

I scowled at him and complied.

We had very little equipment for this jump. Portable recorders, torches, that sort of thing. This was record and document only.

'Right,' I said, seating myself at the console. 'Everyone set?'

'All present and correct,' said Sykes, fizzing with excitement.

'Stop that,' I said.

She immediately adopted the world-weary stance of the historian who's seen it all. I looked down at the console so I couldn't see Major Guthrie grinning.

'Computer, initiate jump.'

'Jump initiated.'

The world went white.

We landed neatly and cleanly.

I gave everyone a moment to get themselves together while I checked the console. Everything looked normal, so I handed control to Miss Sykes and sat back while she organised herself and her teams. She confirmed the coordinates, checked the proximity alerts, made them carry out the com check, and harried the grinning security team. They let her do it, which was a point in her favour. She lined everyone up in their teams and waited. A host of expectant faces were looking at me.

I'd quietly verified everything as well and gave her the nod. We were good to go.

The ramp came down and we stared out at our first prehistoric landscape.

Bloody hell, it was cold.

And empty.

And desolate.

And lonely. Very, very lonely.

The very few people around at this time lived in small, isolated pockets scattered around this barren landscape. It was perfectly possible that they could be born, live their lives, and die, never once having seen anyone outside of their own small group. And if there were people here, who would we see? Homo sapiens or Neanderthals?

I stared around me. How had the human race managed to survive in this environment? It wasn't just the temperature or the face-numbing wind; it was the sheer, awful emptiness of it all. Mile after mile after mile of colourless, tundra-like landscape stretching to the empty horizon. There were a few small trees – stunted, twisted, and bare. A slight covering of snow lay over the ground, through which coarse brown stalks of dead grass rustled in the wind. We circled slowly, the Security people herding us together for safety, all consulting their proximity alerts.

'Nothing,' reported Major Guthrie.

I indicated with my eyes that he should talk to Sykes.

'In which direction do we proceed, Miss Sykes?'

I saw her start slightly and, if possible, grow an inch or so.

'East.'

Evans pulled back his hood. 'Is it just me or can anyone else hear water?'

We could. A small, deep, black rill wandered around tussocky humps of grass and the god of historians was in the office today, because it was flowing more or less in the right direction.

'Follow the water.'

So we did, backs to the wind, following the bubbling stream. Guthrie was at the front; Evans and Gallaccio brought up the rear. We strode out briskly. The terrain was easy to navigate and we knew roughly where we were going. Archaeological records showed an ancient site some half mile to the east of us. If there was anyone there.

There was. Unbelievably, there was.

The camp was a little to the north of its estimated position. We could see their campfires, the only bright spots in this dull landscape on this dull day. A moment later and we could smell the smoke.

Sykes split us into our three teams and we made the rest of the journey separately, wriggling across the ice-cold landscape on our bellies. My team halted a couple of hundred yards away and sheltered by the occasional rock or dip in the ground, we broke out the equipment.

I let Atherton get on with it and attempted, with hands that trembled with both cold and anticipation, to focus my viewfinder. Because this was the burning question of the day. Homo sapiens? Or Neanderthals? Which would we see? Being St Mary's, there was a great deal of money riding on this.

I rested on my elbows, took a few deep breaths, and focused. Here we go!

I could see dark shapes moving around the campfires. They were too far away to make out any details. I tried to slow my breathing and fumbled with my viewfinder. Who were they? What was I about to see?

Everything slowly swam into focus. I could see clearly and the answer was there before me.

Neanderthals.

Standing motionless by the fire, looking down at something I couldn't see, stood a short, stocky figure, swathed from neck to knee in skins and furs, although his arms were bare. The low brow-ridge, together with the short arms and legs were unmistakeable. Even as I watched, he turned his head and held out a hand. Another figure approached, proffering what looked like a hand axe. They stood together, inspecting it carefully, turning it over in their hands, and seemingly weighing the balance.

'Wow!' said Atherton beside me, uttering the traditional historian exclamation of wonder and amazement and I could only agree. Because this second man was not a Neanderthal. He was a modern human. Homo sapiens. There could be no doubt about it. A good head taller, longer in the arms and legs –

this was one of our ancestors.

I could hear Sykes and Lingoss, two hundred yards to my left, similarly wowing. There was silence from Hoyle and North, off to my right. Both of them were far too cool ever to wow. Because there it was. Proof at last. Incontrovertible proof. A Stone Age site, inhabited not by Neanderthals nor Homo sapiens, but a mixture of both. The two peoples co-existed. And not just co-existed. At this site at least, they co-habited. Peacefully. The implications were huge.

I tried to count heads, not easy, since they were moving continually, and clouds of smoke billowed across my line of sight, but I estimated about fifteen to twenty people that I could see, although there may have been many more in the shelters built in a semi-circle around the camp fires.

There were children, too. And this was interesting. From the small sample available, there seemed to be two sorts of children. Two different physical types. I'm not an expert – most of them looked like normal children to me. But two weren't. They were very obviously Neanderthal and the most notable thing about them was their disproportionately large heads. They huddled together around the fire, performing some task I couldn't make out. Everyone worked. There was no childhood here. Life was too short.

'Can you see them?' asked Atherton. 'This is amazing.'

Fired-up historians were dictating at machine-gun speed. Atherton was describing the children. Lingoss was speculating on whether this was a permanent camp or simply a hunting group, following their prey across the frozen landscape. True, the site didn't look particularly permanent, but it's hard to make skin-draped structures look long lasting. North was focusing on the construction of the shelters and who had built them. Tradition says Neanderthal skills were limited – that they only dwelt in caves. Not so, here. There were no caves. I felt a pang of regret. I would have loved a glimpse of some cave art. There were no trees, either. On what had they draped the skins?

'Mammoth bones,' said Atherton beside me, unknowingly answering my query. 'Look. Tusks and longbones, covered with skins and pelts. I wonder how they secured them.' He began to fiddle with his equipment.

'Yes,' I said, trying to ignore the biting wind as I took off my gloves to adjust the recorder again. 'But this opens up a whole new can of worms, doesn't it? Is this a permanent site? Look – over there, planted in the ground. There's a row of mammoth tusks and they're decorated with something. Feathers, perhaps, or some kind of decorative stones? I can't see ... Maybe they're religious offerings. Do they decorate the tusks to ensure future success? And if they do, is this a portable shrine that they carry with them to bring them success?'

'Or maybe a tribe totem,' he said, in excitement. 'Wouldn't that be great?'

Guthrie rolled his eyes.

'And,' said Sykes in my ear. 'I don't know if you can see from where you are, but they're burning mammoth bones. Can't you smell it?

'Of course they would be,' said North, loftily. 'Use

117

your brain. There's no wood here. And the fat would give out a much greater heat.'

'Take your word for that,' said Sykes and the huffy silence rang loud and clear. North really was going to have to grow a sense of humour. And soon.

As far as I could see, the two species were completely integrated. Mixed groups of people sat around each fire. Tools were passed around and examined.

I focused on a Neanderthal man sitting cross-legged and working on something on his lap. As far as I could make out, he seemed to be making himself a hand axe. He seemed dexterous enough, using both hands impartially. I could hear the ringing sound of flint on flint. Chippings flew. Another man, hairy, but modern, leaned over to look. The two of them were communicating. This was extraordinary.

The most recent thinking is that Neanderthals weren't anything like the shambling apes so often depicted in films and holos. Their brains were actually bigger than ours were, but functioned differently. Their larger eye sockets took up frontal lobe space, making them less able to adapt to changing circumstances. More importantly, it restricted their social thinking which meant they tended to live in smaller groups. Smaller groups meant a much lower survival rate in these harsh times. Was it possible that co-habiting benefited both species? Neanderthals were tough, strong, and excellent hunters – Homo sapiens were adaptable and more able to think their way through a problem. They all had communication skills. I could see them, if not talking, at least communicating. There may not be words, but a combination of sound and gesture was enough to convey meaning.

Thirsk were going to be ecstatic when they saw our footage. I couldn't wait to get back and send this little lot off to them. This was sensational stuff, although I suspected Markham would be disappointed at the lack of fur bikinis.

We were still in our three groups around the camp. With our coms open I could hear them muttering to each other as they worked – how cold they were, to get this shot or that shot, to get a close up of what that woman was doing, bloody hell it was cold, and so on. The day wore quietly on. We recorded everything in sight. The Security team watched our backs because we'd certainly forgotten to.

The sun, not that strong to begin with, disappeared behind a low ceiling of grey cloud. The wind sang mournfully amongst the dry grasses. I was bloody grateful I lived in the time of central heating, mugs of hot tea, and chocolate. The average life expectancy of anyone, man or woman, Homo sapiens or Neanderthal, was well under thirty. I should have been dead years ago.

I was just easing my cramped and freezing feet for the umpteenth time, and beginning to wonder if I'd possibly been a little hasty in rejecting Professor Rapson's heated boots, when there was a sudden shout from the camp. People leaped to their feet and grabbed the weapons that were never very far away. Everyone stood staring.

Away in the distance, a figure stood atop a small

hill. He shouted and waved his spear in a particular manner, turned, and disappeared.

There was a moment's stillness and then the entire camp was galvanised into action. Within seconds, what seemed like every able-bodied person was trotting, single-file, armed and purposeful, out into the darkening afternoon.

'Max? What do you think?' said Guthrie.

'Well, obviously they've seen something. Possibly another group of humans – although that's not likely given the tiny population at this time, so more likely, they've seen something worth hunting. Boar or bison, maybe. Something big enough that it needs all of them to bring it down.

'A mammoth?' said Atherton, and his eyes sparkled with excitement. 'Could it be a mammoth?'

'Not *a* mammoth,' I said. 'They travel in herds. Many mammoths. Major, please tell your people they're in charge of my lot now and their priority is to prevent over-enthusiastic trainees ending up as an unpleasant stain on the landscape.'

I could hear him issuing instructions and I did a little of that myself. 'From this moment you take your instructions from your Security escort. Record and document by all means but anyone getting themselves trampled or gored to death will answer to me later on.'

I stowed my gear and scrambled to my feet. This was better than we could ever have hoped for. We might be about to witness a prehistoric hunt. And it could be anything – spotted hyenas, woolly mammoths, woolly rhinos, cave bears, giant deer.

What was their quarry today?

I did experience a slight qualm but how could we be expected not to take advantage of this opportunity? Besides, we weren't the ones out hunting. We would only be observing. We'd be well out of danger. What could possibly go wrong?

Seven

We moved out, following the hunters, taking care to stay well back because it would be catastrophic should they ever catch sight of us.

From what I could make out, both men and women hunted. The little woman did not stay at home tending the kids. The older people did that. All able-bodied people turned out, regardless of sex. If you could walk – you could hunt.

They joined up with another small group of four men and one woman. They must be the spotters. There was a great deal of gesticulating and then they set off. So did we, speculating as we went.

'Mammoth,' said Atherton. 'Please, please let it be a mammoth.'

The god of historians must have been smiling, because, as we cautiously crawled to the top of a small rise in the ground, there they were. Ahead of us and off to one side. Strung out across the tundra, but all moving slowly in the same direction. I've no idea whether fifteen mammoths constituted a large herd or not. I think I had in mind the North American bison thundering over the plains in herds so vast they took two days to pass. However, fifteen mammoths still managed to be very impressive.

We crouched behind a small rocky outcrop. Guthrie and his people kept watch while the trainees recorded and I abandoned my supervisory duties and checked out the mammoths.

The first thing I noticed was that they were both like and unlike elephants. They had very small ears, probably to avoid loss of heat. There were the distinctive domed heads and massive shoulders, falling away to a sloping back. As woolly mammoths, they were well named. They were hairy. Really hairy. Great long matted dreadlocks of dingy brown and grey swung as they walked.

All ages and sizes were represented, from the big matriarch at the front, to the little ones in the middle. The biggest stood about ten feet high at the shoulder and almost all of them, apart from the very young, possessed the most imposing sets of tusks I'd ever seen. Forget elephant tusks, with their smooth curves. These were jutting, angular monster tusks so long they almost swept the ground.

They were magnificent. Truly wonderful. Giants of the earth. They moved slowly and with great dignity. Lying on the ground, I could feel the earth shake as they passed.

I turned my head slightly to look at the hunters. I estimated about nineteen or twenty of them altogether which wasn't many to take down something the size of a mammoth. And they were social animals – attack one and you probably got the rest of the herd for free. Surely these poorly armed people could never bring down something that size.

Yes. Yes, they could. Because not only did they have fire – wonder of wonders, they had dogs, too. Not dogs as we know them – these were not domesticated in any way. They were wolf-like animals, lean and evil looking who, suddenly unleashed, hurled themselves towards the herd, baying as they went.

The herd picked up the pace, lifting their trunks high and trying to close ranks. One or two stamped the ground when the dogs got too close.

These people were experienced hunters. They knew exactly what they were doing. They were going for the weaker animals. Over to the right, one group of people and their dogs surrounded two members of the herd. They were both adults, but one had a very small youngster at her side. Trying to protect it was slowing her down. Expertly, the hunters spread out and began to separate the three from the herd. Shouting, waving with their spears, they strove to push them in another direction.

I stood up to get a better view, taking care to remain out of sight, but I needn't have bothered. All the hunters' attention was on the herd.

'I think,' I said slowly, clamped to my viewfinder. 'Yes. Pits. There are pits ahead. Don't know if they're natural or not. We can check that out later. North and Hoyle, your team stay with the herd. Sykes and Lingoss, your team stay with the smaller group. I particularly want coverage of the dogs but do not allow yourselves to be seen. Or trampled. Don't miss anything. Atherton, you're with me.'

The noise was tremendous. The dogs were howling

like the wolves they had been up until very recently. People shouted, waving torches and spears. Sparks arced through the air. Mammoths bellowed and trumpeted.

The herd broke into a shambling run, away from the lights and noise. All except for two huge matriarchs, who turned at bay as the herd thundered past them, rearing up and stamping the ground. I could feel the impact of their landing. When that failed, they lowered their heads and charged straight at the band of hunters following them.

The group of people immediately split into two, fanning out to the left and right and let them charge through, closing in behind them. This group was the distraction. Their purpose was to distract the matriarchs while the others closed in on their quarry. A wonderful example of cooperative thinking. Atherton was gabbling away into his recorder.

Slowly, and not without a great deal of resistance, the other mammoths were being driven backwards towards the pits. They must surely be of natural origin. How difficult would it be to dig something that deep in this almost permanently frozen ground?

I made a note in my recorder to fix the position and pass details to Thirsk. The contents of these pits should be investigated.

Guthrie, Atherton, and I carried on wriggling over the frozen ground, keeping our heads down. To reveal ourselves to these people would be incredibly stupid. Apart from the damage we could do to a developing culture, I could just see the look on Dr Bairstow's face as I attempted to explain that certain members of his unit were currently being worshipped as gods.

All this crawling around at ground level took time and when we were eventually in a position to start recording again, we could see that the dogs and people working together had succeeded in moving the two smaller mammoths some considerable distance from the herd. I couldn't see the calf anywhere. I had no idea what had happened to it because I was watching the ring of hunters as they slowly backed the two mammoths towards the pits.

The animals bellowed, making a sound very similar to that of a modern elephant. Their cries reverberated around the empty plain. Every predator in the neighbourhood would know what was occurring here. How long before they were prowling around on the edge of things, awaiting their chance?

Holding their trunks out of harm's way, the two mammoths lowered their heads, swinging those massive tusks from side to side. The dogs bayed furiously, closing in to snap at their feet and then dart away again. One dog wasn't quick enough and was heaved, yelping, into the air.

The people milled around, shouting, jabbing, and stabbing with their spears, slowly forcing them backwards. Those who held them waved flaming torches at the mammoth's trunks. As the matriarchs had done, they reared up, pounding their forelegs into the ground. I estimated some twelve to fifteen people here, with maybe another half-dozen taking on the rest of the herd. It seemed a pitifully small number to deal with such enormous animals. I was surprised they were willing to take the risk. On the other hand, one kill this afternoon would feed the whole group for weeks, to say nothing of providing skins for warmth and bones for burning.

I was recording, Atherton was dictating. As always, all our attention was on what was happening in front of us – this was a golden opportunity and we weren't going to miss a second – leaving Guthrie to cover our rear and save us from stray spear thrusts, dog-bites, being trampled by an enraged mammoth, or accidentally torched by an over-enthusiastic contemporary. No one ever said life in the Security Section was easy.

I could hear Guthrie talking into his com. He was in contact with the other teams. 'Everyone's fine,' he said, resuming his watch over my shoulder, breath clouding in the bitterly cold air. 'Hoyle and North are still watching the group driving off the big mammoths. Sykes and Lingoss were apparently nearly flattened by that calf we saw. It's run away and they're keeping an eye on it and will try to drive it back to the herd.'

I nodded absently. No one was dead or dying. That would do for the time being. The climax to the hunt approached. The two mammoths had nowhere to go.

For a moment, one teetered on the brink and then, with one final, huge, despairing bellow, it toppled slowly backwards into the pit and disappeared. Whether in desperation or what, the second put her head down and charged straight for her tormentors. People threw themselves out of her path. It was brought home to me just how perilous a business this was. Fatalities must be frequent. Serious injury a way of life. The odds were with the mammoth every time. The only thing in our favour was a little human ingenuity. Trumpeting victoriously, she stamped off into the growing darkness.

In the far distance, the matriarchs seemed to realise it was all over with. They dropped back to the ground. The other people, realising they had their kill, pulled back at once. The matriarchs turned and headed back towards the herd, as did the one who got away. I hoped the little one had made it back as well, although how likely was it that something so small could survive without its mother?

I turned my attention back to the pits. Some three or four people jumped down out of sight. I heard one last terrified bellow. The death cry. And then silence.

The carcass was butchered amazingly quickly. Of course, other predators would have heard that final scream. How easy it would be, even now, for a couple of sabre-tooths to drive off the humans and benefit from their efforts. I could imagine that happened a lot. All that effort and energy expended, injuries incurred, only to be robbed of weeks of good eating at the last moment. The despair of returning to camp empty handed. In this climate, one or two missed meals could be fatal for the very old and the very young. Looking around at the hostile environment and the killers that lived in it, it really was a miracle the human race had survived at all.

Except, of course, that a part of this group wouldn't. I was focusing now on the close-ups as they began to sling lumps of bloody meat up out of the pit. The majority of these people were modern Homo sapiens. In this group of hunters, the Neanderthals were in a minority and the few that were here were older. There were no Neanderthal youngsters here. The only children I'd seen had been back at the camp. Those children with the strangely large heads.

Atherton was doing a fine job of recording so I sat back and had a bit of a think. It really was useless to speculate armed with no more information than could be gathered from one very small sample group, but look at the facts.

In this group, the ratio of Homo sapiens to Neanderthal was about 4:1. Of all the children I had seen, only two were Neanderthal and both of those had big heads and, as far as I could see, no mothers. Suppose the mothers had not survived the birth – which could have happened for any number of reasons, but suppose … just suppose …

Human beings have soft spots to enable their heads to pass safely through the birth canal. Suppose Neanderthals didn't have some or any of those fontanels. Because their frontal cortex wasn't large enough to need them. At first, it wouldn't matter, but suppose that as the Neanderthal species prospered and their bodies grew bigger, their heads grew too. And then, suppose they reached a size where it was impossible for mother and baby to be safely delivered. Because of a problem with the fontanels. Suppose … just suppose … the reason for Neanderthals slowly dying out was failure to reproduce successfully. Because the child, the mother, or both died at birth. No species survives failure to reproduce.

Many of us carry Neanderthal DNA, so some successful interbreeding must have occurred. Human children survived. Those with mixed parents sometimes survived. Those with Neanderthal parents rarely survived.

I made another note to recommend further research.

A bloody tusk was handed up out of the pit, followed seconds later by the second. That they were removed almost before the butchering had begun was an indication of their significance. The reverence with which they were handled convinced me the decorated mammoth tusks had some religious significance.

They were butchering the bodies on site, but only a few people actually worked on the carcass. A few more wrapped the meat for transportation, but the majority of them stood around the pit, facing outwards, spears raised, silently watching for anything that might appear out of the twilight. One or two were nervous, turning their heads from side to side and sniffing the air. They bundled the meat up in the bloody skins, which were heaved over people's shoulders.

The second group turned up. The ones who had been dealing with the main herd. One was cradling an arm, but otherwise they all seemed unscathed. There was some shouting which I took to be a greeting. Or possibly some boasting.

Eventually, as the cold, dark night began to crawl across the landscape, one barked a harsh sound and immediately, everyone climbed out of the pit, shouldered what they could carry, and set off back to camp. They travelled fast, in single file. Two men ran at the front, a group of them in the middle carried as much as they could, but most of them were at the back, scuffing up the snow, casting anxious glances all around. What were they watching for? Bears? Wolves? Sabre-tooths? Anything that would rear up out of the dark and snatch their hard-won kill. It could easily happen. There was no respite. These people had no claws or teeth. They were at the very bottom of the food chain. Everything was a threat. Far off in the distance, I thought I heard a roar.

'It's almost dark,' said Guthrie softly. 'They won't want to be far from home when the light goes. Look at the amount of blood spilled here. And they haven't butchered the entire carcass. Clever. They've left the remains as a decoy. They're hoping that predators will gather here to feast on the remains and leave them alone.'

I allowed us to spend a few minutes at the edge of the pit, filming the site and the remains. Two of the wolf-dogs hadn't made it and we got shots of those, too. Guthrie was right, there was a lot of blood around, and although we did our best to avoid it, obviously, we trod in it, knelt in it, and generally got a great deal on ourselves.

Not a wise move as it turned out.

I heard another sound in the night. Not that far away this time.

Guthrie's head went up.

'Everyone – sound off. Now.'

'Maxwell,' I said softly. Atherton, Hoyle, North, Gallaccio, Keller, and Cox followed suit.

Evans reported that he, Lingoss, and Sykes had lost the youngster in the darkness and were close to the pod.

'Get them inside at once,' ordered Guthrie. 'Don't let them leave. We're on our way back to the pod. Historians pack your gear. Now.'

We did. Just for once, there were no arguments.

'Right,' said Guthrie, 'the first thing is to get away from this place. Every hungry predator is on his way here at this very moment. I'll lead, Keller in the middle, Gallaccio and Cox to bring up the rear. Single file. Max – watch your knee.'

'Copy that,' I said, and off we went into the dark.

We trotted because that was the best way to cover the ground. Not running, which would leave us breathless and unable to hear properly. Just a gentle trot that ate up the miles, gave us time to see where we were going and if we did fall, we weren't going fast enough to do ourselves any real damage. The terrain wasn't that rough and the moon was up. We weren't overburdened with kit. We could do this.

My knee was holding up well. I loped along with the others, feeling the beat of my heart and hearing my own breath in my head as we jogged over that lonely landscape all those tens of thousands of years ago.

We halted for a position check. Far, far away in the distance behind us, I could see the glow of prehistoric campfires. I wasn't sure, but I thought I could smell roasting meat on the wind. I looked up at a wide sky whose brilliance would never be seen again. A thousand million stars glittered across the heavens. A huge golden moon hung over the horizon, casting long black shadows behind us. The wind still moaned. The grasses still rustled. There was snow in the air.

And still something dogged our footsteps.

Cox and Gallaccio both had their blasters on full charge. I could hear them whining.

'Not far,' said Guthrie. 'A little over half a mile. Everyone all right?'

The question was rhetorical. We had no choice other than to be all right. If we weren't all right and whatever was behind caught us up then we would very shortly be even less all right.

I heard another sound and the night was suddenly bright and hot as Cox fired a short burst into the darkness. I saw eyes. Everywhere. Golden, glittering eyes.

I pulled out my stun gun, although it's only effective at close range, so I'd have to be half way down a sabre-tooth gullet for it to be effective in any way. The trainees weren't armed because if I was doing my job properly they shouldn't need to be. I was completely unsurprised therefore, to see Atherton pull out a nasty looking and completely illegal flick knife which, for all I knew, was standard issue for those in the banking profession, and awarded him another couple of points. Hoyle had a pepper spray. The canister was blue and ours were red, so God knows where he'd got that from. Never mind. I awarded him a point for ingenuity. We all looked at North who unzipped a pocket and flourished a small gold capsule.

'You're going to lipstick them to death?' enquired

Cox, grinning.

'One of those sonic anti-rape things,' she said, expressionlessly. 'Please approach and allow me to demonstrate.'

'Time to go,' said Guthrie.

We set off again, but something had changed. The owners of those glittering eyes were level with us now, keeping pace. Guthrie flashed a torch.

I've only ever seen lions in a zoo and I've never seen a real tiger at all. But I was seeing one now. It stood bigger than a table, with a browny-gold pelt, its eyes coldly glittering. Above all, I remember those huge, curved fangs. It crouched in the beam and snarled, lifting its lip to reveal teeth not very much smaller than its fangs. For some reason I was fascinated by its paws, which were big and soft and spread out to give it a good grip in the snow. These cats were fearless – no human could threaten them. I saw its muscles bunch to leap and then Cox directed a beam of liquid fire at its feet. It leaped back from the flame and disappeared into the night.

'There's more than one,' shouted Hoyle. Of course there would be. I've seen *Ice Age*. They hunt in packs. And they were hunting us.

'Stay together,' shouted Guthrie. 'Do not let them separate you from the others. Tight clump. Don't run. Don't panic. Stay together.'

We did. We did everything right. We stuck together. We trotted faster but we didn't run. The Security people were flashing their torches around. I could make out at least three and probably four big cats keeping pace with us. There would be others behind us.

'We're nearly there,' panted Guthrie. 'They don't like the blasters. We're going to make it.'

We nearly did make it and then Atherton stumbled. Hoyle ran into the back of him and I ran into the back of them and we all three fell to the ground. I rolled over, stun gun at the ready. Someone pulled me to my feet. All around, the security team were firing controlled bursts into the night. There were more eyes now. Something ran at us, snarling. Cox fired, hitting it on the shoulder. There was a terrible smell of burnt cat, a yowl of pain, and it disappeared back into the dark. They were circling closer now. If they only attacked one at a time, then we could hold them, but if they all jumped at once then we were lost. And they were pack animals. They would work as a team. Any minute now ... I watched them sink on their haunches, wriggling a little as a cat does just before it pounces. Although pounces was far too girlie a word for the massive leap that would end in huge fangs tearing out our throats and drenching the snow with our red, wet blood.

Atherton and Hoyle were roaring, jumping up and down and waving their arms. Trying to make themselves look bigger and more threatening. North thrust out her arm and an ear-bleeding tone split the night sky. She pointed it first in one direction then another. Again, they fell back. They didn't go away, however, and the tone was dwindling away, dropping down to a bearable whistle. But she'd given me an idea. I called up the pod. Sykes and Lingoss might not have a clue, but Evans would. If we were close enough to the pod for it to be effective. If it had been installed. Not for the first time, I wished I listened to Leon more attentively. 'Activate the Sonic Scream. Sonic Scream. Quick.'

For a long time, nothing seemed to happen. Were we too far away for it to be effective? Then, there it was. Something nasty on the edge of our hearing. Like nails inside the blackboard of our heads. Like biting into aluminium foil. Like the worst case of airsickness ever. The stars swayed. The ground heaved. I felt an old, familiar pain in my chest.

But the sabre-tooths ran. Bloody hell, did they run. One minute our world was full of giant hungry cats and the next minute they'd fled. I heard Guthrie speak and then, mercifully, the Scream stopped.

The silence was almost as painful as what had gone before. I thought I might throw up anyway. I staggered a little, but a few deep breaths sorted me out. I made a mental note to show my gratitude to Leon in a practical way.

Slowly, we straightened up.

Guthrie opened his com. 'Get the ramp down.' He turned to the trainees. 'Go. It's only a couple of hundred yards or so. Keller, go with them. We'll cover you. Go.'

I could hear them pounding off into the night. We edged backwards, torches and weapons raised and swinging from side to side, covering them, but there was no need. The sabre-tooths had gone.

I heard Evans report their safe arrival and a minute later, we were there ourselves.

They had the ramp down. Evans stood at the top,

blaster raised. Keller waited at the bottom.

We pounded up the ramp, into the warm safety of TB2. Evans closed up behind us. We were safe.

I took a few minutes to get my breath back, hands on my knees, waiting for my head to clear. I still felt sick and disoriented. The floor was not steady under my feet and the walls were waving around in a very disconcerting manner.

When I looked up again, Guthrie was stowing the weapons away and all my trainees were in a little huddle at the far end of the pod.

Something was wrong.

'Everyone present, Miss Sykes?'

'Yes but …'

'Is anyone hurt?'

'No …'

'All equipment accounted for?'

'Yes but …'

'FOD plod done?'

'Yes, but …'

'Right, no reason to linger. Let's get out of here.'

I was in no mood to hang around. Everyone exposed to the Sonic Scream felt like crap and looked worse. I just wanted to get back, have a long hot bath, and thank the god of historians I didn't live in the prehistoric age. Being on the receiving end of the Sonic Scream isn't pleasant. Even Guthrie looked as if he was about to bring up his boots at any moment and the Technical Section gets very irritated when people throw up in their pods.

'Computer, initiate jump.'

'Jump initiated.'

Eight

And here we were – safely home. What an exciting day!

I watched Sykes operate the decontamination lamp and waited for the nasty cold blue lamp to kill off any Pleistocene bugs we'd brought back with us.

I thought they'd be in a mad rush to get their records uploaded. That they'd want to share their experiences and findings. That at the very least they'd stampede into the bar for a well-deserved drink. After the terrors of Sick Bay, obviously. Or possibly because of them.

But they didn't. All right, those of us on the receiving end of the Sonic Scream still looked a bit the worse for wear, but I would have thought Sykes and Lingoss would be raring to go. They weren't. They stood around, fiddling aimlessly with bits of kit.

There was silence.

Something was wrong.

I caught Guthrie's eye. He folded his arms.

I folded mine.

'Right – no one's hurt, are they?'

They shook their heads.

'Let's go then.' I shouldered my bag.

No one moved.

OK. Something was definitely wrong. I let my bag fall to the ground and looked for the weakest link. My first thought was Atherton, but just because he was quiet didn't mean he wouldn't go to the stake for his colleagues. North was the one to challenge. I wondered how quickly she would give them up.

I have to admit that at this stage, I was only thinking in terms of a broken viewfinder or that in the excitement of the moment, someone had forgotten to hit 'record' and missed the hunt. It does happen.

I waited for North to speak and she didn't. She just stared at the floor.

The silence spoke volumes.

And it wasn't just my crew. Evans was also doing his best to become invisible as well.

Finally, it was Lingoss who spoke.

'The thing is … the thing is …' she stopped.

'Yes?' I said testily, still waiting for a bit of broken kit to be guiltily produced. 'What is the thing?'

She fell silent again and then I heard it. A tiny sound in the toilet. Guthrie pulled out his gun and said, 'Back, everyone.'

'No,' said Sykes in a panic, waving her arms. 'Don't shoot.'

A hideous, cold, horrible certainty settled in the pit of my stomach.

I said, 'What have you done?' and even I didn't recognise my own voice.

The silence continued until Guthrie shouted, 'Answer her,' and I didn't recognise his voice, either.

Lingoss stepped forward. 'We didn't mean to but you were in such a hurry. We only meant to give her a few minutes' respite but then we had to leave quickly and we tried to tell you and then it was too late …'

I said again, 'What have you done?'

Guthrie motioned to Cox who strode forwards and grasped the door handle. Guthrie covered the door. 'On three. One. Two. Three.'

Cox pulled the door open.

Shit! Shit, shit, shit!

I actually closed my eyes – as if that would help. Guthrie said, 'Jesus Christ,' and lowered his gun.

Occupying most of the available floor space stood a very young female woolly mammoth. So young that she wasn't so much covered in matted dreadlocks as fluffy ringlets. If this was a Disney film then this was the moment for everyone to say 'Aaawww,' as the protagonists broke into a catchy tune.

No one broke into a catchy tune.

Cox, peering around the door to see what was in there said, 'Bloody hell!' and slammed the door shut.

Strangely, once the door was closed, everyone seemed to take a breath and relax. Except me. I was still staring at the door as if I couldn't believe my eyes. Which I couldn't. Then I couldn't find a voice. Then I could.

I got as far as 'Who …?' when the com squawked and Leon's voice said, 'Everything all right in there?'

'Yes,' I said, amazingly calmly for someone who was about to murder five trainees and then have to go on to annihilate an entire Security team to cover it up.

I wasn't too sure of my ability to take down Guthrie's Security team, and God knows what I'd do with all those bodies afterwards, but I'd make bloody sure I'd spread trainee guts and gizzards from one end of TB2 to the other and maybe hang a few of their soft, wobbly bits from the ceiling as well. Like wind chimes.

'OK then,' said Leon. 'See you in a minute.' He closed the link.

This time I got as far as 'What ...?' before I was interrupted by a tiny, tinny trumpet from the toilet.

'I think she's a bit scared,' said Sykes.

'She,' said Guthrie, significantly, 'is not the one who should be scared. Have you any idea of what you've done?'

'But we didn't do it,' began Lingoss.

'Oh really? She wandered in and got herself locked in the lavatory like the three old ladies in the song?'

'We think she followed us. Perhaps she thought we were her herd. Perhaps she was looking for shelter and thought the pod was a cave.'

'So,' said Guthrie, turning to his people with a very nasty expression. 'The ramp was down and unguarded?'

'No!' said Lingoss hastily. 'But we – I – persuaded them to let her stay for a few minutes.'

'Just to rest,' said Sykes with the air of one struck with inspiration. 'She was very frightened.'

The toilet trumpeted again.

'They'd killed her mother,' said Lingoss, 'and those things were after her, so we thought ...' She tailed off because it was very apparent none of them

142

had thought at all.

'And then ...?' prompted Guthrie.

I looked at Hoyle who had to decide whether or not to go down with the sinking ship.

'They – we pushed her into the toilet in case she ... dirtied the pod,' was his reluctant offering. 'And then you turned up and we had to leave in a hurry and ...'

'They tried to tell you,' finished North, making sure all the blame was allocated as far away from herself as possible, 'but you jumped and ...' she tailed away.

I groped for the left-hand seat and sat down. Lingoss started to speak.

'Shut up,' I said, put my head in my hands, and tried to think.

Pods won't jump with anything contemporary on board. We can't bring anything back from the past. But – and it's a big but – we can rescue items that are about to be destroyed because they have no future influence on the timeline. Last year, we'd rescued three Botticelli paintings from the Bonfire of the Vanities. We'd even jumped back to Alexandria and saved a tiny part of the Great Library as it was being burned by command of Pope Theophilus in 391AD. That we'd been able to jump with this little creature on board meant she had no future. She would have died if she'd remained behind.

Guthrie waved them all down to the other end of the pod and took the right-hand seat.

'I understand,' he said, quietly, 'but you did this yourself, once. You jumped back to 1666 and rescued

I can't remember how many dodos. This is no different. And she would have died. Realistically speaking, she wouldn't have lasted an hour out there on her own. You saw what was on our trail. Remember how quickly the humans legged it back to their own camp? They even left part of the carcass behind to distract predators.'

I nodded.

'Let them live, Max.'

'It's not them I'm worried about,' I said bitterly. 'What on earth do we do with her?'

'Send her back.'

'If we jump now then everyone will know something was wrong and Dr Bairstow won't rest until he finds out and then they'll be out and I'll be ...'

I tried to think what I would be. At the very least, I'd be known as Maxwell the Mammoth Murderer for the rest of my probably very short life.

'Well, we could leave her in the toilet and jump back later.'

'Techies will be all over this pod the minute we're out of the door. One of the first things they do is empty the toilet. They're not bright – don't tell Leon I said that – but even they're going to notice a mammoth the size of an Irish Wolfhound in there.'

'Well, there you are. Tell them it's an Irish Wolfhound.'

'With an eighteen-inch-long nose? Who can trumpet? You're not being very helpful.'

He grinned. 'No, I'm not, am I?'

'And your people let them do it,' I said nastily,

which wiped the smile off his face.

Sykes approached, not exactly on her knees, but the general impression was there.

'Um – we've had an idea.'

'It had better be an improvement on your last one.'

'Oh yes, it's quite neat, actually.'

'I doubt that,' I said, bitterly. 'Go on then.'

'The Pleistocene Park.'

Oh my God – the Pleistocene Park!

Half of me thought, bloody hell that's brilliant, and the other half … the other half had packed it in for the day.

'What's the Pleistocene Park?' asked Guthrie.

Sykes hastened to explain. 'It's a nature reserve in north-east Siberia where they're trying to recreate an Ice Age ecosystem. They already have reindeer, bears, horses, wolves, moose and so on, but … but …' she was beginning to gabble in her excitement, 'they're planning to extract DNA from mammoth carcases and recreate mammoths but they've got problems because they don't have an intact string of DNA. They need a live mammoth and now we actually have one. It's perfect.'

Guthrie looked at me. 'Is this legal?'

'A bit of a grey area.'

'You're as bad as they are.'

'We can turn disaster into success,' said Sykes. 'It'll be amazing.'

'They won't cut her up, will they?' said Guthrie, displaying an unexpectedly warm and fluffy side.

'Of course not,' said Sykes. 'It would be like cutting up the Koh-i-Noor to make industrial diamonds.'

'But how will they look after her? What will they feed her on?'

She shrugged. 'I don't know. Hay? Grass? Elephant milk? But if anyone can work something out, they can. We have to do this, ma'am. We can't keep her here and we can't take her back to die. Her best chance of survival is the Pleistocene Park.'

'We can't jump now,' I said. 'There's a whole army of technicians waiting out there and they're not going to go away.'

'No, we've thought of that. We take her out on a flatbed ...'

'Thus ensuring that everyone in the unit gets a good look at her,' I said sarcastically. 'We might as well have a parade.'

'We throw a cover over her.'

'She's not a bloody budgie!'

My voice reverberated around the pod.

'I bet she'll stay quiet,' persisted Sykes. 'I bet if we cover her up then she'll stand still as good as gold. If young animals can't see, they don't move. Survival instinct. We'll pile our equipment all around her and take her to R&D.'

It was like arguing with myself in a mirror.

'Why there?'

'Have you seen the place? There's a working Iron Maiden, several half-bandaged mummies, a clockwork catapult, two Roman chariots, a scale model of Clifford's Tower, a plaster cast of Oliver Cromwell's warts, a ton of dinosaur coprolites, and a map of Atlantis. They'll never notice a mammoth in the corner.'

Guthrie was doing that thing he does when he's trying not to laugh.

'And then,' she continued, enthusiasm unabated, 'we collect her later and ship her off to the Pleistocene Park. To their experimental facility. They've been trying to clone mammoths for years. And now, they'll have a whole one. It's as if it was meant to be.'

I put my head in my hands. Again.

'Are you ever coming out?' said Leon's voice in my ear.

'Training session,' I said. 'Give us another few minutes.'

'OK.' He closed the link.

'We'll hammer out the details later. First things first, let's get her out of this pod.'

'I'll get a flatbed,' she said, and disappeared.

Believe it or not – and I didn't – it went without a hitch. Note to mammothologists: if you drape a blanket over a baby mammoth, she stands like a statue. We camouflaged her as best we could, piling odd bits of kit around her to disguise the outline.

Hoyle, North, and Atherton were despatched to Sick Bay with instructions to say the training session wasn't quite finished yet but everyone was on their way. Guthrie and his team surrounded the flatbed and did their best to obscure anyone's view. Sykes and I wheeled everything to the heavy goods lift and took it all straight to R&D. Lingoss had nipped on ahead to explain and we were met by a slightly bemused

Professor Rapson.

'Max, this is astonishing. I can't thank you enough for the opportunity.'

'Don't get excited, Professor, she's not stopping.'

'No, of course not, but nevertheless, just to get a glimpse.'

'Where do you want her?'

'Oh, through here, through here.'

We trundled her into a small room that had previously been used as a storeroom. The door seemed solid enough and there were no windows. Someone had put a blanket on the floor. It was pink. I despair sometimes.

'There's water,' he said, indicating a bucket. They'd chalked 'Mary the Mammoth' on it.

'I don't know why they did that,' he said, bemused. 'She can't read and I don't drink water. Anyway, someone's bringing up a bit of hay. She should have milk, of course, but we don't have any mammoth milk' – he seemed to take that personally – 'and she mustn't drink cow's milk. Very bad for her. We must shift her as soon as possible or she won't survive.'

'Will she survive at the Pleistocene Park?'

'Who knows. But I think they're her best chance.'

I turned to Sykes.

'Sykes, Lingoss, get yourselves off to Sick Bay. Try to look normal. Be aware Dr Foster is currently suffering a certain amount of emotional stress. Back here asap. Go, before I disembowel you on the spot.'

'A little harsh, Max,' said Professor Rapson, watching them disappear out of the door.

'It's been a long day.'

I was on my way to Sick Bay for my own check up when Leon spoke in my ear.

'Should I be alerting Dr Foster to the dreadful medical condition one of you seems to be suffering from?'

'What?'

'There's the biggest pile of excrement I've ever seen in my life on the floor in the toilet and it's still steaming. What the hell have you all been eating?'

Shit …

'Oh yes, it was Lingoss.' Well, it was all her fault anyway. 'She said she felt a little queasy. She must have eaten something that disagreed with her. Obviously, she didn't make it to the toilet in time. Poor thing.'

There was an overlong silence.

'As you say,' he said. 'Poor thing.'

'Leave it,' I said, suddenly seeing my way clear. I was being presented with an excellent excuse for them all being in TB2 later on. 'That's a bit above and beyond for your section. I'll send her and her fellow half-wits to clear it up later on.'

Another long pause. I did not marry an idiot.

'Very well,' he said eventually. 'Shall I pull my people out until it's done? We wouldn't want them … being exposed to anything contagious.'

'Excellent idea.'

'I thought you'd agree.'

I had to jump with them, of course. They couldn't go

alone and I wasn't about to implicate anyone else. Professor Rapson obtained the location of the Pleistocene Park, and I used my time in Sick Bay to work out the coordinates.

Then, all we had to do was get her back to Hawking again.

For once, everything went really well – most people were in the dining room – and just as I was thinking we might possibly get away with this after all, just as we were exiting the goods lift, there was the Boss, leaning on his stick. Not what you want to see when you're trundling around a baby mammoth heavily disguised as cleaning materials.

Paralysis set in. We all looked at each other.

'Good evening,' he said, despite all the evidence to the contrary.

There was a polite chorus of good evenings. And a pause.

'Please continue,' I said calmly to Lingoss. 'Unload into TB2 and wait there for me.'

'Yes, ma'am,' she said, equally calmly, and they all set off, trundling an illegal, pink-blanket-draped baby mammoth back to Hawking.

Dr Bairstow and I looked at each other.

'Dr Maxwell, has someone been playing a musical instrument in my unit?'

Bollocks! He'd heard her trumpeting. He knew. I knew he knew. Did he know I knew he knew? Stop that, Maxwell. Insanity beckons.

'Very possibly, sir. I believe Miss Prentiss plays the piano and Mr Bashford's attempts to render the "Moonlight Sonata" on the triangle have been described as – unique.'

'No. This instrument has more of a bovine quality about it.'

'I'm no expert, sir but I don't think many cows can play musical instruments.'

He changed tactics. 'There appears to be a very peculiar smell in my unit.'

'Ah. That might be the History Department, sir.'

He blinked. 'Are you sure? This seems amazingly pungent even for them.'

'Mammoth shit, sir,' I said, grasping the nettle. After all, in how many jobs do you get to use that phrase on your boss? 'Some of us made intimate contact on our last assignment.'

'Indeed?'

'Professor Rapson asked us to have a bit of a dig around, sir, should we encounter any significantly sized specimens. You know, clues as to diet and so on. We did our best to firkle away with sticks and things, but sometimes you just have to get right in there and … delve.'

He stared at me. The silence lengthened.

'Was there anything else, sir?'

'Apart from a fervent reassurance from you that you all washed your hands thoroughly afterwards, no, I don't think so.'

I opened my mouth and at that moment, a tiny trumpeting sound emanated from far, far away.

'Ah', he said, unsmiling. 'Miss Prentiss getting to grips with the Trumpet Voluntary, no doubt. Or possibly Mr Bashford bringing astounding range and volume to an instrument previously known only for its percussive qualities. How extraordinary are the talents of the History Department.'

He knew. I don't know how but he always knew. I did my best not to look innocent because that's always a bit of a giveaway. He regarded me for a long moment. 'Perhaps you could pass the word that this is not a music conservatory. Musical instruments are all very well in their time and place but I think we both know this is not their time and place. Sort it out, Dr Maxwell. And quickly. While I do not relish the thought of seriously inhibiting ... musical prowess ... if I have to, I will.'

He limped away into the shadows whence he came.

Leon had been as good as his word. Hawking was deserted. I had considered taking Leon's pod, but I didn't want to involve him. The Time Police were never far away from my thoughts. And anyway, five trainees, one harassed training officer, and one mammoth all crowded together in a single-seater pod would bring new definitions to the word 'overcrowded'.

I bundled everyone and everything into TB2, and began to lay in the coordinates for the Pleistocene Park.

'When will we arrive?' said Lingoss, peering at the console.

'Real time,' I said, gritting my teeth, because the rule breaking was getting out of hand and even I was beginning to worry.

'We can do that?'

'No.'

She had the sense to shut up.

'Jump initiated.'

The world went white.

'It's dark,' said North, peering at the screen.

'Too bloody right it's bloody dark,' I said. 'Do you really want people seeing us materialise from nowhere, deposit an illegal mammoth, and vanish again like the backward-flying bird of legend?'

They shook their heads.

'Thought not.'

Even with night vision there wasn't much to see. A cluster of oddly shaped buildings, some built off the ground. Of course, you can't dig into permafrost. I saw chimneys and large cylindrical tanks.

'What do we do? Knock on the door and run away?'

'Why not?' I said.

'But ... OK.'

We got the ramp down and trundled her outside. It was bloody freezing. She was going to feel right at home.

We manhandled her off the flatbed and stood her on the ground.

'Get back to the pod,' I whispered. 'Quick as you can.'

I waited until they'd all disappeared, prised up a small stone, and tossed it at the nearest building. There was the sound of shattering glass.

Shit! Sorry! St Mary's owes the Pleistocene Park a window.

No time to hang around. Floodlights came on and

lit up the area with a sharp white light. I ran towards the pod, remembered the blanket, turned back, whipped it off her, and legged it out of there as fast as I could.

The ramp was down but obviously they'd left the lights off and I ran slap into the side of the pod, which bloody hurt, I can tell you. I cursed a bit, fumbled my way around the pod, and eventually found the ramp. Atherton closed it behind me.

I seated myself at the console and rubbed my forehead and nose. Lingoss opened her mouth.

I said, with what I thought was admirable restraint, 'No one wearing grey should speak to me for a little while.'

They fell silent. As they bloody well should.

We landed back in Hawking. Ten minutes from start to finish. Not bad. If anyone ever has an illegal mammoth to dispose of, St Mary's should be your organisation of choice. The trainees clustered around the ramp, all set to go.

'Well,' said Sykes, casually, 'I must get on and write up my report.' Which is St Mary's speak for see you in the bar in ten minutes.

I laughed brutally, opened the toilet door, pointed to the still-steaming heap, said, 'My compliments to Professor Rapson,' and left them to it.

Finally, back to Leon who very pointedly asked no questions for which I was hugely grateful because it had been a long day. I didn't get off scot-free, however. Thinking I would have a nice cup of tea and then a long hot bath, I was strongly given to understand that that order of events was unacceptable. Apparently, there was a strong smell of over-excited … something.

'I really think I should alert Sick Bay,' he said, keeping his distance. 'I can't remember the last time you smelled that bad. Whatever has the poor girl been eating?'

'It's mammoth shit incurred in the line of duty.'

He grinned. 'What is this curious obsession historians have with body waste?'

I gave him a hard look on my way to the bathroom. He was enjoying himself too much.

'You should get used to it. I've lost count of the number of times I've been the victim of Peterson's urinary exuberance.'

He stared at me frostily.

'Not a phrase I ever thought to hear from a wife of mine.'

'Why? Whose wife did you expect to hear it from?' and slammed the bathroom door behind me.

I emerged after some thirty minutes' heavy-duty scrubbing and he again recoiled.

I was not amused. 'Now what?'

'What on earth did you put in your bathwater?

'The entire contents of the bathroom. Magnolia, aloe vera, honeysuckle and jasmine, ylang ylang, lavender oil, something from your end of the shelf that according to the TV advert apparently renders the wearer completely irresistible to members of the opposite sex – I should ask for your money back if I were you – and some stuff from that anonymous green bottle under the washbasin that is probably drain cleaner.'

He sniffed delicately and then put his arms around me. 'Perhaps you could do with some Mr Muscle?'

I snorted. 'If you're involved then Flash might be more appropriate.'

He sighed. 'That settles it. My next wife will be tall, blonde, and elegant, will look like an angel and will never, ever dream of eating sausages in the bath.'

I wrapped my arms around him. 'She sounds very dull. Still as one approaches the quieter years of one's life, that sort of thing must become more appealing. *My* next husband on the other hand ...'

'Yes?'

'Oh, I'm nowhere near as particular as you. So long as he's six foot two and ripped, I'm quite happy.'

'How very undemanding.'

'Well, at my age, you're just grateful for what you can get.'

'Yes, I can imagine you must be fairly desperate. That riot of red hair, those golden eyes, those curves ... What man could possibly want you?'

'Exactly,' I said calmly, but my little heart was going like an engine. 'In fact, I suppose I should be grateful you've hung around for so long.'

'I was brought up to be kind to those less advantaged than myself. Now, speaking of sausages ...'

I gave them the next morning to recover and write up their findings, and then I summoned them to the smaller training room for a real bollocking, because we needed to get this sorted out now. You can't go around not telling senior officers things. How can we do our jobs properly if we don't know exactly what's going on at all times?

On reflection, it is, perhaps, a minor miracle that I'm never struck down on the spot.

I waited in my office until I knew they were all there and then swept into the training room, quietly closing the door behind me.

I made them wait. I arranged my files, opened and closed a few drawers for the look of the thing, and then stood silently in front of them, leaning on my stick so they would know this was a formal occasion. I had prepared an indictment that would strip the flesh from their bones – metaphorically speaking, of course – although I was quite prepared to be literal if anyone happened to say the wrong thing. It occurred to me, not for the first time, that perhaps I wasn't the best person in the world to be in charge of young minds.

Silence settled, along with the dust.

I stood in front of my desk, took a deep breath, and suddenly changed my mind. They had an important lesson to learn today and I had to get this right.

I kept my voice down. Shouting doesn't help. People don't listen. But they do if you speak very quietly.

'Today, we shall begin by reviewing the history of St Mary's.'

That surprised them. They had that *braced for a bollocking* look, but I wanted them to think, not just listen.

'Some little time ago, this unit was visited by the Time Police. We shall be discussing their role more fully in another session, but today, all you need to know is that they are responsible for ensuring St Mary's behaves itself. On this occasion, they were convinced that St Mary's had broken the biggest rule of all – that St Mary's had somehow removed a contemporary from their own timeline. You don't need me to tell you how serious is that charge.'

I paused so they could reflect on that.

'They're not a pleasant organisation – they can't afford to be – and they have their own ways of extracting the truth. The subsequent enquiry was not pleasant. We managed to convince them their fears were groundless, but they returned, in strength, shortly afterwards, with the stated intention of arresting Dr Bairstow and his senior staff.'

I crossed to the screen and brought up images of bodies, wounded people, and devastation, flicking from one to the other in silence.

Sykes said, hoarsely, 'What happened?'

'Eight people died is what happened.'

They sat in silence, staring at the screen, which showed the final, shocking picture of the Great Hall. The roof was on the floor. People sprawled everywhere like broken toys. Clearly visible in the foreground lay Mr Strong, his face covered in blood and dust.

North cleared her throat. 'And did you?'

'Did we what?'

'Bring back a contemporary from their own time?'

'Fortunately, we were able to convince them that

we had not and eventually matters were resolved to more or less mutual satisfaction.'

I wondered if they would notice that I hadn't actually answered the question.

We all looked at each other. I was in the awkward position of the not-completely blameless, but this really was a case of 'Do as I say, not as I do.' I had no choice. We'd all had to learn the hard way. The really hard way. The purpose of today was to ensure they themselves never had to learn the really hard way as well.

'I was once a trainee myself. I too, on many occasions, have shrugged my shoulders and said, "They're not my rules – why should I care?" but the point I am making is that whatever you have done or will do in the future, I, or my colleagues, are already guilty of something similar. You will understand, therefore, that I know of what I speak when it comes to rule breaking. The voice you are listening to is the voice of experience. Yes, my job is to train you up. It is also to try, as best I can, to ensure you don't make mistakes that have already been made.'

I pointed to the screen. 'Eight people died that day. That's more people than there are in this room right now. Part of your training consists of understanding the concept of cause and effect. I invite you to spend some time contemplating what *could* have been the effect of yesterday's ... cause.'

I stopped speaking and waited, wondering what would happen next. The silence lengthened. I looked at the seating layout.

Sykes and Lingoss on one side.

Atherton in the middle – the peacemaker. The buffer zone.

Hoyle and North on the other side.

This was going to be interesting. What would they say and who would say it?

Sykes stood up. 'As mission controller, I want to apologise, Dr Maxwell. We didn't mean any harm, but that's not the point. Harm was done. I think a lesson has been learned. I'm sorry.'

'No,' said Lingoss. 'The fault is all mine.' She looked very white. 'I didn't stop to think it through. I should accept all the blame. Mine was the idea to bring her inside the pod. Sykes, quite rightly, was reluctant, as was Mr Evans. I hope he won't be punished for my fault. But I didn't mean to bring her back. I didn't realise we would jump so quickly.'

I said quietly, 'You should always be prepared for a quick getaway. Serious injuries, tidal waves, volcanic eruptions …'

'Yes, I realise that now. I'm truly sorry.'

'We should have told you,' said Atherton. 'No, that's wrong. We shouldn't have done it in the first place. I'm sorry, too.'

There was a long, long pause. I let it linger.

Eventually, North stood up. 'I regret that the offence occurred.' They all looked at her. She swallowed. 'Should there be any unfortunate repercussions, I shall, obviously, be willing to bear my share.'

Well, that was masterly. Almost an apology but not quite. Just enough to make it clear she didn't want to be involved but is solid with her colleagues. You have to admire someone who always says and does the right thing. You have to. I don't.

Unfortunately, that was as far as we got. Mr Hoyle was quite adamant. 'It wasn't my idea. I didn't want to be involved,' thus effortlessly rendering himself absolutely correct and completely unlikeable. It didn't seem to bother him at all. Even after all this time, our Mr Hoyle was still an unknown quantity.

Nine

The next day, I was sitting in my office, trying to work up some enthusiasm. I felt weary and it wasn't like me to be so knocked out by one assignment, even if we had had a bit of drama afterwards. For the first time, I wondered if Dr Bairstow had been right. His one fear had been that taking trainees on jumps this early in their career might be risky and how right he'd been. On the other hand, we'd brushed through things reasonably well. The timeline was intact. St Mary's was intact. Dr Bairstow had stayed his hand and I'd had an opportunity to teach them a valuable lesson.

Mrs Shaw, bless her, had taken one look, gently placed a mug of tea in front of me, and left the room. It was just me now, listening to the ticking clock, and wondering whether I should admit I had been wrong and look at revising my training programme.

The door opened. I made myself look up. It was Leon.

'Hello,' I said, so pleased to see him. 'What are you doing here?'

'I'm on a break and thought I'd pop in,' he said, picking up my mug, taking a sip, grimacing, and handing it back to me. 'Is there any tea in all that sugar?'

'I need the energy.'

'Tired?'

'A little.'

'I think you should consult Dr Foster.'

'I think she has enough on her plate at the moment.'

'True, but promise me you will go and talk to her.'

'I'm not ill.'

'I know.'

'Just a bit tired.'

'I'm not surprised.'

'Stop being so considerate and reasonable. You know how it pisses me off when you say and do exactly the right thing.'

He laughed. 'Why are you sitting here all by yourself?'

'I'm waiting to see what happens after yesterday. I had to walk that fine line between putting the fear of God into them and not terrifying them to the extent they hand in their notice.'

'How do you think you did?'

'Not sure.' I sipped my tea and said jokingly, 'You didn't happen to see any of them lurking in the corridor on your way here, did you?'

He stopped laughing.

I sighed. 'Oh God, no. Really? Who?'

'I'm sorry, Max. All of them. They seemed to be plucking up courage.'

Shit. Shit. Shit.

There was a knock at the door and he stood up. 'I'll stay if you like.'

'No, it's OK. If I have to murder any of them and conceal the bodies afterwards, you'll need plausible deniability. But thanks anyway.'

He crossed to the door. 'Talk to Helen.'

I nodded.

He held open the door. 'Come in, please.'

They filed into the room. He gave me one last smile and closed the door behind him.

I crossed to my briefing table so we could all sit together. They made a big business of sitting down and shuffling their chairs around. I let them take as long as they liked, determined not to speak first. Finally, silence fell. We all looked at each other. I wondered who would speak.

Predictably, it was Atherton. The peacemaker.

'Good morning, Dr Maxwell.'

'Good morning.'

He shifted in his chair.

The others murmured their good mornings.

I nodded.

We were just using words to fill up the empty space while we worked our way towards the important stuff. I was determined not to speak. Never make it easy for people to do something you don't want them to do.

The silence dragged on.

Eventually, Lingoss stirred. 'Actually, Dr Maxwell, it's me that wanted to speak to you. The rest of them are just here for – support.'

Well, now they had achieved a team spirit. Bloody typical.

'I've been thinking about what you said yesterday.

About the consequences ...' she stopped.

I waited.

Nothing happened, so I said, 'Yes?' in what I was convinced was an encouraging tone.

'Well, I ...'

I smiled. 'Surely I brought you up better than this, Miss Lingoss. Start at the beginning. Begin by stating the purpose of the interview. Detail the issues to be discussed. Propose your solutions and make your recommendations.'

'Very well. Ma'am, with enormous regret, I'd like to leave the course. I don't think it's right for me.'

'Is this because of yesterday?'

'Oh, no.'

Of course it was because of yesterday, and the sooner she admitted that to herself, the better. I must admit, I was a little surprised she was deceiving herself like this. I would have thought that of all of them, Lingoss was the realist. Yes, she'd made a mistake, but she'd owned up and acknowledged her fault. As far as I was concerned, the incident was closed.

She took a huge breath. 'To tell you the truth, ma'am, I ... I ... The work is not as interesting as I thought it would be.'

What?

What?

Like Tarzan swinging through the jungle, I veered from sympathy to outrage.

Not interesting?

Not *interesting*?

What?

Some of this must have shown on my face, because, ever so slightly, they were all leaning away from me.

I made a huge effort for calm.

'Not ... interesting?'

'No, no, that's not right. I expressed myself badly. I should have said ...' she stopped.

'Oh, for God's sake, Connie,' said Sykes, exasperated, and I made a note to remember to tell Peterson he'd been right about that.

'Well,' I said, swallowing hard and doing my best to present an appearance of reason and concern, 'perhaps we could discuss the reasons you want to leave St Mary's and ...'

'Oh no,' she interrupted, 'I don't want to leave.'

Reason and concern flew out of the window. 'Yes you do. You just said ...'

'No I didn't.'

'Yes you did. You said ...'

'I said I didn't want to be an historian any longer. Because ...'

'The work isn't interesting enough. Yes, you said. Although frankly, Miss Lingoss, it's probably better you do leave. I should tell you now, things are unlikely ever to be more interesting than yesterday.'

'You're making a complete dog's breakfast of this, Connie,' said Sykes. She turned to me. 'This is why we came, ma'am. She's pants at this sort of thing.'

'No, I'm not,' she began indignantly, and at the same time, Atherton started to speak.

'Everyone shut up,' I said. 'You.' I turned to Lingoss. 'Clarify.'

She gripped the table. 'I don't want to leave St Mary's. I really like it here. But I don't think I want to be an historian. I've been talking to Professor Rapson and ... I want ... with your permission, ma'am, I'd like to transfer to R&D.'

I was speechless. Yes, it does happen.

Atherton hastily got to his feet. 'We'll leave you to discuss this.' They disappeared. Actually, they couldn't get out fast enough.

I struggled to take this in. I'd heard the bit about not wanting to be an historian first and it was only a few fury-filled moments later that the other sentence had turned up. I was still struggling to reconcile the two and not climb over the desk and wallop her with my lamp when she spoke again.

'Are you all right, ma'am?'

I found a voice. 'You want to transfer?'

'If possible.'

I found another voice. 'To R&D?'

'Yes.'

'You want to transfer to R&D?'

Because sometimes I have to have things made easy for me.

'Yes.'

'Why? Why on earth would you want to join that bunch of unpredictable, dangerous, reckless, unsafe, anti-social misfits ...?'

I trailed away. I'd answered my own question. Of course. Where else would she want to be? Unconventional and independent, she was made for R&D. And she could keep the Mohican.

This was a huge blow. So huge that I had no idea

168

what to say to her. I knew she'd disobeyed instructions during the Valley of the Kings assignment. I knew she wasn't guiltless in the matter of Mary the Mammoth. I knew she'd probably been the instigator of the Let's Bomb the Rat disaster, all of which, as far as I was concerned, made her ideal historian material.

I didn't make the mistake of saying, 'Are you sure?' or attempting to change her mind. She was tough. She'd looked after herself all her life. She knew what she wanted. And she knew what she didn't want, as well.

I said slowly, 'I'm very sorry you don't feel the History Department is right for you, Miss Lingoss. I'm not aware of any problems you may be experiencing. Your exam results are excellent. Your practical work is of an extremely high quality. You seem quite at home at St Mary's.'

This was a bit of an understatement. She'd taken to St Mary's like a duck to water. With the possible exception of Sykes, I would have said she fitted in here better than anyone did. She was popular. The techies and Security people liked her enough to take instructions from her. She had a real future in the History Department.

'Have you spoken to Professor Rapson?'

'Only to ask if he would have me. There was no point in pursuing the matter if he wouldn't.'

'And what did he say?'

'Oh, he seemed quite excited. Then he said "*Quomodo cogis comas tuas sic videri?*" but I got the gist. Then he asked me if I knew anything about linothorax. Then he asked me if I happened to have a crochet hook on me. Then he asked if you knew about me wanting to transfer out and then he said I had to check with you first. So I am.'

Well that was good of him. Just wait until I got my hands on that staff-stealing, people-poaching, trainee-tempting, devious old … I pulled myself together.

'I will discuss this with Professor Rapson and either or both of us will speak to you tomorrow, Miss Lingoss. In the meantime, please do not discuss this with anyone else other than your colleagues.'

'Why not?'

'Seriously? You want Dr Bairstow to hear this from someone other than you or me?'

'Oh. No.'

After she'd gone, I sat in a state of mild shock for about half an hour, turning things over in my mind. Good points emerged. Professor Rapson would owe me for the rest of his life. I'd see to that. I'd have a half-trained historian in R&D on whom I could call if necessary. She wasn't actually leaving St Mary's. She could have her Mohican back. She was prime R&D material. I was beginning to talk myself around and then Mrs Shaw came rushing in and turned on the screen.

'Look, Max. Such excitement. You won't believe what's happened.'

And there she was. A still picture of Mary the Mammoth, standing in a small wooden shelter, surrounded by some half dozen hugely smiling people. Christmas had not only come early for the

Pleistocene Park, but was never going to go away again. Ever. There was our tiny mammoth. For whom Christmas had also come. For some reason, I'd never given a thought to the publicity.

I became aware of the newsreader's voice '... a stunning scientific discovery in Siberia's Pleistocene Park. Reports are coming in that, unbelievably, what looks like a live baby mammoth has been found wandering just outside the station. Scientists say she's in remarkably good condition and cannot have been separated from her mother for any great length of time. At present, she is being cared for at the facility, while expeditions are mounted to locate at least her mother and with luck, the rest of her herd. Tonight, experts from all around the world are heading to the Siberian tundra where this astonishing discovery has been made. Over now to our science correspondent for more details ...'

I sighed. Maybe the day hadn't been such a dead loss after all.

Ten

On to our next assignment.

I'd chosen Herodotus because – well, who could pass up the chance to meet the first historian, the Father of History. Or the Father of Lies, as he was also known. All right, some of his stuff was a bit far-fetched, but the important thing to remember is that he was the first person ever to try to account for historical events in a realistic way and not put everything down to godly intervention. He traced the causes of wars, marriages, deaths, and painstakingly wrote everything down in his *Histories*.

He's been criticised because he wrote down *everything*, believable or not, and possibly embellished things slightly along the way, as well. For some time, he was considered the world's first tabloid journalist – or so the world thought, until back in the 20th century, it was discovered that what had always been regarded as a particularly imaginative bit of reporting, concerning giant Persian ants who dug up gold dust as they excavated their burrows was true after all. Someone discovered there were actually marmosets that did that, and the word for marmoset is very similar to that for ant, so it turned out the old boy probably knew what he was talking about after all.

Anyway, after his travels, he settled in Thurii, a Greek colony on the Tarentine Gulf, and sat down to pull together his *Histories* and that was where we were off to. To catch a glimpse of the great Herodotus himself. I pictured him, sitting alone in the dappled shade of a pine tree, wearing a pristine white robe, with snowy beard and hair, meticulously recording his findings. Or possibly sitting in the agora, surrounded by admiring acolytes, giving a public reading of his works.

Either way, a quiet assignment. No weather or geographical catastrophes were involved. Scorpions and snakes aside, the wildlife was comparatively harmless. The town was not in the middle of any sort of political upheaval. Everything should be fine.

The aim of this assignment was to meet and interact with contemporaries and I gave it to North, to see what she would make of it. I thought there might be some gender-based protests from Atherton or Hoyle, but Atherton was too good-natured and Hoyle, as usual, had nothing to say. Whether his enforced years in America had taught him to keep his mouth shut and his head down, I don't know. I do know that here at St Mary's, where the concepts of mouths shut and heads down (unless Professor Rapson was in the vicinity of course) were virtually unknown, he stood out like a small golden nugget of truth in an assembly of politicians, bankers, and estate agents.

We assembled for her briefing.

She started with the life and travels of Herodotus,

then went on to describe the town of Thurii, its history and layout.

We were going as a party of travellers who were just passing through on our way from A to B. There would be six of us. The four trainees, Markham, and me. Three men and three women.

'Please remember,' she said, 'Greek women rarely appeared in public. Upper-class Greek women, that is. Economic circumstances sometimes forced other women to be on the streets. For one purpose or another.'

Her tone left no doubt as to which class she belonged. I suspected her family might be one of those who claimed their ancestors had come over with the Conqueror. If mine had been there as well, then the females had probably offered services of a horizontal nature, while the men sold dodgy three-legged horses with low mileage.

I stood up. I had a point to make. Not that I was going to let any of them out of my sight even for a second, but a warning was still in order.

'Miss North makes a very valid point. I cannot over-emphasise its importance. And not just the women. For all of us. Our watchwords will be discretion and unobtrusiveness … ness'

A bit of a panic there as I felt the word getting away from me.

'Unobtrusiveosity?' suggested Sykes, straight-faced.

I stared down at her. She beamed helpfully at me. Disgraceful behaviour. I distinctly remember I was never anything other than polite and helpful when I was a trainee.

We were recalled by North, laser-focused as always, wrapping up her briefing and ordering everyone off to Wardrobe for their fittings. She had been brief and to the point. I had uncharitably imagined her boring on for hours, enjoying the sound of her own voice, but she'd resisted the temptation. Grudgingly, I had to admit I couldn't have done much better myself.

They all traipsed off to Wardrobe to be kitted out and I took the opportunity to grab a word with Markham.

'Just the one security guard?'

'Yes, but that one is me.'

'Is it some sort of punishment?'

'Only for me. After your last effort with the mammoth, Major Guthrie made us draw lots.'

'And you won?'

'Nearly right.'

Completely wrong as it happened. Only an hour after the briefing, he had presented himself to Sick Bay for his latest round of vaccinations, or inoculations, or whatever they had to do to him to render him fit for purpose, and the silly sod had some sort of allergic reaction to something and broke out in giant red lumps. We all traipsed along to laugh at him but they wouldn't let us in, which was disappointing.

Anyway, there being no one else available at the moment, we got Leon instead.

'A technician?' said North. I swear I saw her lip curl.

I turned slowly. 'I'm sorry?'

She had the grace to back down. 'Well, it's not his area of expertise, is it?'

'For your information, Miss North, not so very long ago, that particular technician saved our world. I forgive your ignorance because we haven't dealt with this subject yet, but against overwhelming odds, he instigated and led the rebellion against the Time Police. All the Time Police, up and down the timeline. He commanded the rescue team that saved St Mary's and was, in fact, Director of this unit until Dr Bairstow recovered from his wounds. You were not to know that and so, on this occasion, I shall forgive your rudeness.'

I hadn't realised I was shaking with rage. Because he is a quiet man who doesn't say a lot in this over-gobby unit, those don't know him tend to underestimate him. He didn't get that nasty scar across the bridge of his nose for nothing. He was still second in command of the unit. I know Dr Bairstow consults with him on every important issue. He was the man I had chosen. And most importantly, he was the man who had chosen me.

'I'm sorry,' she said, stiffly. 'Obviously we're lucky to have him.'

'Yeah,' I said. 'You are.'

We all walked down to Hawking together. We were dressed as travellers. The men wore knee-length tunics, sturdy boots, thick cloaks, and wide-brimmed hats. We women wore long tunics, stout shoes, and voluminous stoles to cover our heads and conceal our faces.

I'd wanted to bring Peterson along as well, to act as the head of our party, and because he spoke excellent Greek. He was too busy, however. He'd promised to come on the next one.

We traipsed up the ramp. TB2 still smelled, very ostentatiously, of disinfectant and pine air freshener. I could feel my sinuses shutting down in self-defence. With what passed for a sense of humour in that sorry department, the Technical Section had put an extra bucket in the loo. I resisted the urge to pitch it straight back out again.

I shunted Miss North out of the left-hand seat – nice try, but no banana, Miss North – and checked over the coordinates. While I did that, she made them check over their coms and their recorders and criticised Sykes's hair. Sykes scowled and rammed in another few hairpins. I could sympathise.

North turned to me. 'All present and correct, ma'am.'

In the background, Leon nodded.

'Very well. Initiating jump.'

The world went white.

It was a beautiful day. The sun shone from a cloudless blue sky and dazzled the eyes. The sea glittered invitingly. This was a pleasant spot. I could see why people would want to live here.

We turned our attention to the town.

All the colours of the Mediterranean were here. Blue, green, ochre, terracotta ... Blindingly white buildings were arranged in a modern grid pattern. All the walls facing the street were blank but for large, wooden doors, some of which stood open. I could smell pine trees, hot dust, and mimosa blossom. In the far distance, I could hear the sea.

It was very hot and very quiet. I wasn't sure if that was good or bad. The few people on the streets moved sedately from one patch of shade to another. We stood out, but on the other hand, no one was challenging us. We seemed able to move around easily enough.

Atherton led the way. North seemed unable to get her head around the fact that even though she was mission controller, she was a woman and should stay well back. I sighed. You couldn't fault her academically, but she had to understand it's perfectly possible to lead from the rear. Eventually, after a certain amount of jostling for position, she consented to walk at Atherton's shoulder.

Hoyle and I followed on behind and Sykes and Leon brought up the rear. I would actually have preferred to have Sykes in front of me where I could keep an eye on her, but in the words of the song, we can't always get what we want.

The streets were very clean. Even without the grid system, you could tell this was a modern town. There were no twisting lanes or sinister alleyways. No weeds sprouted between the paving and most streets were paved. No litter lay around, no broken pots, no dubious stains down the side of immaculately whitewashed buildings. The occasional cat sprawled on a roof in the sun, or a dog trotted past, intent on his own business. We could hear voices on the other side of walls as we passed. Women's voices mostly. Someone was cooking something that smelled really good.

There were some women on the streets, examining goods on market stalls, or standing in groups, talking. And there were plenty of female slaves drawing water, or sweeping steps. No high-class women around obviously, but women in a small party, supervised and chaperoned by their menfolk, appeared to be socially acceptable. We were just dusty travellers looking for a meal and a night's rest. We didn't push it anyway, drawing our stoles around our faces and keeping our eyes downcast.

Atherton detached himself and approached a group of men standing talking in the shade of yet another high, white wall. His Greek wasn't as good as mine was – actually, it was excruciating – but there was no way I could approach a group of strange men. They seemed to understand him, however, and pointed away up the street. He nodded his thanks and we set off. At the end of the street, we halted.

'Just down there,' said Atherton. 'If I understood them right.' He nodded to a high wall on our left, broken by a pair of sturdy wooden doors. One door stood open. Squinting through the gap, I could make out a courtyard, two sides of which consisted of a flat-roofed, L-shaped house. I could hear female chatter. Someone was shaking a rug. I could see a few pots against a wall with straggly herbs trailing over the edge.

'Right,' said North, before I could speak. 'Is everyone ready? Recorders on? Is everyone aware of their role?'

Training Officers aren't allowed to slap their recruits. I'd checked with Peterson. Twice, actually, just in case the rules had changed recently. However, to maintain solidarity, I nodded obediently and ignored the carefully blank-faced Leon.

Atherton and Hoyle stood at the front. The rest of us clustered behind them and peered in through the open gate.

There he was. Right in front of us. Over by the far wall, in the shade of a stunted pine tree, just as I had always imagined, sat a stocky, middle-aged man in an unbleached tunic. A nearby table was laden with scrolls and amphorae. Several scrolls lay on the ground at his feet. I could hardly believe our luck. Surely, this was going to be the easiest assignment ever. We'd have thirty minutes of so observing the Great Man and then be back home in time for tea.

We stood in the gateway, looking in at the peaceful and scholarly scene. The next minute, an amphora sailed through the air and smashed against the wall beside me. I jumped a mile and an enraged voice bellowed, 'Bugger off out of it, ye randy little ginger git!'

For one ghastly moment, I thought he was shouting at me and then a skinny ginger tomcat, lightning fast, zipped past my legs, out through the gate, and away.

We all stood frozen. Not so much because of the low flying amphora – people chucked things at us all the time, we were used to it – but the words had been spoken in English. Modern English. With a broad

Scouse accent.

At the same time, he caught sight of us and froze. We all stared at each other.

This second look was much less favourable than the first. I saw a man approaching middle age with wide shoulders and powerful forearms. Probably from throwing all those amphorae around. He was short and dishevelled, his crumpled tunic was covered in wine stains and with a thick, greasy leather belt. His bare feet were very dirty and he was showing a great deal of forehead because he had very little hair, and the little he did have was matted and greasy. His beard had bits of food in it. He was drunk. I could smell him from here.

And he was English.

It was all a bit much to take in.

All right, yes, he was sitting at a table under a pine tree – I got that bit right – but that seemed to be it. He was about as far from my picture of a scholarly historian as it was possible to get.

I dragged my gaze back to his face, which was flushed with wine and good living. He had the coarse red-brown complexion of the Englishman abroad and spread across the top of his head, presumably to protect his bald pate from the sun, was the world's worst fashion faux pas – the knotted handkerchief.

We all stared at each other.

He struggled to sit up and said in abysmally accented Greek, 'Yes? What do you want?'

I pushed my way to the front and said in English, 'Mr Herodotus?'

I could practically see his mind working. I saw him

consider the possibility of pretending he couldn't understand me. I saw him remember he'd shouted at the cat in English. I saw his shoulders slump. He sat back on his stool and said, 'St Mary's, I presume. Don't suppose any of youse got a ciggy, like?'

Eleven

It was Leon who rose magnificently to the occasion. Good job we brought him because I was just too gobsmacked to speak.

He ushered us all into the courtyard, carefully pulling the gate to behind him.

At a word from the man, the two women shaking the grass mats stopped what they were doing and disappeared back into the house.

'Um … You are Herodotus?'

'The very same.' He rose, tried to bow, lost his balance, clutched at the table and one of the jugs went over with a crash. Empty, fortunately.

We gaped. It was just too much to take in. I know that meeting a cherished idol in the flesh is often a disappointing experience, but for God's sake, when you travel back through time to meet the Father of History, the great Herodotus himself, you don't expect to be confronted by some badly dressed, cat-hating, fat bloke from Liverpool with personal-hygiene issues and a drink problem. At this rate, any minute now, we'd discover The Beatles were Mesopotamian temple prostitutes.

I opened my mouth but never got the chance to

speak.

'I'm not going back.'

'Pardon?' said Leon.

'You can't make me. I won't go.'

'No, we don't …'

I began to have a bad feeling. I stepped forwards, saying, 'Sir …' but he wasn't listening.

Grabbing an old broom, he took up a threatening position which I ignored because, frankly, he was so pissed he could hardly stand up, let alone hit anyone.

'Sir, please put the broom down. We've come …'

'I know why you've come. You'll never take me back. I'm warning you – I'll shout the buzzes. Get out of here while you still can.'

This was not good news. The last thing we needed was to be involved with the local authorities. At this time, there was no equivalent of a modern police force. Order was maintained by a bunch of publicly owned slaves. In Athens, they were known as the Scythian Archers and there was no reason not to assume the founding fathers of Thurii wouldn't have implemented the same system here. They dealt mostly with public order and surveillance of foreigners. We came under both categories. At any moment, we could expect a bunch of rod-bearing thugs through the gate, all set to cart us off to wherever they held people guilty of a breach of the peace. We were foreigners and he was an important man. Suddenly, this was serious and I needed to calm him down.

'Sir, we haven't come to take you back anywhere. Trust me when I say that no one from St Mary's has any idea you are here.'

'Never mind St Mary's. What about those bastards in the Time Police?'

'Believe me, sir, we're on a simple training jump and are as surprised to see you as you are to see us.'

He made a noise that sounded like humph, which was something I thought only happened in books and slowly lowered the broom.

We stared at each other some more. Whatever he was thinking, he came to some sort of decision. He made a huge effort to pull himself together and said, 'Well, I can see some sort of mistake has been made. I wouldn't want to keep you from your assignment, but perhaps I can offer you some wine before you go?'

I wasn't enthusiastic. Greek wine is the Hellenic world's answer to battery acid. Even inhaling the smell was usually enough to turn my stomach. But this was Italy and maybe wine would taste better here.

Before I could politely decline, he shouted and the two women scuttled back into the yard. One bore a tray with beakers. The other carried yet another jug of wine.

He fussed around with stools and things. Now that he'd got used to us, he seemed anxious for us to stay. He poured and the women handed round the beakers. I noticed that both of them had bruises on their arms. One had another, older mark on her cheekbone.

He saw me looking so I took a few sips to be polite. I'd been wrong about the geographical location improving it any.

Leon put his beaker down untouched. He kept watching the gate. 'Sir, we mustn't trespass on your hospitality any longer.'

'Oh, must you go so soon?'

His voice had a false ring to it. I looked from him to Leon. I could see he was unhappy and if Leon was unhappy then we should go. And now.

The trainees put down their beakers. I said something polite – I forget what – and Leon, overriding Herodotus' protests, had us on our feet and out of the gates before he knew what was happening.

'Back to the pod, everyone,' he said, pulling the gate closed behind him. 'Quick as you can.'

'Why?' enquired Sykes as we trotted off down the street.

'For someone who wanted us to leave, he was suddenly very keen that we should stay, don't you think?'

We moved as quickly as we could without attracting attention. The sun continued to beat down on our heads and I was suddenly conscious of a certain amount of internal discomfort, which I suspected was my body's usual indecision regarding from which orifice it should expel the recently imbibed wine.

We were in a pristine public street. There was nowhere to go. Literally. We trotted on until we rounded a corner and ahead of us was a small olive grove with a conveniently situated clump of myrtle bushes. The moment became urgent.

'Wait here,' I said. 'I'll be back in a minute.'

'What on earth ...' enquired Atherton.

'Greek wine.'

'Ah.'

'You lot sit in the shade,' ordered Leon. 'Nobody moves from this spot.'

I pulled him aside. 'You should stay with them.'

'No one goes anywhere alone. Your orders. Trainees wait here. Miss North, you are in charge.'

He cast an anxious glance around, but no one was in sight anywhere. 'Come on.'

We trotted down the goat path and I worked my way into the centre of the myrtle bushes. Leon waited on the path.

It's all very well for men and their outdoor plumbing. I had to manoeuvre myself into the appropriate position, manage vast quantities of fabric, avoid prickly plants, and manage not to wet my own footwear.

All this takes time and when I eventually emerged, triumphant, some time later, Leon was sitting on a nearby rock. He checked no one could see us, put his arm round me and we walked back through the olive grove. I listened to the birdsong and the insects and thought about how peaceful life was here.

They'd gone. All four of them. They weren't here. They weren't bloody anywhere. Any of them. I couldn't believe my eyes. Where could they possibly have gone?

We stared about us. The landscape was empty.

This was a disaster. A complete disaster. All right – if I'd just lost one or two I could have fudged the registers and possibly no one would have noticed, but not all of them. Sooner or later, someone was going to realise I was a training officer with no trainees. I looked all around us. I think I might even have looked up, because you never know.

'Shit,' said Leon. He pushed me against a wall. 'Stay here. Do not move from this spot.' He ran to the end of the street, looking left and right.

I opened my com and said, 'Miss North? Can you hear me? Are you safe to speak?'

She responded immediately, speaking very quietly. She sounded breathless.

'I think we've been arrested.'

Oh, for God's sake.

'For what?'

'Theft.' A pause. I could hear men's voices around her. I waited until she judged it safe to speak again. 'Something in my basket. Heading towards harbour.'

That bastard Herodotus. He'd planted something on her and then called the authorities. And he was a founding father. They'd knock themselves out for him.

Leon and I stared at each other in dismay.

'Come on,' he said. 'No, not that way,' as I set off downhill towards the sea. He nodded significantly back the way we'd come. 'That way. Atherton, Hoyle, do not let them separate you from the women. Insist on staying together. Max and I will get you out. You know the drill. Do as you're told and keep your mouths shut. Stay out of trouble and await rescue.'

Atherton said, 'Copy that.' He sounded anxious. I didn't blame him.

'And don't let Sykes bite anyone. We're on our way.'

'Yes sir,' I could hear the smile in his voice.

'This is my fault,' I said bitterly closing my link.

'No, actually, it's not. It's the best thing that could have happened. If you hadn't nipped off for a minute then they'd have all of us and we'd all be in trouble.'

I never thought I'd live to be grateful to Greek wine.

Herodotus was exactly as we'd found him. Half asleep against the wall with a beaker of wine in one hand. Only the randy little ginger git was missing.

No she wasn't.

I was there in two strides and knocked his beaker away. Wine sprayed up the wall.

'Hey! That one was full.'

'You had them arrested for theft?'

'I told you – I'm not going back to St Mary's.'

'You bastard!'

'They'll be all right,' he whined. 'They'll just be locked up for the night and escorted to the town gates tomorrow morning.'

He was lying.

I seized two great handfuls of his greasy tunic and began to bang his bloody head against the bloody wall.

'No they bloody won't. Especially the girls, you greasy bastard. Get them released now – this minute – or I'll drag you back to St Mary's by your balls – always supposing we can find them – and let them deal with you, you scrofulous toe-rag.'

He looked over at Leon. 'Are you going to let her talk to me like that?

'Nothing to do with me. Let me know if your arms get tired, Max, and I'll take over.'

He sagged. 'All right.'

'Who's got them?'

'Well, you could call them the police, I suppose.'

'What did you tell them?'

'That I'd been robbed by a group of strangers.'

'Where would they take them?'

He folded his arms and threw out his chest. The inference was obvious. He wasn't going to assist any further. Which was stupid of him. There are rules and regs that even I have to obey when dealing with contemporaries. Herodotus – or whoever this pillock was – was no contemporary. He was St Mary's. I could not only do with him as I pleased, I could be creative with it.

I know when to step back.

'Chief Farrell, please take whatever steps you feel necessary to induce Mr Herodotus to provide the information we require.'

Herodotus just had time to register that maybe things weren't going to go his way after all, when Leon whipped out his stun gun and zapped him. Only lightly, but enough to put him on the ground. So – taking a moment to sum up – four missing trainees and the world's first and most important historian twitching at our feet. Well down to our normal standards so far.

He lay flat on his back, arms and legs outflung and a stream of drool running down his chin. His tunic had ridden up. He looked, if possible, even more unattractive than ever.

'Yuk,' said Leon, hastily covering him up. 'Why am I suddenly thinking of Markham's dead chicken at

Troy?'

'I'm pretty sure only a mental health professional could unlock the secrets of your mind and even then only when wearing protective clothing.'

'Shall I put him in the recovery position?'

'Not if a kick in the slats will bring him around more quickly.'

It did.

'Jesus,' he said, one eye going east and the other west. 'Youse two are a right pair of bastards.'

'What a coincidence,' said Leon, pleasantly. 'We were just thinking the same about you.

'Again,' I said. 'Where have they been taken?'

Silence. I took another threatening step forwards.

He curled up in a protective ball. 'To the harbour area. There's a lockable storehouse where they keep people prior to …' He stopped.

'What will happen to them?'

He shrugged. 'Dunno. Lads put to work as galley slaves, I suppose and the girls …'

We all knew the answer to that one.

'Come on,' I said to Leon. 'And bring him.'

'What for?' said Herodotus, panicking. 'You don't need me.'

'You got them in – you can get them out. You will explain it's all been a terrible misunderstanding. And if you don't,' said Leon with quiet menace, 'we can spend some time discussing the phrase "multiple fractures" and its implications.'

He swallowed, sat up groggily, and started whining. 'This is not my fault. I didn't ask you to come here. I'm doing perfectly well in the here and now. I'm fulfilling History. In fact,' he continued, and I could practically hear his brain working, 'if anything happens to me then there's no more Herodotus and you've got a big problem.'

'We should take him back,' said Leon, playing bad cop. 'The Time Police will be pleased as punch to get their hands on him and we could do with the credit.'

'You don't frighten me,' he said truculently, 'I'm Herodotus the historian. You can't take me anywhere.'

He had a point. If he truly was Herodotus – and I had a horrible feeling he was – then he was one of the most important men of his age and there was no way we could do anything that would prevent him from finishing his *Histories*.

'True, but you've settled down now. Your travelling days are done. Your notes are complete. Anyone could finish them off. In fact,' I looked at Leon. 'I can think of any number of historians who would jump at the chance of six months in the sun, with unlimited amphorae and servant girls thrown in.'

'You bastards.'

Leon hauled him to his feet and then wiped his hands on his tunic. I didn't blame him.

I looked around the courtyard. There was no sign of anyone else anywhere. Either his household staff was in hiding or, more likely, no one liked him enough to come out and save him. I remembered the two women who had served us wine. And their bruises. I could imagine what being a female slave in this household must be like.

'So, where's the real Herodotus?'

'You don't get it, do you? I'm the real Herodotus.'

'All right, where's the man who was born in Halicarnassus?'

He shrugged. 'Set off on his travels and never came back. I found myself in Athens, up to my neck in trouble. They asked me my name and this was the only one from this period I could remember.' He shrugged. 'My speciality is actually the Etruscans so I said the first name that occurred to me and suddenly I was a star. Comfy billet, good food, and as much wine and women as I could handle. People tell me things, I write them down. Any gaps and I make it up. I'm an important man and I tell you now, I'm not going back to St Mary's. It's too bloody dangerous and my director was an absolute bastard. No, I'm staying here.'

Leon stared at him. 'Why can't you go back? What did you do?'

'Nothing,' he said, feebly and unconvincingly.

'Where's the rest of your team.'

'Went off without me,' he said, trying to look hard done by and only succeeding in looking shiftier than ever.

'I don't blame them,' said Leon. 'But why would they do that? You know the drill. We never leave our people behind.'

He shrugged. 'They might have thought I was dead.'

I stared at him. 'Why might they think that?'

'I might have ... accidentally ... come across a body and swapped the clothes.'

Leon said suddenly, 'You killed a contemporary?' and slammed him so hard against the wall that it was a miracle his teeth didn't come loose.

'Ow,' he said. 'Jesus. No need for that.'

I was in no mood for sympathy. 'Tell the truth, you lying piece of shit. Did you kill a contemporary?'

'No, no. Nothing like that. He was dying. I think. There wasn't anything I could do for him, anyway. Then he died. So I swapped clothes and ...'

He stopped suddenly.

Leon hauled him to his feet again. 'And ...?'

'And burned the body. They thought it was me.'

'Why? Why would you do such a thing? What sort of a monster are you?'

'Not my fault,' he whined again. 'Things got out of hand. St Mary's was a bitch to work for. And I owed some money. Not a lot. Well, not to begin with but it was a lot after a little while. Then there were some people looking for me so I took a long-term assignment to Athens, gave the rest of St Mary's the slip, changed my identity, and took a ship to Italy. It was easy.'

Leon doesn't often lose his patience. He jabbed his elbow in Herodotus' mid-section – a nasty, street-fighter's move that doubled him over. 'I've seen worm-ridden turds I liked better than you,' he said, and let him drop to the ground. We left him coughing and moaning in the dust while we had a bit of a think.

'We need to get them back,' I said. 'The sooner the better and definitely before nightfall.'

'Agreed. And bollock-brain here can help us do it.'

'Fuck off,' said the Father of History, still face

196

down in the dirt.

Leon kicked him. 'You're an important man and a founding father. You could get them out.'

'Fuck off,' he said again.

'Fine,' I said. 'If that's your final word. Leon, get him on his feet. We'll take him back to St Mary's and hand him over to the Time Police. Let them sort him out. We'll come back with Major Guthrie and a team and break them out after nightfall.'

'Good plan,' said Leon and hauled him upright again.

He wasn't as hurt as he'd led us to believe. Possibly realising there was no escape now, he struggled, breaking free of Leon's grasp. The two of them squared up to each other. We were between him and the gate but he was a solid man and he knew it.

'You're younger than me, son, but I could take you with one hand behind my back. Or one shout from me, and the whole town will turn up and you'll join our friends in gaol. So you just let me go and we'll say no more about it.'

All the evidence to the contrary, I'm actually quite a nice person. All right, I was a little unstable these days, but being Training Officer can do that to you. Mrs Nice Guy went straight out of the window.

I picked up the broom. 'That's enough from you, you pus-filled pile of shit. I'm sick to death of you and your ugly face so listen up. We can spend all day threatening each other and getting nowhere, or maybe there's a way for everyone to get what they want out of this. You cooperate. We get our people back and leave you to end your days in peace and prosperity.

Or – if you don't co-operate – you can just end your days. Period.

'Trust me,' said Leon. 'It's quicker and easier to eat your own legs than argue with her. Better men than you have tried and died. So what's it going to be?'

He stood quietly for a while, turning over my offer.

Leon passed me some water. 'Better get a move on, mate,' he said, in his new role as decision facilitator. 'If we don't return on time there'll be more St Mary's people here than you can throw a dead dog at. Maybe even Time Police as well. Think how pleased everyone will be to see you again. Or – you help us, we forget we ever saw you, and everyone gets what they want.'

Both of us shut up and stood quietly while he turned things over in his mind. Eventually, he came to a decision, shouting over his shoulder.

'Woman! Bring me my sandals.'

We emerged again into the bright sunshine of the lane behind his house.

'Do you know exactly where they're being held?'

'Yes.'

I could see Leon working himself up to saying something.

'Max, I think you should stay behind.'

I turned slowly. 'What did you say?'

'I think you should stay out of this.'

'Because?'

'Because if anything goes wrong then one of us is

still able to get back to St Mary's.'

'I appreciate your reasoning, but if we all end up under arrest then a mature and respectable female can more easily facilitate our path to freedom.'

'Not sure we'll be able to find one at this short notice.'

'I'm going to ignore that comment.'

We trotted down the lane and around the corner.

I said to Herodotus, 'How much trouble are they in?'

'Hard to say.'

'Try.'

'No, I really don't know. What passes for a police force here deals mainly with public order and trading offences. And this is a very law-abiding town.'

Until we got here, was the implication.

I contemplated trampling him into the ground.

'I wouldn't worry too much,' said Leon. Just for one moment, he put a gentle hand on my shoulder. 'No one messes with North if they know what's good for them and they don't call her Psycho Psykes for nothing.'

'Do they?'

'Personally, Max, I think we should get a move on and rescue the good people of Thurii before North and Sykes cause some sort of international incident and we have to explain things to Dr Bairstow. Or the Time Police.'

'Agreed,' said Herodotus.

'No one asked you.'

Twelve

None of Thurii was unpleasant or squalid – it hadn't yet had time to develop any sort of character – but you could see the harbour area would be the first to slide.

There was the actual harbour itself, with some two dozen fishing boats pulled up out of the water. Women squatted around them, gutting fish and tossing the unwanted bits into a pile. A number of mangy and probably very closely related cats sat waiting.

Set further back from the sea were ten or twelve anonymous buildings. These were not so brilliantly whitewashed as the other parts of town. Dogs and women bustled about. Washing was draped over a low wall to dry in the sun. Fishing nets hung on poles to dry, or were being mended. Various stalls had been set up displaying a variety of fishing-related equipment and domestic goods, including a table selling cooking pots and implements. Battered stools and wobbly tables stood in the shade of a grove of eucalyptus trees where a large number of men sat comfortably watching their womenfolk work.

Over on the far side, in its own little huddle of

buildings, stood a single-storey thatched structure with no windows. I'd already guessed that was the place, even without the sound of North's sharp as cut-glass tones raised in complaint and echoing across the water. You had to hand it to her. She was a hundred yards away, locked away in solidly built stone building with solidly built wooden doors and still they could probably hear her in Athens.

'You should shut her up,' said Herodotus, nervously. 'They're going to go in and sort her out in a minute.'

Leon made himself comfortable on the wall. 'We'll wait.'

'What for?'

'It's always easier to rescue someone if you don't actually have to break down the door yourself.' He touched his ear. 'We're right outside, Miss North. Whenever you're ready.'

'You don't need me, then,' Herodotus said, turning to go and unfortunately running slap into one of my hairpins.

He really wasn't having a good day.

'The fuck was that for?' he said, rubbing the fleshy part of his upper arm.

'You're not going anywhere.'

'What are we waiting for?'

Even as the words left his mouth, I pointed and said, 'That.'

I wasn't the only one pointing. Those in the café had seen it too. A shout went up.

'Fire! Fire!'

The thatched roof was smouldering.

'Bless her,' said Leon, stretched, and got to his feet. We strolled over, a muttering Father of History between us.

I could hear our people kicking the door and shouting to be let out.

Slaves ran towards the building. These must be their guards. They wore thick tunics and heavy boots. Heaving up the bar, they wrenched the door open. Out tumbled my happy band of pilgrims, a little smoke streaked and coughing, but otherwise, alive and well and very much kicking.

Fat lot of good it did them. They were immediately recaptured. More rod-bearing slaves simply rounded them up and corralled them against a wall while their colleagues organised a bucket chain.

Herodotus smirked. 'We're not stupid here, you know. How easy did you think it would be?'

Leon nodded at me. Time for the real Plan A.

I snapped. 'This easy,' and nudged him sideways with my hip. He was a solid bloke but years ago, back in the mists of time when I was a trainee myself, Major Guthrie had taught me a very useful trick. I'm short. I think I've already said I have the muscle tone of lettuce. I can't rely on brute force, so Guthrie had taught me that it's all just a matter of balance, and suddenly, Herodotus didn't have any. He staggered sideways into the cooking-pot stall, which didn't stand a chance under his weight.

We left him thrashing around amongst broken planks and shattered pots and creating the sort of diversion that money just can't buy while the female stallholder screamed and cursed at the top of her voice.

They were forming a bucket chain from the sea. Many men were joining in. The building was in no danger. Easy enough to replace the thatch. I was glad we hadn't done any permanent damage.

Quite close to us, another group of people were heaving up what looked like the cover to a well and forming a second chain.

And then disaster struck.

I saw it happen. As they always do in a fire, people were running in all directions. Some running away. Some running towards. In all the confusion, right in front of me, I saw a little kid knocked sideways by a man who probably never even noticed him.

One moment he was there. The next moment he was teetering at the edge of the well – and then the next moment he was gone.

I shouted and ran forwards. I wasn't the only one. A woman started screaming. Real screaming, not the running around in circles waving your arms screaming.

She couldn't get anyone to listen. The slaves were busy making sure their prisoners couldn't escape, the woman at the pottery stall was yelling at Herodotus who, by struggling to extricate himself, was making things much worse. A crowd was gathering there as well. There were angry voices. Founding father or not, I wondered again how popular he actually was.

I ran to the well, pulled the woman down on her knees so she wouldn't be knocked in too, and we both peered down into the watery depths. A draught of cool, damp air rose out of the well. It wasn't that far down – only about ten feet or so. My relief was overwhelming. If it had been about forty feet deep we'd have been buggered.

I could see the little boy, head straining out of the water, eyes screwed tight shut, scrabbling at the stone sides, which were green and slippery. He couldn't get a grip. I could hear him whimpering and gasping for breath. The water slapped loudly against the sides as he thrashed around in a panic. If he couldn't swim or somehow keep his face out of the water then he wouldn't last long.

We needed rope. This was a harbour, for God's sake. There were ships. Where there are ships there's always rope.

Leon was suddenly at my side, peering down the well. Our priorities had rearranged themselves. The trainees would have to wait because you can't let a contemporary die. The consequences could be massive. We needed to sort this out – fast.

'Rope,' I said.

He looked around at the flailing riot at the pot stall and the crowd surrounding the burning building. No one was paying any attention to us.

'No time. Give me your stole.'

I ripped it off and held out my hand for the woman's girdle. She was bright. She pulled it off and handed it over.

'I need more,' said Leon.

Sykes and North weren't that far away, pushed against a wall. I shouted, 'Give me your stoles.'

The stared for a minute and then began to unwind themselves. In public, too. If we hadn't been guilty of something before, we certainly were now.

Not without some trepidation, I approached the guards slowly and carefully and gestured at the stoles on the ground. They stared at me for a moment, then back at the woman on her knees at the well side, crying and wringing her hands, and then suddenly, they got it.

I ran back with the stoles and handed them over to Leon who began to knot them together and when I looked up, the slaves had joined us and were also peering down the well. The woman continued to shout at the kid to hold on. I think his name might have been Amyntas.

Bits of burning thatch were floating through the air and the riot at the pot stall was approaching meltdown.

Presumably not wanting to let them out of their sight, the guards had helpfully brought their prisoners with them.

'I'll go,' said Sykes, hanging dangerously far over the edge.

'No you won't,' I said, hauling her back.

'I'm smaller, lighter, and younger than you,' she said, winning no friends at all as far as I was concerned.

'You're a trainee. You're not allowed to endanger your life. You have to wait until after you're qualified for that.'

'Neither of you is going,' said Leon. 'I'll go. They'll pull me up.' He gestured to the slaves who obviously understood and nodded. He wasn't as small and light as Markham, but he was considerably smaller than the guards. We all were. There were mountains smaller than those guards.

He tied the stoles around his waist and handed the other end to a big bugger with a shaven head whose stubble was just beginning to grow through again. He wore a washed-out grey tunic stretched tightly across his enormous chest. He got the idea, nodded, and planted his feet. His two colleagues did the same, seizing his belt and bracing themselves.

Leon slowly lowered himself over the edge. Hoyle and Atherton lay on their stomachs shouting advice. I stayed with the young mother, who couldn't bring herself to watch.

'Has he got him yet?' I said, completely unable to see what was happening.

'Nearly,' said Hoyle.

The big slave, muscles bulging, was taking the strain easily enough. He was as big as a house. Actually, he reminded me of Dieter, a little bit.

A shout from Leon below and now the three of them began to heave him up. Atherton and Hoyle hung over the edge, directing operations. North and Sykes hung on to them, just in case they fell in too, and I hung on to the mother. A real team effort.

Leon's head appeared first, and then the kid's, eyes still screwed tight shut. His hair was plastered to his head and two skinny brown arms clung tightly around Leon's neck.

Atherton prised the kid loose. 'Here you go, sunshine,' and handed him, dripping wet, to his mother. We all heaved Leon out and over the edge, where he lay, gasping and making a puddle in the dust. If they arrested us all now there wouldn't be anything we could do about it.

The knotted stoles had ridden up under his armpits. I struggled with the wet knots.

The big guard flexed his shoulders a couple of times in relief and then took out a knife.

I tensed. What I thought I would do is a mystery, but fortunately, I didn't have to do anything. He sliced through the sodden material, pulled Leon to his feet, and fetched him a slap on the back that made him stagger. Someone passed Leon a wineskin. The young woman, complete with child, flung her arms around him. He staggered backwards under the onslaught. I laughed at him.

Now what?

I was contemplating quietly gathering my team together and just casually strolling out of the war zone when a scream from the pottery stall caused heads to turn.

Everyone has their tipping point. The moment when the straw breaks the camel's back and the camel turns round, spits in your eye, and then eats you.

It would appear that our Miss North had had enough.

I'd only taken my eye off her for a second, but in that time she'd managed to find some sort of wooden tray – from the wine shop, I guessed – and was beating the hapless Herodotus around the head and shoulders with more enthusiasm than I would have thought her capable.

It would seem that while you can take the girl out of the 21st century, it's more difficult to take the 21st

century out of the girl.

'You bastard! You total bastard!'

'She doesn't seem very happy,' observed Leon. 'What's the problem?'

Herodotus lay on his back, hopelessly entangled in the awning, broken planks, broken pottery, and with his tunic unattractively up around his waist again. I wondered if he ever regretted abandoning trousers.

'Well he did grass us up, I suppose.'

That, however, did not appear to be the issue uppermost in her mind.

'I spent hours on this bloody assignment, you arsehole. Days, even. I planned it all down to the minutest detail and then you come along and everything goes straight down the drain. This was supposed to be the perfect assignment. This was my moment and thanks to you, it's been a bloody shambles. A bloody bollocking shambles, you pathetic little worm. Give me one – just one – reason why I should allow an obnoxious piece of excrement like you to continue polluting the planet, because I can't think of any. And for heaven's sake, pull your tunic down and cover up that disgusting object before it evaporates in the sunlight.'

She was belting him so hard that pieces of wooden tray were flying off in all directions. Apart from curling himself into a ball and shouting, 'Gerroff,' occasionally, there wasn't a lot he could do. He was completely at her mercy.

No one was making the slightest move to save him. Clearly my doubts about his personality had good grounds. People were standing, grinning. At any moment, they would be pulling up chairs and calling for more wine.

We're really not supposed to beat up contemporaries. As a cautious and prudent leader, I should do something. Sometimes the bluebird of wisdom does deign to flap gently over my head and release a small dollop of something appropriate.

I walked over as slowly as I could. She'd had a trying day. She deserved a small treat.

I said gently, 'Miss North.'

I don't think she heard me.

I said again, 'Celia.'

She dealt him one final blow and desisted, but only because the tray had finally disintegrated in her grasp. She flung the last piece to the ground and stood, chest heaving for breath, staring around her.

It was just bloody typical, wasn't it? Our Miss North, despite being arrested for theft, starting a fire in a public building, and laying into the Father of History like an avenging Fury, had managed to emerge pristine and unmarked. Her hair was immaculate. Her robe spotless. I didn't dare look down at my own clothing. Sometimes life just isn't fair.

She stepped from the wreckage like Dido from the ruins of Carthage. An avenging goddess, eyes flashing fire. An over-enthusiastic Valkyrie. She stared challengingly at the watching crowd. You could see every man of them suddenly remembering why they never let their women out of doors if they could help it.

She put her hands on her hips and glared at them.

'Are you looking at me?'

Sykes and Atherton surged forwards before the crowd could come to any harm.

She kicked aside what little remained of her tray, tucked a stray wisp of hair behind her ear, and picked her way delicately towards us. We stood respectfully silent as she joined us.

'Dr Maxwell.'

'Miss North.'

'We should go,' said Leon, hastily and Hoyle and Atherton nodded enthusiastic agreement. 'Before they discover who started the fire. And before Herodotus comes to his senses and does us some real damage.'

I looked around.

The storeroom-cum-gaol roof was blazing merrily away.

The young mother appeared to be crushing the small boy to her bosom while simultaneously boxing his ears. An impressive feat that only mothers seem able to achieve.

The skinny cats, unable to believe their luck, had abandoned the fish entrails and were in among the unguarded baskets of fish. They darted about, seizing something tasty and racing off through the crowd, tripping several people up in their haste to get away.

Someone's donkey was having a kind of seizure by the sound of it. Or perhaps they always sound like that.

There were even two old women screeching at each other from their sitting positions against a wall. They were only prevented from doing each other actual bodily harm by the fact they couldn't stand up without assistance. Their screeched insults were clearly audible over the shouts, yowls, breaking pots, roaring flames …

You could tell St Mary's was in town.

We gathered ourselves together, put up our hair, and rewound our wet stoles. Leon wrung out his tunic.

Herodotus had been pulled out of the remains of the pottery stall and propped up against a wall. He looked terrible – face the colour of boiled shite and spotted with big blue bruises. He had a glorious black eye and blood trickled from both nostrils. He opened his eyes as we approached.

'Go away. Just … bloody … go away, will you.'

'We're going now,' said Leon. 'And you're going to facilitate our departure by telling everyone it was a misunderstanding. That you were too drunk to know what you were doing. They'll believe that.'

He looked at us. 'What about you? What are you going to do?'

'We're going,' Leon said. 'And we're never coming back.'

He nodded.

I'd been thinking.

I turned back again. Herodotus peered at me groggily and visibly braced himself.

I said softly, 'Look, you were an historian before you came here. Now you're Herodotus. The greatest historian of all. Why don't you tidy yourself up a bit? Lay off the wine. Get those notes written up. Write that book. You chose a famous name. Live up to it.'

He wiped his nose on the back of his hand, looked

at me, and then spat a gob of bloody mucus at my feet. I washed my hands of him.

I just wanted to get us all back to the pod, but even as I thought about getting them moving, an elderly man hobbled cautiously towards us, gave us all the once over, and picked Atherton as the most approachable. Or the most normal. He began to talk furiously, gesturing towards us, and plucking at Atherton's tunic.

Leon was herding us all together like an anxious sheepdog. 'What's going on over there?'

'Don't know. We might not be out of the woods yet. Be prepared to make a run for it.'

We stood in a tight little group, expecting the worst.

Eventually Atherton extricated himself and came over.

I said, 'What was that all about?'

'Well, I'm not sure I got all of it, but I think I might have been offered half a goat for Miss North.'

Sykes pricked up her ears. 'Really? Which half?'

We limped back to the pod. North was nearly in tears.

'The whole thing was a disaster. Could it have gone more wrong?'

'Hard to see how it could have,' said Sykes, cheerfully.

'Not helping,' said Atherton.

'How much trouble are we in?'

'None at all,' said Leon. 'What makes you think that?'

'I beat up the Father of History.'

'Yes, you did,' I said in admiration.

'But I was mission controller. I should have ...'

If she was going to start on what she should have done, we'd be here all day.

'Listen,' I said, 'You handled your team, yourself, and the situation well. I'm not sure I could have done better.'

She seemed genuinely surprised.

'The aim was interaction with contemporaries and we more than achieved that objective. No one said it had to be friendly interaction. Not everyone in History is nice, you know.'

She nodded.

'Just try not to be quite so ... inflexible. It's all very well to have a stated goal, but you should realise there are many paths to that goal. And if things go horribly wrong – and you must be prepared for the fact that they frequently do – then you must be able to think on your feet and get there another way.'

'So I haven't failed this assignment?'

'No. We frequently have missions that turn to crap. The measure of success is how we deal with that.'

She turned that over in her head. I rather got the impression this was a completely new concept to her. Dealing with the unexpected, I mean.

'You should think about this, Miss North. Anyone can meticulously plan and there's nothing wrong with that, but in our job, we have to expect the unexpected. It's how we cope with the unforeseen that is the measure of our success. You have all the makings, and if you can learn to be a little more flexible – learn to adapt to rapidly changing circumstances – you could be an excellent historian.'

She smiled suddenly. 'Really?'

I nodded. 'Yes, really.'

And perhaps if I stopped looking for things to criticise and looked for things to praise her for instead, I might become at least an adequate training officer. Something for me to think about, too.

We drank our tea – except for the heathen Hoyle – and tried to tidy ourselves up a bit. Historians never go back looking scruffy. Injured – yes. Dead – occasionally. Scruffy – not if we could help it. Looking around, some of us were a little smoke damaged. Some were wet. Apart from Miss North, all of us were muddy. By the time we'd finished, the pod looked as if a small war had been fought inside it. I could see Leon compressing his lips. It was obvious whose fault this was going to turn out to be.

'Everyone set?' I asked.

The world went white.

Dieter opened the door, took it all in at a glance, and grinned at me. 'So, how did it go?'

'Perfectly,' said Leon. 'The locals were completely unaware of our presence.'

Isn't he wonderful?

I began to shut things down. They picked up their gear and filed out.

'We'll be out in a minute,' said Leon to Dieter. 'I just need to have word with the Training Officer about certain aspects of this assignment.'

Oh dear.

Sykes looked back. 'Should we stay?'

'No,' he said calmly. 'None of what follows will be suitable for young people or those of a nervous disposition.'

She cast me a sympathetic glance and followed the others outside.

He closed the door behind her. And locked it.

I looked up. 'Leon, what are you doing?'

He said nothing, just looking at me across the pod, holding my gaze. Not looking away. At all. I couldn't tear my gaze away, either.

'Well,' he said softly. 'Wasn't that just like old times?'

My breathing was suddenly all over the place. The ventilation system had obviously packed up because suddenly I just couldn't get enough oxygen into my lungs. And the heating system had gone into overdrive.

He crossed the pod in two long strides, took hold of my wrists, and pushed me up against the lockers, crushing my body with his. His blue eyes were very dark. I could feel him hard against me. He grasped my hair and pulled my head back, kissing the base of my throat. I could feel his breath on my skin. His lips were very hot.

As was I.

He kissed me hard. Eagerly. He tasted of dust and sweat and Leon. I pushed against him as hard as I could. I could feel the heat of his body even through his damp clothes.

He pulled my tunic down off my shoulder. And then the other one. I got my arms free. Slowly, very slowly he dragged his muddy hand across my breast, leaving a long smear, dark against my skin. We both stared at it for a moment and then he said softly, his breath hot in my ear, 'You are a very ... very ... dirty girl.'

I sat quietly while Dr Bairstow read through our reports.

He flattened the data stacks and sat back in his chair. 'So, to sum up. You jumped back in time, encountered the venerable and respected Father of History, discovered that he was actually an escaped historian from the future, got yourselves arrested for theft, burned down a gaol, started a riot which resulted not only in a young child falling into a well, but extensive damage to a pottery stall, and grievous bodily harm to the aforementioned Father of History as well.'

I nodded.

'Impressive,' he said, meaning anything but. 'You were there for less than three hours.'

I know when to remain silent.

'What was his real name?'

'I forgot to ask him, sir. He wasn't ... capable ... a lot of the time.'

'And none of you would know anything about that?'

'It wasn't just us, sir. Other people had a go at him too. He wasn't a popular bloke.'

'So I gathered.'

He remained silent, drumming his fingers on the desk.

'We really can't allow him to remain there.'

'Agreed, sir.'

'We'll give him time to finish off his *Histories*. The date of his death and location of his grave are unknown, which makes things easier for us. The Time Police will remove him. It will be quick and quiet.'

I shivered. Then I thought of the bruises on his slaves' arms and the death of the contemporary he'd 'accidentally' encountered. And he'd grassed us up without a second thought. God knows what would have become of us if we hadn't managed to escape.

'What will happen to him, sir?'

He didn't answer and I didn't ask again.

Thirteen

We were half way through the programme. Only one down so far – Miss Lingoss – and even she was still alive so, as I cheerfully argued to Dr Bairstow, that didn't really count. He countered by handing me the mid-term assessment paperwork and telling me to get on with it.

I sighed. You lose some and then you lose some more.

There's an accepted routine for trainee assessments. The trainee enters the room and fixes the training officer with a glance that effortlessly combines blinding innocence with solemn dedication and hard work.

The training officer, for her part, lets them sweat for a minute or so then lifts her eyes from their file and regards them coldly.

The trainee, transfixed by the awfulness of this soul-penetrating glare, immediately confesses to every guilty sin he/she/it has perpetrated since the moment of conception and earnestly promises to do better in the future.

The training officer, magnanimously allowing him/her/it to live, extracts promises of even greater commitment in whatever future she allows the trainee to enjoy and sends him/her/it on his/her/its way.

Good fun, I think everyone will agree.

I can't begin to say how badly it all went. See below for selected highlights.

Me:
(at this point, still full of fire and drive):

So, Miss North, tell me about your ambitions. Where do you see yourself in five years' time?

North:
Oh, I want your job.

Me:
Training Officer?

North:
No, Chief Operations Officer.

Me:
(slightly astonished)

You actually want to be Chief Operations Officer?

North
(slightly astonished at my slowness)

Yes.

Me:
Well, if you stop getting up people's noses, lose the attitude, adjust the tone, and just generally stop being a pain in the arse, you might make the long list. Until

then, no chance. Next!
Yeah, that could have gone better.

Sykes was the next one through the door.
I had noted, when reading through her file, that it was the Security Section who had christened her Psycho Psykes. Considering that between them, they enjoyed nearly every personality disorder known to man, and in Dr Foster's opinion, at least two of them should be sectioned, I was inclined to believe they knew what they were talking about.

Sykes:
(bounding cheerfully through the door):

Good afternoon.

Me:
(now not quite so full of fire and drive):

Good afternoon, Miss Sykes. Please si …

Sykes:
(hurling herself into a chair)

So, Dr Maxwell, how do you think it's going so far?

Me:

Well, I …

Sykes:
(enthusiastically)

Great.

Me:

Well, I …

Sykes:
(plonking a data cube on my desk)

I've finished my report on the Herodotus assignment.

Me:

Jolly goo ...

Sykes:
(plonking another data cube on my desk)

And I hope you don't mind but here's a list of future assignments I think the History Department will find useful.

Me:

Tha ...

Sykes:
(plonking a third data cube on my desk)

And Lingoss and I put our heads together and here are some ideas for the future.

Me:

Yes, but ...

Sykes:

So how much longer before I'm qualified?

Me:
(feeling the question was irrelevant because I was going to be dead long before then)

Well ...

Sykes:

Only there's so much to do, isn't there?

Me:

Ye …

Sykes:

(managing to bound with enthusiasm while still in a sitting position)

Only I hope I'm doing well because I think it's really great here, and I'm sorry Dr Maxwell, but if I'm not then you've got a problem because you're going to have to dynamite me out of this place.

Me:

(alarmed at the mention of dynamite in this context)

No, I …

Sykes:

Well, that's good then. Was there anything else?

Me:

God, no.

Sykes:

OK. Bye!

Me:

Mrs Shaw, do we have any aspirin?

And on to today's mystery guest, Laurence Hoyle.

Me:

Well, Mr Hoyle, you've been here three, no four months now. Any comments?

Hoyle:

Is it always like this?

Me:

(looking around in case I've missed something)

Like what?

Hoyle:

This ... this ... turmoil. This bedlam. The noise. The explosions. The shouting. How does anyone get any work done? Nothing works properly. Nothing goes according to plan. You're like irresponsible children, noisy, reckless, and lacking all respect. No one takes anything seriously.

Me:

(quite indignant at this slur but conscious of not being on solid ground)

Of course we take things seriously.

Silence.

Me:

Is this a problem for you?

Hoyle:

I don't know. It's not what I was expecting.

Me:
(hackles rising)

What were you expecting?

Hoyle:
(gloomily)

Not this.

Me:
(expecting my nose to grow at any moment)

I think you're worrying unnecessarily, Mr Hoyle. While I admit that, on rare occasions, things might look a little chaotic, I can assure you that here at St Mary's we are always completely on top of things. Furthermore …

And, of course, that was the moment chosen by Rosie Lee to stick her head round my door and announce (looking anything but) that she was sorry to disturb me, but did I know the History Department had concealed a baby in a warming pan and were carting it all around the building and it didn't sound very happy.

'No, they haven't,' I said, fingers crossed under my desk. 'It'll be just a bag of flour or something.'

'Very possibly,' she said, 'but it's making a hell of a racket for a sack of self-raising.'

Bloody hell. Now what?

I said without hope, 'Thank you, Mr Hoyle, that will be all,' but of course he followed me out onto the Gallery, where a crowd of historians were trailing behind Prentiss, Lingoss, and Bashford rather in the manner of clouds of dirty smoke from an old banger that had just failed its emissions test. Prentiss, with some difficulty, was heaving around a warming pan and Bashford clutched the inevitable clipboard.

I could hear the sounds of vigorous academic debate.

'And might I point out,' Bashford was saying severely, 'that the key points of baby smuggling are to be quick and quiet. Neither of which you seem capable of. How much do you reckon the average newborn weighs?'

Prentiss rested the warming pan on the balustrade. 'Well, I'd say this seems to be about seven pounds. Plus the weight of the warming pan itself. And the long handle makes it quite tricky to carry. And he won't stay still which is really making my shoulders ache. In my opinion, they couldn't have carried him very far without their arms dropping off. Or somebody noticing. I mean, look at the crowd following us around.'

They stopped dead as they saw us, politely stood aside, and said, 'Good afternoon, Max.'

I returned the greeting because I'm polite, too. Hoyle just stood with his mouth open. With misgivings, but not yet completely given over to despair, I enquired what was up.

'Just checking whether it's possible to smuggle a baby into a royal birthing chamber inside a warming pan,' said Bashford, cheerfully.

Ah – James Edward Francis Stewart. Son of James II and Mary of Modena, who, after years of unsuccessful reproduction, suddenly and suspiciously produced a healthy son. Rumour had it that on producing yet another stillborn child, a live baby had been smuggled into the queen's room in a warming pan.

'And is it?' I enquired.

'Not sure yet,' said Prentiss. 'It's bloody heavy, I know that. Max, how much do you think a baby weighs?'

'No idea.'

'Well, setting aside the fact my arms are practically dropping from their sockets, I would have thought the pan was too shallow *and* you have to ask yourself, isn't someone trundling around with a warming pan in September just a little bit suspicious?'

She hefted the pan for a better grip. The lid lifted slightly and a faint cry could be heard.

I felt rather than saw Mr Hoyle's agitation.

'Bloody hell, we'd better get a move on if you don't mind,' said Bashford. 'He's trying to get out again.'

'He?' said Hoyle, in horror, completely missing the important word, which was *again*. 'You haven't – you surely haven't got a real baby in there?'

Silence. They exchanged looks with each other and grinned.

'Have you?'

'No, of course not,' they said unconvincingly.

The warming pan tilted alarmingly.

'Look out,' he shouted. 'You'll drop him,' and made a grab for the lid.

'Don't open it, for God's sake,' yelled Bashford.

Too late.

The lid was thrust aside revealing an enraged ginger face and bristling whiskers.

Vortigern, the kitchen cat, who normally spent his days cocooned in the safety and security of Mrs Mack's office, had not taken kindly to enforced deportation. Hissing, he lashed out, leaped from the pan, and disappeared back to safer regions.

'Ow,' yelled Hoyle, flapping a badly scratched hand. Bashford and Prentiss were unsympathetic.

'What did you take the lid off for, you idiot?'

'I thought you had a real baby in there.'

'Seriously? Where would we get a real baby from?'

'How the hell should I know? If Lingoss can requisition a dead pig and a coffin then I would have thought a baby would be easy.'

I left them all deeply embedded in the process of blame allocation.

And on to Atherton. Lovely, normal Atherton.

Me:
(losing the will to live)

Everything OK with you, Mr Atherton?

Atherton:

Yes, fine, thank you.

Long pause.

Me:
(surprised and suspicious)

Anything you wanted to say?

Atherton:

Nope.

Me:
(still not quite believing)

So everything's all right?

Atherton:

Yep.

Me:

Well, thank you, Mr Atherton. Good afternoon.

Always quit while you're ahead.

Having brushed through the mid-term assessments I bounced back to Dr Bairstow's office with the completed paperwork. Mrs Partridge waved me through. 'He has Miss Lingoss with him at the moment, but they're just finishing. You may go straight in.'

They were talking together in the window. Today's hair extravaganza was purple. Hers, I mean. He didn't have anything like enough hair to compete with the magnificent mauve madness of Miss Lingoss. He would come second place to an egg.

'Ah, Dr Maxwell. Do come in. Miss Lingoss is just about to explain the reasons why there is a dead pig occupying the car parking space next to mine.'

'The disabled spot was occupied, sir,' she said cheerfully.

'With some curiosity, I enquire why there is a dead pig in the car park at all.'

'We didn't think you'd want it inside, sir.'

'I congratulate you on your perspicacity,' he said, 'but we are still no nearer to ascertaining its purpose in the scheme of things.'

'William the Conqueror, sir.'

'Yes, I feel I may need more details.'

'He was enormously fat, sir.'

'One or two more, perhaps.'

'The coffin was too small and as they tried to squeeze him into it, his corpse exploded.'

'Disconcerting.'

'To say the least, sir. I am attempting to reproduce the circumstances leading to that unfortunate event.'

He stared at her.

'Why?'

She appeared genuinely bewildered. 'Why not?'

He sighed. 'Very well, Miss Lingoss, thank you.'

She bounded past me, grinning broadly. I grinned back. An exploding pig in the car park. Something to look forward to.

I know I've made it sound as if I was bearing the trainee brunt alone, but others were actually doing their fair share too. Clerk and Prentiss had escorted them to 884AD, to watch the Vikings sail silently and menacingly up the River Medway, emerging out of the early morning mist to attack the city of Rochester. They'd enjoyed that and no one had been skewered by a Viking arrow.

Two weeks later, they'd jumped back to Granada, 1492 to record Isabella and Ferdinand receiving the keys of the city as the final part of the Reconquista and they'd all survived that one, too.

And now, Major Guthrie had them down for another Outdoor Survival exercise.

I was thrilled at the thought of a couple of days without them, until it became apparent it wasn't just the trainees involved in this one. He was expecting me to participate as well.

I fixed him with my best reproachful puppy look.

He laughed at me. 'Wasting your time.'

'After everything I've done for you, Ian.'

'*To* me, don't you mean?'

I let my bottom lip quiver.

'You can pack that in as well' he said, heartlessly. 'It won't work. I've been through the records and for one reason or another you haven't actually completed one of these for ...' he pretended to consult his clipboard as if we didn't both know the answer to that one, '... Never. Anyway, now's your chance,' he continued. 'The weather is lovely. You'll enjoy it.'

I abandoned reproachful for heartrending.

Let me put it this way, Max, if it's the last thing I ever do, I will ensure you actually participate in an Outdoor Survival event.'

'It could be the last thing *I* ever do, too.'

'There's always a silver lining. 08.00 tomorrow. Do not be late.'

The dreaded Outdoor Survival exercise is the one where we take our trainees, drive them to some inhospitable wilderness, and leave them to die of starvation and exposure. Unless, of course, by using a combination of skill, endurance, and blind luck, they manage to find their way back to St Mary's again.

For various reasons, I'd never actually participated in one, but obviously the time had come when the traditional excuses of rank, pressure of work, absence in another time period, pretended sickness, actual sickness, injury, or death were unavailing and I was actually going to have to complete the bloody thing.

I boarded the transport under the 'I'm on to you, Maxwell so don't even think about it,' eye of Major Guthrie and his smirking clipboard. We drove for a hundred years. I was the first to be dropped off. They pushed me out, drove away laughing, and left me to die.

Just for once, however, the weather was good and it was quite a pleasant spot, although my actual location was still a complete mystery to me. I could have been on one of the outer moons of Jupiter for all I knew.

I stared around at the green rolling hills. Somewhere, high in a powder blue sky, a lark was giving it everything he'd got. It was just like that piece of music by Vaughan Williams, which was nice, but not particularly helpful. I had just under forty-eight hours to get back to St Mary's, or be exposed forever to ridicule and general mockery.

I think I've said before that I've never really considered the god of historians to be quite up to the job, so any requests for assistance (apart from being uttered in a hurry and at the top of our voices) usually have to be accompanied by fairly explicit instructions as to what's required to remedy the situation. The response isn't always quite what we had in mind, but, occasionally, every now and then, on an apparently random basis, the god of historians really, really comes through.

A white van appeared from nowhere, cruised to a halt beside me, and asked if I was OK. I mean, obviously, the driver asked me. I'd only been out here about ten minutes or so and certainly wasn't yet so far gone as to be imagining talking Mercedes Sprinters.

He asked if I was in the army and was it one of those survival things?

He was half-right, so I nodded and climbed in. He took me to the nearest town, dropping me on the ring road. I was staring in baffled incomprehension at a road sign when a huge artic pulled up. I heaved myself in and grinned at the driver. She took me to Rushford.

From there, I took a taxi, shamelessly quoting Dr Bairstow's account number because we were supposed to be using our initiative. There would be trouble later on, but deal with the now. With luck, I'd be dead before the future turned up.

The taxi dropped me just outside the village and I cut through the woods, enjoying the shade and the birdsong. I signed in at the South Gate, laughed at their surprise, skirted the lake, pushed my way through the reed beds, crossed the grass, climbed in through one of the Library windows, grinned at an astonished Dr Dowson, and headed straight for the bar.

I entered to stunned silence. With my track record for catastrophe, they certainly hadn't expected to see me for at least a week and probably only then to the accompaniment of sirens and significant numbers of the emergency services, but here I was. I'd hadn't been gone much more than a couple of hours. Major Guthrie and the transports weren't even back yet. This was a record that was never going to be broken.

Ordering a celebratory Margarita, I took a seat by the window, heaved my pristine and unused backpack to the ground with a crash, put my feet up, made myself comfortable, silently raised my glass to the god of historians – and waited for Guthrie to return.

Obviously, someone had told him and I'll never forget the look on his face as he strode into the bar, stopped dead on the threshold, and stared. Such was the depth of his emotion that he very nearly dropped his clipboard.

Considering that every member of St Mary's who wasn't actually out on assignment had found a good reason to be in the bar at that specific moment, the silence was remarkable. He just stared. I could practically hear his mind working until one of the bar staff tapped him on the arm and handed him the double scotch I'd ordered for him earlier. I raised my glass and grinned at him, because I'm told that's really annoying.

And that, folks, is how you effortlessly pass into St Mary's legend.

However, enough of me. The point I'm meandering towards is that I was back – and not only was I back, but I was back hours, days, weeks even, ahead of schedule and this was probably why Miss Lee was taking advantage of my absence to use my empty office to have a really good cry.

Now I knew exactly how Major Guthrie had felt. Another occasion so unexpected that the world is flipped upside down and everything is topsy-turvy.

I stopped on the threshold, gobsmacked, and she leaped to her feet and glared at me as if everything was my fault. Which, to be fair, it usually is.

I really wasn't sure what to do. Tactfully ignore her? Ask her what was the problem? Turn around and walk away? I tried to remember that this was my office after all, and sat down behind my desk.

She'd obviously been at it for some time. Her face was blotchy, her eyes swollen, and her nose was running. My first thought was – my God, could this be guilt? Was I right? Was Rosie Lee the traitor and was she now experiencing remorse? Admittedly rather late in the day, but better late than never. Well, whatever the reason, there was obviously something very wrong with Rosie Lee today.

Actually, that's an inaccurate statement. There's something wrong with Rosie Lee every day.

Reactions to her vary from mild dislike to outright hostility with a little bit of irritation thrown into the mix for good measure. As far as I knew, she had no friends, nor any desire for any. I had no idea what she did with herself when she wasn't in the office (actually, I didn't have much of an idea of what she did in it, either). I didn't know where she went or whom she was with. I was just grateful it wasn't me.

However, there might never be another opportunity so I moved smoothly into interrogation mode.

'What's the matter with you?'

All right, not subtle, but a direct question sometimes prompts a direct answer.

She trumpeted into a completely inadequate bit of tissue and threw it into my bin where it landed with a squelch. Fortunately, she had enough sense not to say 'nothing', which is so irritating when there obviously is *something* and you have to play that stupid guessing game.

She sighed. 'I've had a bit of a falling-out.'

I was a teensy bit surprised. Not that she'd fallen out with someone – that happened twenty times a day and they always came to complain to me afterwards – I mean surprise that it had obviously upset her so badly.

'With whom?'

She shuffled her feet around a bit and then muttered something.

'Can't hear you.'

She sighed again and said, in defiantly ringing tones, 'David Sands.'

So, nothing to do with the death of Schiller. Or was it? I would have to probe further. But first things first.

'I have to hand it to you, Miss Lee, you possess a rare gift. How can you possibly argue with David Sands? He's one of the nicest blokes on the planet.'

Stupid question. She could argue with a corpse and reduce Patience herself to foaming, blood-red rage.

I got up and made the tea, having discovered long ago that making it myself was the safest option. The rumour at St Mary's is that the last person to ask her to make the tea got it at head height some forty-five seconds later. No idea if that's true but who wants to take the risk? There's enough drama in my life without having to spend the working day ducking low-flying tea.

Anyway, back to the plot.

'What on earth could you find to argue about with David Sands? Was it one of his stupid knock-knock jokes?'

She tossed her head, defiantly. 'We've been going out.'

I tried not to look gobsmacked and failed miserably.

'Yes, I know what you're thinking. He's tall, he's handsome, he's popular, and everyone likes him, so why would he be interested in someone like me?'

Exactly the question I *was* asking myself, but saying so would probably not be helpful. Since I couldn't think of anything to say, I said nothing and obviously this was the right way to go because without any prompting from me, she was off again.

'I mean, look at me. Why would he even bother? What could he possibly see in someone like me? Does he think I'm easy? Is that it?'

God knows where she got the idea that anyone would think she was easy. Personally, I would have said she was the most difficult person ever born.

'Or does he just think I'm grateful?' she continued bitterly. 'It's not as if anyone else is ever going to take us on, is it?'

There are no words to describe how far out at sea I was at this point. There were rafts in the mid-Atlantic that were less at sea than I was. However, my duty was clear. She was having a vulnerable moment and it was up to me to exploit it with powerful and penetrating questions.

I said, 'Do you want some tea?'

She blew her nose again and nodded. So far so good. I kidded myself I was winning her confidence.

Shoving a steaming mug towards her, I sought to push the conversation in the right direction.

'Is this because you didn't fight for St Mary's last year?'

'What?' Her head reared up. Oh God, I'd annoyed her and she was about to attack me. 'Where did that come from?'

'Well, I was wondering. For some reason, you seem to feel you're not good enough for him and I wondered if it was because you didn't fight for St Mary's. And,' I continued, with that reckless madness frequently experienced when risking life and limb, 'you subconsciously feel guilty because that was when he lost his foot and – '

There was a crash as her mug hit the wall. Tea splashed everywhere. I jumped a mile and decided that in the not-unlikely event of Dr Bairstow chucking me out one day, relationship counselling was a field I should probably avoid. I almost began to wish I were back in the great outdoors again, battling for my life in the warm afternoon sunshine.

She was on her feet. 'You! You're no better than the rest of them. I know what they say about me but I never thought you were saying it as well.'

I was now so far out at sea I was practically dropping over the horizon. 'Right,' I said, suddenly losing patience. 'Stop. Sit down. No, never mind the china. We'll sweep it up later. Sit down, take a deep breath, and tell me what you're talking about.'

'Well, at the moment, I'm talking about being pissed at you because of what you implied because I didn't fight for St Mary's.'

'Yes,' I said, suddenly getting back on track. 'Why didn't you?'

Silence fell heavily.

She said nothing.

I waited, every muscle tensed in case she made a break for it. I swear, if she so much as twitched a muscle, I'd be over the desk and pounding her into the ground. My mind flew back to that dull, grey day when we found Schiller's body, all yellow bones and tattered clothing with that small, neat bullet hole in the centre of her forehead …

Go on, Rosie Lee. Just give me an excuse …

She took a deep breath and straightened her shoulders.

I braced myself. This was it.

She put her clasped hands on the table and said very quietly, 'I didn't fight because of my little boy.'

The world span around me. I had to replay the sentence several times before I could make any sense of it. To gain time, I said stupidly, 'Because of your little boy?'

She nodded.

I pulled myself together. 'You have a child?'

She nodded.

I sat back in my chair. I really must learn to listen better. She was a single parent and had a child and because of this, she'd thought Sands would think she was easy. Or that she would be grateful. She'd said, 'No one would ever take *us* on.' For God's sake, Maxwell, learn to listen!

All right, that answered the question about why she hadn't fought. She was on her own. If anything had happened to her then her child would be all alone in the world. An acceptable reason. Unfortunately, it was also the reason for her obvious shortage of money and an excellent reason for her to accept a bribe – a substantial bribe, probably – to betray us all to Clive Ronan.

On the other hand, she'd made her confession easily enough. If she were guilty then surely she wouldn't have mentioned the kid at all.

It struck me that I was pretty rubbish at this.

And who could the father be? Assuming she hadn't eaten him during the act. Like a praying mantis, that is. Not a bad idea actually, and certainly one that could do with being more widely adopted.

'Um ... Who's the father?'

She read my mind. 'No one here. Nothing you need worry about.'

'So where is he in all this?'

'Gone.'

'Ah.'

'His parents didn't like the look of me.'

I suddenly experienced a complete change of view. Who did they think they were? 'You're probably better off without him. You're certainly better off without them.'

'I thought so, yes.'

'Does he send you any money?'

'Of course not. Everyone knows if you ignore this sort of problem then she goes away.'

'But there are agencies for ...'

She sighed impatiently. 'There are different worlds for different people. People who have rich and powerful parents live in a different world from people like me. There were demands for paternity tests, investigations into my past history, and allegations of promiscuity ... and then they said they could bring my baby up better than me and I should hand him over, so I backed off.'

'You're definitely better off without him.'

'That's what I said when I told him and his mother to fuck off. I even tried to get a solicitor to draft them a letter telling them if they came within a hundred yards of me and my son I'd take legal action.' She shrugged. 'He wouldn't do it.'

'What did you do?'

'Forgot them and carried on with my life.'

241

'Does anyone here know?'

'No one knows. I took two months' unpaid leave. I told people I had a once-in-a-lifetime chance to visit relatives in Australia.'

'But where is he? The kid, I mean?'

'Rushford. Where I live.'

Oh my God – the coat hanging behind the door. Right in front of me for all this time. I'd noticed the shabbiness but the important fact had escaped me. If she lived at St Mary's then why would she bring a coat to work? Because she didn't live here. She lived in Rushford with her kid and that was where the money went. Rent, transport, and childcare.

I took a deep breath. A very deep breath.

'I'm going to ask you a question. I have a good reason for asking it and I'll tell you why afterwards.'

She looked wary. 'All … right.'

'Answer me truthfully. This is more important than I can say. Has anyone … anyone at all ever offered you money in exchange for information about St Mary's?'

I don't know what sort of reaction I was expecting. She slowly shook her head. 'No, no never,' and then the implications sank in and she flushed red with rage. Genuine rage. She wasn't faking it.

'Steady on,' I said, quickly. 'Let me live long enough to explain.'

I gave it to her in a few sentences.

She sat back and looked long and steadily at me. 'We have a problem, don't we?'

I appreciated the 'we'. 'Can you shed any light?'

She shook her head slowly. 'I wish I could, but no.

I can see why you think it … might have been me, but it wasn't. I would never —' She broke off and fell silent.

I was silent myself, thinking what her life must be like. I had Leon. At the end of a bad day – and sometimes even during a bad day – he was there. Always. A word, a look, a cup of tea – whatever was needed. I suddenly realised how much I'd grown accustomed to having him around and remembered again that special feeling that warmed my heart whenever he was near. I remembered how, whenever he entered a room, I was the first person he looked for. I remembered how he would smile, just for me alone. I remembered the sound of his voice, the touch of his hands, his solid warmth.

Rosie Lee had none of that. Rosie Lee was so alone in this world that she'd been pregnant and no one had noticed. She'd given birth and no one had noticed. She lived alone in Rushford. Did anyone know? Mrs Partridge? Dr Bairstow? How could this happen? How could anyone be so isolated from those around her? And what did that say about us?

However, there was a solution. Which brought me back to the original topic of conversation – the handsome and charming David Sands.

'Does he know?'

She had no difficulty working that one out and nodded defiantly. 'Just about the first thing I told him.'

Yes, I could imagine her flinging the information at his head.

'How did he take it?'

'Well, I think it was a bit of a shock. He just stared at me. I said I'd give him a week to think about it and let me know what he wanted to do and he came to see me the very next day and asked to meet him.'

'Him?'

She stuck her chin in the air and said defiantly, 'Benjamin.'

'Benjamin Lee. Nice name,' I said, vaguely, because I was still thinking.

While I was doing that she got up, picked up the bits of broken mug, and put the kettle on again. 'What are you going to do?'

'What?' I said, still thinking.

'What are you going to do? Are you going to tell Dr Bairstow?'

'No, of course not, but it would be a good idea if you did.'

She recoiled. 'No.'

'Rosie,' I said gently, 'there's nothing in the rules and regs about having kids. You haven't broken any laws. You don't even have to disclose any information about the father if you don't want to, but it is possible he can do something to make your life a little easier.'

'Such as?'

'No idea, but I have every confidence he'll think of something. And you should give Sands the benefit of the doubt. You've given him every opportunity to run away and he hasn't. Nor has he told anyone about Benjamin. Why don't the two of you take some time and just talk to each other? He's a decent man. You could do a great deal worse.'

She put another mug of tea in front of me. God knows I needed it.

We sat and sipped.

'Sorry about the wall,' she said, indicating the giant tea stain. 'I'll get Mr Strong to paint it over.'

'No need. I quite like it. I'm going to tell people it's a giant Rorschach test and get them to tell me what they see.

'Tell them it's a bloodstain,' she said, cheerfully.

'Or I could tell them it's the remains of my last personal assistant who passed away under mysterious circumstances.'

There was a slight pause. I couldn't help myself. Curiosity was eating away at my very bones.

'So how did you two – get together? You and Sands?'

'Do you remember our celebration dinner, the one after the Battle of St Mary's? The one last year?'

'No, I didn't attend. I was unconscious, remember?' I should point out that I was unconscious because I'd been shot, not because I'd self-medicated on an entire jug of Margaritas. Just to be clear.

She swallowed. 'I arrived late. Everyone was already sitting down. I couldn't see a seat anywhere. No one would catch my eye. Suddenly, everyone was too busy talking to their neighbours to see me and there wasn't any room.'

No, there wouldn't be. The civilian staff had stepped up and won the day. At some cost to themselves. People hadn't liked Rosie Lee before the battle. They certainly didn't like her afterwards. But that was no excuse. My anger was tinged with guilt.

245

For how long had this been going on? How difficult were they making her life? There are a thousand small ways to make someone's life a misery. And how typical of her not to mention it.

She was continuing. 'Anyway, I thought bollocks to the lot of you, and turned around to walk out and go home and I ran slap bang into David Sands. I knocked him over. He went flying. He still wasn't very steady on his legs then.'

No, he hadn't been, then. His balance was fine, now, but he'd been a bit wobbly for a while and people were always picking him up off the floor. I suspected he usually arranged things so his pickers-up were female and pretty.

'I said I was sorry, and instead of telling me I was the clumsiest ass on the planet and why didn't I look where I was going because he was six feet tall, for God's sake, and how could I not see him, which is what he would have said to someone he liked – and possibly hit them with his crutch as well – instead of all that, he just said it didn't matter and everything was fine.

'I said, could I help, and he said no, just let him get on with it, but he couldn't because his foot kept slipping on the parquet floor so I went to help but he slipped again and I fell down on top of him and he said bloody hell, woman, you're heavy and I smacked him on the arm and he said why was I beating up a cripple and Mr Clerk and Miss Prentiss walked past and Mr Clerk said oh bad luck, mate, meaning, I suppose, that he'd rather be on the floor with anyone other than me and then he kissed me – Mr Sands, I mean – and Clerk said to get a room for God's sake and he said – Mr Sands, I mean – that he intended to one day and I didn't know what to say and they helped him up and I wanted to go home but he took me in to dinner and made me sit with him and then …'

She tailed off, possibly to draw breath, and I had a bit of a think. I needed to look into this ostracism of Rosie Lee because I wouldn't stand for it. I had no idea what I would do about it, but I'd think of something.

She was staring at the floor, hot and angry.

'So,' I said, fascinated by someone else's romantic entanglement, 'then what happened?'

'We talked.'

I stared at her. I knew David Sands very well. 'Are you sure?'

'Well, you know what I mean. He talked and I listened. But he seemed to be enjoying himself. And it was a nice thing for him to do. To sit with me, I mean. And then the dinner finished and he could legitimately have gone off with the other historians into the bar, but he didn't and we sat a little longer while they cleared up around us and the next day he sent me a note thanking me for my company at dinner.'

You have to hand it to male historians – they have charm in spades. Peterson, with his thatch of brown hair and lazy grin; Roberts, squeaky and endearingly unsure of himself. Even Markham, of course. Not strictly a member of the History Department, but grubby, disreputable and unfailingly likeable. It would appear our Mr Sands had been exercising his charm all over Miss Lee. You can add bravery to his list of qualities.

'Anyway, the next night, we went for a drink in Rushford. And the night after that. And then we went out to dinner …' she trailed away.

Bloody hell!

I made an effort to get things back on track. 'So, have you had a disagreement? Is that why you were …?'

She nodded and blew her nose again.

I tried to imagine anyone falling out with David Sands.

'Was it about Benjamin?'

'He says he doesn't mind although I don't see how he can't. I mean, he must do, mustn't he? And then he started on about …'

'His foot,' I finished.

'Yes. Did I mention he's a complete idiot? Apparently, it's all right for him not to care about Benjamin, but he can't believe I don't care about him missing a foot. He makes me so angry.' She sniffed again. A tear rolled down her cheek.

And we were back where we started.

Except that we weren't. I had more or less eliminated Miss Lee from my list of suspects. And I'd had a fascinating insight into someone else's love life. And she'd actually made me a cup of tea. All that, coupled with my staggering success in the Outdoor Survival thing – I was really on a roll today.

'Right,' I said, in my newfound role as agony aunt. 'Talk to him.'

She shook her head. 'He won't listen. He just thinks I'm being kind.'

'No,' I said without thinking. 'Even Sands isn't that stupid.'

She blinked in surprise and then, even as I thought my last moment had come, she began to laugh. I joined in. I couldn't help it.

'Well,' I said. 'You know what to do. Talk to him.'

She shook her head.

Time to lie. 'You've got better powers of persuasion that that. He's a great guy. Very attractive. Trust me, if you don't work at it, someone else will. Whatshername from IT is always going on about him.'

'He won't even talk to me at the moment.'

'Then you talk to him. For God's sake, you're Rosie Lee. Your reign of terror is second only to Dr Bairstow's. Get out there and hunt him down. Pin him to the ground and make him listen. If you don't, Whatshername will.'

Silence. I was never going to heaven.

She smiled tentatively and nodded. 'All right, I will. Thank you, Max.'

I picked up my mug and toasted her. 'An honour and a privilege, Miss Lee.'

For one instant, I thought we were about to enjoy a rare moment of peace and harmony, and then there was a scream of warning from the car park outside, followed by nasty, soft, wet noise and something huge, purple, and wobbly impacted against the window, making us both jump.

'What on earth –?' she said and rushed to the

window. 'Oh my God.'

'Don't panic,' I said. 'It's just Miss Lingoss' pig exploding in its coffin.'

'What coffin?'

I was seized by the cold hand of dread.

'The coffin in which the pig is interred?'

'No,' she said, craning. 'I can't see a coffin anywhere.'

'Tell me,' I said, as casually as I could. 'Is there much damage?'

'Mostly to the car parked in the next space.'

The hand of dread tightened further.

'How bad?'

'Impossible to say. You can't actually see the car for dripping pig.'

'Miss Lee, could you nip along to R&D please. My compliments to Miss Lingoss. Tell her there's been premature pig precipitation in the car park and she shouldn't stop to pack.'

Fourteen

In all of our training courses, there comes a moment when the full impact of what they do has to be brought home to the trainees. When they realise that a large part of the job is watching people die, because History is not pretty. We call it the violent death assignment.

After some consultation with Peterson, I'd selected Rouen, 30th May 1431. The death of Joan of Arc.

Everyone knows the story.

Towards the end of the Hundred Years' War between England and France, things were going badly for the English. There were three reasons for this. Firstly, the early gains of Crécy, Poitiers, and Agincourt were all but cancelled out by the premature death of Henry V; secondly, the new French king wasn't as mad as the previous one; and thirdly, the inspired leadership of a young girl called Joan, who appeared from nowhere and set about pushing the English out of France.

Under her command, the French were regaining their territories and everything was going well until she was captured by the Burgundians. Inexplicably, the French king, on whose behalf she had laboured so

251

hard, refused to pay the ransom and the Burgundians, not ones to miss a good business opportunity, sold her to the English instead for the sum of 10,000 livres.

Unwilling to risk hostility in their occupied holdings, the English handed Joan over to an ecclesiastical court in Rouen where, because she had cut her hair and wore men's clothing, she was accused of and tried for the crime of heresy, rather than praised for handing the English forces their arses at the battles of Patay, Meung-sur-Loire, Montepilloy, and Lagny. The French king still did not come to her rescue and eventually, she recanted, which didn't suit the English at all.

If ever a person was stitched up, it was Joan of Arc. During her time in prison, she was continually threatened with sexual assault by her captors. Rumour had it even the Earl of Warwick was involved. Whether it happened or not, Joan resumed her men's clothing in self-defence. Just as the English had intended.

The church swung into action again, calling her a lapsed heretic, the punishment for which was death. By burning. She would be executed on the morning of 30th May 1431 in the Vieux Marche in Rouen and her burning supervised by the Bishop of Beauvais, Pierre Cauchon. And we would be there.

Atherton had this one. I took him aside.

'You may feel I've sold you a little short on this one, Mr Atherton. We won't be venturing outside. This is a record and document only assignment. Your main task will be that of observing your colleagues. Being burned at the stake is not a good way to die. No one will enjoy this. Keep an eye on them as well as what is happening outside.'

'If it's that bad then why go?'

A good question.

'Joan will burn whether we're there to observe it or not. And it all happened six hundred years ago. Does that help put it in perspective?'

He nodded.

'However, this will not be pleasant. Be aware.'

'Yes, ma'am.'

Peterson invited himself for this one. 'Time I checked out what sort of a job you're doing. I see you're one down already.'

'I don't count that. Miss Lingoss has not actually left the building.'

'And we're getting Randall back.'

'Oh, that's good news. How is he?'

I felt a little guilty. I'd had two messages from Mr Randall, requesting the pleasure of my company in Sick Bay and not only had I not gone, I'd been avoiding him ever since. It embarrasses me to be thanked. He'd got the message and the requests had ceased, to my relief.

'He's fine. He's coming along on this one just to ease himself back in again. We're not going outside so I imagine even we'll find it difficult to balls this one up.'

I grinned at him. 'You underestimate us.'

We assembled in Hawking. No need to check everyone over – no one was in costume. Once inside, we tested our recording equipment very carefully. We have to get things right first time. If we screw up then for everyone on that jump the opportunity is gone forever. You can never visit the same time twice. Two versions of the same person in the same time is very bad news. In the way that no two objects can occupy the same space without catastrophic consequences, so no two versions of the same person can occupy the same time. No one's quite sure what form the catastrophic consequences would take. Whether the two versions would simply cancel each other out – permanently – or whether it would be the equivalent of matter meeting anti-matter and the subsequent explosion would annihilate the universe and everything in it, we just don't know. Anyway, Atherton made them check all the equipment very thoroughly. His instructions were delivered quietly and without fuss. Just like the man himself. Effective without being pushy.

I took the left-hand seat. Peterson made himself comfortable in the other. Randall eased himself into the corner.

I turned round. 'Welcome back. Good to see you. You OK now?'

He nodded. 'Right as rain. Looking forward to this one. I thought I'd have a bit of a snooze in the corner while you lot do your historian things.'

I sighed. 'Typical Security Section. All these years and you still don't have any idea what actually goes on at St Mary's, do you?'

He settled himself back comfortably. 'I'm sure I will have when it becomes important. Wake me if you need me.'

So here we were.

We'd landed well before dawn, settling ourselves in a dark corner of the market square, the Vieux Marche. We were gambling on the fact that the crowd would be so dense they wouldn't notice the small shack in the corner that hadn't been here yesterday.

We were in Number Eight, my favourite. Quite a small pod, but TB2 was far too big for today. We were a little crowded, but nothing to complain about. Although that wouldn't stop us. Peterson and I stepped back from the console to give them room to work.

Early we might have been, but the scaffold was already erected and by the dim, pre-dawn light, English soldiers were unloading densely packed bundles of firewood from the continuous line of carts snaking around the Vieux Marche. They were in a hurry, shouting impatiently at drivers and horses alike. The drivers picked their teeth in silent contempt, and the horses apparently went to sleep.

More English soldiers were filing into the square. Hundreds of them had been drafted in as crowd control. They were expecting trouble. Records say the day passed reasonably peacefully, but the records are wrong. There was trouble. For everyone.

Atherton switched off the proximities before we went deaf because there would soon be enormous numbers of people in this place. North aligned the cameras. Sykes split the screen and started recording. Hoyle was monitoring the sound levels.

I touched his shoulder. 'Not too loud, Mr Hoyle.'

He nodded.

We didn't have long to wait.

As soon as the enormous bonfire was built and the carts withdrawn, the soldiers started allowing the citizens into the square.

The four trainees clustered around the console. I stood to one side where I could see what they were doing. Peterson stood at the other, and Randall was at the back against the lockers.

We were ready.

'Begin, please,' said Atherton.

I watch people die for a living. I don't like it – and not getting involved is always difficult, but that's what I do. I watch people die.

I try to achieve a small amount of detachment. I try to tell myself that these people died hundreds, sometimes thousands of years ago. That nothing I can say or do will change that. Or *should* change that. That I'm simply here as a witness. Nothing more. Nothing less.

Mostly, I can do that. Sometimes I have to go away somewhere quiet afterwards. Sometimes I need to be on my own for a bit. Or, in extreme cases, I have an overwhelming urge to take what I've seen and felt and splash it across a canvas or a wall somewhere. Surprisingly, Dr Bairstow's pretty good about that. The point is, over the years, I've learned to deal with it, but these people hadn't. Yet. Peterson and I would monitor this assignment very carefully and Dr Foster and her team would keep an eye on them afterwards while they came to terms with what they were to see here today.

According to records and eyewitness accounts, the English were in a hurry to get this over with. Joan was hustled into the market place with some speed.

She wore a simple white robe that was far too long for her. Either she'd been praying, or she'd fallen down because it was stained around her knees. Her short thick brown hair had grown a little, but not enough to plait. She wore it gathered at the nape of her neck in a stubby ponytail. Her escort, Martin Ladvenu, a priest of the order of Saint Dominic, walked with her, carrying a cross on a long pole. The priest murmured to her as she walked. She seemed very calm, but the bailiff on her other side was sweating heavily. Huge dark rings stained his tunic around his neck and under his arms and he regularly dragged a sleeve across his forehead.

The crowd made very little noise as she was marched across the square, although eight hundred English soldiers might have been the reason for that.

The little procession halted at the base of the scaffold and Joan bowed her head as the sermon was read out. My middle French isn't good, but it was all being recorded and someone would get it translated.

I was surprised they let her speak, but it seems to be a fixed tradition at executions – the accused always has the right to address the crowd. Joan spoke. Again, I couldn't make out her words. She spoke with a heavy accent, her voice high and piping in the early morning air. She seemed to speak for a very long time. I know, again from the records, that she was asking people to pray for her. Throughout the crowd, women were openly crying. The English grew restive. They wanted this over with.

She was still speaking as they started pushing her towards the scaffold. The drums rolled. Now, she showed some signs of agitation and the crowd began to murmur. There was some shouting from the rear. Officers bellowed commands and the soldiers used their pikes to push people well back from the scaffold. They were not gentle. There was going to be trouble.

One soldier turned to her and gestured her towards the scaffold. She spoke to him, urgently. He gestured again. She seemed to be pleading with him.

The man, a common soldier by his gear, looked around for a moment, then bent and picked up a stick, which he broke across his knee. Pulling a leather lace from his sleeve, he lashed the two pieces together in the form of a rough cross and handed it to her.

The transformation was amazing. At once, she became tranquil and calm.

I'm a bit cynical when it comes to religion, but it did seem to me that if a heretic requested a cross at her execution then a compassionate church, grateful to have saved another soul, could easily have found one for her from somewhere. Apparently not, however.

The English had had enough by now. They heaved her to the top of the pile and secured her to the stake. Men stood ready with lighted torches.

They shoved Martin Ladvenu roughly out of the way and before the sentence could be read, or she could make any further statement, the drums rolled and the fire was lit.

They must have drenched the wood with oil because it went up like a rocket.

The crowd cried out and the friar, a good man, picked himself up off the ground and stationing himself perilously close to the leaping flames, raised his cross high where she could see it.

She didn't die easily. She didn't die easily at all.

There are three ways in which you can die at the stake.

The first is for the executioner to ensure there is enough smoke for the victim to inhale, lose consciousness, and die while mercifully oblivious. The second is to pay him a small sum of money and he will strangle his victim from behind early on in the proceedings. Many stakes had a ring specially built in for the cord or chain to pass through.

Joan burned the third way. The worst way.

She was conscious as the skin on her calves blistered and then began to char. She was conscious as the hem of her robe caught alight. She was still conscious as the flames roared around her thighs and began to creep up her body.

Burning people bleed.

They scream, too.

She held out for a long time, but in the end, she screamed.

She screamed 'Jesus' just as all the chronicles reported, but it wasn't a plea to take the pain away, or a reproach for being abandoned, or even a demand for help. It was a simple statement of her faith.

It didn't end quickly for her, despite the furious shouts from the crowd. She suffered greatly. I was angry for her. She'd served her God and the King of France and where were either of them today when she needed them?

I wasn't the only one. The people didn't like it, either. They were becoming restive again. There was movement in the crowd as waves of people began to surge forwards, shouting angrily, pushing at the line of soldiers holding them back. The soldiers became nervous. At a command, they held their pikes at the ready. The shouting increased. Someone threw a stone. This was becoming ugly. Well, uglier.

Another stone flew through the air and hit a soldier. He reversed his pike and knocked a woman to the ground. The next minute, we had a full-scale riot on our hands. There's no mention of this in the history books but history is written by the winners and perhaps the English wouldn't want it known they'd lost control today.

Women and children were screaming and trying to run away. Soldiers, with no orders to let them go, pushed them back into the square again, where they collided with those still trying to get out. Chaos reigned.

Still the flames blazed and still she screamed. I'd heard that some burnings could last for up to two hours. It was unimaginable that she could endure for so long. That she should have to endure for so long. I could turn off the screen, but that would be a betrayal. To look away when something terrible is happening does not mean that the terrible thing ceases to happen.

Someone should bear witness to this. Someone must. Most people read about Joan of Arc at school. The chapter always ends with 'and she was burned at the stake in 1431' and then the bell rings and we pack up our books and move on to something else.

Nowhere does it mention that her skin blackened and fell away. That the hot chains seared hideous patterns into her skin. That her hair burned like a flaming halo. That a hideous, greasy, grey smoke lingered everywhere. Or that she screamed and screamed until her voice gave out and the only sounds she could make were barely human.

I seriously thought about pulling the plug and getting us all out of there.

I turned the sound down and in the sudden silence, heard a movement behind me.

I'd been so busy monitoring my stony-faced trainees for any signs of distress that I'd forgotten about Peterson and Randall. Especially Randall, only just back on the active list and by no means as recovered as everyone had thought.

He turned away from me, but not before I caught a glimpse of his face, white and haggard. He began to rummage around in one of the lockers and I couldn't think what he was doing until he pulled out a gun and slapped home a clip.

Even then I didn't get it. I think I just stared at him with my mouth open. While I was pulling myself together, he pushed past me towards the door and suddenly I knew what he was going to do.

He looked back once, daring me to say something. Which I should have done, but my throat closed and words wouldn't come. The voice in my head was screaming at me to do something. To stop him. Now. Before any real harm was done.

Too late.

He slapped the switch and slipped through the door. I can't describe the smell that flooded into the pod. I nearly heaved and by the time I'd steadied myself, he'd disappeared and we were suddenly in a world of trouble.

Peterson, his face cold and set, pulled out a blanket and wrapped himself in its folds, covering his blues..

All the trainees' attention was still on Joan of Arc. There are no words to describe the noises she was making.

I put my hand on Peterson's arm and whispered, 'You must get him back before it's too late.'

He nodded and let himself out of the door.

Atherton looked around.

'What …?'

'Disregard,' I said. 'Please continue with your assignment.'

North peered closely at the screen and said, 'Is that …?'

'Yes,' I said calmly. 'They've gone for close ups. Did you want to go with them?'

She looked at me for a moment, her face expressionless. She was very pale. I could see a line of sweat across her top lip. 'No.'

I watched the trainees watching the screens. The light flickered across their faces. Occasionally one would make a minute adjustment to the controls. No one was speaking. They were watching the execution.

I was watching for Randall and Peterson and I couldn't see either of them.

I honestly don't know whether Randall fired or not. I certainly didn't hear the shot, but abruptly, those terrible, tortured cries ceased.

'Thank God,' whispered Sykes. 'Is she finally dead?'

A small wind blew the shifting smoke and flames aside just as she spoke, and for one moment, I caught a glimpse of a body, robe burned away, hair gone, legs and body black and bloodstained, but now, mercifully, hanging limply forwards from the stake.

She was dead. Had Randall killed her? Had Peterson been too late? And where were they now?

Whatever had occurred and whoever was responsible, it was finished

I had no idea what was to come.

The fire would continue to burn for some time. The executioner, on instructions from the English, would rake away the wood to show her burned body and then her bones would be burned twice more before being flung into the Seine. They wanted no martyrs made this day.

All this would work in our favour. No bones would ever be found. There would never be any evidence. No evidence of a possible fatal shot. I would never say a word. Nor would Peterson. And the trainees, whatever they suspected, would never know for sure.

I forgot that History knows everything.

Atherton was issuing instructions to start shutting things down. They turned all the cameras to monitor the crowd. I scanned the screens anxiously. Where the bloody hell were they? They might be taking a moment to get their breath and pull themselves together before struggling back through the crowd to the pod.

The cameras were still running, but the execution was finished. There was nothing more to see. English soldiers were still fighting with the crowd, trying to keep them away from the fire. Even though it would be hours before the bones were cool enough to touch, they didn't want anyone trying to pick them up as relics. They would be thrown into the river. No physical trace would ever remain of the young girl whose scorched soul was even now – as they say – in a better place. Looking at the still-leaping flames of her funeral pyre, it was hard to see how she could be in a worse one. I hoped she found her God, although if it had been me, he would have been getting a right ear bashing.

North said suddenly, 'What's that?'

At the same moment, Atherton said, 'Who are they? Look. They're coming this way. Who are they?'

Shit. Not only had I forgotten about History, I'd forgotten about the bloody Time Police as well.

Fifteen

The Time Police.

What can I say?

A long time ago in the future, in one of those bizarre coincidences that drives all the conspiracy theorists into a frenzy, the secret of time travel is discovered by several countries almost simultaneously. Governments, as usual, see things only in relationship to their own benefit. The urge to rewrite History in their own favour is too great and for a while, the timeline is so tangled that it's touch and go. The Time Police are formed to sort things out. They're given a wide remit and unlimited powers. And they do sort things out. Make no mistake, disaster is averted only because of the Time Police and their efforts. Unfortunately, although the problem goes away, the Time Police do not and now they travel up and down the timeline monitoring and enforcing. They look for anomalies and it was possible that today they'd found one.

The trainees were all looking at me. I hoped I looked better than I felt. The important thing was not to let them know that anything untoward had just taken place. That their training officers had just broken one of the most important rules of all. I fell back on my lecturing voice.

'These, ladies and gentlemen, are the Time Police. We have already touched on this subject. I don't know why they are here. Neither do you. Do not speak unless spoken to. Confine yourself to answering their questions. Do not volunteer information.'

North said, 'Are we in trouble? Did we do something wrong?'

'Not that I am aware of.'

At the console, Atherton said anxiously, 'Shall I let them in?'

'That would probably be wise, yes.'

There were three of them, clad in their traditional black uniforms, their only concession to historical accuracy being the all-enveloping black cloaks they wore. I opened the door to Captain Ellis. An old acquaintance. Things could be worse. I'd once saved his life and he'd saved mine.

He rolled his eyes. 'Max. Why did I not guess?'

I knew why he was here. My job was to get rid of him asap. Before Peterson and Randall made their way back through the riot and fell into the hands of the Time Police. I couldn't warn them. I couldn't do anything to prevent them returning and walking straight into this trap.

Ellis stepped into the pod, gesturing one officer to remain outside. I like to think it was because of overcrowding, but more likely it was so he could pick up anyone who, for instance, might be making their way back to the pod after doing something horribly illegal.

'So,' he said, stripping off his gloves and looking around. 'What's happening here?'

I gestured at the screen. 'Well, it's Rouen 1431, and Joan of Arc, having successfully led the French forces against ...'

He interrupted. 'No, what's happening here in this pod?'

I looked around in what I hoped was well-simulated bewilderment. 'Training assignment. Four trainees. One handler. May I introduce Miss Sykes, Miss North, Mr Hoyle, and Mr Atherton.'

They nodded politely.

'No security?'

'We're not going outside so it wasn't considered necessary.'

He wasn't stupid. He knew me well. He was also in a position to see the console. 'And yet, the door has been opened.'

Bugger. Yes, it had.

'Well, we let you in, of course.'

'Other than that?'

'Ah. Yes.'

I assumed an expression of complicity, gestured with my head and we moved away. Well, as far away as we could get in a small pod. Sykes and the others politely bent over the console, pretending not to listen.

I lowered my voice. 'This is the assignment when they must witness something nasty. You know what I mean.'

He nodded. 'You mean the violent death

assignment. Well, it doesn't get much nastier than what's happening out there. And you opened the door because …?'

'You've been out there. What was the first thing you noticed?'

'Oh, right. The smell.'

I nodded.

'How many actually threw up?'

'None yet, but I'm still hopeful.'

'You've really thrown them in at the deep end, haven't you?'

I shrugged. 'They have to learn. They're no good to anyone otherwise.' I took a gamble. 'Good to see you again. Time for a cup of tea?'

'No, but thank you. Just as a matter of interest, do they know who we are?'

'We've touched on the Time Police briefly. I'm quite glad to see you, actually. You can be my next session. Would you like to bark at them? Threaten them with your futuristic weapons? You know, just to add a little colour.'

'Again, thank you, but no. I do, however, want to have a quick look at your logs before I depart.'

'Of course,' I said, panicking like mad on the inside and desperately trying to remember if Peterson had made any sort of log entry during this jump. My stupid mind, however, refused to cooperate and all I could do was stare helplessly at the console.

The other guard stood by the door. Admittedly, there was very little space and unless he kept an eye on us from inside the toilet, there really wasn't anywhere else for him to stand. A pod is not your traditional time-travelling machine. We are, if anything, smaller on the inside than the outside, and, effectively, we were trapped. Whether they intended it or not, we couldn't get out.

I turned to Atherton. 'Mr Atherton, please make our logs available to —' I got no further.

Sykes leaped from her seat and collided heavily with the guard.

'Let me through. Let me through. Oh God, I'm going to be sick.'

And she was. A great stream of vomit spewed down his front. He stepped back instinctively, bumping into Captain Ellis and while they were sorting themselves out, with a really unpleasant retching sound, she threw up over the console as well. Leon was not going to be a happy man.

Looking on the bright side, now the former smells of burning meat, cabbage, and stale people were completely obliterated.

'Oh God,' said Atherton and now he bolted for the toilet. More unpleasant sounds came through the door. My own insides heaved. North had her hand over her mouth. Not the world's greatest actor, but she was managing to convey her meaning through the medium of mime. Hoyle just stood by the lockers. Queen Victoria was back.

'Oh for heaven's sake,' I said crossly and banged on the toilet door. 'When you come out, bring a bucket of water, will you?'

Turning to Ellis, I said, 'Any chance of some help clearing this lot up?'

There was the sound of renewed retching and I'm

one of those people who vomit in sympathy. I could taste the bitter fluid in my mouth.

Sykes burst into tears. 'I'm sorry, I'm really sorry, but I want to go home.'

I'd found an old bit of tissue in a pocket and was dabbing at the console, smearing the stuff around all over the place. Why are there always carrots?

Sykes sank back into her seat and was sobbing away to herself. North awkwardly patted her shoulder.

I turned to Ellis again. 'This is all your fault.'

'Mine?'

'Just look at this place. It's a bloody shambles.'

'You can't blame us for that. That's down to you, Max. Frankly, I think you're teaching them to run before they can walk.'

'What? We were doing fine until you turned up. Typical Time Police. You've been here just five minutes and one trainee has covered the pod in wall-to-wall vomit, one's locked himself in the bathroom, two of them are in tears ...' North obediently sniffed, 'and the other one's in a state of shock.'

Hoyle's expression did not change. I despaired of that boy.

I stormed on regardless. 'The least you can do is ...'

'Nothing to do with us. Not our job.'

'Yes, talking of that. Not that I'm even remotely interested, but why are you here?'

'Not sure. Report of an anomaly to check out. I didn't think much of it at the time, but now I see that you're here ...'

'Well,' I said, folding my arms. 'I never thought I'd get to say this, but it wasn't us.'

'No?' he said, thoughtfully, surveying the wreckage of our assignment.

'Have you thought …? I mean …'

'What?'

'I know that according to the Time Police, everything is my fault, but this is an important historical event. We might not be the only ones here.'

The other guard, in some hurry to escape this stinking pod and now presented with a face-saving reason to leave, looked at him hopefully. In the silence, I could hear Sykes's sick dripping to the floor.

I didn't dare say another word but if they didn't get a move on … Peterson and Randall would be back any minute now … and they'd walk straight into a trap.

From the toilet came sounds of Atherton apparently bringing up a hairball the size of a kitchen table.

'We'll go and check it out,' Ellis said.

'What do you mean, you'll go and check it out? You can't just barge in here, wreck my assignment and then push off and leave me on my own to …'

'Yes, we can,' he said, and gestured his man outside.

I stood in the doorway and tried not to look over his shoulder for Peterson.

'I know it's you,' said Ellis, very quietly.

I opened my mouth.

'Don't bother. Quit while you're ahead.'

I grinned at him. 'Nice to see you again.'

'And you. A word of warning. You might have a problem with one of your trainees. And I don't mean the one who can, apparently, projectile vomit at will.'

'Hoyle?'

'The quiet one? Yes. Don't like the look of him. Too intense.'

I nodded and stepped back into the pod.

They wrapped their cloaks around themselves and disappeared into the milling crowd.

I slapped the door shut and called, 'You can come out now, Mr Atherton.'

Sykes was wiping down the console with her sleeve. I passed her a drink of water. 'Neat trick.'

'Thank you,' she said, beaming. 'I haven't actually done anything I didn't want to since I was about six. Parents, teachers, police, social workers – I've vomited over some of the finest in the land.'

'And now the Time Police,' said Atherton, emerging. 'Is there no end to your talents?'

'No,' she said, modestly.

'Look out there,' said North suddenly. She'd been staring at the screen. 'Oh my God.'

They were never going to get back to the pod through this. The riot had worsened. The crowd surged back and forth, as the English battled to regain control. People were prising up cobbles to throw at the soldiers. I could hear cries and screams as people were knocked to the ground and trampled. A voice bellowed instructions and the English soldiers, who surely could not be expecting a rescue attempt at this late stage, formed an outward facing ring around the bonfire, pikes bristling.

I instructed Atherton to split the screen and all of us were staring as if our lives depended upon it. The confusion made it difficult to pick out any individuals. About the only good thing we could say was that there was no sign of the Time Police. I had to place all my reliance on Peterson to keep them both safe. They'd keep their heads down and work their way quietly back to the pod.

'There they are,' said North, suddenly, pointing at the screen and my heart lurched. Something had gone horribly wrong.

I thought at first that Peterson was supporting Randall. Then I thought it was the other way around. Then I saw that they were holding each other up, staggering unsteadily as they were buffeted this way and that by the crowd. Both their blankets were covered in blood, although whether theirs or someone else's was impossible to say. Even as we looked, Randall dropped to his knees, dragging Peterson down with him. The crowd closed around them. They would be trampled in the riot.

Before I could say a word, Atherton and Hoyle were heading for the door. I drew breath to stop them, but they were outside before I could speak.

'Break out the medkits,' I said to the other two. 'Be prepared for emergency extraction.'

Atherton and Hoyle were ruthless, shoving people aside without hesitation and fighting their way to the spot where we'd last seen them. They heaved Peterson and Randall to their feet and dragged them back towards the pod. I stood by the door, waiting, ready to go to their aid.

Both of them were dead weights. North came to assist and even then, it was a struggle to get them in through the door. With one last heave, we got them inside. Sykes slapped the door control and shut out the riot outside.

'Get them on the floor,' I said. 'Quick. Where are those medkits?'

None of it was good news.

The blood was Peterson's. He had a huge wound to his upper arm. I could see bone.

Randall was worse. He lay white-faced, eyes rolling around in his head. A trickle of blood ran from one ear. His breathing was all over the place. Occasionally, he twitched.

I was quite calm. I don't remember feeling sick or frightened or panicky. I don't remember feeling anything. I could see clearly what had to be done. I issued a torrent of instructions and while they were scurrying about opening medkits and fetching water, I retrieved the gun from the folds of Randall's blanket and kicked it under the console.

The first thing was to stabilise the pair of them before getting them back to St Mary's. There was no point in taking back a couple of corpses.

'We need to stop Peterson's bleeding. Atherton, make a fist and apply pressure to the brachial artery. Press down as hard as you can. North, get those medkits open. I want sterile dressings. All of them. And clotting agent. As much as you can find. Quick.'

She scrambled to comply.

'Sykes. You take Randall. Clear his airways. Find

out if any of this blood is his. Hoyle. Check his skull. He's had a bad knock to the head.'

They bent over Randall.

'Oh my God,' said Hoyle, in horror, his voice sliding up the scale in panic. 'Max, the damage is ... huge. I can feel the bone moving under my hands. It's ... squishy. How is he still alive?'

'Never mind that now. He is still alive. Keep him that way.'

I cut off Peterson's sleeve, sprayed the clotting agent, and started packing sterile dressings. The blood soaked through within seconds. I sprayed each dressing before I applied it. It was useless. He was dying under my hands.

'Atherton, can you apply any further pressure?'

He looked up at me. I remember his uniform was wet with Peterson's blood. 'I'm using my whole weight.'

'Do not stop. Even for one second.'

'No, ma'am.'

'Apart from the head wound, is there any other damage, Miss Sykes?'

'Not that I can find. But he's all tangled up in this blanket. Difficult to see.'

'Don't try to move him. I'm calling for emergency extraction. Brace your patient and yourselves.'

'Ready,' they said.

'Computer. Emergency extraction. Now.'

Nothing happened. Nothing bloody happened. Shit. Now what?

There are several reasons why a jump can fail. The first is mechanical failure – a fault with the pod itself.

Not likely in this case. Leon is ruthless in his quest for pod perfection and anyway, the computer itself would tell us if the pod was at fault.

Secondly, and worryingly, the safety protocols would engage if our destination no longer existed and therefore the jump could not be made. Hugely unlikely, but this was St Mary's after all. Home of the unscheduled explosion. Disaster capital of the western world. It was always possible that something cataclysmic had occurred there and we had no St Mary's to go back to.

Thirdly, and most likely, we'd picked something up. Quite inadvertently. It could be a natural object such as a fir cone (that had happened before), something manufactured, even something alive – a mouse, a moth. Anything. In which case we had to locate and eject it as quickly as possible.

They were all panicking, their voices shrill and jerky. 'Why aren't we jumping? What's gone wrong? Is the pod broken? Why didn't we jump?'

I swallowed down my own fears, fighting to keep my voice calm. 'Quiet please, everyone. Computer, state cause of jump failure.'

'Foreign object detected.'

'Mr Hoyle. You will find this foreign object. Search everyone. Begin with Randall.'

He was staring helplessly at Randall, his eyes wide with shock. I spoke sharply to galvanise him into action. 'Now, Mr Hoyle.'

I didn't dare take my eyes off Peterson or stop work even for a second, but I felt Hoyle crouch over Randall, patting, searching through his clothing. It could be anything. I had no idea what to tell him to look for.

North was still ripping open sterile packs. Her hands shook. There weren't that many packs left. Peterson's arm was just a blood-soaked mess. His breathing was very fast and shallow as opposed to Randall's which was noisy and irregular.

'Mr Hoyle, have you found anything yet?'

'No. Atherton, give me your knife.'

I heard the sound of tearing material as Hoyle desperately cut through Randall's clothing.

His voice was cracking with panic. 'I can't find it. I can't find anything. There's nothing here. I can't see why we're not jumping. He's dying and I can't find it.'

I kept my voice quiet. 'Keep calm. Begin at his feet and work your way up.'

'Wait. Wait. I've got it. I've got it. Oh shit.'

There it was. Embedded in his ribs. A rough home-made blade with a bone handle.

'What do I do?' Panic in his voice. 'What do I do?'

And then, for me, everything stopped. The world receded. Sound died. Movement ceased. My hands stopped working.

Because I knew what we should do.

What I should do.

What I had to do.

As long as that knife was in this pod, we couldn't jump. I needed to get it out of the pod and if I pulled it out, Randall would die. If I didn't pull it out then they would both die. And it would have to be me. I couldn't ask anyone else to do it. Nor should I.

They were all looking at me. I remember the silence as they all looked at me.

I pushed all thought away.

'Miss North, take over here.'

'What are you going to do?'

'Pull it out.'

'But you can't. It will kill him.'

'Step aside, Mr Hoyle.'

'You can't do this.'

'I must.'

I knelt beside Randall. His skin was paper white. I never knew he had freckles.

I did not think of all the years I'd known him. All the missions we'd been on together. All the dangers overcome together. Quiet, steady, dependable Randall. His eyes were open, struggling to focus. I had no idea if he could see me.

I leaned over him, saying gently, 'I'm so sorry, Will.'

I had no idea if he could actually hear me.

His eyes were rolling everywhere. Blood had collected in his ears. His hand jerked around, trying to grasp at my sleeve. More blood ran from the corner of his mouth.

I must do this. I must do it now. If I delayed then Peterson would die too.

He was trying to speak.

'Trynunstan.'

Bollocks to everything. I took a moment just for him. He was about to die. He deserved a moment. Gently, very gently, I smoothed back his hair.

'It's all right, Will. Just close your eyes. It's time to go to sleep now.'

My voice was shaking. Someone was crying. It might have been me. It might have been all of us.

'Mustrynunstan.'

His eyes closed. Heavy breaths rasped his throat.

'I'm here, Will. Everything is fine. I'm going to make everything better, I promise you. Sleep now.'

I took a deep breath and grasped the blade. 'St Mary's thanks you for your service.'

I pulled.

It came out surprisingly easily.

One huge surge of hot blood over my hand.

And then, silence. Randall had stopped breathing.

'No,' screamed Sykes. 'You are not allowed to die.'

She and Hoyle started CPR. I could hear them counting.

'Four, five, six ...'

I turned back to Peterson and said to North, 'How is he?'

She dragged her eyes from Randall. 'Still breathing.'

'Thirteen, fourteen, fifteen. Breathe. And again.'

'One, two, three ...'

They never stopped. It was useless but they wouldn't stop.

Atherton was still being a human tourniquet. North had used the last of the dressings and was lashing everything into place with triangular bandages.

'I'll take over here, Miss North. Get rid of this blade, please. And for God's sake don't let anyone in.'

She stared at me. Eyes wide with shock and fear, tears on her cheeks, trembling on the verge of panic.

I kept my voice very calm and quiet.

'Do it now, please, Miss North.'

She picked up the knife, holding it at arm's length. I could hear her sobbing with shock. I don't think she knew she was doing it. She crossed to the door and opened it. The sights, sounds, and smell of today came as something of a jolt. I had forgotten all about what was happening on the other side of the door.

I heard the door close again and silence fell.

'Right. Brace yourselves everyone.'

I leaned across Peterson, holding him steady.

'Computer, emergency extraction. Now.'

The world went black.

Sixteen

I've had some awful emergency landings but this one wasn't too bad. We managed to stay on the plinth this time. We were home but we weren't out of the woods yet.

'Miss North. Initiate decon procedures. You know what to do.'

The blue lamp came on.

I heard her declare a medical emergency. Her voice was high with stress, but they were all holding it together.

I was reduced to ripping up towels. Still packing Peterson's wound. Still trying to staunch the flow of blood. Don't die, Tim. Don't die. His face was so white as to be transparent. I could see the blue veins under the skin. He was shaking uncontrollably. His breathing was very fast and very shallow.

And Randall wasn't breathing at all.

'Ten, eleven, twelve …'

I felt as if everything had stopped. That the world was divided into the time when they had been whole and alive and the time when they weren't. Where were the bloody medics? I spared a glance at the screen just in time to see Helen and her team flying down the hangar. Seconds later, the door opened.

I hadn't given a thought to her possible reaction when she saw Peterson lying in his own blood. They'd been together in their own peculiar fashion for as long as I could remember.

She stopped dead in the doorway and her team all cannoned into the back of her.

I told myself I was too busy to look at her face.

'Report.' Her voice was perfectly calm.

I replied, 'Randall. Massive head trauma. Puncture wound to his left ribs. Stopped breathing on his own about two minutes ago. Peterson – laceration on his upper left arm. Major blood loss. Atherton's applying pressure to the brachial artery and I've packed the wound. We've all decontaminated.'

'Any other wounds?'

'None found.'

'Get your people out. Report to Sick Bay. Wait there until someone comes to you.'

Hunter pushed past her to get to Randall.

'It's all right,' she said softly to Hoyle and Sykes. 'I've got him now.' They climbed stiffly to their feet, red patches of Peterson's blood on their knees. They stood blindly, unsure what to do next.

Leon and his team stood at the doorway.

He stretched out his hand to them one at a time. 'Come along, Miss Sykes.'

Slowly, she put her bloodstained hand in his. He handed her to Dieter and put out his hand for Hoyle.

I eased back from Peterson, my legs not completely under control. Pretending to stretch my arms, I reached under the console and palmed the clip. Atherton helped me up. North was already outside.

I looked back into the pod. There was a huge pool of dark red blood on the floor. Peterson was soaked in it.

Randall lay unmoving. Hunter was working on him but I could tell by her face. They closed the door.

The hangar was completely silent. I made a huge effort because I had trainees to deal with.

I caught Leon's eye and nodded to tell him I was fine. He nodded back.

Guthrie appeared, crossed to the pod, and went in. And came back out again, his face unreadable.

I took a deep, ragged breath that hurt my chest. 'Right, everyone up to Sick Bay.'

We set off. Every trainee had an escort. Someone talking gently to them. Sykes was sobbing. With anger, I guessed. And helplessness. Dieter put a gentle hand on her back. I swallowed a lump in my throat and concentrated on what had to be done.

Sick Bay was silent and deserted. There were no medics in sight. Everyone was either with Randall or with Peterson.

Sykes suddenly grabbed a chair and sat down hard. 'Sorry.'

'It's all right,' I told her. 'It's perfectly acceptable to fall apart afterwards so long as you keep it together when you have to.'

We made some tea and finally a junior nurse appeared. Nurse Fortunata.

We were despatched for a shower and remanded for the statutory twelve hours' observation. Just for once, it was justified. They'd not had a good day. They'd seen Joan of Arc die. I still wasn't sure whether they were aware of Randall's possible role in her death. I hoped to God not.

They'd watched their leader lie through her teeth to the Time Police.

Then they'd had to deal with the catastrophic injuries to Randall and Peterson. And then Randall had died. We all knew he was dead. They'd fought for him, they'd done everything they could, but he was dead. He'd used his last minutes to get Peterson back to the pod. He'd done his job and it had killed him.

Guthrie appeared in front of me, grim-faced. 'Everyone else all right?'

I nodded.

'What happened? You weren't supposed to go outside. That's why I only sent one guard. How did he and Peterson get injured?'

I'd had time to think of an answer.

'Peterson wanted a better angle than we could get in our corner. We were rather hemmed in by people. And then there was some sort of riot we didn't know anything about and they were both injured. I'm sorry, Ian. Truly, truly sorry. I've known Randall a long time. He's a good man.'

He shook his head. 'They should never have gone outside.'

No, they shouldn't. I should have stopped him. I was mission controller and I should have stopped him. Joan would have died anyway. The only difference was that she'd died a little sooner than she should have. A little less agony to endure. But we're not supposed to interfere. History doesn't like it. History will do anything to prevent that happening. I remembered the riot. The one not in the History books. The one in which they were both injured. Because today we had interfered with History and there's always a price to pay. Today it had been Randall. And it might still be Peterson as well.

Snapshots of the aftermath of that dreadful day are seared into my memory.

The trainees – my trainees – staring into their empty mugs.

Atherton, very pale and quiet.

Hoyle, hard to read as always. He was pale and quiet to begin with.

North, shocked and shaking, but determined not to show it.

Sykes, angry at what she saw as her failure to save Randall.

The sudden crash of doors and raised voices as they brought up Peterson and Randall.

Helen issuing instructions.

Doors opening and closing.

Machines beeping.

Standing in line with half of St Mary's, all of whom wanted to give blood. Peterson was universally liked.

Snatching a moment's respite with Leon before he went off with Guthrie.

Talking quietly to Dr Bairstow who, unlike everyone else, got the full story. He listened without speaking, hands crossed on his stick.

Finally, he drew a long breath and lifted his head.

'Sir, I need to speak to the History Department. They'll want to know what's happening.'

'I'll see to that, Max. Please concentrate on our trainees. They need you.'

I nodded.

Would any of them leave because of today? I could happily do without North who wound me up just by being in the same room as me. Almost immediately, I felt ashamed of the thought. When the chips were down she'd been what she always was – bloody perfect.

He nodded over my shoulder. 'What do they think happened?'

'That they stepped out for a better view. The only other person who knows that isn't true is Peterson and he's …' My lips stopped working.

He put his hand on my shoulder. Just briefly. Just for a moment.

'And the Time Police?'

'Know that something was going on but chose to look the other way.'

'One thing to be thankful for.'

We stood in silence for a moment.

'You see to your people, Max and I'll see to all the arrangements.' He permitted himself a small, sad smile. 'It's going to be a long night for both of us.'

I sat with them while they ate. Or rather, while they picked at their food. Even I had no appetite. The smell of charred flesh was still in my nostrils. I had a quick word with Fortunata who came back with a small jar.

'Here,' I said, 'try some of this.'

'What is it?' said Sykes, listlessly.

'Menthol rub. Put a dab over your top lip.'

'Smells awful.'

'Better or worse than Joan of Arc?'

We dabbed away and soon the fresh smell of menthol filled the room.

I waited until they were settled for the night and then went out to the nurses' station. Fortunata was there, writing up her notes.

'Everything OK?'

I nodded. 'I can't sleep. You don't mind if I wait here?'

'No problem.'

Hours passed until finally, in the small hours, just when the human spirit is at its lowest, they wheeled Peterson back through. His face was the same colour as the sheet.

I waited some more until Hunter appeared, apparently for the express purpose of yelling at me for not being in bed, and then handed me a mug of tea.

I waited some more.

Finally, Helen appeared, still in her scrubs. I've never seen her look so tired. She stared at me for a while and then jerked her head in the direction of her office. Once there, she sank into her chair and put her head in her hands.

I rummaged through her desk until I found her

secret stash. I knew she'd have one somewhere.

'Here you go.'

She lit a cigarette. She'd obviously given up giving up.

I gave her time before asking, 'How is he? Will he lose his arm?'

She shook her head wearily. 'I don't know. I've done my best. It may not be good enough. So yes, he may.'

She sat wreathed in smoke. I listened while she talked, blaming herself.

Then she blamed me. I sat quietly and let her get on with it. There wasn't anything she could say to me that I hadn't already said to myself.

Then she cried. Which was worst of all.

We sat for a long time in silence and I realised she'd fallen asleep. I carefully draped a blanket around her and went back to the nurses' station. Telling Fortunata I needed some fresh air, I headed to the door. I was lucky. Hunter would never have let me get away with it. I slipped outside.

Shivering in the pre-dawn chill, I made my way towards the lake. I stood amongst the willows, took out the clip, and hurled it as far away as I could. I heard the faintest plop in the silence.

I never checked to see if any shots had been fired. I didn't want to know.

We were released the next morning. I sent them for breakfast and went straight to see Dr Bairstow. From there I went to speak to the History Department. They were all in the Hall, waiting for me. I gave them the edited version, because, out of respect for Major Guthrie and the Security Section, no one was ever going to hear what Randall had done from me, and we talked for a while.

I was at a loss to know what to do next. No one was in a fit state to go out on assignment. And what of the trainees? I couldn't leave them while I spent time with the History Department and I so badly wanted to see Leon.

I had a bit of a brainwave and called him up. Could he take the trainees off my hands and keep them busy for the rest of the day?

He could, so I sent them off to the Technical Section and then remembered Kalinda. She and Peterson had been partners once.

I spent a very careful thirty minutes on the phone with Kalinda and when I'd finished, Leon called me.

'Leon, how are they?'

'Losing heavily against my people at five-a-side, but they're OK.'

'Thanks for this. I appreciate it.'

'Not a problem. It's doing my people good, as well.'

'How's Guthrie?'

'Not too bad. Markham and Evans managed to set fire to the oily-waste drum and by the time he'd finished shouting at them, I think everyone felt a little better. Why don't you get something to eat and I'll see you later.'

Doing as I was told – just for once – I wheeled into the dining room and the smell of roast meat hit me in the face and I wheeled straight back out again. I just wasn't hungry. I still couldn't get the smell of burning flesh out of my nostrils.

I went back to Sick Bay. They'd put him in the isolation ward. He was still asleep. Helen sat by his bedside. We looked at each other and then I pulled out a chair and sat at the other side.

Out of the blue, she said, 'There was a problem with your last scan. The one from Thurii. Get another one.'

I nodded.

We sat for an hour, just listening to him breathe.

I was in that strange state between sleeping and waking when I heard the change in his breathing. Helen sat up, immediately alert.

He opened his eyes. Oh God, he opened his eyes.

Helen bent over him.

I left them together.

Seventeen

Half way along the long corridor back to the main building, I had a message that Dr Bairstow wanted to see me.

I toiled back up the stairs again. Leon seemed a very long way away for someone who was only just down the corridor.

Dr Bairstow was waiting for me in his office. Mrs Partridge sat behind him. She doesn't often smile, but it's always worth waiting for and she smiled gently at me now. The weight lifted a little.

Dr Bairstow began. 'I understand Dr Peterson is awake?'

'Yes, sir.'

'Dr Foster says it's too soon to be sure, but the early signs are good. We must be hopeful.'

I said again, 'Yes, sir,' and tried to be hopeful.

He continued. 'I shall be appointing Mr Clerk as temporary head of the History Department, but you will supervise him. Together, of course, with your duties as Training Officer. I'm sorry, Max, but I think your period of light duties is over.'

'Well, I wasn't enjoying it very much, sir. Was there anything else?'

'Actually, yes. Would you sit down, please?'

I didn't like the sound of this. It got worse. I heard a tap on the door, and Mrs Partridge got up and ushered in Major Guthrie.

We sat in silence. What was this all about?

Dr Bairstow began. 'As you know, all members of this unit lodge their wills with me, together with any private correspondence concerning matters that may arise after their death and it is my responsibility to carry out any instructions they may have for me.'

He paused, opened a drawer, and pulled out an envelope.

'I have today, opened a letter Mr Randall left for my attention. I should warn you …' He paused again and pulled himself together. After a moment, he continued. 'I should like you to be privy to its contents and so I shall read you what he has to say.'

He paused, adjusted spectacles I never knew he wore, and began to read.

Dear Sir,

I left this letter to be opened after I'm dead. Also with this is my will as per your instructions.

This is very hard to say but if I'm dead, I suppose it doesn't really matter. I have to tell you. If you don't already know. It was me. It was me who told Ronan we were going to St Paul's. I didn't think at the time I had a choice because he knew something about me I didn't want anyone else to know. I was afraid of people finding out and he knew it. Then he said he'd give me money as well and I said I'd do it. I didn't want the money for me. It was for someone else. I thought I could use it to put things right so I said yes. I swear on the Bible he told me no one would be hurt and as it happened I never got the money and when the bastard tried to kill us all at St Paul's I saw what a fool I'd been but it was too late then.

I nearly went to the Major a couple of times to tell him what I done but then they found Schiller and after that I was too scared. So I just carried on as best I could. The only thing I could do is write it all down for you ready for when I was dead.

Before I was in St Mary's I was in the army and something happened. She was a nice girl and too scared to tell anyone but we all knew who done it and one night we caught him behind the sports block and gave him a right good seeing to. Only we went too far and he ended up paralysed.

We were scared to death they would find us but they never did. We got away with it. We were never even questioned. A couple of years later I came to St Mary's and I'd almost forgot what we did. Ronan must of found out somehow because I got a message saying he'd tell you unless I did what he wanted and I'd go to prison. I can't lie. We went too far with that bloke but I thought maybe I could send him the money and it would make things better for him, so I told Ronan where and when we were going.

It was stupid. I know that now. He never kept his end of the bargain. I never saw any of the money and the next thing I was locked in St Paul's with everyone else. He told me he was just going to steal our stuff and no one would be hurt. And then there was

Schiller dead and I wish I'd of died myself. And I would of said something but everyone was so angry and I didn't know what to do so I'm just going to try to do my job as best I can. Perhaps in some way that will make up for what I did.

I'm sorry, sir, because I've been with you since the beginning. Please tell the Major for me that I'm sorry and I let him down. If there's any money coming to me please can you send it to the bloke we injured. The name of the place he's at is in my box of things under my bed.

Yours,

William Randall.

He folded the piece of paper and put it back in the envelope. A dreadful silence followed.

'Is it true?' asked Guthrie, hoarsely.

Dr Bairstow nodded. 'I have checked. Every word is true.'

Silence again.

I was staring at the faded pattern on Dr Bairstow's carpet. I'd known Randall for years and I'd had no idea. If he hadn't written the letter himself, I would never have believed it. I just knew him as a quiet, conscientious person who'd been on any number of assignments with me and never let me down. And when his own actions in Rouen had placed both him and Peterson in harm's way, he'd managed to get them both back to the pod, probably at the cost of his own life. And yet, he and others had once beaten a man so savagely that he'd been permanently and badly injured. How could one man do both? Saint and sinner. Hero and coward. Perhaps his saving Peterson had been one last attempt to pay a debt that could never be repaid. I don't know. Can a lifetime of hard work and dedication to your job pay for one mistake? And then I remembered he'd betrayed us to Ronan. And then I remembered the people he'd helped save over the years. And then I saw Schiller's body again. And then I just didn't know.

Beside me, Guthrie got to his feet and kicked his chair across the room, sending it clattering against the wall. I'd seen him angry before, but I'd never actually seen him lose control. It was over in a second.

Dr Bairstow sighed. 'I have thought long and hard over this and I have come to the conclusion it is better to say nothing. Let people continue to think Randall died in the line of duty.'

Now I was angry. 'What about Schiller? People should know who was partly responsible for her death.'

Guthrie turned to me. 'No, Max. I'm sorry, but no. Dr Bairstow is correct. It's vital that people feel they can trust the Security Section. We can't have people staring at us and wondering whether another one of the very people responsible for keeping them safe will betray them for money. I'm sorry, but you must see that.'

I clenched my fists, fighting off an irrational desire to burst into tears.

Dr Bairstow said, 'Please sit down, both of you. I'm afraid Major Guthrie is correct, Max. And we must also consider how vulnerable Mr Randall would have been to any future attempts by Clive Ronan to obtain information.' He sighed. 'You may, if you wish, share this information with Chief Farrell, but otherwise, nothing leaves this room. Is that understood?'

I nodded.

'A small service will be held for Mr Randall, as usual. I would like you to attend, if you would. He did save Dr Peterson and perhaps that is the best way to remember him. I think, at heart, he was a good man. He just lost his way a little.'

Guthrie and I left together. We paused on the gallery, looking down into the Hall. The History Department was sitting around a table, talking quietly.

Guthrie leaned his elbows on the balustrade and sighed. 'I should have picked up on this, Max.'

I couldn't blame him. Now, far, far too late, I remembered that Randall had, on several occasions, asked to speak to me and I'd avoided him. Had he intended to confess? We'd never know now.

'I should have seen what was happening right under my nose and I didn't because my mind was on other things.'

I didn't pretend to misunderstand. 'You and Grey, you mean?'

'How could I have missed this? I shouldn't have missed this.'

'It's not going well, is it?'

Now he didn't pretend to misunderstand.

'I thought that when I saw her again – I thought we

could just pick up where we left off and —'

'And you're not the person she remembered,' I finished for him. 'It's been ten years, Ian – it would be a miracle if you were.'

'I know,' he said. 'God, all I ever wanted was to have her back and now she's back and ...'

He stopped again. His mouth turned down in a bitter grin. 'We should be careful what we wish for.'

My heart went out to him. Can there be anything crueller than being reunited with your lost love after a ten-year separation, only to find she's not as you remembered. Or imagined. To meet the right person in the wrong time.

I had what was, for me, an inspiration.

'Ian, I think you should stop pursuing something that doesn't exist any longer. End it. Draw a line and move on.'

He was shocked. 'But ...'

'And then start again. Begin anew. She'll come back from Italy. When she returns, introduce yourself as if you've never met. Don't try to pick up where you left off ten years ago. Accept that you are not the same people and start again. See what happens.'

He stared at me. 'You're quite wise, aren't you?'

Well, that was a surprise. People have used a 'w' word to describe me on several occasions and that word has never been 'wise'. Deep down, I felt a small stirring of warmth. As if something good had finally emerged from this dreadful week.

That night I lay with Leon curled around me. After a while he said, 'You're not asleep, are you?'

'No. Can't sleep.'

'Peterson will recover. He's not going to die.'

'I know. But his arm …'

'It's too soon to know. Wait until Helen can actually say.'

'If he has to leave, I'll probably leave too.'

'No, you won't. You won't leave Dr Bairstow without any Senior Historians. You won't leave the History Department without a Chief Operations Officer. You won't leave four trainees half-trained. Like it or not, there's no way you can leave at the moment.'

Unusually for him, there was a bitter note in his voice.

'You're wrong,' I said, my voice trembling a little in the dark. 'I would do any or all of that without a second thought if I had to. What I won't do is leave you.'

There was a short silence and then he said, 'Would you leave if I asked you to?'

'You know the answer to that one.'

'I'm not sure I do.'

'Yes, you do. It's like the king and parliament.'

Now there was a different kind of short silence.

'It's like *what*?'

'You know – the king and parliament.'

'I am aware of both. I'm just slightly confused by their appearance in our conversation.'

I heaved a sigh. 'The king has the power to say no, so parliament ensures he never has to. It's constitutional something or other.'

'I always thought your failure to comprehend the

properties of electricity was the most frightening thing I had ever encountered. Today you have plumbed new depths.'

'Hey. We did constitutional history at school, you know.'

'I daresay, but did you actually attend any of the classes?'

'Not the point right now.'

'I'm rather at a loss to remember what the point of this conversation was.'

'You were telling me to get some sleep and then for some reason you veered off and started jabbering on about the king, constitutional history, electricity, and my truanting past. You know I love you dearly but I do feel that sometimes you should strive for more focus.'

I could feel him smile in the darkness. 'Feeling better now?'

'A little.'

'No need to thank me.'

'Wasn't going to.'

'Ingratitude, thy name is Max.'

'Can I ask you something?'

He sighed. 'Sleep never really happens when you're around, does it?'

'Do you think I'm turning into Isabella Barclay?'

Even more silence. A very long silence.

'Why aren't you saying anything?'

'I'm trying not to laugh.'

'Thank you for taking my issues seriously.'

'Is this about North?'

'Is it that obvious?'

'Not at all, but the other day when you burst through the door, pitched your boots down one end of the room, threw your training notes up the other, and swore you would swing for that bloody woman one day, I had a bit of an inkling.'

'Can I compliment you on your sensitivity and perception?'

'You can. And what is this problem with North? You apparently deal quite successfully with Miss Lee so why not Miss North?'

'I don't know. I don't know if it's the voice, or that she never gets dirty, or that everything about her is perfect, I just don't know. I do know that I'm beginning to look for faults where none exist. Like Barclay used to do with me. And I worry that I might be turning into her.'

He dropped a kiss on my shoulder. 'Allow me to put your mind at rest. You are not turning into Isabella Barclay.'

'Well, that's something, I suppose.'

'And Peterson will survive.'

'Do you think so?'

'I'm convinced of it. Anything else you want to get off your chest?'

'You don't have to be nice to me just because I've had a bad day, you know.'

'That's a relief. I was beginning to worry I wouldn't be able to keep it up and now I don't have to.'

Eighteen

I went to see Tim the next day. He was sitting up, his bandaged arm resting on a pillow. I've never seen him look so bad. Not even after he'd been lost in the Cretaceous Period. Or the time he was blown up by the Time Police. The pain in his eyes hurt my heart.

'Hey.' He tried to smile.

'You look awful.'

'Not half as awful as I feel.' He turned his head on the pillow and looked out of the window.

'The fault is mine, Tim. I should have stopped him leaving the pod..

'Yeah? And how exactly would you have done that? You're only about three foot six. Even in high heels. No, sorry, Max. Nice try, but this one's on me.'

I didn't know what to say. I didn't know what Helen had told him. He might not yet know that Randall had died of his injuries.

'Can you remember what happened?'

'Oh, yes. Every blood-soaked moment of it. I remember the smell of her burning and the sound of her screaming. I remember the way she slumped against the stake. I especially remember the sound of Randall's skull breaking. Have you ever dropped a melon? It sounds just like that. You wouldn't think so, would you? You'd think it would crack or crunch or something but no, it's not like that at all. It's a kind of splat and …'

'Tim, stop it.'

He looked me straight in the eye. 'By the time I got to him she was dead.'

I thought of the secret I was keeping and nodded.

'And now he's dead, too' he continued. 'Because I didn't get to him in time. You can't say that wasn't my fault.'

'He was the one who made the mistake,' I said.

'Well, he won't ever do that again, will he? Thanks to me.'

I thought for a while and then said carefully, 'Do you remember a conversation we once had?'

He stared at me, expressions of anger, exhaustion, self-loathing, bafflement, all slithering across his face. 'What?'

I held his gaze. 'I'm sure if you think carefully you will remember the one I mean.'

He turned his head away again. 'Is there an award for worst hospital visitor ever that I can nominate you for?'

'You must remember. I forgot them. The trainees. You had to remind me.'

I saw him frown for a moment. 'Do you mean when we talked about …?'

I cut across him quickly. 'When I forgot the trainees. Yes, that's what I meant. That's probably something I shouldn't talk about. There are some things that should not get around the unit.'

He stared at me. 'Yes, I remember talking about …'

'That matter has resolved itself.'

I waited while he worked it out.

'Are you telling me that Randall...*Randall*...was...?'

'I mean, we wouldn't want that getting around, would we? Imagine how people would feel if they knew what had happened.'

He was still staring at me. 'Are we still talking about you forgetting the trainees?'

'Obviously. What else could we be discussing? But sometimes, as I say, everything resolves itself. And now the matter is closed.'

I remembered those slurred, desperate words. 'Trynunstan.' Try to understand. I tried to soldier on, my voice wobbling all over the place.

'I mean, such a dreadful mistake to have made. To have to live with. And such repentance afterwards. Nothing can change what was done, of course, but sometimes, it's possible to pull yourself together and do your job as best as you can and ensure nothing like that ever happens again. To try to atone.'

My voice failed. He reached out and took my hand. I hadn't realised there were tears on my cheeks.

'I understand what you're telling me,' he said softly. He squeezed my hand feebly.

'We all make mistakes, Tim. But you and I have friends to help us through them.'

Now, I needed to see my trainees. There were no lectures until next Monday, but I wanted to make sure they weren't completely traumatised. Yes, people can deal with shock, but they have to be given time to process it. Our last assignment had been one hammer blow after another. I still felt my stomach slide sideways whenever I thought of Peterson. How must they feel?

We met in the small training room. They looked a little subdued, but none of them was actually clutching a letter of resignation.

'Good morning, everyone. You'll be pleased to hear Dr Peterson is awake and doing well. A service for Mr Randall will be held the day after tomorrow. Best uniforms for those attending. Our sessions will recommence on Monday at 09.30. Until then, your time is your own. My advice is to clear off to Rushford and do normal things. See a holo, visit a couple of bars, late-night curry. The sort of things normal people do. Does anyone have any questions?'

They shook their heads and filed out. Except for Mr Hoyle.

'Mr Hoyle? Was there something you wanted to say to me?'

'Yes.'

I sat at the data table next to his and hoped my people skills were up to the challenge. It struck me now that when I first arrived at St Mary's all those years ago, that it was a struggle for me to look anyone in the eye and say good morning. These days, people actually sought me out and asked me for advice on personal relationships, romantic problems, and social issues which, quite honestly, is a bit like asking an anorexic for recipes.

We sat in silence while he wound himself up for whatever he wanted to say to me. I knew the signs. I couldn't rush him.

He opened his mouth several times and nothing came out so I said gently, 'What's the problem, Mr Hoyle?'

'Not a problem as such – it's – well, I don't want you to take this as a criticism but don't you think this might not have happened if you all took your jobs a little more seriously. If everyone just stopped messing about?'

I was really, really angry. Really angry. Really, really angry.

I sat back, crossed my legs, adjusted my scratchpad as it bumped against my knee, and said quite mildly, 'I'm not quite sure you really understand how things work at St Mary's and that's not something I can teach you. If you can't work it out for yourself – and it doesn't look as if you can – then there may be no place for you here after all. I do think, after everything you did to get here, that that would be a shame. A great shame. But I'm not surprised to hear your comments, Mr Hoyle. St Mary's is the sort of place into which either you fit or you don't. It has nothing to do with academic ability. We look for a certain type of person here. Mrs De Winter obviously thought you were the right match for us, but even she gets it wrong occasionally.'

So far so good. I was still giving him a chance to live.

He blew it. 'But I'm so ... disappointed in this place. There are important issues out there and you all behave like a pack of children. There's no discipline, no serious research, no dedication – it's all so –

amateurish. Sometimes I don't think any of you deserve to work here.'

I resisted the urge to do him a serious injury. Even after the events of the last few days, he still didn't have a bloody clue. My voice was icy.

'Do you have any idea what it's like to crouch under a cam net in the direct line of fire, waiting for the Light Brigade to charge, knowing that in an hour's time, every bright, brave young man down there who is terrified out of his wits but doing his duty regardless, is going to be blown to pieces? Literally reduced to a pulp of flesh and bones before your very eyes? Do you have the imagination to know how that feels? And we can't flinch or look away – we do our duty too. So as far as I am concerned, if St Mary's wants to set fire to their own feet, or conceal a cat in a warming pan, or blow up the septic tank, then as far as I'm concerned, it is my privilege to allow them to do so.'

I paused and waited for my breathing to slow. 'We have a few days before we pick things up again. Why don't you spend the time thinking seriously about whether you have a future here.'

All right, I know I was furious, but I honestly thought I'd been reasonably gentle with him. Even so, I was completely taken aback by his reaction. I thought he was going to burst into tears.

'No, no. I meant no criticism. Well, I did, but it was more of a question. I didn't mean to cause offense. I certainly don't want to leave. It's just that the working methods here aren't quite what I expected, but that's not your fault. Perhaps I've just spent so much time abroad that I'm unfamiliar with the way things are done here. I apologise.'

He was practically gabbling by the time he'd finished.

I heard Captain Ellis' voice in my head. 'You have a problem. He's too intense.'

He had been right. The quiet ones are often the worst.

I calmed myself down, forced a smile, and said, 'Take your days off, Mr Hoyle. Come back on Monday. We'll take things from there.'

He backed out of the door, still gabbling.

I really should have taken time to have a bit of a think about that.

I had lunch with Leon. We sat in the sun outside Hawking. He brought sandwiches for us both and chocolate for me. This was something we'd done on and off ever since I started at St Mary's. Recently, because of the pressure of work, more off than on. It was good to feel the sun on my face, the warm wall behind my back, and breathe in the smell of fresh-cut grass as Mr Strong nurtured the pitiful remains of the South Lawn. Rumour had it he was petitioning Dr Bairstow for permission to convert the crater into an ornamental pool.

'Is he insane?' said Leon. 'We'll have Professor Rapson knocking up the Claw of Archimedes before lunchtime. Or breeding his own Plesiosaurs. Or recreating the sinking of the *Mary Rose*. It's just asking for trouble.'

He unwrapped his sandwiches and passed me one.

'How are you feeling?'

'Oh, I'm fine. Keeping my chin up.'

'Keeping everyone's chins up from what I hear.'

I smiled.

'Don't get so caught up with everyone else that you forget to take care of yourself.'

I smiled again. 'That won't happen. I know I'm a bit high maintenance sometimes, but I also know I always have you.'

He took my hand and kissed it and we sat together in the sun, holding hands and not talking very much.

I spent the afternoon with Clerk, looking over the History Department's assignment schedule and then, in the evening, went back to Sick Bay to see Tim, who didn't look much better.

I entered just in time to hear him say, 'I might never be able to hold Helen's hands again.'

'You won't have to,' I said, closing the door behind me. 'She'll hold yours.'

'Or draw a bow.'

'Learn to use a sword,' I said, although I just wanted to cry for him.

'Or even peel an orange.'

'Oh, for God's sake,' said Markham in exasperation. 'I haven't peeled an orange for years. I just hand it to the nearest pretty girl and look pathetic.'

'Second nature to you, I should imagine,' I said. 'Besides, who could possibly think anyone from the Security Section has the physical coordination to peel an orange without breaking a window?'

'Ha! Well, I've got you there,' he said, triumphantly. 'When it comes to physical coordination you're looking at this year's winner of the one-handed-bra-unfastening competition.'

We stared at him.

I found a voice.

'Security has a bra-unfastening competition?'

'*One-handed* bra-unfastening competition,' he said, reprovingly. 'And it's not easy, I can tell you.'

'I'll say,' said Peterson, thoughtfully. 'I struggle with two.'

'I don't want to hear any of this,' I said.

Markham gently patted my back as if I was a nervous horse. 'Calm down, Max. We don't use real women, obviously.'

I'm not often struck dumb, but – seriously?

'I don't believe anyone can unfasten a bra one-handed,' said Peterson, suddenly sounding tired. He lay back on his pillows. 'And you're the most cack-handed person I know.'

Markham sat back and grinned evilly. 'Really? Max?' He wiggled his eyebrows at me.

I stared at him for a moment and then gave myself a small experimental flex.

'You bastard!'

I stormed into the bathroom to refasten my bra, slamming the door behind me. When I came out, Markham was rummaging through his many pockets, pulling out a black lacy specimen.

'That's a bra,' I said, stupidly stating the obvious, but come on …

'Whose?' enquired Peterson. 'It's not …?' and he

nodded towards the space he imagined Nurse Hunter was currently occupying.

'Well, of course it is,' said Markham, indignantly. 'It's certainly not mine.'

'Are you mad?' I said in a strangled whisper, as if she could overhear me. 'If Hunter finds out ...'

'She won't. Now, Max, can you get me some tissues. And I need a pillow, too. Come on, don't just stand there.'

'I am a Chief Officer, you know,' I said, haughtily, but no one was listening.

When I came out of the bathroom, trailing reams of toilet paper behind me, he'd fastened the bra around a pillow. I handed him the toilet paper and he began to tear off great handfuls, which he stuffed into the cups.

You want to look away, but you just can't.

'There,' he said, head on one side, adjusting things to his satisfaction.

They propped the bra-wearing pillow up beside Peterson. Markham, having established his credentials, took on the air of a mystic, imparting the secrets of brassiere manipulation to an acolyte, but Peterson was laughing and had a little colour in his face.

'Go on,' said the Grand Master. 'Give it a go. Just remember what I said about keeping your ring finger curled under.'

The door opened and I braced myself for a life-saving leap from the window, but it was Leon.

He stood stock-still. I didn't blame him. Peterson and Markham on the bed together, wrestling with a bra-wearing pillow. You couldn't make it up.

I stood up. 'For God's sake, Leon – take me away from all this.'

He held the door open for me.

'See you, guys.' I left them to it.

Outside, I bumped into Hunter.

She nodded over my shoulder. 'How's it going in there?'

Enlightenment dawned. 'You and Markham set all that up.'

'Well, of course we did, Max. You don't seriously think I would let him wander around all day festooned with women's underwear, do you?'

'With you two,' said Leon, darkly, 'I never know what to think.'

She sighed. 'You wouldn't believe what I had to promise him to get him to do that.'

'Don't tell us,' said Leon. 'Some things are better never spoken about.'

She laughed. 'I have to go in there now and yell at the pair of them. For their own good, of course. Come back tomorrow, Max. He looks forward to seeing you.'

We left.

I was half way down the stairs when the tears finally came. My legs gave way. I sat down with a bump and sobbed. Sobbed for Randall who had spent his life trying to atone for one mistake. Sobbed for Tim whose life would never be the same again. Sobbed for Markham and his peculiar ideas of physiotherapy, but who had said and done exactly the right thing, when I had been so useless. Sobbed for

Leon, whole and healthy beside me, who scooped me up in his arms and held me until I was too tired to cry any longer.

Nineteen

I was busy these days. I now had two departments to manage, and I'd have to be careful how I went about it. Clerk was in nominal charge of the History Department and it was a great opportunity for him but they were still fairly shaken up over Peterson. I wanted to give him every opportunity to shine but not be overwhelmed. To feel he was in control but not exposed.

We'd spent time going over the assignment list and temporarily postponing anything that looked even mildly hazardous and now the rest of the department were on their way to help set up a tentative timetable.

I had, of course, re-inherited Miss Lee who, for some reason, was sitting on the floor of my office, apparently dismantling something with brute force and a lot of bad language. I just let her get on with it. Easier. Quicker. Safer.

The door opened and the rest of the History Department appeared, a little quiet, but ready for action. Mr Sands halted on the threshold and stared at her. 'What are you doing?'

'Repairing my hairdryer.'

That was useful. If she was successful, she could

fix mine.

He frowned. 'Give it to me.'

'Why?'

'Well, not to put too fine a point on it – this is men's work.'

He was suddenly a man alone. The rest of the department, showing a respect for Health and Safety I would never in my wildest dreams have suspected, was clustered in the far corner, geographically as far from him as they could get.

She was holding a screwdriver. I mentally reviewed the medical procedures for sharp-force trauma. To be fair, she did give him an avenue of escape. She must really like him.

'I don't understand.'

'What I'm saying is that if you had a man in your life, you wouldn't be sitting cross legged on the floor in the early stages of electrocution.'

It was going to be interesting to see just how far a screwdriver could be inserted up someone's nose before encountering a sinus.

To the relief of all present she put the screwdriver down.

'Seriously? A man? I think we both know that even if I was stupid enough to possess such a thing he would, at this very moment, be stretched out on a sofa somewhere, beer in one hand, himself in the other, watching *Match of the Day*. And I'd still be here trying to fix my stupid hairdryer. By myself.'

He picked up the hairdryer and threw it out of the window.

'Sorted. I'll buy you a new one. Morning, Max.'

The rest of the meeting proceeded peacefully. Miss Lee took notes and did not, even for one moment, lift her eyes from her scratchpad.

This was the trainees' final assignment. We were entering the home stretch. All I had to do was get them through this last jump without major loss of life or limb. Not that difficult, surely.

I formally appointed Hoyle controller of this mission and at last, there it was. A flicker of reaction. He turned hastily away and strode off. I let him go. He'd had to wait a long time for his assignment. It wasn't his fault if his stiff upper lip was having a bit of a quiver.

This final assignment was more in the nature of works jolly. Part of a long-term and continually ongoing industrial history assignment. We already had Stevenson's *Rocket* under our belt, including the unfortunate death of the MP, William Huskisson, who had somehow, at some point in the proceedings, managed to get himself run over.

Now we were off to see if one of us could manage to fall off the Clifton Suspension Bridge. Any takers?

We assembled outside Number Five. Atherton, Hoyle, North, Sykes, Markham, and me. I spared a thought for Peterson who should have been with us on this one. He was slowly recovering the use of his arm, thanks, he said, to constant and dedicated physiotherapy. Although Nurse Hunter had warned him that if he tried it on her he'd lose the use of another appendage.

We checked each other over. I couldn't help comparing this occasion to their first jump, nearly six months ago. How much more assured they all were. More confident. More of a team. Atherton, North, and Sykes stood around like old hands, exchanging jokes and laughing at each other's costumes which, since we were off to the Victorian era, were pretty laughable.

As usual, we women had come off worst. While the blokes were able to get away with sack coats, waistcoats, and trousers, sadly, we'd arrived at the age of the crinoline. And colour. The invention of mauve and magenta shades had caused a minor sensation and, being Victorian, the fashion industry had picked up these colours and run with them. In addition, our crinolines were stiffened with gauze, under those, we had starched petticoats, and under those, of course, the inevitable corset.

'Not too tight,' I'd pleaded. 'I really like to be able to move occasionally. And bend down. And breathe.'

Mrs Enderby had done her best but I'm short and this was yet another occasion when my width far exceeded my height and yes, my bum really did look big in this.

In fact, everything was big. Pagoda sleeves over wide undersleeves, a big lace collar that was supposed to make me look demure and failed. And as if none of that was enough, over everything, I wore a knee-length fitted jacket heavily trimmed with purple braid, and a matching bonnet.

Sykes and North emerged, similarly encumbered, in vast pink and purple skirts, with three-quarter-length capes over the top. I've never seen so many ribbons.

'Bloody hell,' said Sykes, ruining the demure Victorian maiden effect, 'this lot weighs a ton. Why do my skirts look like those Austrian blinds?'

'Looped up to keep them out of the mud,' said Mrs Enderby. 'I beg of you, please try to keep them clean. And most importantly, please don't bleed on the material. It's very difficult to shift blood sometimes.'

I pulled on my gloves and picked up an umbrella. It was England. Of course it would be raining.

'Will we be able to get you all in?' enquired Atherton, looking at our skirts. 'It's not a big pod, you know.'

'If we can't then you and Mr Hoyle can draw lots to decide who to leave behind,' said Sykes, cruelly.

'What?' said Hoyle sharply, from inside Number Five. 'What did you say about leaving me behind?'

'Nothing,' I said reassuringly, stepping through the door. 'No one's being left behind.'

He certainly needed some sort of reassurance. Far from recovering himself, his hands shook as he moved them over the controls, checking everything.

I took him aside and said quietly, 'Mr Hoyle, are you all right?'

He made a huge effort to smile reassuringly. 'Yes. Oh, yes. Sorry. Just a little nervous. This is a big moment for me.'

I was so relieved to see he could actually experience some emotion that I took this at face value and carried on with my own checks. I wasn't concerned over this one. We were going to witness a glorious festival celebrating a stupendous engineering feat. The Bristol Riots were long since done. No civil disturbances of any kind were reported. It would be a happy, family day, full of civic pride. Nothing could possibly go wrong.

The opening of the Clifton Suspension Bridge is well documented. On Wednesday 8th December 1864, the city of Bristol did not so much push the boat out as fire it from a cannon. Events would kick off around half past nine with a military display in Queen's Square, after which the troops would march along Broad Quay Park and up to the Downs.

Meanwhile, the Trade and Friendly Societies had assembled in the Old Market, to display samples of their workmanship and products before joining in the procession which, by now, was about half a mile long. There can't have been anyone in Bristol who didn't have a relative or know someone who was taking part in the parade, and was there to cheer them on with enthusiasm and, above all, volume.

We were up near the Downs in a position carefully chosen to enable us to experience the maximum enjoyment from the parade and still witness the opening ceremony. And have our eardrums perforated, of course.

By the time it reached us, the procession was nearly three miles long and comprised several thousand people. It would take nearly forty-five minutes to pass.

We joined in with huge enthusiasm (with the exception of Mr Hoyle, of course, from whose dictionary the word enthusiasm was definitely missing), clapping and shouting ourselves hoarse as each individual exhibit passed by, striving to make ourselves heard over the sounds of more than twenty brass bands.

Bringing up the rear to enormous admiration and applause was a vast float pulled by eight huge, glossy black horses, all decked out in red, white, and blue ribbons. The float depicted a seated Britannia, surrounded by figures representing Europe, America, Asia, and Africa. Possibly, at the beginning of the proceedings, she had been as quiet and demure as society demanded, but by the time she got to us, she was flourishing her trident at the crowd, and waving and smiling fit to bust. The crowd, appreciating her commitment, roared and waved back again.

And all this time, the rain was pouring down. Umbrellas became entangled. I couldn't believe no one lost an eye. The streets were slippery. Drains and gutters were clogged with straw, litter, discarded flags, and the occasional drunk. Giant puddles of muddy water were slowly spreading across the roads. My petticoats were sodden and splashed with mud nearly to my knees. I was enveloped in the smell of wet people and wet horses.

The records say there were around one hundred and fifty thousand people on the streets that day and I was convinced that every single one of them stood on my feet at one time or another. We were so tightly squeezed together that we could barely lift our arms to wave the little Union Jacks Markham had procured for us. He didn't say where he'd got them from and I didn't ask. The crowd was very good-natured and cheerful despite the awful weather, but trust me, there's only so many times you can take having your bonnet knocked over your eyes before you contemplate wielding a hatpin.

It wasn't just the clamouring, cheering, shouting people. All across the city, church bells rang, seemingly in some sort of frenzied ecumenical bell-ringing competition. Multi-coloured flags and bunting criss-crossed the street to the alarm of horses in general. Crowds of shouting people hung from every window or clung precariously to roofs and gables. As far as I know, unbelievably, no one died that day.

After an hour or so, with my legs and ankles feeling as if they were on fire, I stepped back a little to watch the trainees. Sykes, her face alight with excitement, was waving her flag with wild abandon. Even North was politely applauding each exhibit as it marched past, her head inclined as Atherton attempted to shout something into her ear. Hoyle was staring down the road, his arms wrapped around himself, although whether for protection or not, I had no idea.

We followed the procession, attempting to get as close to the bridge as possible. Actually, we had very little choice – we were carried along rather like salmon being swept upstream by their uncontrollable urges. Speaking of uncontrollable urges ... I looked around. There were people from here to the horizon. There was no chance. Plait your legs, Maxwell.

There was an enormous amount of milling around as the procession halted for the ceremonial opening of the bridge. We clung together as best we could, because if we were separated now, it could be a good twenty-four hours before we saw each other again. We were far too far away to hear the actual speakers – hardly anyone was close enough to hear the speakers – but such small details didn't stop the crowd applauding and cheering each one as if they'd heard every word.

The Downs – that lovely open space at the top of the Avon Gorge – had been packed with people since early morning. A large area was lined with stalls selling foodstuffs that wouldn't taste anywhere near as good as they smelled. Markham counted out some enormous copper pennies and purchased a pie.

He and Atherton took a turn at one of the shooting galleries. I'd have liked to have a go myself, but it was generally reckoned that such things were too much for the gentle sensibilities of women. Both of them scored badly and retired, affronted and muttering about the sights being crooked. We patted their arms in a soothing manner, which, for some reason, annoyed them even more. We watched acrobats and tumblers, and did our best to avoid pickpockets, cutpurses, and ladies whose affection could be purchased by the minute. There was also a large number of small boys, all hiding behind the observatory, and apparently trying to kill themselves on cheap cigars.

I was quite surprised to find I was really enjoying myself and I wasn't the only one. With the exception of Hoyle, who obviously didn't know how, everyone was relaxed and happy and apart from bruised toes and minor crush injuries, we were all having a great time.

Below us – far below us, actually – the River Avon was filled with gaily decorated steam ships all the way back to the Cumberland Basin, all sounding their whistles as hard as they could go. It was all quite a sight.

Around about noon, the rain stopped and the sun came out and the serious business began.

The military marched into position. The civic dignitaries approached in stately procession, the Lord Lieutenants of Gloucestershire and Somerset, the Mayor of Bristol, a couple of bishops, the company directors, everyone who had even the remotest connection with the bridge was there. The bands played. The four cannon set up in Leigh Woods fired a twenty-one gun salute, which made me jump out of my skin and caused ladies everywhere to scream. The crowd roared approval for every shot. Music, cannon fire, and huge cheers. St Mary's itself couldn't have made more noise.

The procession marched across the bridge and then, to everyone's amusement, turned around and marched straight back again.

'Just like the Grand Old Duke of York,' said Markham.

They raised the flags. The soldiers presented arms. All twenty bands played "God Save The Queen" to which the crowd sang with enormous gusto and enthusiasm – and finally, the bridge was open.

'Dear God,' said Markham, still waving his Union Jack. 'I've seen battles won and lost with less fuss.'

'Oh come on,' said Sykes, her bonnet askew. 'You loved every minute of it.'

They all had. They were damp, dirty, hungry, thirsty, but just for once, everything had gone completely according to plan and we had some great footage. I smiled at them. 'Job well done, guys. It took us a while, but we finally got it right.'

'I'm desperate for a cup of tea,' said Atherton, proving that they were indeed, true historians.

All the important people were disappearing fast for a bit of a civic knees-up and we were free to find ourselves a watering hole. And nobody did high tea like the Victorians.

'No,' said Hoyle. 'We should get back. It's dark, the wind's getting up, and every tearoom for miles around will be packed. Let's go back to the pod.'

He was a killjoy but he was right. And some of us were desperate for a bathroom break as well. The crowds were beginning to disperse and so did we, but slowly, so we could enjoy the fireworks on the way.

Hoyle walked in front, arm in arm with North. They didn't appear to have much to say to each other. I walked in the middle with Atherton, and Sykes and Markham brought up the rear. I could hear them chattering away to each other.

The rain began again and the pod was further than we thought. Hoyle quickened his pace. It was all very well for him; he wasn't encased in four and a half miles of starched petticoats. I could hear North complaining at him. Atherton was silent and I whiled away the time wondering who would pair up with whom. Normally, on a training course, you get an idea of who gets on and who doesn't. People are naturally attracted – or repelled – by their fellow trainees. Relationships are built that can last a lifetime – however long that may be – but I had no clues with this bunch. The traditional pairing is one man and one woman, because there are always places women can go and men can't – and vice versa. We had two of each, but how they would divide themselves up was a puzzle. Usually, we don't interfere. We don't assign people to each other. The best and strongest partnerships are between those who choose each other. If asked to hazard a guess – and Dr Bairstow would almost certainly ask me to do so – I would pair North with Hoyle because then they could cancel each other out, so to speak, and Sykes with Atherton. I tried to imagine Sykes and Hoyle together and gave that up. And Sykes and North would probably kill each other. I'd just have to wait and see.

The pod was warm and welcoming after the crowds and the rain. We stamped our wet boots and divested ourselves of soggy capes. There was a stampede for the bathroom, which is not something you ever see in movies or holos about the glamorous life of time travel. Those who had to wait argued over whose turn it was to make the tea. Or coffee, in Hoyle's case.

We dried ourselves off a little. I seated myself at the console and a strange little silence fell, broken only by the sounds of the kettle coming to the boil.

'What?' I said, suddenly uneasy.

There was some shuffling and then Atherton stepped forwards. Interesting. Not North, despite all her best efforts to become their leader. Not Sykes, with her easy, breezy confidence. Definitely not Hoyle, who had seated himself alongside me and was scanning the readouts. Atherton. Quiet, capable Atherton. Good choice, guys.

He cleared his throat. 'On behalf of all of us, we'd like to thank you for everything you've done for us and to present you with this.'

With a flourish, he produced two envelopes – one big, one small.

I didn't know what to say.

Behind them, Markham grinned at me.

I said, 'Um, thank you. This is very unexpected.'

They urged me to open them.

The first contained a card, signed by all of them. Even Lingoss. 'She didn't want to be left out,' said Sykes. 'And she's coming to our celebration tomorrow night.' She paused shyly. 'You're invited, too. And Mr Markham, of course.'

'I'll be there,' he said quickly.

'And Dr Peterson too, if he's well enough.'

'He will be if there's alcohol involved,' said Markham, with confidence.

'Open the other envelope,' instructed North.

The second envelope contained membership to an organisation known as ChocAss. The Chocolate Association.

I laughed. 'You're kidding.'

'It's great,' said Sykes, enthusiastically. 'I've been a member for years. Every month they send you a selection of chocolate. You have to eat it –'

'Obviously,' said North.

'You have to eat it,' continued Sykes, throwing her a Look, 'and then there's a questionnaire for you to complete. You know, flavour, appearance, texture, whatever, and then you send the paperwork back for them to evaluate the products. So you're carrying out valuable and important work.'

'If you can be bothered,' grinned Atherton. 'Alternatively, you pursue the Sykes method of research which is to sit down, scarf the whole lot in one evening, and then throw the paperwork in the bin. They don't really care.'

I was truly touched. To cover my emotion, I opened the card again, read the signatures very carefully, and then examined the small certificate, which said I was indeed now a member of ChocAss and carrying out valuable scientific research in the exciting world of chocolate. I thought about how Leon would laugh when he saw that.

'Thank you,' I said, eventually. 'It's the perfect gift. You shouldn't have. I'm not sure we haven't transgressed some rule or reg here, but I'm very glad you did. Thank you so much.'

Markham handed me a much-needed mug of tea and we all slurped busily.

'So what happens next?' said North, making herself comfortable on the floor, her skirt billowing elegantly around her.

'Well, you get tomorrow and the weekend off. You've already learned the basics of calculating coordinates. There will be a lot of work in the simulators while you get that sorted out, but it's necessary. I remember on my course, a colleague managed to land himself in the middle of the Spanish Armada. Literally. They still haven't worked out how he managed to do that. From there, you go on to simulated situations, when they'll throw everything they can at you to see how you cope. It's a lot of work, but now that you have these jumps under your belt, it should make a lot more sense than doing things the other way around as we used to.'

Markham got to his feet and took down the Instructions in the Event of a Fire notice.

'What are you doing?'

'Well, basically, all it says is that if there's a fire to put it out, and if you can't then to exit the pod with all speed. I think we can work that out for ourselves. And if we are on fire then who's going to stop and read the instructions anyway?'

He stuck my card up in its place where it looked very pretty and I suddenly realised that I was going to miss them. Technically, they would continue to be mine, but the day-to-day supervision was passing to others and I found that now that the time had come, I was actually quite reluctant to part with them.

I looked around the pod. So, here we were at last. Final assignment completed. No one had fallen off the bridge. No one had been run over by a runaway carriage. Despite enthusiastically consuming stall-bought lemonade and several animal-product pies, none of us had died of anything horrible. We hadn't drowned, nobody had managed to set fire to the Suspension Bridge and we had tons of good footage.

Atherton had followed my thinking. 'Surely this must be our most successful assignment ever,' he said, tempting fate beyond ... well ... temptation, because at that moment, Mr Hoyle dramatically whipped out a pistol and in a voice oscillating between terror and determination, equally dramatically announced that he was now in control.

A stunned and slightly perplexed silence fell.

'You're already in control,' I said, not a little exasperated. 'You're mission controller, remember?'

'That mission is over with,' he said, his voice cracking. 'Forget it. You ...' he pointed his gun at North, remembered her tantrum at Thurii when things hadn't gone as she had decreed, pointed it at Sykes, remembered that she was a psycho, and finally pointed it at Atherton, who despite his good nature, looked none too pleased at being last on the list of those being threatened.

I looked over at Markham who shook his head very faintly. The message was clear. He was on the far side of the pod, sitting on the floor. He couldn't get to Hoyle in time.

The silence in the pod was complete as we all stared at him. No one moved. Something clicked on the console as a read-out updated itself and he jumped a mile. The pause was going on too long. He was too strung up. Whatever he was steeling himself to do – now that the moment had come, he was shaking with nerves. With everyone still staring at him, the gun began to tremble a little. That impassive exterior was beginning to crack. That's the problem with these quiet, intense types. When they finally lose it – which they always do – they really lose it. Now that his moment had come – whatever that moment was – he was losing control of himself. This was becoming dangerous. Firing a gun in a pod is even more hazardous than firing a gun in a passenger aircraft at thirty thousand feet. You don't want high-velocity bullets impacting the working bits, leaving you stranded and with no means of getting home. Even worse if they actually hit someone and I'd seen enough blood-soaked bodies on the floor to last a lifetime.

'Very well,' I said. 'You are indeed in control, Mr Hoyle. Please indicate your next move.'

He rummaged for a slip of paper, gun pointing everywhere. I glanced at Markham, who again shook his head. Play along. I turned my attention back to Hoyle who had found what he wanted and passed it over to me.

I turned the paper around and played dumb. 'What's this?'

'Coordinates.'

'I am aware of that. Where and when are these for?'

He blustered. 'You don't need to know that. Just lay them in and make the jump.'

'You really are the most incompetent hijacker in the entire history of hijacking,' I said. 'How long have you been at St Mary's? In which lecture did I ever give you the impression that historians are stupid enough to jump blindly to a set of coordinates of which they know nothing?'

'Is that a serious question?' he said angrily. 'Because the serious answer is – all of them. And accompanied by cats disguised as babies, kidnapped livestock, fire, disaster, and any number of small explosions as well. So lay in the coordinates and make the jump.'

He flourished the gun. At least, I think he did. He was so strung up that his arm seemed to be waving around the place on its own. I could see his finger, white on the trigger. Time to slow things down a bit. I sat back and spoke quietly.

'You won't use that in here. You can't risk damaging the pod and you can't shoot me because I'm the only person authorised to operate this pod.'

Wisely passing over Sykes, who would have eaten him if he'd tried it with her, he pointed his pistol at North and said, 'No, but I can shoot her.'

North ignored him and faced Sykes. 'I told you he was an oik.'

'Yeah, you did,' she admitted. 'Looks like you were right.'

Some sixth sense must have warned him because he spun around towards Markham who had already started to move. At the same time, Atherton jumped at him. The three of them collided heavily and crashed to the ground. North and Sykes jumped back and flattened themselves against the lockers and I swung my legs out of the way.

I could hear Markham shouting. 'Put it down. Let go of the bloody thing, will you? Before someone gets hurt.'

And then the gun went off.

Everything went horribly silent and still.

Twenty

I had a terrible sense of *déjà vu*. I saw again the blood-soaked floor. Randall, limp and lifeless. Peterson with his terrible wound. All I could think was – no, not again. Please God, not again. Time ticked on and no one was moving.

After a hundred years or so, Atherton rolled off the top of the heap and lay on his back, staring up at the ceiling.

I swallowed. 'Are you all right, Mr Atherton?'

'Yes, I'm fine,' he said, pulling himself slowly to his feet.

On the floor, Markham and Hoyle lay locked together in some dreadful parody of a fond embrace. The gun was an inch from Markham's right eye. As far as I could see, they were both unhurt.

Hoyle sucked in a deep ragged breath. 'Lay in the coordinates or I'll shoot Markham dead. Do it now.'

I know it's traditional to say, 'Over my dead body' or something similar, but believe me, the phrase, 'Over someone else's dead body' is far more frightening. And compelling. Besides, as I once said to Leon – the priority is always staying alive. Being dead seriously limits your options. I wanted Markham alive and functioning. With him by my side, anything was possible.

'Very well,' I said quietly. 'But first, is anyone hurt?'

There was a ragged chorus of shocked no's.

'It doesn't matter,' he said, impatiently. 'Just make the jump.'

'If that bullet has penetrated the console and damaged the boards then we're not going anywhere,' I said. 'Whether you want us to or not. And since you're only ever going to get one try at this, Mr Hoyle, you'd better make sure you get it right first time.'

Still on the floor, he nodded.

I slipped off the seat and pulled the front off the console. 'The rest of you look around. If the bullet's not inside any of you then it must be somewhere else. Find it.' I pulled out the boards and carefully inspected each one.

There was no need. I could tell by the lack of acrid smoke and shrieking alarms that they were undamaged, but while I was busy with this, someone else might have a plan.

I think everyone else must have thought the same about me because two minutes later North had discovered the splintered hole in the bathroom door, and Markham still had Hoyle's gun in his eye and no one had a plan.

'Well,' said North with admirable cool, sticking her head around the bathroom door to inspect the damage. 'The toilet's shot.'

'That's actually very funny,' said Sykes. 'Who'd

have thought?'

'Mr Hoyle, please allow Mr Markham to rise. Nobody is to make any sudden movements. Both of you get up slowly, please.'

Very, very slowly, the two of them climbed to their feet and faced each other. Markham flicked his eyes at me for instructions. He might have been saying he could disarm him but I wasn't taking any chances. Besides, we wouldn't be historians if we hadn't been born with more than our fair share of terminal curiosity.

'Right,' I said. 'What's this all about?'

Hoyle was staring at Markham, not taking his eyes off him, stubbornly saying nothing.

'I could beat it out of him,' said Markham, helpfully, peering at me from around the pistol.

'And me,' said Sykes. 'I'd like to have a go too.'

'No one's beating anyone,' I said, exercising my primary function as peacemaker and keeping everyone alive. 'Just tell us what all this is about, Mr Hoyle.'

'You don't frighten me,' he said, his voice trembling. 'I'm not saying anything.'

'Look,' I said. 'I'm not a nice person. I didn't want to be Training Officer. I've nursemaided you lot for what seems like forever and I'm sick of it. This was your final jump. On Monday, I hand you over to Chief Farrell and Professor Rapson for the last part of your training and I'm buggered if I'm going to let anything stand in the way of getting rid of you at last. I've never liked the look of you, Hoyle, and as far as I'm concerned, if you don't tell me what's going on right this moment, you *will* be involved in an unspecified but unfortunate accident this afternoon. We will be unable to bring back your body for burial, and everyone will be very sad for about ten minutes, and then we'll all go to the bar and this time next week no one will even remember your name.'

All right, possibly a little harsh, but I really wanted to know what was going on.

'Can I still give him a bit of a kicking?' enquired Sykes, hopefully.

'I don't see why not.'

'Trust me,' said Markham to Hoyle. 'I've known Maxwell a long time now and she really doesn't mess about when she's seriously pissed. And all she has to do is ask the computer to identify the coordinates so why don't you just do yourself a bit of good and tell us what this is all about.'

He stepped back as he spoke. At the same time, I swivelled the right-hand seat for Hoyle and sat back, hands clasped unthreateningly in my lap.

He moved slowly, and sat at the console, pointing the gun at me. 'You. No sudden moves.'

'You've obviously never worn a crinoline,' I said. 'No one's making any sudden moves, I give you my word. Sit down, everyone. No one moves until I say so. That's a direct order.'

They all moved back and reluctantly sat down. Sykes and Atherton were still glaring at Hoyle, and North was looking at him as if he was something found at the bottom of a grease trap. Just for once, I was in complete agreement with her.

'Come on, lad,' said Markham. 'What's the game

here?'

For a moment, I didn't think he would speak. Finally, he said, 'It's a long story.'

'Better make a start then,' I said. 'Begin with these coordinates.' I laid the paper in front of him. 'What is so important and so secret you couldn't just put in a request in the normal manner?'

'I couldn't take the chance. If I did that and permission was refused ... That would have tipped you off and I would never have been able to ...'

I said, through gritted teeth because I really was getting pissed off now, 'To what? Where and when are these coordinates?'

He still said nothing.

I turned back to the console. 'Computer.'

The computer chirped its response.

'No, no, I'll tell you. It's ... I wanted ... I'm sorry, this isn't easy. I've been planning this for so long, and it's so important and I've just ...'

'Oh for God's sake,' said Sykes. 'Don't make me come over there.'

The fight went out of him. 'All right.' He took a deep breath. 'My full name is Richard Neville Laurence Hoyle.'

He stared defiantly around the pod, possibly a little disappointed at the lack of response.

'Yes?' said Atherton. 'So what?'

I felt some sympathy for Hoyle. It had obviously never occurred to him that whatever fanatical beliefs had driven him to be here and now, those beliefs meant nothing to anyone else.

He twisted his hands together around the gun and

335

looked sideways at me in a suddenly very familiar pose ... That expression ... Richard ... Neville ... I had one of those blinding revelations that either drives you into the arms of religion or the bottle. Or both. The two often seem to go together. Because now – now that it was far, far too bloody late, of course – now I knew who he reminded me of. There it was. The famous pose. The face in three-quarter profile, the hands clasped together, although in the painting, I always think he's nervously twisting a ring. Dark hair hanging around his face, the intense gaze, the wide, sensitive mouth.

'Bloody hell,' said Sykes, who'd seen it too. 'It's Dick the Turd.'

That did it.

'Don't say that,' he shouted furiously, leaping to his feet. Sykes, alarmed at this sudden violence, did the same. As did Markham. And Atherton. Even North.

'Stop,' I shouted, terrified someone was going to be shot. 'Stop. Everyone ... sit ... down. Just sit down. Good.' I turned back to Hoyle. 'And you too, please, Mr Hoyle. You can relax, too. I give you my word we'll sit tight.'

I turned to the rest of them. 'Don't make a liar out of me.'

They sat.

Hoyle sat.

Nobody had been shot. A minor miracle.

'Now. Start at the beginning, Mr Hoyle. What's this all about?'

Even now, he couldn't bring himself to tell

anyone. I suspected years of secrecy were proving difficult to overcome.

'Come on,' said Markham encouragingly. 'Big breath and off you go.'

'It's about ... it's about ... him.'

'You mean ...' began Sykes, and Atherton kicked her before she said Dick the Turd and set him off again. 'Richard III,' she finished.

'Yes, him. I've worked for years. To get here I mean. To be in a position to be able to ...'

'Yes?' said everyone, somewhat impatiently, but it was like trying to get a straight answer from a politician.

He drew a huge breath. 'To be in a position to get to the Battle of Bosworth Field.'

I was gobsmacked. I think we all were.

'Is that all?' demanded Sykes in disbelief, dismissing the final, devastating battle of the Wars of the Roses, the end of the three-hundred-year-old Plantagenet dynasty, and the beginnings of the Tudors with a disparaging flick of the wrist. 'All this just for bloody Bosworth Field?'

'There's no *just* about it,' he shouted angrily. 'It's where he dies.'

'But it's only a battlefield,' she stormed. 'You could have just put in for the jump. Or waited. We were bound to get there one day.'

'Oh yes,' he shouted, contempt dripping from every word. 'Sit quietly and twiddle my thumbs while you lot crash around blowing things up, setting yourselves on fire, getting yourselves injured – or killed. They said it was only a matter of time before

337

someone steps in and sorts you all out.'

'Someone like you, I suppose?'

'Well why not? At least I appreciate the full potential.'

I didn't like the sound of this at all. What potential? And who were 'they'?

'Why don't you start at the beginning?' I said.

'Why don't you make the jump?' Up came the gun again, wavering away in a manner far more terrifying than if he pointed it straight at me.

I sighed. 'Let me put it this way. Tell your story and there's a chance you'll get to Bosworth. Don't tell your story and you'll never get there. Your choice.'

'Yeah, right.'

'No, I told you. I gave my word. Everyone's sitting down. No one will interfere. Tell us your story.'

He sighed 'My name is Richard Hoyle. I'm not American. Or Canadian. I was born in Derbyshire. I'm descended from Richard III. And proud of it.'

'Yes,' I said soothingly, before he went off on one again. 'Now that I know, I can definitely see a resemblance. We all can.'

'I was supplied with papers and a cover story.'

'By whom?'

'Them.'

I couldn't decide if he was being reticent or whether he genuinely didn't know. 'Why?'

'So I could go to Bosworth Field, of course.'

I exchanged a glance with Markham. Poor deluded boy. Someone had targeted him because of his obsession with Richard III. Someone who knew about

St Mary's had offered him a chance to be at Bosworth. To see it. To experience it at first hand. To see his ancestor. How could he resist? And what did he have to do in return?

'Who's "them"?' said Markham, interrupting my train of thought, which was a pity because I was nearly there.

'The people who paid me to come here.'

'To St Mary's?'

'To Bosworth.'

'Why?'

'So I could witness the battle, of course,' he said impatiently. 'Which I'm not doing yet,' he continued significantly.

'Yes, but how does that benefit them?'

He shrugged, blinded by his tunnel vision. He'd probably never even given that a thought. Never queried why someone was doing this for him. Or what they would want in return. Although to be fair, how many of us, suddenly offered an opportunity we'd previously thought unobtainable, would question the motives behind the offer? When we get what we want we don't often look any further.

'Where did these conversations take place?'

'London.'

'Have you ever seen any of these men since?'

'No. The money and papers appeared, just as they said they would, and off I went to Thirsk.'

'Actually,' said Markham to me, 'that's rather clever. They invented the story of him escaping from America and gave him obviously forged papers and we never looked past that. If you're going to falsify documents, disguise them as falsified documents. Neat.'

'Have they made contact with you in any way since?'

'No.'

'Were you *ever* in America?' demanded Sykes.

'No.'

'So everything – every single thing you told us about yourself – was a lie?'

He nodded. 'They said if I'd come from America on obviously forged papers then no one would look at them too closely.'

I refrained from looking at Markham. So much for the Security Section's supposedly rigorous background checks.

'So just to make sure I'm clear. You were provided with money and papers and a backstory for the sole purpose of enabling you to get to Thirsk so that you could join St Mary's?'

'Yes.'

'And from there, jump to Bosworth?'

'Yes.'

'*Why?*'

His eyes shifted. 'They didn't tell me.'

There was a long silence while I stared at the console and had a bit of a think.

'All right,' I said. 'Here's what I'm prepared to do. We return to St Mary's, drop off the trainees and Mr Markham, and then I take you on to Bosworth Field.'

'No! We go now! No more delays.'

'Unacceptable. I won't risk …'

'You can't go without us,' said Sykes, indignantly.

'We want to be hijacked too.'

'You're trainees,' I said, exasperated. 'I'm not allowed to …'

'And you're definitely not going without me,' said Markham.

I shot him a look. He grinned at me.

'That's settled, then,' said Hoyle. 'You said you would go. They all want to go. I want to go. No reason to wait any longer.'

I was left, as usual, without a leg to stand on.

'So,' I said, knowing I was going to regret this but trying to make the best of a difficult situation. 'Bosworth Field it is.'

We didn't jump immediately, of course. Even I'm not that stupid. I confirmed the coordinates with the computer and insisted on holding a briefing as to what to expect once we arrived.

Everyone knows about Bosworth Field. The 22nd August 1485. The end of Richard III, the 'Crookback' of Shakespeare's play. Or Dick the Turd if you were a member of the Sykes School of Slander.

This was the final battle in the decades long struggle between the Houses of Lancaster (Red Rose) and York (White Rose). The causes of the war are complex and bloody and go back a hundred years.

Edward III had too many sons. Not a problem at the time, but his grandson, Henry of Lancaster, usurped the throne as Henry IV. He was vulnerable throughout his short reign but his son, Henry V, hit on the bright idea of reviving the traditional English claim to the French throne and shipping the whole squabbling bunch of troublemakers over to France.

Things were going well and then he stupidly died of dysentery and the whole thing began to fall apart.

Slowly, the English lost their French possessions. The long minority of Henry VI was a disaster and he was so useless when he did grow up that most people probably wished he hadn't bothered anyway. The country was broke and, with the exception of Calais, had nothing to show for it.

His truly unpleasant wife, Margaret of Anjou, managed to turn the relatively neutral Richard of York into an enemy by treating him as one and he rose in revolt, citing his superior claim to the throne.

The Wars of the Roses were a tragedy for nearly everyone. Richard of York was killed. His second son, Edmund of Rutland, was killed. The king's only son, Edward of Westminster, was killed. Huge numbers of the aristocracy were killed. In fact, the only reason Henry Tudor ever had a crack at being king was because he was almost the only Lancastrian left.

There was no doubt these two branches of the Plantagenet line hated each other with a fierce and deadly loathing and the whole thing was about to come to a head on a marshy piece of land between Shenton, Market Bosworth, and Sutton Cheyney. The end of a thirty-two-year war, the end of a dynasty, and the end of a king. The end of the Middle Ages, as well, if you like. The decline of the overmighty medieval barons and the feudal system, and the beginning of the Tudors, the middle classes. And a new religion.

Everything would be different after today. Henry Tudor and his forces march up from Milford Haven. Richard marches from Leicester and ranges his forces along a ridge – probably Ambion Hill. Henry's forces face him across the Redemoor Marsh. Outnumbered, Henry keeps his army together. Richard divides his into three, headed by himself, the elderly Duke of Norfolk, and the Earl of Northumberland, who was in charge of the rearguard.

The really important people, the treacherous Lord Thomas Stanley and his brother Sir William, stand off to one side unwilling to commit themselves either way. Waiting to see how they can twist the events of this day to their advantage.

Everyone knows what happens – Richard, in an effort to prevent Henry Tudor approaching the Stanleys to persuade them to fight for him, leads an all-or-nothing charge of probably less than two hundred knights straight at Henry himself, gambling everything on one reckless throw of the dice.

He doesn't make it. The Stanleys, seeing their chance, fall on him from the rear. Northumberland refuses to come to his assistance. Richard loses his horse in the marsh and is killed. His crown, which he wears to distinguish himself to his own troops is, supposedly, found in a hawthorn bush and placed on Henry's head by Sir William Stanley himself.

Game over for the Plantagenets.

So we were jumping to a battlefield. Not the ideal place to take a bunch of trainees. I seemed to be the only one worried by this. Everyone else was jumping with excitement.

I checked the coordinates very, very carefully and then I did a parallel calculation, which I passed to Atherton for confirmation.

Hoyle was shifting impatiently in his seat, but had the sense to keep quiet. It wouldn't benefit him if we landed in the wrong place at the wrong time.

I asked him if he'd calculated the coordinates himself.

'No, but I verified them and they are correct.'

Yes, they were. They were spot on, 22nd August 1485; slightly to the south of Ambion Hill. Right in the middle of the action. I wondered whether the people who had supplied these coordinates had expected Hoyle to survive. Or even wanted him to.

Never mind Hoyle. Would we survive?

As I saw it, there were two areas of concern. Firstly there was the battlefield itself, although we should be safe enough inside the pod. Unfortunately for us, inside the pod was our unstable hijacker, highly strung, twitching with nerves, and armed. On reflection, we might be safer outside after all.

I turned to Hoyle.

'Your plans on arrival?'

'To observe. Stop procrastinating. Get on with it.'

I couldn't delay any longer. Slowly, hoping some sort of inspiration would strike within the next twenty seconds or so, I laid in the coordinates and had Atherton check they were correct.

He nodded and sat back down again.

Hoyle pointed the gun at me.

'Now.'

'Computer, initiate jump.'
The world went white.

Twenty-one

This was not my first battlefield.

Nor was it Markham's.

It was the trainees', however.

The first thing that always strikes you is the noise. There were over twenty thousand men gathered here today. Orders were shouted. Drums rolled. Horses neighed. Even now, only minutes before the battle commenced, smiths and armourers were still busy at their forges, hammering away at weapons and armour. Grooms were getting replacement mounts ready. Pages and squires ran to and from with spare weapons and last-minute helmets, weaving their way through the chaos. The whole area seethed and hummed like a beehive.

As far as I could make out, we were somewhere within the Redemoor Marsh. And marshy it was. Not just the boggy wetness of badly drained land, this was real marshland. I could see patches of murky standing water interspersed with clumps of coarse, reedy grass. Stands of straggly willows would give us some cover, and I could see fallen, rotting tree trunks and spindly birch trees scattered around. It could have been worse. We weren't completely exposed.

'Good grief,' said Markham. 'We've landed in the Great Grimpen Mire.'

Atherton stared at him. 'When did you read *The Hound of the Baskervilles*?'

'Fell off the stable roof.'

Atherton waited, but no more was forthcoming.

I could see the Yorkist banner, Richard's White Boar, high on the ridge above us. What I assumed was the Earl of Northumberland's rear guard, under his banner of red and white, was stationed behind the hill.

Henry Tudor's army, fighting under the Red Dragon, faced the Yorkists in a solid block, under the command of the Earl of Oxford, who had forbidden his men to fight more than ten feet from this banner, fearing that if they split up, they faced being ridden down by Richard's knights.

Off to one side lay the boggy ground in which we were concealed and that would prove so fatal to Richard, and opposite that, forming the fourth side of the square, Lord Stanley and his brother waited to see which way the cat would jump.

It was very quiet inside our pod as three trainees and one hijacker suddenly came face to face with the realities of war.

I said quietly, 'Well, Mr Hoyle. Now what?'

He stood up and moved towards the door. 'You can go now. I don't need you any longer.'

'What?' gasped Sykes, outraged beyond words. 'We're not a bloody taxi service, you know.'

He slapped the door control and suddenly the pod was full of the sounds of men and horses and the smells of sunshine, bruised grass, and slightly stagnant water.

Markham stood up. 'I'm coming with you.'

'We're all coming with you,' said Atherton.

Up came the gun again. 'No, you're not. Stay back, all of you. I'm here now. I won't hesitate to shoot. Remember, I don't need you any longer.'

I believed him. His gun was swinging back and forth, trying to cover us all at once and he was vibrating like a badly balanced washing machine.

'Are you sure?' said Markham. 'You're the one trembling like an aspen.'

North stared at him. 'Trembling like a what?'

'An aspen. It's a tree.'

'Don't you mean an ash?'

'They make coffins out of ash,' said Sykes helpfully.

Markham turned to her. 'No they don't. That's pine.'

Sykes opened her mouth to respond, and possibly for the first time in her life, was silenced.

'Shut up!' shouted Hoyle and his voice cracked with emotion. 'Shut up! Shut up! For God's sake. All of you. For once, can't you all ... just ... shut ... up.'

Well, there you go. We'd finally managed to push him over the edge. Not exactly the recommended procedure when trapped in an enclosed space by a madman with a gun.

Not taking his eyes off us and swinging the gun from left to right, he backed out of the pod and the door closed behind him.

'Is it just me,' said Sykes in the silence, 'or was he

a bit unbalanced there at the end?'

'Sorry, Max,' said Markham. 'I was hoping for an opportunity to grab him.'

'Me too,' said Sykes.

Atherton grinned at her. 'You?'

'Why not?' she said, shifting her weight ever so slightly.

'No reason,' he said hastily. 'He's gone, anyway, that's the main thing, and it's not our fault he's got the life expectancy of a cliff-top lemming. What harm can he possibly do?'

'He's got a gun,' I said, flatly, and silence fell.

'What do you think he's up to?' said Atherton, turning to me.

'At a guess,' I said, 'he's going to try and prevent Richard's all-or-nothing charge towards Henry. That was certainly the turning point of the battle.'

'Jesus, Max. How can he possibly hope to get away with that?'

'No idea. Speaking as his primary trainer, I'm slightly annoyed at his failure to absorb anything I've said over the past months. I tell you, if – when – I get my hands on Mr Hoyle, he's a dead man.'

'It might come to that,' said Markham seriously, and I nodded. It might. If we couldn't stop him then we'd have to kill him. Because if we didn't, History would. And probably us as well.

I sighed. 'Mr Atherton, please take off your trousers.'

'There you go, Phil,' said Sykes. 'Another fantasy fulfilled.'

He went scarlet and climbed out of his trousers.

I ripped off my coat and giant skirt. It took both Sykes and North to get me out of my corset. Sykes resorted to a sharp implement and when she'd finished, no one was never going to be climbing into that corset again. I closed my mind to the grief I was going to get from Mrs Enderby and scrambled into Atherton's trousers.

'Braces? Belt?'

'Here,' he said, handing me his cravat. I tied myself into his trousers and Sykes rolled up the bottoms for me. I thanked the god of historians for my boots.

Markham wrenched open a locker and pulled out a tag reader. Because Hoyle was tagged. We all were, in case we were lost or injured. Actually, there's no 'in case' about it. 'When' is probably the more accurate word. Anyway, to help us locate lost or injured historians, we had tag readers, which, in theory, can home in on the lost or injured etc. The reality is that they're bloody useless. They actually only sound off if your target is about six feet in front of you. We generally find that jumping up and down shouting, 'Hoi! I'm over here, stupid,' is much more effective.

He also took pair of stun guns. Tossing one at me, he headed towards the door.

I turned to the console. 'Computer. Additional authority Atherton. Authority Maxwell. Five zero alpha nine eight zero four bravo.'

'Confirmed.'

I turned to the trainees, who were standing open mouthed.

'Listen to me very carefully. You will stay here. You will not leave this pod. I don't know what Mr Hoyle is up to but it is my job to find out. Markham's job is to protect me while I do it. Your job is to stay here. I know you're not happy about that. I wouldn't be either but I can't function properly if I don't know you're safe. Therefore, your instructions are to remain inside the pod. Document and record by all means, but if anything goes wrong – and it will – your second priority is to declare an emergency evacuation. The pod will get you back to St Mary's where you can brief Major Guthrie and assist in any rescue. You will not be able to do that if you are dead or dying on the battlefield out there. It's hard but unavoidable. There will be plenty of opportunities in the future for you to die a painful and messy death. Just not today. Mr Atherton, you have command. Close the door behind us.'

I stepped out of the door straight into a bog. I looked down and watched my feet sink up to my ankles in brown water. It was just one of those days.

I don't know what arrangements appertain to the formal opening of a battle. There's never any clearly given signal that I can see. It's almost as if there's some sort of gentleman's agreement. 'So that's agreed then, chaps. Kick-off at eleven. Unless it's raining, of course, in which case the whole thing's off and we'll try again tomorrow.'

Because at the exact moment we exited the pod, trumpets sounded and over to our left, the Red Dragon banner began to move. Henry's army was advancing. I could feel squidgy earth moving under my feet. The battle had begun.

Markham pulled me down. 'You stay with me, Max. I'll get us wherever we need to be but you stay behind me at all times.'

I nodded.

I could hear Atherton in my ear.

'We've split the screen. North is covering Henry Tudor. Sykes has Richard. And I will keep my eye on the trainee formerly known as Laurence Hoyle.'

'I like Atherton,' said Markham, confidentially. 'If you don't want him, I bet Major Guthrie would snap him up.'

'Please ask Major Guthrie to keep his thieving hands off my trainees.'

Atherton said, 'Um, you do know we can hear you in here, don't you?

Barely had the words left his mouth when a huge fusillade of cannon shot sounded from the lower slopes of Ambion Hill. White smoke drifted across the marsh. Horses everywhere screamed – whether in panic or battle fury was unclear. The king's army had opened fire.

The battle was on.

There aren't many advantages to lying in a bog while a battle is fought over your head. About the only one is that you're left to enjoy sole occupancy of the bog while everything happens elsewhere.

I said, 'Mr Atherton, any sign of him?' Because you can't see much when your head's only six inches off the ground and you're hiding behind a tussock of reedy grass.

'Yes. Fifty yards ahead of you and slightly to your right. He's on the move again.'

And so were we, slinking along on our bellies. I could smell wet earth, muddy water, gunpowder, and horses. There were insects everywhere.

'Where's he going?' said Atherton, suddenly, and I could hear the alarm in his voice. 'No. He's going the wrong way.'

'What?'

'He's not heading towards Richard. Where is he going?'

'How should I know? We can't see a bloody thing here.'

Smoke from the cannon fire was still drifting across the battlefield, obscuring our view. And hiding us, of course, for which we should be very grateful.

'Stop a minute,' said Markham, pulling me behind some sort of coarse bush. 'Let's just get our bearings and work out what's happening. Atherton, report.'

'Oxford's trying to get his forces around the bog so they can get to grips with Richard's army. That's happening to your left. They're being hampered by cannon fire, but they'll be clear in a minute. Hold on.'

I could hear North yammering away in the background.

'Another part of Richard's army is on the move. It's Norfolk. He's moving to engage the Lancastrian forces. Bloody hell, Max, you have to get out of there. You're going to be right in the middle of it.'

'Not without the cause of all the trouble. Can you see him anywhere?'

'No. And the archers are moving up. Watch your

heads.'

'This is stupid,' muttered Markham. 'We can't see a thing and we're going to die. Stop and think, everyone. We have to work out what he's going to do and where he's going to go and put ourselves there ready to intercept him. Thoughts?'

'Well,' said Atherton, in my ear, 'according to the computer records, Oxford's men hold their ground and some of Norfolk's men run away. Richard orders up Northumberland to reinforce them but he doesn't move. Henry rides towards the Stanleys to persuade them to fight for him and Richard decides to risk everything on one throw of the dice. He charges Henry. If Hoyle somehow persuades him not to do so …'

'But how?' demanded North. 'Who's going to believe some idiot who wanders in off a battlefield and says not to do it? He'd never get anywhere near the king. It's madness. He can't possibly hope to succeed.'

'No,' I said slowly, as the thought that had been tickling the back of my mind slowly coalesced. 'Not Richard. Henry. Oh my God. He's not heading for Richard. Of course he's not. It's Henry Tudor who's his target.'

'He'll never get to Henry,' said North, scornfully. 'It's well known that Henry Tudor stayed safely at the back.' Her tone of voice implied he was the sort of man to drink his own bathwater as well.

'Except when he left his army to persuade Stanley to fight for him.'

'But Hoyle would have to fight his way through

the main part of the battle *and* Stanley's forces. He'd never survive long enough to get close. It would be suicide.'

'He doesn't have to,' I said. 'He's got a gun.'

Silence. I mean, I know there was a battle going on but all I remember is complete silence.

'He's going to kill Henry,' said Markham, quietly.

'Henry's armoured,' said North, quickly.

'He'll shoot his horse,' said Sykes. 'That's what I'd do.'

I made a mental note never to cross her.

'I'd shoot his horse,' she continued, 'and then, when he's helpless on the ground, someone else will kill him.'

'Just like Richard,' said Atherton. 'He lost his horse and they closed in and killed him. Hoyle's planning to do the same to Henry. Max …'

'Don't panic,' I said, panicking like mad. Nobody heard me. They were all panicking as well. Everyone was talking at once.

Atherton's voice sounded in my ear. 'Shut up, both of you. Max, he's on the move again. To your right. He's heading towards Ambion Hill.'

It was hard going. We were blind-sighted and completely reliant on Atherton's instructions. I wasn't even sure in which direction we were crawling. I know we were very close. All around us, I could hear the sounds of men fighting and screaming and dying. The clash of steel upon steel. Little red ribbons of blood began to colour the water around me. Cannon fired, causing the soft ground to shudder with every shot. The smell of gunpowder seared my nostrils. I could feel the sun, warm on my back. Elsewhere – away from here – it was still a lovely summer's day.

We floundered around in the wet soil. I was really glad I'd had the forethought to divest myself of acres of petticoats. I said to Markham, 'Can you see him?'

Very cautiously, Markham raised his head. The tag reader bleeped faintly which meant we were reasonably close. For the first time, I gave some thought to how exactly we would get near enough to stun an armed man in the middle of a battlefield. Nothing sprang immediately to mind.

'This way,' said Markham, and we dropped back into the mud again.

Suddenly, there he was.

And he wasn't the only one.

Twenty-two

You get them in every area of conflict. From the massive set pieces of Waterloo all the way down to an impromptu pub fight. People who hang around on the fringes, talking the talk, and then at the first hint of trouble are straight out of the toilet window and walking the walk off down the street.

Deserters.

They line up with their mates and as soon as the arrows start flying, they melt away. In this instance, they'd had the same idea as us and were crawling through the boggy ground. The only difference was that we were crawling towards and they were crawling away. There were three of them, all moving slowly through the long, reedy grass. They'd abandoned their cumbersome pikes in favour of short, wicked-looking daggers. And all of them were on a collision course with Hoyle, who, concentrating on events elsewhere, had no idea of his peril.

'Well,' said Markham softly. 'Does this solve our problem for us?'

Did it?

If we did nothing and Hoyle got a dagger between the shoulder blades, then we could all go home. I could hear my report to Dr Bairstow now. 'He was attacked by three blokes, sir, while we stood by and did nothing.'

Somehow, even given that it was his own bloody fault, it didn't sound good.

But – and it was a big but – he had a gun. If he turned his head and saw them – or us ... He'd already committed at least one capital crime today and if he really was prepared to shoot Henry then the slaughter of three seemingly unimportant contemporaries wouldn't cause him any concern at all. We had to intervene.

'You take the one on the right.' said Markham, reading my mind. 'Right is the side away from the battle.'

'Very funny.'

We stood up and ran. They heard us coming and wheeled around. Markham had his stun gun ready and before his target could get his dagger up, he'd zapped him one. The man crumpled back into the mud.

I was grappling with the one on the far right. The two of us fell to the ground, scrabbling and splashing in the warm mud.

My world was full of heavy, grunting men and that's not anything like as much fun as it sounds. I was underneath one of them. The one who smelled of onions and sweat. He had a knife. I'd dropped my stun gun and had both hands grabbing his wrist in the approved manner because, for some reason, I couldn't see a thing, when I heard a clunk, and he went limp. I heaved him to one side and tried to sit up.

'You do know you forgot to take off your bonnet,

don't you?' said Markham, hauling me out of the mud.

I pulled it out of my eyes and looked around. 'Where did Hoyle go?'

'To your left,' said Atherton in my ear. 'I have him about twenty yards away. Heading away from you.'

I surveyed the three groaning men.

'Leave them,' said Markham. 'They only attacked us because we went for them. They won't bother us again. All they want to do is get out of this.'

They weren't the only ones, but in the interests of morale and setting a good example to others, I said nothing.

Usually, when we observe any sort of conflict, we do it from higher ground, or from a safe distance, or from inside the pod. This was the first time I'd ever actually been inside a battle. How anyone was able to work out what was going on was a mystery to me.

There were no neat lines tidily engaging each other face to face. I saw a struggling melee of men, none of them wearing any discernible uniform or badge. There wasn't even a great deal of swordplay. Most of them just seemed to be pushing away at each other as the two armies struggled to gain ground. The whole thing was actually like a giant rugby scrum from which injured men and horses struggled to drag themselves away to safety. The noise tore at my ears. Cannon boomed. I couldn't see where the balls landed, but each explosion was greeted with fresh screams and shouts.

The faintly comforting smells of wet earth and water were slowly being overwhelmed by the stench of hot horses, gunpowder, and blood. A nasty, metallic mixture that made my nostrils twitch and dried my mouth.

Arrows rained down seemingly indiscriminately. To me, everything seemed chaos and confusion. This was the defining battle of the age and from where I was standing – admittedly up to my ankles in a bog – I had no idea who was who and certainly no idea who was winning.

Thank God for Atherton. A fresh fanfare of horns broke out.

'I think that's the king calling up Northumberland's forces from the rear,' said Atherton. 'You don't have to worry about him. He doesn't move today.'

No, Northumberland refused to obey the king's summons. Whether from treachery or because he simply couldn't manoeuvre his men around the boggy area is still disputed today. Whatever the reason, his forces were one small thing we didn't have to worry about.

We needed to get a move on, however. At the moment, Henry Tudor was safely ensconced at the rear of his forces, but the moment he emerged to call on the Stanleys for support, he was vulnerable. We had to find and neutralise Hoyle. Because if we didn't then History would take us all out.

I pulled Markham to the ground. 'If you were Hoyle, where would you go?'

'Higher ground, if I could. To see what's going on and get my bearings.'

'Yes,' said Atherton. 'He's stopped. Your two

o'clock. Between thirty and fifty yards.'

'Copy that,' said Markham. 'Max, watch our backs.'

We set off again, crawling with a little more speed now. The ground was firmer and drier. We were moving away from the safety of the marshland.

'You need to hurry,' said Atherton, urgently. 'Henry's army is opening ranks. He's on the move towards the Stanleys.'

And so was Richard. We could hear the horns and shouted orders as Richard gathered his knights around him for that final, gallant, doomed, hopeless charge at Henry. He would so nearly get there. But nearly was not good enough.

'We must move now,' I said, frantic with anxiety. 'Hoyle will attack Henry before Richard loses his horse.'

'Just wait. Wait until Hoyle's attention is on what is happening.'

We inched forwards. Viewing a battle at ankle height is one of the scariest things I've ever done. I kept thinking what would happen if the tide of fighting suddenly turned in our direction. Everything out there would just sweep straight over the top of us.

'There,' said Markham. And there was Hoyle, crouching in a stand of stunted, waterlogged birches, craning his head left and right. Looking for his target.

'Surely he's too far away,' I said. 'He can't have a range of much more than twenty yards,' and even as the words left my mouth, he stood up and began to run. Towards the fighting.

Markham muttered a curse that made the air

bubble around us and set off after him. I embellished the curse and set off after him. I'd say we flung caution to the wind, but that implies we'd been acting with caution in the first place. There are many words to describe the actions of two idiots crawling through a major battlefield in search of a fanatic with a gun but believe me, cautious is not one of them.

Markham pulled away from me. I'm not a sprinter. I dared not spare even a glance for what was going on around me. I ran after Markham. Who ran after Hoyle. Who ran towards Henry. Who was galloping towards Lord Stanley.

And then everything happened all at once.

The king's forces swept down in a tidal wave of thundering hooves, wild-eyed horses, and armoured knights, their arms rising and falling as they slaughtered everything around them, pounding after the king's banner as Richard tore towards his enemy. They were unstoppable. Shouting incoherently, Henry's escort broke up in confusion.

At the head of the charge, Richard himself, easily recognisable by the crown on his helmet, bore down on Henry Tudor. Men and horses scattered before him and even though I knew how this would end, for one treacherous moment I honestly thought Richard was going to be successful. That he would actually reach Henry after all and the entire course of History would be changed.

Henry's bodyguard moved to surround him. Not a warrior Plantagenet, he was hiding behind them, making no move to engage the enemy in personal combat. Not so Richard, who was well to the front of the charge, falling upon Henry's standard bearer, Sir William Brandon, with such ferocity that he shattered his own lance.

At that moment, only one person stood between the king and his target and that was the gigantic Sir John Cheyne, one of Henry's bodyguards, at six feet eight inches tall, easily the biggest man on the battlefield and probably in all of England as well. In one smooth movement, Richard wheeled about and using the momentum of his horse, slammed the remains of his lance into Sir John's head, striking with such vigour that both Sir John and his horse crashed to the ground.

And there he was. Henry Tudor. Alone. Exposed. Vulnerable.

With a roar that was audible even over the clamour of battle, Richard drew his sword and charged. And then, just as he was poised to fall upon Henry, to overrun his small force, when victory was literally within his grasp, the Stanleys finally made up their minds. Trumpets sounded. With a roar that drowned out everything happening around us, the front ranks began to move, smashing into Richard's tiny force from the rear.

It is very possible that until that moment, Lord Stanley himself had had no idea to which army he would commit his support. To Richard's threat to execute Stanley's son unless he joined the attack on Henry, Stanley had contemptuously replied that he had other sons. When Henry sent messages asking for his aid, he had returned a vague response, refusing to commit himself either way.

Now, with Richard far from his own lines, isolated and vulnerable, he had seen his chance. With his actions, suddenly the tide of battle turned.

Things went very bad very quickly.

The fighting was brutal. Everyone out there today had everything to lose. No quarter was asked and certainly none was given. The world was a violent place. Men screamed and fell. Horses trampled them into the mud and then fell themselves, hamstrung or pierced by arrows. The ground ran thick with blood.

Richard himself, still horsed, was laying about him, right and left. His visor was raised, but I couldn't see his face. His golden crown glinted in the sunlight. Beside him, his own standard-bearer, Sir Percival Thribald, went down as his horse was cut from underneath him.

Shouting, 'The king lives! The king lives!' he struggled to his knees, keeping the White Boar flying high. A rallying point for Richard's beleaguered forces.

Three men turned on him. At no time did he seek to defend himself, devoting all his efforts to keeping the king's banner flying.

'The king lives! The king lives!'

He disappeared in a sudden scrum of armoured men.

When they drew back. Sir Percival lay in a pool of his own blood. Both his legs had been hacked off. He was screaming all the while, but still he kept Richard's standard upright. Keeping the White Boar flying, providing reassurance to his followers that the king still lived and that while the banner flew, there was hope.

There was no one to come to his aid. Richard's tiny band was hopelessly outnumbered. Knights fell from their horses and did not get up.

'The king lives. To the king. Protect the ki—'

A sword swung. The banner tilted. The sword swung again. Even as I watched, the White Boar dipped for the last time and then slowly, very slowly, fell sideways into the bloody melee.

And Hoyle, whom, believe it or not, I had nearly forgotten about, stepped from his hiding place and raised his gun.

Markham pushed me aside, stood up, and shouted, 'Hoyle!'

He spun around and fired. Or rather, the gun went off. I wasn't sure he was in complete control of himself.

I didn't hear the sound of the shot, but beside me, Markham went down. I ran straight at Hoyle. I didn't stop to think about anything. I just flew at him. My weight carried him backwards and we both crashed to the ground.

He fought like the madman I was pretty sure he was, but we were both desperate. We both had everything to lose. I clamped myself around his gun arm and hung on as best I could. I had no idea whether Markham had been hit or not. Whether he would be able to come to my aid ... If I could just prevent him from firing that shot. He slammed his fist hard into the side of my face and for a moment, everything went fuzzy. I felt myself falling to one side and then, miraculously, Markham was there, pulling him off me. I left them to it. My priority was the gun. I groped around as the two of them struggled, standing on me, falling over me, rolling around. Markham's language was appalling. Hoyle was alternately cursing and crying. Someone stood on my hand.

There it was. I crawled forwards and one of them kicked it away from me, sending it spinning into a shallow pool of water.

'Bollocks!'

'What's going on?' shouted Atherton on the com, 'What's happening?'

I had neither the time nor the breath to reply.

I lunged for the gun, scooped it up, made it safe, wondered what to do with it, and had a brainwave. I pulled off my bonnet, stuffed the gun in the high crown, and jammed it back on my head. Who says historians can't improvise?

That done, I turned my attention back to Markham, who was not faring well. Whether fuelled by fear or desperation, Hoyle was definitely coming off better in this particular struggle. Markham was underneath, slowly sinking down into the liquid mud and water.

I swung a rotting piece of wood, which disintegrated on impact, but did the job. Hoyle went down, falling sideways with a splash.

That done, I collapsed alongside them and took two or three deep breaths, which was all I allowed myself before attending to Markham.

'Are you hurt? Please tell me you're not hurt. I can't possibly take you back again with yet another injury. Hunter goes mad, you know.'

He opened the one eye that wasn't swollen shut. 'Does she? She told me she didn't care.'

Hoyle stirred. Markham rolled him onto his front and pinned both his hands behind his back. That done, we sat on him and took stock of each other.

He nodded at my face. 'That's going to sting in the morning.'

'It bloody stings now,' I said grumpily.

There are people who bear their troubles bravely and then there's me.

'How is he?'

Hoyle was in a bad way. Wet, muddy, bloody, unfocussed, and desperate. He kept twisting around, trying to see what was happening, alternately cursing and begging to be let go.

'Let me see. For God's sake, let me see. I can't be here and not see.'

Markham and I exchanged glances and let him sit up.

'No sudden moves,' warned Markham.

He nodded, wiping a trail of blood from his nose. His hands were swollen, bruised, and shaking. Tears merged with the snot and blood. I thought all the fight had gone out of him.

We crouched amongst the rotting trees and watched. The fighting had surged sideways, right up against the edge of the marsh and it was probably safer to stay put than try to make a run for it. Whoever had calculated those coordinates for Hoyle had done a cracking job. I'd never been so close before. The action was brutal and bloody. Only yards away, men were literally being hacked to pieces or trampled into the mud. I saw an arm, still clutching a sword, fly through the air. The ground was red. Men lay pinned beneath horses, screaming for aid.

Someone set up a cry. 'The king is dead!'

'No,' shouted Hoyle in a sudden panic. 'No, he's not.'

He was right. Not yet he wasn't. Away to our left, Richard, still easily recognisable despite being liberally splattered with mud and blood, was fighting like a man possessed. His sword arm rose and fell relentlessly. Men fell beneath his fury as he spurred his horse forward. Henry Tudor was only a sword's length away, frantically pulling his horse backwards as his bodyguard disintegrated around him.

I couldn't see his face – unlike Richard, he never raised his visor – but I could see him kicking at his horse, trying to find space to turn him in this mad melee. So desperate to escape that he hadn't even drawn his sword.

Richard was standing in his stirrups, roaring at him to stand and fight. His horse, trained to fight for him, was trampling those who sought to stand in his way as the king urged him on through blood and bodies, fighting his way towards the seemingly helpless Henry Tudor.

This was the deciding moment. How could he fail? Richard was, literally, only feet away, desperate to get to grips with the hated Henry Tudor. Henry would fall, surely. No one stood between him and Richard's ferocity. The king, teeth clenched, was literally straining every muscle to reach his hated adversary. The last Lancastrian. Henry would fall and the

Plantagenets would endure. How could it be otherwise?

And then, in the blink of an eye, everything changed. Blinded by his overwhelming urge to kill the usurper, Richard had allowed himself to become separated from the main body of his already beleaguered forces. His desperation and fury had driven him far beyond his fellow knights and then, suddenly, seemingly from nowhere, he was surrounded by Stanley's men – all stabbing and swinging their weapons, circling him, cutting him off.

His horse, splattered with blood and gore, wild-eyed and foaming, reared up, seeking to escape. His back legs sank deeply into the soft ground. At the same time, Richard leaned over to despatch another man at arms. There was a flurry, I couldn't see exactly what happened – his horse was thrashing around in panic, trying to break free from the bog – and the next minute, the king was unhorsed. He thumped face-down onto the ground and his helmet, with the crown still attached, rolled free across the trampled grass.

A massive roar went up. Henry's men closed in for the kill.

Hoyle struggled, shouting incoherently. It took all our strength to hold him down in the mud. The fight had not gone out of him after all.

'A horse!' he shouted, voice cracking with emotion. 'A horse! For pity's sake, someone give him a horse. There. There. Look.'

I looked over my shoulder. There was indeed a spare horse, standing miraculously quietly, reins trailing on the ground.

My momentary hesitation was all Hoyle needed. With a massive effort, he threw us both aside, scrambled to his feet, and started to run towards the horse.

Two mounted men came out of nowhere. Moving fast. The leader slammed into Hoyle's chest, knocking him clean off his feet. He flew through the air and crashed heavily to the ground. Without pausing, the second rider rode straight over the top of him.

I never saw where they came from and I never saw where they went. I saw no badges. They carried no banners.

We crawled over to where he lay, white-faced, spread-eagled in the mud. I stared in horror. The damage was … extensive. I didn't even know where to begin. There was no way anyone could make this right.

'Jesus,' whispered Markham, looking down at him. 'Max?'

I shook my head.

He was trying to speak.

'Lift him up,' said Markham, quickly. 'He wants to see.'

So we did. We carefully raised his shoulders and Markham knelt behind him to support his weight. So that he could see the end.

Richard was up on his feet.

Brandishing his sword, he swept a vicious circle about himself, bellowing, 'Treason! Treason! Treason!' His voice rose above the sounds of battle around us.

No one came to his aid.

He was surrounded by Henry's men, but no one moved. For what seemed a very long time, no one moved. No one wanted to make the first move against the king.

'A horse,' murmured Hoyle, bubbles frothing on his lips as he spoke. 'All he needed. No bastard brought him a horse.'

No, they didn't. There are many who say he was a good king. That he didn't kill the princes in the tower. That he didn't murder his wife to marry his niece. That he was a good man. A good soldier. A good king. But when the chips were down – when men had a choice to make – no one came to his aid. No bastard brought him a horse.

But no one had the balls for the final attack, either. We were some distance away, but I could hear men panting, see their chests heaving as they struggled to get their breath. Circling the king. Waiting for an opening. This was a pivotal moment in History but no one wanted to be first one to strike. To kill a king.

Richard was turning with them, sword still outstretched. Still dangerous. He was smaller than I had expected and very slender. Frail, almost, but he was a formidable fighter and everyone knew it.

I saw a pale, mud-splattered face. Dark eyes. Hair, dark with sweat, plastered to his head. At his feet, the White Boar lay twisted and bloody in the mud.

Then, although no word was spoken that I could hear, they all moved at once.

Richard had nowhere to go. There was no one to

come to his aid. This was the end and he must have known it, but still he fought. He swung once. A man fell into the crowd and was trampled.

The first blow caught the king across the forehead sending him off balance. He staggered but stayed on his feet.

A moment later, behind him, a man swung his halberd in a wild, wide circle. The impact sliced off the back part of Richard's skull.

Blood and brain matter sprayed a pink arc in the sunshine.

The sword fell from his hand. He dropped to his knees, swaying slightly, but still not dead. His lips moved.

With a roar of frustration, another nameless man stepped forwards and thrust his sword through the base of his skull.

He twitched – once – twice – and then slowly fell forwards onto his face in the mud.

Suddenly brave, they fell on the body with cries of triumph, hacking and stabbing. There were so many of them they got in each other's way. Everything and everyone was red with blood.

They tore off his armour. Even the padded jerkin and linen he wore underneath. Everyone was scrabbling for a souvenir. Fights broke out. Men were kicking his naked body around. Someone drew a sword.

'We should go,' I whispered, and Markham nodded. It would do Hoyle no good to see what they did to him next.

He stifled a cry of pain as we heaved him to his

feet and with an arm over each shoulder, we splashed back to the pod.

Behind us, I heard a shout of laughter.

The battle had disintegrated into chaos. Everyone was taking up the shout. 'The king is dead. Richard is dead.' Men and horses were running in all directions. Many of them fled into the bog, blind in their panic. Twice, someone barged into me, leaving me floundering around in brackish water, struggling not to bring Hoyle down on top of me. The water smelled awful and tasted worse.

Everyone had taken up the cry. 'Richard is dead. The king is dead.'

We'd have been lost if it wasn't for Atherton who guided us back. The pod wasn't as far as I'd thought. We'd spent so long crawling around and hiding in the bushes that I'd completely lost my sense of direction.

We didn't try to hide. We just put our heads down and moved as fast as we could. Hoyle's feet dragged behind him. We tried not to, but we hurt him – I know we did, but he hardly made a sound. Once he tried to tell us to leave him and Markham told him to shut up. I wondered myself why we were doing it, but we're St Mary's and we don't leave our people behind.

He was a dead weight. I struggled in the soft ground. We might none of us have made it back but for Atherton, who disobeyed instructions, left the pod, and came to meet us. I was too thankful to relinquish Hoyle to argue. Pulling out my stun gun, I covered our backs, but I needn't have bothered. It wasn't a retreat – it was a rout. Men were flinging down armour and weapons and running for their lives.

375

Desperate to get away. To escape the new king's vengeance.

Somewhere back there, Sir William Stanley was pulling Richard's crown out of a hawthorn bush. Henry Tudor would leave the battlefield as Henry VII.

Richard would leave naked, slung across a horse with a sword rammed between his buttocks. The humiliation wound.

'Why are you here?' I said to Atherton, in mild exasperation. 'Does nobody listen to a word I say?'

'I came to get my trousers back,' said Atherton. 'If anything happens to them I'm in dead trouble with Mrs Enderby, and you know how brutal she can be.'

He had a point.

We laid Hoyle gently on the floor, propped him up, and angled the screen so he could see what was happening outside. He watched the rout. The king's army fleeing the field in all directions. We saw Henry stand over Richard's body, sword in hand. Men cheered as if he had actually done something brave. The traitors stepped up to receive their rewards from the new king.

Richard's body was mercifully obscured. Hoyle shouldn't see what they had done to him.

Tears ran down his face, but not from the pain.

We knelt around him. They were all looking at me and there was nothing I could do. Except get him back to St Mary's. And for what? To me, there's always been something wrong with nursing someone back to health so you can execute them with a clear conscience.

And it wasn't completely his fault. Someone had taken advantage of his obsession and sent him here to die. Someone knew there was no way History would ever allow him kill Henry Tudor. Someone sent him here to get St Mary's into trouble. He'd been used. We all had.

I caught Markham's eye. His face was grim. His thoughts were following mine.

'Why?' he said softly.

I shrugged. 'He said it himself. So someone who appreciates the full potential of St Mary's can take over.'

'He's dying, isn't he?'

I nodded.

Hoyle coughed, more blood bubbling from his mouth, and pulled at my trousers. 'Please. I don't want to go back. Made a mess of things. Leave me here.'

I looked at him. Impact with the first horse had crushed his chest. The second horse had trampled him. Destriers aren't light. You have to be a powerful horse to carry the weight of a knight and his armour. His chest was the wrong shape. He could barely breathe. He couldn't possibly have very long.

What should I do?

'Leave me here,' he whispered. 'They can bury me with all the others. Near Richard.'

I sat back on my heels. The fallen were buried at St James's Church, Sutton Cheyney. Richard, as we all now know, was buried at the church of the Grey Friars in Leicester.

I sat quietly and had a bit of a think.

'Leave me here. Please. Everyone hates me.'

'Of course we're not leaving you,' said Markham indignantly. 'What sort of people do you think we are?'

I looked at his fellow trainees. They didn't hate him. Atherton was cradling his head. Sykes was gently washing his face with water. North was covering him with a blanket. I felt a sudden glow of pride. They were going to make great historians.

I made a decision.

'Richard,' I remembered to use his proper name. 'I've been thinking and there's a greater service you can perform for him than ... well ... the one you had in mind today. What do you say?'

He nodded, slightly.

'Mr Atherton ...' I began to issue instructions.

Markham listened with his mouth open. 'Well, I'll be buggered. Max ...'

'It'll be fine,' I said with only the slightest twinge of guilt.

Twenty-three

I instructed North to interrogate the computer. Sykes and Atherton started working on new coordinates. Markham stayed with Hoyle while I rummaged through the med kit.

I shot Hoyle with every pain-killing med I could find. The combined effect would probably kill him, but he wouldn't live long enough for that to matter.

I set Markham to check the read-outs. We'd had two jumps. One to Bristol and one to Bosworth and we should still be fine, but I wanted to make at least two more. There should be no problem with the cells, but pods need frequent aligning. There's no other reason for keeping the Technical Section around. If you don't align them then they start to drift. And anything can set them off. When I first arrived at St Mary's there was a rumour that an historian had changed a light bulb in the toilet and the pod kept drifting a decade to the left until some genius had worked out why. I'm still not sure I believe that one.

We made Hoyle as comfortable as we could and I joined the others at the console.

'How's it going?'

Atherton brought up his calculations. 'We're

cutting it fine.'

'We have to. Go back too far and it won't be there. Go back too soon and we'll run afoul of the hundred-year rule. We have to get it right on the nose ...'

They nodded.

'Does everyone know what to do when we get there?

Markham and Sykes held up the canisters of the anti-bacteriological paint we used on the decontamination strips. 'Yes.'

'Mr Atherton, do you have the exact position?'

'No. But I think I have it to within about ten feet.'

'Close enough for St Mary's work. Miss North and Mr Atherton, you will remain in the pod with Mr Hoyle. Should anything go wrong, you are our backup.'

They weren't just backup. Hoyle didn't have long and no one should die alone.

They understood and for Hoyle's benefit, pretended they didn't. Besides, they wouldn't be historians if they didn't argue.

'Why? Why do we have to stay here?'

'Well, for a start, Mr Atherton isn't wearing any trousers.'

He looked down and went scarlet again. 'Give me back my trousers this minute.'

I pulled off Atherton's trousers and began to struggle back into my skirt. Something had gone wrong with the crinoline, and I was now considerably higher on one side than the other. Mrs Enderby was going to stare at me reproachfully.

Atherton was regarding his trousers with horror.

'What have you done to them?'

'Nothing. They're just a bit ... wet.'

There was a great deal of muttered complaint, the gist of which was that thrusting your legs into wet trousers is neither pleasant nor agreeable. I told him not to be such a baby and were the coordinates ready yet?

'Are we doing something illegal here?'

Markham grinned at him. 'How long have you been at St Mary's?'

We checked the coordinates twice. We had to get this right. Hoyle wasn't going to last much longer.

I was sitting with him on the floor, explaining what would happen next and enjoying the very faint smile he'd managed to muster. Sykes read out the coordinates. Atherton laid them in. North checked them over. What a team! And with all this extra-curricular activity, they were cutting great swathes through their upcoming training schedule as well. When they'd finished, they turned to me expectantly. Everyone looked at me expectantly.

'Are we sure about this?' said North. 'Suppose someone paints over it?'

'They won't,' said Markham confidently. 'This is a local government car park. Council officials everywhere head the charge in the battle against entropy. Resisting change with every fibre of their beings. They'll still be renewing it when the sun explodes.'

Everyone's familiar with the story. You can read it for yourself in the *Leicester Mercury*. Because, ladies and gentlemen, 'R' marks the spot. Yes, it does. Really. Back when they excavated the council car park, looking for Richard's remains, there was a faded letter 'R', painted on the tarmac. It wasn't really near a parking space. It didn't line up with anything. It was just there. It had been there forever. No one knew for what purpose or even when it had appeared. It had just always been there and when they were looking for somewhere to start excavating someone said, '"R" marks the spot.'

And it did.

Or rather, it was going to.

I said, 'Computer, initiate jump.'

The world went white.

Well, here we were. A certain car park in Leicester.

We'd landed at night because we're reckless but we're not stupid. OK – disregard that last statement. But we had to do something for poor, dying Richard Hoyle. Give him a little comfort as he started out on his last journey.

Given the one-hundred-years rule, we had calculated the jump to the very closest date we thought we could get away with and for some reason, either the pod was becoming unreliable, or because we were tired, we got it wrong. Badly wrong.

We'd aimed for mid-20th century. I had no idea when we actually did land and there was no time to check because the second we touched down, a klaxon went off and frightened the living daylights out of all of us. Red lights flashed everywhere, even in the ex-toilet.

'Warning. Extreme hazard. This jump is not within permitted parameters. Emergency evacuation in four minutes, fifty-nine seconds.'

'Bollocks,' said Sykes. 'Will we have long enough?'

'We have to,' I said. 'Sykes, Markham. Do you have your canisters?'

'But what about the safety protocols,' said North, her voice effortlessly audible over the shrieking klaxon. 'We should check the proximities and ...'

'No time,' said Markham, already shoving Sykes out of the door. 'Move.'

'Good luck,' said North.

We exited the pod in a hurry.

There were no lights in the car park. I wasn't even sure it was a car park. The ground beneath my feet was solid, so it was either concrete or tarmac, but it could easily have been a school playground or someone's back garden.

Dark clouds scudded across the sky and it was cold. A light breeze stirred the short hairs around my head.

And North had been absolutely right, we should have checked the proximities, because just as we were dashing across the car park in our bedraggled Victorian gear, a voice shouted, 'Hoi!'

'Bollocks,' said Sykes again, and I mentally awarded her another couple of points for correct use of language in a hazardous situation.

'You two go on,' I said. 'Get it done. I'll talk to whoever it is.'

It was the police. Of course it bloody was. You'd

think they'd have something better to do than patrol deserted car parks in the middle of the night. There were major criminals out there. Bank robbers. Burglars. Motorists somewhere were probably approaching the speed of light even as we spoke. Why weren't they pursuing them instead of harassing very nearly innocent historians? I'm not fond of policemen. It's nothing personal, but a couple of them did once try to arrest me on my wedding night. That sort of thing leaves mental scars, you know.

There were two of them and they were upon me before I knew it, which was bad because I had no time to think up an acceptable reason for a bunch of weirdly dressed people apparently vandalising a perfectly respectable council car park.

'Good evening, officers. What seems to be the problem?'

The played their torches over me and then past me into the night, trying to see if I was alone. I strained my ears for the sounds of urban vandalism and could hear nothing. Whatever they were doing back there, they were doing it in silence. And in the dark.

'What's going on here?'

I decided to go with the truth.

'Good evening. I am Dr Maxwell from the Institute of Historical Research near Rushford. Acting on information received, we are engaged in painting a large letter "R" in this car park, to pinpoint the position of the grave of Richard III. Not immediately, but some years in the future, this area will be excavated and the king's bones located and identified. The old Alderman Newton's school will be converted into a magnificent visitors' centre, resulting in fame, prestige, and much-needed revenue for the city. The story of the discovery of Richard's remains will fly around the world and the fact that they are buried almost directly under this letter "R" – that's the one being painted as we speak – will pass into folk legend. As you can imagine, it is enormously important that we complete our task, otherwise the course of History will be changed, with catastrophic results. I estimate they will require another minute and then we will be gone and you will never see us again.'

They stared at me. 'What?'

I was done. I just couldn't think of anything else to say. I sent up a mental prayer for help and the god of historians responded with a bolt of inspiration, which, typically, missed me and hit the two fine representatives of the local constabulary standing before me instead.

One of them started to laugh. 'It's Rag Week, isn't it?'

Why the bloody hell hadn't I thought of that? The god of historians was fired on the spot.

'Yes. You're right. It's Rag Week. Can I interest either of you in making a contribution to ...' I tried to remember when I was and what were the issues of the day, '... pulling American troops out of Vietnam? Banning the Bomb? Ending apartheid in South Africa? Equal rights for women?'

They stared at me again in complete bafflement. 'What?'

All right – I admit it. I'm not good with stuff after

1485.

I was rummaging for something to say when Markham appeared out of the dark. Somehow, he'd straightened his cravat and slicked down his hair. He looked nearly normal.

'Ah, there you are, mother.'

What?

'Thank you officers, I can take it from here. It's her age, you know. Normally she's as good as gold, but sometimes she does take it into her head to go for a bit of a wander. Was she talking about Richard III again? A bit of an obsession with her, I'm afraid. Come along now, dear,' he continued, raising his voice slightly and skidding closer to death with every word. 'The car's just around the corner. I'll take you home, make you some nice Horlicks, and you can listen to *The Archers*. You know how you like that. Goodnight, officers.'

He took my arm, and before they could say a word, he turned me around, and led me off into the night back to the pod.

'*Mother?*'

'Come on Max, pick up the pace or the pod will go off without us.'

We broke into a trot.

'*Mother?*'

'We don't want to be stranded here, do we? We're in enough trouble as it is.'

'*Mother?*'

'We got it done. Nice big "R" as close as we could get to where he's buried. Well, within about ten feet, anyway. Not a bad effort, all things considered. Sykes is back in the pod. '

'*Horlicks?*'

'Yes, yes,' he said soothingly. 'You can murder me later, but for now we need to move.'

They had the door open ready. I could hear the countdown. We had over thirty seconds to spare. That's practically a lifetime. Where's the drama in that?

Hoyle lay on the floor, staring up at me with eyes that were far too large for his face. Atherton was cradling his head and North and Sykes were bracing him as best they could.

I knelt at his side and took his ice-cold, bloodstained hand in mine. 'We've done it, Richard. We've marked the grave. Richard III will be discovered. All thanks to you.'

Not strictly true, but what would you have said?

He nodded, his eyes cloudy. He didn't have long.

I went to get up but he clutched at me.

'I get it,' he said, his voice barely audible.

'Get what?'

'I get why you do it. The shouting. The chaos. It's ... how you cope, isn't it? It's how you deal with ... what you've seen. How you deal with people dying. All the stuff you watch and you ... can't change a single thing. You can't help a single person. It's how you yourselves don't explode.'

Atherton said urgently, 'Max, we have to go. Now.'

I said, 'Computer, override emergency evacuation. Jump to pre-programmed coordinates. Now.'

And the world went white.

Hoyle died somewhere between the council car park in Leicester and Bosworth Field. North covered his face with the blanket.

We landed back in the Redemoor Marsh. I estimated we'd been gone about an hour. They were still parading the king's naked body around because everyone must see that Richard was dead. The sword protruding from between his buttocks waggled grotesquely at every movement of the horse.

We waited until dark and then very quietly let ourselves out of the pod. Atherton and Markham carried him carefully to the edge of the marsh. We turned away while they gently stripped him of his anomalous clothes. We had no choice. We couldn't leave them here. I hoped he would understand.

There was a long row of bodies already laid out. We simply set him down at the end. Atherton straightened his legs. North folded his hands on his poor crushed chest. Sykes smoothed his hair. No one took any notice of us. There were many other people doing the same. Women included. Battlefields take a lot of clearing away afterwards.

'Would anyone like to say anything?' I said.

'I don't know what to say,' said Sykes, and the other two nodded in agreement. I understood. They had thought he was one of them and then discovered he wasn't. Then they'd changed their minds and decided that maybe he was after all. Or could have been. Until he allowed obsession to get the better of him. Had he even noticed he was being used? Or didn't he care as long as he achieved his ends? Was he good? Or bad? Or like Randall, was he a little of both?

A chill wind blew in off the marsh, bringing with it the smell of stagnant water. Dark clouds scudded across the darker sky. I looked at the scene around me. Lights moved in the distance, rising and falling as people leaned over the bodies, trying to find any that might still be alive. Voices came and went. Somewhere, a priest was intoning a prayer. A woman was sobbing. I can't remember how many died that day. Thousands, I think. I wondered where Henry was and what he was doing now. He'd left the field, anyway. Only the dead and those ministering to the dead remained.

I don't know why we were so reluctant to leave. Was it because, for the first time ever, we were deliberately leaving one of our own people behind?

'If he can be happy anywhere,' said Markham quietly, 'it will be here. Yorkists all around him and his king not far away.'

I nodded, even though by now, it was too dark for anyone to see clearly. 'Richard Neville Laurence Hoyle – rest in peace.'

'Come on,' said Markham. 'Time to go.'

I picked up Hoyle's clothes and we squelched our way back through the bog.

Twenty-four

I can't even begin to describe the grief we got from Sick Bay.

'Isolation,' said Helen, muffled behind a mask.

'What? Why? All right, I'll grant you Markham and I are a little battered, but ...'

'Are you serious? You've been rolling around in a swamp. A medieval swamp.'

'Yes, but ...'

'With insects, mosquitoes ...'

'And poisonous frogs,' interjected Markham, who always has his own reasons for wanting to remain in Sick Bay as long as possible.

She ignored him and Hunter shot him a look that considerably decreased his chances of surviving whatever they had in store for us.

'Cholera. Leptospirosis.'

I tried. 'Yes, but ...'

'E. coli infections. Dysentery.'

I tried again. 'No, but ...'

'Typhoid. Botulism.'

I gave up. 'Yes – all *right*.'

'Tapeworms.'

'Oh, not again,' said Markham. 'I've only just

evicted the last one.'

'Cryptosporidiosis.'

'What?'

'Microsporidiosis.'

'Well now you're just making things up.'

A week later, Dr Bairstow and I stared at each other across his desk. Yes, all right, I'd allowed a bunch of trainees to be hijacked off to 1485, but he'd allowed said hijacker into St Mary's in the first place. In fact, if my memory served me well, I'd had a bit of a protest about our Mr Hoyle and been told, in no uncertain terms, to wind my neck in. Something I would have no hesitation in pointing out to him as soon as the words 'How could you allow this to happen?' floated across his desk.

They never did. Just for once, he neatly sidestepped the vexed question of whose fault all this was – usually his favourite part of any mission debriefing and plunged straight into my nipping off to a council car park in Leicester. And yes, all right, that was my fault. In an effort to deflect him, I strove to convey the importance of the painted 'R'.

He refused to be deflected. 'Would I be right in crediting the appearance of this painted letter "R" solely to the efforts of St Mary's?'

'Do you mean the one that contributed to the discovery of his remains, sir?' I said, trying to paint things in the best possible light.

He regarded me coldly. 'Was there more than one painted letter "R" in that particular car park?'

'Not that I'm aware of, sir.'

'So St Mary's was responsible?'

'It would appear so, sir.'

'You changed the past.'

'No sir, we changed the future. Different crime altogether.'

There was a long pause and then he leaned forwards, suddenly serious. 'You need to take care, Max. Great care. You are beginning to tread the line between what is acceptable and what is not. From there, it only takes the smallest step to find you have stepped over that line altogether. That you have done the wrong thing for the right reasons. I am warning you, in future, to be very, very careful.'

I shivered, suddenly cold. As cold as the night following the battle at Bosworth. As if something had walked over my grave.

Taking a deep breath, I tried to distract him. 'So what happens now, sir?'

He stood up, and went to look out of the window. 'I am not sure.'

'Hoyle was a bit of a time bomb, sir, which is rather appropriate, don't you think? He could have gone off at any time. We were lucky.'

'I'm assuming this is the St Mary's definition of the word luck.'

'It could have been a lot worse, sir. Someone became aware of his obsession and used it to gain whatever it was they wanted.'

'They wanted St Mary's,' he interrupted. 'And a deliberate attempt by one of our own people to assassinate Henry Tudor and change the course of History would have brought everything crashing down around us. We who have always – *always* – maintained History must not be changed in any way, would have been found guilty of our own most serious crime. The Time Police would have come down on us in force and this time, there would have been no escape. You and I would almost certainly have been imprisoned.'

'If the Time Police let us live.'

'If, as you say, the Time Police had let us live. And even if St Mary's had been able to continue, a new regime would certainly have been installed.'

'Someone more able to recognise the true potential of time travel,' I said slowly, remembering what Hoyle had said.

'Yes.'

'Sir, are we in trouble? Again?'

'Specifically, no. Thanks to your prompt actions, no. The threat was neutralised. But generally, yes. There are people who – who feel that St Mary's could … fulfil other functions.'

'Such as?'

He looked at me and said nothing. I understood. Some things were above my pay grade. Actually, there were things that slithered on their bellies that were higher than my pay grade. Wisely, I did not mention this.

'What do we do, sir?'

He shrugged. 'At this moment, there's nothing we can do. But there's nothing they can do, either. History is intact. The assignment records have been destroyed. They will never know what happened to Mr Hoyle and there is no proof.'

'Will they try again?'

'Oh, almost certainly, I think. Don't you?'

I remained silent, thinking about this.

He sighed and said quietly, 'Why did you do it, Max?'

'Sir?'

'Take him on to Leicester. Risk the hundred-year rule.'

I replied, equally quietly, 'He was dying, sir. I wanted his death to have some meaning for him.'

He turned from the window and came to sit back in his chair, his face unreadable. 'Explain.'

I swallowed back a sudden urge to cry. I must be more tired than I thought.

'I'm willing to bet the idea to kill Henry Tudor was not his. His obsession was with Richard. Someone took him aside and said, "But what if Henry died at Bosworth, not Richard." That was probably all it took. The seed was planted. Then, at the end, I think he realised what he'd try to do. What he'd nearly done. How he'd been used by someone who knew that whatever the outcome, he himself would not survive it. He was ashamed. And defeated. And bitter. He had nothing left.'

I swallowed and continued defiantly, 'So I took him to Leicester and told him he'd performed a service for his king. That Richard's body was discovered because of his actions. I like to think he died a little happier because of that, sir. I'm sorry if you wanted to have him shot, but if you'd seen his face, perhaps you might agree with me. If you don't, of course, you'll just have to shoot me instead.'

'A course of action I have not yet discounted, given that Mr Hoyle is no longer here to answer the charges brought against him.'

Well, yes, he had me there, but when I looked up he'd put the file away and was smiling faintly.

'So, you are handing over three trainees, Dr Maxwell. Soon to become Pathfinders.'

'Three exceptional trainees, sir. I think there's great potential there.'

'As do I.' He paused. 'Tell me, does any of this seem familiar to you?'

'Sorry sir, I'm not with you.'

'Well, we have three new historians. Mr Atherton is a natural leader. He possesses a quiet confidence that is impressive. People like him. Then there's Miss North. Tall, blonde, a little terrifying – especially if things don't go as she thinks they should. And Miss Sykes, of course. Short, passionate, energetic, and with the same sense of self-preservation as a mongoose staring down a cobra.'

I stared at him. 'No, sorry sir. I'm not with you.'

'Never mind. It must just be my imagination. Oh, just one final query. Why has Miss Sykes entitled her report, "How Mr Atherton Lost His Trousers"?'

I closed my eyes.

'That will be all, Dr Maxwell.'

Twenty-five

Well, my training course hadn't gone quite according to plan, but all things considered, three out of five qualifying wasn't bad. Hoyle's name had gone up on the Board of Honour. As I argued with Dr Bairstow, if Randall's name could go up then so could Hoyle's. He did agree, but that might just have been so I would stop talking and go away.

They all went on to graduate. We assembled in the Great Hall. Peterson and I sat in the front row. He'd been up and about for some time now, still on light duties, although that didn't stop him sticking his nose in where it wasn't needed. On several occasions, I'd had to give him beer just to make him go away. His arm was supported in a black silk sling, which he thought made him look mysterious and enigmatic. No one had the heart to tell him.

They wore their brand new blues for the ceremony. A little stiff and shiny in places, but they'd soon acquire the patches, burns, and unidentifiable stains that would mark them out as true historians. Atherton and Sykes looked like the rest of us – baggy blue sacks. North's fitted her perfectly. I'd bet what remained of next month's pay that she'd had hers tailored. Sykes was squinting down at her own chest, trying to read her name stencilled across her top pocket, when Dr Bairstow entered and we began.

He read out their names and, to great applause, they came forward for the presentation. Lingoss clapped as hard as everyone else. Today's hair event was blue, in their honour.

Atherton led the way, smoothly taking his certificate with one hand and shaking Dr Bairstow's hand with the other. He'd been up all night practising, apparently.

North was next up, inclining her head graciously. I sighed. Was it too much to ask …?

No, it wasn't. As she turned away, she caught my eye and smiled. She should definitely smile more often.

Sykes was the last one. She bounced up the stairs, beamed blindingly at Dr Bairstow, took her certificate, pumped his hand vigorously, beamed again in case he'd missed it the first time around, and bounded back down again. Just for one moment, the Boss caught my eye. I grinned at him.

He raised his hand and the applause died away.

'I have just one brief announcement before we disperse. I have today heard from Thirsk. The Chancellor sends her compliments and congratulations. The expedition to Belverde Caves has been successful. The Botticelli paintings have been found, more or less intact. A formal announcement will be made tomorrow. In the meantime, I believe appropriate refreshments have been made available.'

This was Dr Bairstow speak for, 'A sum of money has been placed behind the bar. This is nothing to do with me and you should, under no circumstances, expect this to become a regular event. Any physical manifestations of high spirits will be met with mass distribution of Deductions from Wages For Damages Incurred Forms. Dismissed.'

It was a good party. We had a lot to celebrate. The recovery of the Botticelli paintings would lead to even more fame and fortune for Thirsk and a period of very nearly unchallenged funding for us. And we had three new historians. And Peterson was on his feet. His arm would never work properly again, but he had announced his intention of becoming ambidextrous and to this end, was working hard on his physiotherapy. Word had gone out and there wasn't a woman in the building who would turn her back on him. And Markham had been released from Sick Bay only that morning after his latest outbreak of mange had cleared up. Although, as Hunter said, Markham without mange was like Spotted without the Dick.

Glass in hand, I wandered around the room, avoiding Dr Foster, who wanted me for something or other. I had no idea what but it wouldn't be pleasant, so I was ignoring her.

Leon and Dieter were discussing something in the corner. Leon smiled for me alone and then bent his head to listen to Dieter again.

Markham was doing his Madame Zara impersonation over Hunter's palm. Bending over her hand, he was intoning, 'You will meet a short, fair stranger who is nowhere near as contagious as he was this time last week …'

David Sands had backed Rosie Lee against a wall. I turned away, not wanting to intrude, but not quickly enough.

'Knock-knock.'

Oh God, the boy was an idiot. An opinion apparently shared by Miss Lee, as well.

'What?'

He sighed. 'No,' he said patiently. 'Not "What?" You have to say, "Who's there?".'

'How should I know?' she demanded.

'Know what?' he enquired, innocently.

'Who's there?'

'Yes,' he said, triumphantly. 'That's the ticket. I knew you'd get it in the end. You just had to concentrate a little,' and I suddenly realised that he was the perfect person for her. It didn't matter what she threw at him. It all just went straight over his head. Somehow, he could get through her defences without even trying.

I found Peterson, sitting on the stairs, glass in one hand, bottle in the other. He said, 'Helen's looking for you,' waved, and she came over.

I began to melt away.

He poured her a drink and handed it to her. 'I know that to you the entire human race is less than dust but everyone else is partying. You should join us.'

She refused to be distracted. 'Did I see Max with you?'

Behind her, I shook my head and mouthed, 'No'.

'Yes, she's behind you. Did you want her?

She turned. 'Max. Come and see me at 10.00 tomorrow morning.'

'No chance,' I said, aghast. 'It's Saturday tomorrow. As a married woman, I have responsibilities to fulfil on a Saturday morning. Twice on a Sunday.'

'Oh, please,' said Peterson, wrinkling his nose. 'Too much information for an invalid.'

'Stop arguing, Max, and get your arse up to Sick Bay at 10.00 tomorrow.'

'Personally,' I said to Peterson, 'I don't think doctors should be allowed to attend social gatherings. Every time you see one you can't help remembering the circumstances under which you last met, which are always either horribly personal or hideously embarrassing.'

'Or both,' said Peterson, grinning at her.

She blushed and took it out on me. 'Just be there, Maxwell, or I'll do things with a set of electrodes that will make your hair stand on end.'

'Well since you've asked so nicely ...'

I turned up at the appointed time because that was the easiest option. You really don't want Helen Foster roaming the building looking for you.

I was in there for some considerable time because I had to make her say everything twice. And even then it didn't go in properly. She had scan results and printouts and God knows what scattered over her desk, which she flourished at me, mistakenly thinking they would mean something. I sat and watched her lips move, feeling the ground shift beneath my feet.

After she'd finished, she switched on the kettle and ordered me to wash my face. She went to sit on the window seat, lit a cigarette, and puffed the smoke out of the window while I struggled to pull myself together. I wiped away the last of the tears, blew my nose, lifted my chin, and said, 'Now what?'

'Well, that's rather up to you, isn't it?' she said, effortlessly living down to her image of unhelpful disinterest. 'I'll need to see you regularly, of course. You can't just crash around the timeline as you used to. And I'll need to inform Dr Bairstow, as well.'

'I'll do that,' I said.

'Make sure you do.'

'I don't have much choice, do I?'

'Not any longer, no.'

When I'd finished there, I took a long time to be by myself, sitting alone in my office and thinking about things. It was some time before I eventually got back to my room. I opened the door into a little haven of warmth and soft light.

This was *our* room. Our things were here. Our books were lined up on the bookshelves. My red snake dangled from the top shelf. My painting gear stood in one corner. His armchair was placed by the window to catch the morning sun. My no-longer-needed walking stick stood against the wall. Our photo watched us from the bedside table. Bear 2.0 smiled at us from the windowsill.

Leon sat with his feet up, reading. 'There you are.'

I put off the moment. 'What's the book?'

He held up the cover for me to see. '*Temporal Dynamics. Volume IV.* One of Dr Hawking's greatest blockbusters.'

'Oh, wow! Is there sex and violence?'

'More than you would think,' he said, and settled down again.

I once said, long ago, that happiness is like grains of sand. The more tightly you clench your fist, the more it just slips through your fingers. I said that if we just came to rest somewhere and waited quietly then one day we'd look up and it would be there.

He looked up and smiled and I'd been right – happiness had snuck up on me when I wasn't looking and here we both were, in this quiet room, warm and comfortable and safe and together. The heavy rain beat on the windows. Mozart played quietly in the background. I looked at Leon, stretched out on the sofa, *Temporal Dynamics* in one hand, a glass of wine in the other.

There would never be a better moment to tell him.

I couldn't think of anything to say. Words just wouldn't come. I couldn't seem to fight through the tightly clenched ball of something that was hurting my chest. For once, just for once, I was completely overwhelmed. Completely at a loss. Completely, hopelessly ... lost.

I squared my shoulders and lifted my chin.

'Leon.'

It came out more loudly than I intended.

He blinked. 'Why are you yelling at me?'

'I ...'

'What?'

'I ...'

'What?'

Oh, for God's sake. We could go on like this all day.

I caught hold of the table for support.

'I have something to tell you.'

'Yes, I'd gathered that from your "It's all gone horribly wrong and we're going to have to run like hell" look.'

'I have a look for that?'

'You have a look for everything, although at the moment, I have to say I haven't seen you this terrified since our wedding day. Tell me the worst. Is it bad?'

I nodded. Then shook my head. Then nodded again.

'Well, that seems to cover the full spectrum of responses, but could you narrow it down a little for me?'

'I ...'

He sighed. 'And we were making such progress, too.'

I was really struggling. I wanted to tell him but this changed everything, and once spoken, the words could never be recalled and things would never be the same again.

'Leon ...'

Suddenly serious, he said, 'What is it, Max? Just tell me.'

I had to say something. I was frightening him. I took a very deep breath.

'Dr Bairstow is going to be a godfather.'

THE END

406

Jodi Taylor

For more information about **Jodi Taylor**

and other **Accent Press** titles

please visit
www.accentpress.co.uk

Lightning Source UK Ltd.
Milton Keynes UK
UKOW04n0256201015

260973UK00011B/109/P